PRAISE FOR
The Jane Austen Project

"What lover of literature hasn't dreamed of going back in time to meet Jane Austen? In her debut novel, Kathleen A. Flynn brings this dream to life, creating a vivid portrait of Regency England in all its glory and squalor. Flynn illuminates the stark contrasts between that era and our own, and movingly depicts the heartbreak of those who might try to travel between the two."

—Lauren Belfer, author of *After the Fire* and *A Fierce Radiance*

"*The Jane Austen Project* is clever, captivating, and original. I loved it and couldn't put it down! It's been a long time since I've been so engrossed in a novel, or lost so much sleep reading it. Who wouldn't want to travel back in time and meet Jane Austen? Flynn's depiction of Jane Austen is wonderful, exactly as I imagine she must have been. The ending is a shocker and one of the strengths of the novel. It presents a view of time travel—and history—you won't soon forget. A keeper on my Austen shelf."

—Syrie James, author of *Jane Austen's First Love*

"I loved *The Jane Austen Project*. Brilliantly written and a must-read for any Jane Austen fan!"

—Paula Byrne, author of *The Real Jane Austen*

THE
Jane Austen

PROJECT

Kathleen A. Flynn

HARPER ⬤ PERENNIAL

NEW YORK • LONDON • TORONTO • SYDNEY • NEW DELHI • AUCKLAND

FIRST EDITION

Designed by Jamie Lynn Kerner

Library of Congress Cataloging-in-Publication Data

Names: Flynn, Kathleen A., 1966- author.
Title: The Jane Austen Project / Kathleen A. Flynn.
Description: New York : Harper Perennial, 2017.
Identifiers: LCCN 2016035898| ISBN 9780062651259 (paperback) | ISBN
  9780062651266 (ebook)
Subjects: LCSH: Austen, Jane, 1775-1817—Fiction. | Women novelists, English—19th century—Fiction. | Time travel—Fiction. | BISAC: FICTION /
  Historical. | FICTION / Literary. | FICTION / Fantasy / Historical. | GSAFD: Fantasy fiction. | Historical fiction.
Classification: LCC PS3606.L9359 J36 2017 | DDC 813/.6—dc23 LC record available at https://lccn.loc.gov/2016035898

ISBN 978-0-06-265125-9 (pbk.)

17 18 19 20 21 LSC 10 9 8 7 6 5 4 3 2

To Jarek

Go, go, go, said the bird: human kind
Cannot bear very much reality.
Time past and time future
What might have been and what has been
Point to one end, which is always present.

—T. S. ELIOT, "BURNT NORTON"

CHAPTER 1

SEPTEMBER 5, 1815

Leatherhead, Surrey

WHAT KIND OF MANIAC TRAVELS IN TIME? SOMETHING I WOULD wonder more than once before it was over, but never as urgently as that moment I regained consciousness on the damp ground. Grass tickled the back of my neck; I saw sky and tree-tops, smelled earth and rot. I had the feeling that follows a faint, or waking up in an unfamiliar bed after a long journey: uncertain not just where I was, but who.

As I lay there, I remembered that my name was Rachel. Body and mind snapped together and I sat up, blinking at my surroundings, which were indistinct and flatly gray scale, and rubbed my eyes. I reviewed known side effects of trips through wormholes: palpitations, arrhythmia, short-term amnesia, mood swings, nausea, syncope, alopecia. Changes in vision had not come up. Maybe this was new to science.

Wind rattled the leaves, counterpoint to a repetitive squeak that might have been some insect long extinct in my own time. I marveled at the 1815 air, moist and dense with smells I had no words for, reminded of the glass-domed habitat re-creations at the Brooklyn Botanic Garden, where we used to go on field trips. *Once, children, the whole world was like this.*

Liam was about a meter away, same distance as in the air lock, but now facedown and ominously still. Arrhythmia can confuse a heart enough to stop it. And then what? Could I really be so unlucky as to lose my colleague at the start of the mission? I'd have to pose as a widow, the only sort of lone woman entitled to any protection and regard here—

"Are you all right?" I demanded; he did not answer. I slid closer and reached out to check his carotid, relieved to find a pulse. His breathing was fast and shallow, skin filmed in cold sweat. Past him, a clump of white trees, name forgotten, glowed in the gloom. My own heart was banging in my chest; I breathed slowly and stared at the white trees.

Birch! And another word came to me: *dusk,* something barely noticed in my own time, in a life illuminated by electricity. Natural light; we'd learned the vocabulary of that, along with *waxing, waning, crescent, gibbous,* and the major constellations. I saw again in memory the steel-gray corridors of the Royal Institute for Special Topics in Physics, as the year I'd spent there glided before me like a time-lapse video clip: the dancing and riding practice, the movement and music lessons, the endless reading. Our walk to the air lock, last checks, solemn handshakes with the rest of the Jane Austen Project Team.

I was here. We'd done it.

"Are you all right?" I asked again. Liam groaned but rolled

over, sat up, and scanned our surroundings of field, birch, and hedgerow. The portal location had been chosen well; nobody was here.

"It's dusk," I explained. "That's why it all looks like this." He turned toward me, dark eyebrows arching in a question. "In case you were wondering."

"I wasn't." His words came slowly, voice soft. "But thanks."

I looked at him sideways, trying to decide if he was being sarcastic, and hoped so. In our time together at the institute preparing for the mission, something about Liam had always eluded me. He was too reserved; you never knew about people like that.

I stood, light-headed, straightened my bonnet, and took a few stiff steps, brushing dirt and grass off my dress, conscious of the swish of all my layers, the slab of banknotes beneath my corset.

Liam lifted his head, sniffing. He unfolded himself, rising to his feet with a surprising grace—in my experience tall men shamble—stretched his arms, repositioned his frizzy doctor's wig, looked to the right, and froze. "Is that what I think it is?"

My eyes adjusting, I saw a road: a lane wide as a wagon, forking a little way off. And in the Y of the fork, a gibbet: a man-size iron frame, like a sinister birdcage, holding something that— "Oh."

"So they really were everywhere," he said. "Or we are just lucky."

Now identifying one component of what I'd been smelling, I stared in dismay at the corpse, which seemed to gaze back at me, blank-socketed. Not freshly putrefying, not a husk, but in between, though in this light it was hard to say for sure.

Maybe he'd been a highwayman; the people here displayed condemned men near the scenes of their crimes, as warnings to others. And maybe we would end up like him, if things went wrong.

I had forgotten to breathe, but the reek lingered in my nose. I'd been around dead people ever since medical school; I'd autopsied them, but not like this. On one occasion, though, during my volunteer stint in Mongolia, someone had been misidentified and had to be exhumed—

With that, I gagged and bent over, clutching my throat, seized by dry heaves. When they'd passed, I dried my eyes and straightened to find Liam peering down at me, brow furrowed.

"Are you all right?" His long hands, pale at the ends of the dark sleeves of his coat, lifted and fluttered in the fading light, like he was about to touch me but didn't know where. Shoulder? Elbow? Forearm? What's the least intimate part of your opposite-sex co-worker to grab if she's in distress? Unable to decide, he brought his hands back down to his sides; despite the horror of the cadaver, this was funny.

"I'm fine," I said. "Just great. Let's get out of here." We had both turned away from the gibbet. I'm not superstitious, but I hoped our way to the inn wouldn't lead past it. "North. If the sun set over there"—the horizon seemed brighter in one area—"then it must be that way."

"Well, yes, because there's Venus, right?"

"Venus?"

"That bright object in the west?"

I repressed annoyance at not having noticed this myself. "Yes, exactly!"

We turned away, took a few steps, and then Liam stopped and whirled around.

"Mother of god. The portal marker."

I cursed under my breath as I turned too. Could we almost have forgotten something so important? Two disturbances in the grass could only have been the outlines of our two bodies. Liam took the metal marker from an inside pocket of his coat and pushed it as far as it would go into the earth right between them, blue spiral top barely visible. "Spectronanometer?" he asked.

I fumbled for my device, which hung on a silver chain around my neck and resembled a blob of amber, and squeezed. It vibrated to life and beeped to signal proximity to the marker. As I pinched it off, I was shaking. The portal was precise, in time frame and geopositioning; we would never have found it again by chance. Liam had fished his spectronanometer out of another pocket—it resembled a small snuffbox, one that didn't open— and stood pressing it. Nothing happened. He muttered, shook it, and tried again.

"Here." I took the little silver object from him, positioned it in my hand, and tightened my grip slowly. It vibrated and beeped; I squeezed it off again and handed it back. "They're temperamental."

"Evidently."

It was growing darker and colder; time to get moving. Yet we stood in silence at this spot, last link with where we'd come from. How much would happen before we stood here again, assuming we ever made it back?

"Come on," I said at last. "Let's go."

AS WE STARTED DOWN THE ROAD, LIAM'S STRIDE WAS LONGER AND I began to fall behind, though I'm normally a fast walker. Until now, indoors was the only place I'd worn my half boots, hand-made products of the Costume Team. The soles were so thin I felt the gravel under my feet. And then, the intensity of everything: the smells of grass and soil, a far-off cry of an owl, it had to be an owl. The entire world seemed humming with life, a shimmering web of biomass.

The Swan loomed as a whitewashed brick building outlined by flickering lamps along its facade, with an arched passageway into a courtyard and stables beyond. As we drew closer I heard men's voices, a horse's whinny, a dog's bark. Fear swooped up my spine like vertigo. I stopped walking. I can't do this. I must do this.

Liam had stopped too. He shook himself and took a few long, audible breaths. Then he seized my elbow with an unexpectedly strong grip and propelled us toward the door under the wooden sign of a swan.

"Remember, let me do the talking," he said. "Men do, here."

And we were inside.

IT WAS WARMER BUT DIM, A TIMBERED CEILING, AIR THICK WITH smoke, flickering light from not enough candles, and a large fireplace. A knot of men stood by the fire, while others sat at tables with bread and mugs of beer, platters of beef, ham, fowl, and other less identifiable foods.

"Look at all that meat," I whispered. "Amazing."

"Shh, don't stare."

"Do you see anyone who looks like they work here?"

"Shh!"

And he was upon us: a small man in a boxy suit, a dirty apron, and a scowl, wiping his hands on a dirty rag as he looked us up and down. "Are ye just come, then? Has someone seen to your horses, have they now?"

"Our friends set us down from their barouche a bit hence." Liam had thrown his shoulders back and loomed over the man. "We are in want of rooms for the night, and a coach to town in the morning." His inflection had changed, even his voice: a haughty lengthening of vowels, a nasal, higher-pitched tone. We'd done lots of improvisational work in Preparation, yet he'd never given me this eerie sense I had now, of his becoming an entirely different person.

"A barouche?" the man repeated. "I've seen no such equipage pass."

"Had it passed here, they would have set us down at the door."

This logic seemed sound, but the man surveyed us again, frown deepening. "À pied, is it?" It took me a moment to work out what he meant; nothing could have sounded less like French. "And not so much as a bag between the both of ye? Nay, we've no rooms." A party of the three men nearest—rusty black suits, wigs askew—had stopped eating to observe us. "You could sup before you continue on your way." He waved a hand at the room behind. "Show us the blunt first, though."

Was our offense the presumed poverty of showing up without horses, or was something else wrong with our manners, our clothing, us? And if the first person we met saw it, what were our odds of survival here, let alone success? Liam had gone so pale, swaying a bit, that I feared he might faint, a known time-travel side effect.

Fear made me reckless. "William!" I whined, pulling on Liam's sleeve and bracing myself under his elbow to shore him up. His eyes widened as he looked down at me; I heard his intake of breath. I went on in a stage whisper without a glance at the man, and if my mouth was dry, my accent was perfection: "I *told* you, Papa said this was a shocking inn. But if it has no rooms, perhaps it has horses. 'Tis moonlight! A chaise and four, or two, and we will be there by dawn. I said I would visit Lady Selden the instant we got to town, and that was to be last week, only you never can say no to Sir Thomas and his tedious gout."

Liam looked from me to the man and drawled: "My sister's word is law, sir. Should there be coach and horses, I would be happy to show the blunt, and to see what I hope will be the last of this inn." He produced a golden coin, one of our authentic late-eighteenth-century guineas, flipping it into the air and catching it.

I held my breath. What if the inn had no horses in shape to go, no spare carriages? It happened, animals and vehicles being in constant transit from one coaching inn to another. And now we were robbery targets, with Liam waving around gold.

The man looked from me to Liam; his eyes returned to me. I raised my gaze to the ceiling with what I hoped was an expression of blasé contempt.

"I'll have a word in the yard, sir. Would you and the lady take a seat?"

IT WAS COLDER, THE WAXING GIBBOUS MOON UP, BEFORE WE WERE in the post chaise, which was tiny and painted yellow, smelling of the damp straw that lined its floor as well as of mildew and horse.

We'd drunk musty red wine and picked at a meat pie with a sinister leathery texture as we sat in a corner of the room, feeling the weight of eyes upon us and not daring to believe, until a porter came to lead us to it, that there was actually going to be a chaise.

Our postilion swung himself onto one of the horses, and a large man wearing two pistols and a brass horn gave us a nod and climbed into the boot at the back. He had cost extra, nearly doubling the price of the journey—but it was no night to encounter highwaymen.

"You were good back there," Liam said in his usual voice, so quiet I had to lean in to hear him as we creaked out from the yard. One seat, facing forward, was wide enough for three slender people. Drafty windows gave a view of the lanterns on each side, the road to London ahead of us, and the two horses' muscular rumps. "Fast thinking. I know I told you not to talk, but—"

"A hopeless request. You know me better than that by now."

He made a sound between a cough and a laugh and said after a pause, "So you really never acted? I mean, before this?"

I thought of the unscripted workshops we'd done together in Preparation: imagining meeting Henry Austen for the first time, say, or buying a bonnet. "Why would I have?"

We were bumping down the road, moon visible above the black tree shapes, the world beyond the lanterns' glow spookily monochrome and depthless to the eye, but rich with smells. The Project Team's guidance had been for us to spend the first night near the portal site, in Leatherhead, recovering from the time shift before braving town. Materializing in London, dense with buildings and life, was risky. Traveling by night was risky too, but here we were. I wondered what else would not go according to plan.

I DON'T KNOW HOW LONG I WAS ASLEEP, BUT I WOKE UP SHIVERING. Liam was slumped with his head against the window, wig slid sideways, snoring. I pulled my shawl tighter around myself, coveting his waistcoat, neckcloth, and cutaway jacket—a light weight, but wool—and Hessian boots, the tall kind with tassels.

I had lots of layers too, but they lacked the heft of menswear: a chemise, then a small fortune in coins, forged banknotes, and letters of credit in a pouch wrapped around my torso, topped by a corset, a petticoat, a frock, and a shawl, a synthetic re-creation of a Kashmir paisley. I had a thin lace fichu around my shoulders, over-the-knee knitted cotton stockings, dainty faux-kid gloves, and a straw bonnet, but no underpants; they would not catch on until later in the century.

The darkness was becoming less dark. I stared out; when did countryside turn urban? We had pored over old maps, paintings, and engravings; detailed flyover projections in 3-D had illuminated the wall screens of the institute. Yet no amount of study could have prepared me for this: the smell of coal smoke and vegetation, the creaking carriage, the hoofbeats of the horses like my own heartbeat. And something else, like energy, as if London were an alien planet, its gravitational field pulling me in.

Anything could happen to a person in Regency London: you could be killed by a runaway carriage, get cholera, lose a fortune on a wager or your virtue in an unwise elopement. Less dangerously, we hoped to find a place to live in a fashionable neighborhood and establish ourselves as wealthy newcomers in need of guidance, friends, and lucrative investments—all with the aim of insinuating ourselves into the life of Henry Austen, gregarious London banker and favorite brother of Jane. And through him, and the events we knew were waiting for them both this autumn, to find our way to her.

I eased next to Liam, the only warm object in the cold carriage, my relief at getting away from the Swan curdling to anxiety about everything that lay ahead. Queasy as I was from the bumping carriage, with the stink of horse and mildew in my nose, with the gibbet and the meat pie and the innkeeper's rudeness still vivid, the Jane Austen Project no longer seemed amazing. What I'd wanted so badly stretched like a prison sentence: wretched hygiene, endless pretending, physical danger. What had I been thinking?

THE ROYAL INSTITUTE FOR SPECIAL TOPICS IN PHYSICS WAS NOTH-ing anyone like me would know about; I was far out of its Old British ambit of analysts and scientists and spies. I learned of it by accident, in Mongolia, in bed.

Norman Ng, though a conscientious colleague and all-round mensch, was indiscreet. He liked having secrets, but never kept them, as I should have understood before I'd started sleeping with him and found I'd become the subject of salacious gossip among our whole aid team. Though this might not have stopped me; Mongolia was dark and cold and grim after the earthquake, the worst place I'd ever signed on for. Or the best, if your aim was to relieve human suffering; there was no shortage.

Late one night, peacefully postcoital, Norman told me about a friend of his from school, one Dr. Ping, now at a little-known government research center in East Anglia.

"You're trying to tell me that Old Britain—No, that's crazy. You made that up."

"They have mastered practical time travel," he said again. The wind howled; the yurt poles creaked. "Rachel, they are far ahead. People don't understand this, but they will. When they see the results, we will all clamor to be Old British, even more than now. The Chinese will forgive the Opium Wars. The Americans—But you guys apologized already for independence, I forgot." Norman was Old British, with his Cambridge degree and elite ancestors who'd come from Hong Kong just before the Chinese takeover at the end of the twentieth century, but it suited him to play the outsider.

"It's mind-boggling. It's impossible."

"You know about the Prometheus Server?"

I yawned; I'd been up since dawn. "Tremendous energy source, supercomputers, whatever." More of what our world was already full of, in short.

"You sound so casual! An order of magnitude beyond earlier technology! With enough energy, and enough data, you can calculate *anything*. Including wormholes, and probability fields, and simulate every possible scenario. And once you can do that—"

"Okay, let's just pretend this is true. What have they done with this fabulous ability?"

"Research."

He said it so portentously that I laughed. "Can you be more specific?"

"I don't know what all the missions have involved." I couldn't see his face in the darkness, but his tone seemed affronted. "I'll tell you, though, there's one being planned—this is what made me think of it. I don't know the details, but it involves Jane Austen. She's important somehow, to history, I don't know why—"

"Because she's a genius," I interrupted; Norman knew how I felt about Jane Austen. Everyone did.

"And because of Eva Farmer. You know who she is, right?" The name was familiar, but I could not immediately connect it to anything. "One of the inventors of the Prometheus Server? Apparently also a huge Jane Austen fan. She's on the board at the institute, and she's . . . I don't know exactly. She's huge. She's taken a personal interest in the Jane Austen thing." I rolled over on my side, closer to Norman. I was still having trouble believing, but I was interested. "And there's a medical component. They'll need a doctor."

At this, I said nothing for a long while, just listened to the wind and the creaky posts and the sound of my own breath. Something had shifted inside of me: an icy shiver, a portent like a cold finger on my clavicle.

"Norman," I said at last. "You'll give me an introduction to your friend?" The Old British were big on introductions; one did not just show up, self-sponsored, to anything. But the world ran by their rules now.

RHYTHMIC BUMP OF CARRIAGE, CRUNCH OF GRAVEL, TATTOO OF hoofbeats, smell of night, sleep. When I awoke, I saw the sun just up—*dawn*—and what could only be the Thames, a ribbon of silver dotted with boats, a bridge ahead. On the other side, the pastoral persisted: we swept past an orchard, a flock of sheep, a big brick house with a circular drive. Then houses began to cluster thicker, streets to narrow, people to multiply. The dusty air was filling with human voices and the rumble of cargo wagons that clotted the road, along with ragged pedestrians staggering under their various burdens: a heap of cloth, a load of coal, half a pig.

What kind of a maniac travels in time? I was thirty-three the year I went to 1815, single and childless, a volunteer after humanitarian disasters in Peru, Haiti, and most recently Mongolia. Between these, I worked in the emergency department at Bellevue Hospital in New York and liked vacations that involved trekking through mountains or swimming in very cold water, in corners of the earth where such things were still possible. Love of adventure might seem an odd mix with devotion to the wit and subtlety of Jane Austen, but together they are me. What Norman had revealed that night—*Jane Austen, time travel*—was nothing less than what I had been waiting for my whole life. Unknowingly, of course, because who could imagine such a crazy thing?

"We're here," Liam whispered; I had not noticed he was awake. "It's real. Unbelievable."

Now, buildings that I recognized; we were passing Hyde Park, heading down Piccadilly, and there was too much to take in. We pulled into a big square with a fenced-in equestrian statue and our destination, the Golden Cross inn. We'd barely stopped before a man in livery was asking what he could do for us; before we were hurried up a flight of steps, down a dim corridor, and into a private coffee room with a view of the square. Hot water for washing, effusive promises that someone would shave Liam in a bit, and finally breakfast.

THE COFFEE CAME IN A TALL SILVER-PLATED POT, ITS SMELL REviving my optimism about life in 1815. And it tasted even better:

hot, espresso-strong, vanquishing the road dust in my throat. I wrapped my hands around the cup and shivered with pleasure.

Liam picked up a roll and sniffed it. He took a bite. "Hmm." Another.

I tried one. It was like nothing I had ever tasted, and I chewed slowly, poised between analysis and sensual delight: still warm, with a pleasantly elastic texture, tangy aroma, and hint of salt.

Suppressing a groan of ecstasy, I said: "Maybe we just landed on a good inn. And lucky, because who knows how long it will take to find a place to live." As I thought of this challenge, and all the others, my bread-and-coffee-fueled euphoria faltered. "Hard to know where to start."

I meant this as a general comment, but Liam said: "I'm thinking, with clothing. It will take time." He brushed some schmutz off his sleeve. "Tricky to pose as a gentleman when you've only one shirt."

"Our guidance is to go to a bank first. It's more important." Until we deposited our fake money, we had to wear it. "The Project Team was clear on that."

"But we have freedom to improvise, to respond to unexpected developments. Like you did when there were no rooms at the Swan."

"How is deciding you feel like going to a tailor instead of a bank an unexpected development? And anyway, you can't be measured for clothing with all that money on you."

He stood and took off his coat. "Some of it's sewed into the shoulders here—but this, sure they will notice." He was unbuttoning his waistcoat, lifting his shirt, reaching under and back, offering a glimpse of taut, pale, and lightly furred midsection. I dropped my gaze just in time as he turned and tossed a belt like mine on the table: silky fabric, tiny zippers, heavy and thick with its rag-paper contents. "Do you mind? You can add it to yours, just for now. A mantua maker isn't going to measure you around the middle." This was true. The construction of 1815 dresses brought the waist way up, to just below the bustline, with everything below loose and floaty.

"I can't possibly fit this much more under my corset."

There was a pause before he said: "Just today, till we visit a tailor."

"I'm not sure why you think it's such a great idea to deviate from the mission plan on this. Walking around wearing our entire fortune makes me nervous."

Liam, after tucking and buttoning, adjusting and smoothing, returned to the table and sat, resting his head on one hand. His long face was ruggedly unhandsome, with too much chin, a habitually gloomy expression, and a slightly crooked nose. He'd been some kind of actor before going into academia—part of why he'd been selected for the mission—but his looks could not have propelled his career. Only the eyes, maybe: I allowed he had beautiful eyes, finely shaped, a luminous blue, now fixed on my face.

"Me too. But so does visiting a bank. I'm not ready to face one today, Rachel. My clothes might be wrong, my timing's off, I need a bath."

I was silent. Liam had always been chillingly formal during Preparation: polite, giving away nothing. This might have been the most revealing admission he'd ever made, and I was divided between sneaking sympathy and reluctance to strap more money onto myself as he continued:

"The hardest thing we do, at least till we meet Jane Austen, assuming we ever manage that. Not a single thing can make a bank doubtful. If they find us out as forgers, we'll be sent to New South Wales in chains. Or hanged." He added in a whisper, "And we *are* forgers."

A little more time before taking on a bank might not be such a bad idea. I looked down at the table, at the money belt, and rehearsed the series of steps needed to conceal it on myself. Undressing would be easier with help, yet I hesitated to ask. But did undue modesty give the moment an importance it did not deserve, like I was trying too hard to pretend we belonged to 1815? As I puzzled over this, a knock at the door solved my problem: "Barber here, sir; if you'll step down the hall I'll be pleased to shave ye."

Liam stood up, eyes still on me. "You'll manage? Lock the door." And he was gone.

The frock was easy: I could reach the three buttons in the back and ease it over my head. I squirmed out of the petticoat and undid my corset: front and back panels of quilted linen stiffened with whalebone, compressing and shoving my breasts upward for an unfortunate shelf effect and keeping my spine rigid. So I could dress myself in the early days before I had a ladies' maid, the Costume Team had made me a front-lacing model. Over my chemise, my money belt circled my rib cage. I added Liam's below and put the corset back on. To make room, I laced looser, but found the petticoat's unforgiving bodice no longer fit over my less-compressed breasts. I heaved a deep sigh, last one for now, and laced myself up again, tight this time.

OUTSIDE THE INN, WE STOOD BLINKING IN THE DUSTY AIR. IF HALF of London had been awake when we arrived, now the other half was up too, making as much noise as possible.

A line of hackney coaches waited nearby. Also several chair-men in grimy suits, arms folded, next to their sedan chairs. These were little boxes one sat in, to be carried on springy poles by two men, one front and one back.

"Shall we walk?" Liam asked. I envied his rosy, just-shaven gleam. I had washed my face and hands, but still smelled like the inside of the chaise. "We can look at things better."

I agreed this was a good idea, looked the wrong way, and stepped into the street. Liam grabbed my arm and jerked me back from a black blur and a rush of horse-scented air, as a high-set carriage and a standing man in gleaming pale pants and boots as black and shining as his horse flashed past.

An actual Regency buck! Then it hit me I could have died. I imagined compound fracture, amputation, blood and sawdust, the reek of gangrene in a dim room. I would be buried here in 1815—under a cross, my just deserts for posing as a Gentile—and later Liam would go visit my heartbroken mother and describe my last hours. She was used to my risk-taking life, though she had never accepted it.

You could die anywhere, anytime; why did this seem so much worse? I looked at Liam; the color had drained from his face.

He had let go of me, but now extended an elbow. I hesitated, staring down at his dark sleeve, then stepped in closer and tucked one gloved hand under his arm, feeling silly but safer.

Thanks to disaster zones and emergency medicine, I know chaos, yet I had never seen anything like this. The intersection of Charing Cross and the Strand was terrifying, and we stood there agape, as I began to understand why people took sedan chairs.

In the raking light of morning, the dust was visible: particles of coal smoke and dried horse manure, shards of brick and iron and paint and porcelain and leather. It softened the shadows of the stony buildings, swirled in the air, and rose from the torrent of passing vehicles: hay cart, mail coach, curricle. Ragged men courted death dodging between them, while hawkers sidled, crying out their wares in a singsong patter: flowers, beer, snails, milk, sheet music of the latest ballads. The air smelled of baking bread and rotting food and coal fires and unwashed bodies. It echoed with the clatter of iron wheels on cobblestones and the shouts of the hawkers, the overlapping vibrations of lives compressed in one place. The boom of a nearby church bell drowned out all other sounds for the count of nine.

A sailor with a parrot on his shoulder, hurrying with his head down, bumped into us and broke stride to apologize, revealing a mouthful of mossy teeth, while the parrot, jostled, spread iridescent green wings with an outraged flutter. Pushed together by the sailor, we stood close and then, at a break in traffic, seized the moment to dash through the gap, hands clasped. Across the street I leaned against the cold wall of the nearest building. I kept my head low, black spots before my eyes, the roar of the city fading in and out with my pulse.

"Are you all right?" Liam shouted in my ear. I nodded.

A lady in a sedan chair passed, trailed by a tiny African servant, child or Pygmy, followed by a man, naked, dirty, and wrapped in a blanket, screaming about the Last Judgment. So many beggars I lost count, including one-legged Army veterans in uniform and a man without arms, who wore a basket for alms around his neck and held out his stumps mournfully as Liam and I exchanged a look of horror and I dropped a coin in the basket. At corners, old-looking little boys with scraps of brooms walked backward in front of us, sweeping horse manure out of our way and pausing, thrusting out a hand.

I couldn't shake the feeling that everyone was in costume, as if we had assembled for a grimly realistic Regency-themed Halloween party. There was a dairymaid yoked with milk pails; a manservant from a wealthy house in blue livery, white stockings to the knee, and a powdered wig; a flour-dusted baker with a basket of loaves.

THE FABRIC EMPORIUM OF GRAFTON HOUSE WAS AN OASIS OF CALM. Curved windows to the street and a skylight above illuminated the interior, stuffed with rolls of cloth artfully unfurling over the wooden counters. We got in line, watching as shoppers fingered cloth and traded gossip; as shop attendants barked orders to each other and inclined their heads to the customers. The two just ahead of us were having trouble reaching consensus, and I edged closer to listen, hoping for clues to proper shopping conduct and fascinated by this glimpse into the lives of others.

"I do not know if Clarissa will like this," the older woman was saying. "She is so changed since her marriage, I hardly dare guess what she likes anymore."

"She can hardly dislike a good-quality muslin, Mamma."

"Do you not fear the stripes will strike her too frivolous?"

"They are tasteful stripes. Very discreet. One can barely see them," the younger woman said, then, adjusting her tone for the man waiting on them: "Seven yards of this one." She continued: "And if she does not like it, she will say, and I shall use it myself."

"She will not say. She does not confide in me as she did before her marriage." Her daughter gave a faint sigh, and turned the discussion to ribbon.

An assistant had materialized and was asking Liam something.

"No, we shall need that, as well as a great deal else," he said, in a tone nearly as pompous as the one he had used at the Swan, and the man began unrolling varieties of linen. It was a commodity, bought in bulk for the shirts and sheets that were sewn at home, chiefly by the ladies of the house, even in wealthy families. Liam deliberated before he chose the most expensive one, and was congratulated by the clerk on his discernment, as I watched in silence, amused by his new persona of textile-savvy dandy, taken aback at being left out. After a lengthy discussion about the best materials for waistcoats, jackets, and pants, a formidable heap of cloth had accumulated on the counter and we could turn to my fabric needs. I quickly chose a dress's worth each of eight kinds of muslin, happy to be doing, not watching.

We arranged to have most of our purchases delivered to our inn, keeping some with us so we could get started on having people sew. The clerk, who had been totaling everything on a long sheet of paper, looked up. "And how would you pay for that, sir? Are you running an account with us already, or would you start one?"

I had been so caught up in the task that I had forgotten to be afraid, but suddenly I was. Liam hesitated and pulled a few banknotes from an inner pocket of his coat, peeled off one, and passed it across the counter. It was ten pounds, drawable on the Bank of Scotland. My heart was pounding as the clerk held it up to the light, moistened his thumb and tried to smear the ink in a corner of the note, fingered the paper, then nodded at Liam—

"One moment—" and disappeared through a door into a back room.

The Project Team was confident its forgery was too skillful to be detected: relatively small sums spread over many banks, with meticulous attention to ink, paper, and surviving examples of real banknotes. But we had trusted the Artifact Fabricators with our lives in a way I had not fully appreciated until this moment. I looked up at Liam, who was watching the door where the clerk had gone. Expression blank, he might have been anyone waiting for his change.

As the minutes stretched out, sweat trickled down between my breasts and came to rest on the money belt. "If he doesn't come back, I'm making a run for it," I whispered. Where would I go? Could I even get out of this store? It was more crowded now, and we were crushed up against the counter. I smelled tobacco and unwashed hair.

"Do not even think such thoughts," Liam breathed, adding audibly: "Remember, we have to ask about tailors when he comes back."

The man returned, not to have us arrested, but to apologize; there had been trouble finding change. To write down, on a torn-off piece of the brown paper used to wrap packages, information about tailors. The one specializing in jackets was famous: on St. James's Street, patronized by Beau Brummell himself, who had risen from obscure origins to become the arbiter of male fashion, essentially inventing Regency menswear. Another tailor, almost as renowned, specialized in pants, and then several mantua makers for me.

"What about shirts?" I asked. "Can any of these people make a shirt? I do not sew fast enough."

The clerk glanced at me, scratched his head, and wrote something else.

BY THE TIME WE WERE BACK AT THE GOLDEN CROSS, THE LAMP-lighters were at work. We had visited the shirt tailor, the pants tailor, the jacket tailor, and a mantua maker. We'd bought stockings, hats, shoes, gloves, and two trunks to hold it all; quills, ink, paper, tooth-cleaning sticks made of marshmallow root, and a first edition of *Mansfield Park,* passing several five-pound notes from the Bank of Ireland.

In my bedroom, I noticed that all the coins in my reticule, a sort of handbag, were gone, though I had tied the string tightly and kept it close, or so I'd thought. It was less than one pound, but the loss was jarring. I tried to console myself by supposing that my pickpocket needed the money more than I did, but this led to a worse thought: What if his getting it altered history?

The institute's guidance was that we were to interact as little as possible with anyone but our target subjects, for fear of significantly disrupting the probability field, possibly influencing macrohistoric events in unforeseeable and damaging ways. Yet the McCauley-Madhavan theory had established that the field could survive some disruption—our mission would have been impossible otherwise. Of the previous thirty-six missions to the past, twenty-seven teams had returned more or less unscathed, while six had required some memory modification, and three had never come back. So far, no one had changed history in an important way. But our mission was unprecedented in how close it would require getting to the people we'd come to find.

"You must resist the temptation of involvement," I remembered Dr. Ping, the Project Team leader, saying. "It is a seductive age, despite its many disgusting aspects." Yet could we resist involvement and still—what? Have money stolen? Patronize a shirt-making tailor who looked on the verge of starvation? Maybe we'd saved his life today, with Liam's order of twenty-one shirts.

I studied my dress in the dim light and decided to take it off. We'd been nearly back when a passing wagon went through a nearby puddle, sending a clot of mud onto the lower section of my dress and through it to my petticoat, as well as onto Liam's boots. All I could do was rinse that part in my wash water and hope for the best.

The inn had given us a sitting room adjacent to our two bedrooms. I checked that the hall was clear before hurrying out in corset and chemise, thinking as my hand touched the doorknob that I could have grabbed my shawl as well, but I didn't go back for it. The prospect of appearing before my colleague in underwear had given me pause only that morning, but now I was too tired to care; had I not routinely worked out in the institute's gym wearing less? And I saw my earlier concern for what it was: the affectation of an 1815 attitude, a self-indulgence in going native, or imagining I had. I would have to watch out for that.

"What a day, huh?" I surveyed the offerings on a table by the hearth where a coal fire burned: a slab of meat pie, a chunk of boiled meat, boiled cabbage accompanied by boiled potatoes, and a boiled pudding thing draped in bacon. And wine, fortunately.

Liam was by the window, looking out; we had a view of a dim alleyway. His boots were gone—he must have sent them for cleaning—and his coat off. He had removed his neckcloth and wig, and seemed to have just dipped his head in his washbasin.

"Here," I said, handing him his money belt. Taking it, he shot a glance at my outfit. And a second one before he averted his eyes, saying nothing but turning pink, sitting down at the table and resting his head in his hands.

"Are you all right?" I asked, remorseful. We had to work in close quarters for a long time; I needed to be careful about boundaries, respectful of other people's taboos. Many of the Old British were prudes, another revival of their Victorian glory days.

He lifted his head and poured us wine. "It was quite a day, but—maybe we'll get used to it. Would you like some of this? No saying which animal, but thoroughly boiled."

Our own world was vegan from necessity, food the product of technology, not nature. You could synthesize something like meat, but it was unpopular, part of the lost world before the Die-off, that era of chaos and selfish mistakes no one wanted to remember. We had eaten it, though, as part of Preparation, to get used to it.

I took a bite of the boiled pudding thing, which was soft yet unyielding, and chewed and chewed, willing myself to swallow; the faux meat of Preparation was nothing like this. My knife felt heavy and cold; my fork had the dullness of pewter and only two tines. But I attacked the food with determination. And wine.

As we ate in silence, I revisited the day's events, their intensity softened by firelight, quiet, and alcohol. "That was smart, to start spending banknotes. A test. If one aroused suspicion, we could have pretended to be victims of fraud ourselves. Which would be much harder in a bank, with a couple thousand." I poked the boiled thing with my fork: what made it so springy? "And you were wonderfully calm." Liam shook his head. "You were nervous?"

"You weren't?"

"You never showed it."

"If you showed everything you felt," he said, and paused, chewing and chewing the same piece of food, finally spitting out a chunk of gristle and depositing it on his plate, "it wouldn't be the world of Jane Austen, would it?"

"Very true." I raised my tiny wineglass in homage to this notion, drained it, and poured us each more. "But you were an actor before, right? That must help. You never said much about that." He'd never said much at all about himself; this was a good time to learn more, before we would be surrounded by servants and in character at all times. "What's your favorite Shakespeare play? What sort of actor were you?"

Liam looked wary. "The usual sort, who couldn't find work."

"But you went to drama school?"

"I did."

"In London?"

"In London."

I paused, stymied. "And did you enjoy it?"

"Mostly." He blushed again and ventured, "More fun than medical school, I imagine."

"*I* enjoyed medical school."

"Fair play to you, then."

"But I would have enjoyed studying drama too. It fascinates me. I don't see the big dichotomy between art and science people seem to insist on. Why can't you love both?"

"No reason." He leaned back in his chair and tilted his long head at me, rolling his empty glass in his hands. "Is it how you ended up in this? Love of literature?"

"Yeah, short version. Love of Jane Austen."

"She is a wonder." We considered this, and Liam went on in a lower tone, "And to think she's alive. Now! And that we might meet her and—God willing and we don't wreck it—"

"We won't."

"You sound very sure of yourself."

"I didn't go through all this to fail." Liam said nothing. I served us each a piece of the meat pie, hoping it would be better than the one at the Swan. How could it be worse?

"What's the long version?"

"What?"

"You said—" He was looking down at the table. "And so—"

"I had an in, thanks to someone I knew—I mean, I might not have been the most obvious choice, being American and all—but I was the best, and in the end they had the sense to see that. Unrivaled Jane Austen nerd, used to practicing medicine in primitive conditions, proven audacity, whatever." I paused. "And you?"

"No proven audacity, no."

"How did you—?"

"I got lucky."

False modesty annoys me. Liam had written a biography of Beau Brummell's valet that proved he had a graceful prose style and a sly wit, at least on the page. He went on: "Herbert Briand was my professor. My mentor, really." I must have looked puzzled. "He found the letter."

"Oh, right." After all surviving letters of Jane Austen should have surfaced, the annotated volume of them in its eleventh edition, another had turned up in a long-removed-from-circulation copy of *Ivanhoe* in library storage in Croydon. Written in 1815 to Jane Austen's friend Anne Sharpe, the letter was explosive. A novel supposedly started and abandoned around 1804, decades later published in a fragment titled "The Watsons," had, in fact, been completed. In the letter, Jane Austen explains why she won't publish it and plans to destroy it. Too personal, she says; too dark. "He encouraged you to apply?"

"He made it possible."

"I'm sure your own merits had some role. But it was generous of him. You'd think he'd want to go himself."

"He's an old man; not well."

"Nice of him to back you, though. It will be huge for your career, right?" Time travel was secret; if we succeeded in returning with "The Watsons," the institute would concoct a narrative of a scholarly discovery. It would be a big deal, for the Old British revered Jane Austen and considered her short life and small output a tragedy not unlike the destruction of the library at Alexandria.

"It would be the making of me," Liam said in a tone so solemn I suppressed a laugh. "Life can start, you know, after that."

"I think life's started already." I waved a hand around the room. "This is crazy, right here, 1815. If this isn't life, what is?" My earlier dismay was gone; I was burning for things to get started. To meet her, to *know*. The Jane Austen Project was going to be amazing. I shivered despite the fire; it was also going to be cold.

"You're right. I misspoke."

"But you meant something by it. Perhaps you can be the

one to prepare the manuscript for publication?" I refilled our glasses. "Imagine. Reading her handwriting! Her cross-outs, her substitutions!"

"That would be something." He sounded as if the idea had never occurred to him. Yet I knew he'd gone to Oxford some-time after drama school; his book had been long-listed for some prize; his mentor had backed him for the project. And there was something else too, but the memory glided away. I crossed my arms over my chest to conserve heat.

"Is that what's driving you?" I realized I was slightly drunker than was ideal. But here was a mystery, and now a good time to unravel it. "Worldly ambition? Academic renown?"

Liam looked at me. "Do you want my coat? Aren't you cold?"

Since I was, I accepted the oversize garment, turning back the sleeves in search of my hands. There was a pause, during which I hoped he would not comment on how short I was, and he didn't, before I said: "I was trying to clean my dress. The mud."

"My surmise was correct."

"Not part of my plan to go through 1815 partly clad." I'd hoped for a laugh, but he merely nodded.

I raised my glass. "To the mission."

"To Jane Austen."

"To 'The Watsons.'"

Our glasses met. A gust of air from the open window swirled through the room, making the fire flicker and throw shadows, and I shivered again. I had a sense of being there and yet not, as if I were watching the scene from far away, as if time had stut-tered and stopped and gone on, like a momentary disruption in a heart's rhythm. Sometimes I see us there still, all innocence and ignorance, everything before us.

CHAPTER 2

SEPTEMBER 23

33 Hill Street, London

SURPRISINGLY SOON, THE STRANGENESS OF 1815 BEGAN TO FEEL normal. With the help of newspaper ads, a house agent, and ready money, we had a suitable house—fully furnished, indoor privy, fashionable West End address—on a six-month lease. We'd hired three servants, commissioned more clothes, and started the scary work of depositing the fake money. But there was so much to do, and no time to lose.

Routines were established; habits began to form. I would meet Mrs. Smith, our cook-housekeeper, downstairs daily to review menus, plan the shopping, and go over accounts. A stout woman with mild dark eyes and smallpox scars, she had a gentle way of explaining even things that must have seemed very obvious to her.

One morning, though, she threw me a new challenge as soon as I sat down in her dim little room down the hall from the kitchen. "Grace tells me, miss, the drawing room chimney is smoking."

"Is it? I suppose she knows." Grace was the maidservant.

"Have you not noticed?" I had no idea. Coal smoke was one more thing the house smelled like, along with the beeswax candles, the turpentine and vinegar as cleaning products, the lavender that scented my bedsheets. "When you met the house agent, did he say when these chimneys had been cleaned last? I think the fire in the kitchen is not drawing as it should either."

"We have to clean them?" I thought of *Oliver Twist,* and the scene where little Oliver narrowly escapes becoming a climbing boy.

Mrs. Smith blinked slowly, her way of repressing amazement at how little I knew. The institute's solution to our having no family, friends, or acquaintances—in an England where the gentry all seemed to know each other or be within a few degrees of separation—was to make us orphaned siblings, the children of a Jamaica planter. It was not an ideal biography, but it could explain away a lot, like ignorance about chimneys.

"At your order, miss, I will send Mr. Jencks to find a sweep." I must have still looked confused, for she added, "At this hour, they are in the streets, crying out their trade."

"But tell him to get only one who uses brushes. Not one with a boy."

She blinked. "Brushes?"

"Some have special brushes with long handles that go all the way into the chimney."

"I've not heard of such a thing."

"Even so, they exist." I was feeling surer of this. "Make a point of it when you speak with Jencks." I talked to Jencks, the manservant, as little as possible myself; my dealings with him were always unpleasant. "He doesn't like me," I had complained to Liam. "Whenever I ask him to do something, he sneers at me and finds a reason it's impossible." Liam had looked skeptical; Jencks was always fawningly polite to him.

I WAS THINKING ABOUT JENCKS, AND ABOUT THE AWKWARD NECESsity of having servants at all, later in Green Park; a morning walk was another routine we'd established, a time to discuss things without fear of being overheard. That day, though, we hadn't been talking much, just walking in brisk silence down an alley of plane trees. It was sunny but cold, with a subtle change in the slant of light suggesting autumn. A gust of wind had caught falling leaves and was swirling them in the air above us.

"It's time I wrote to Henry Austen," Liam said, apropos of nothing. "Don't you think?"

I looked at him in amazement. "Uh, yeah."

It was what I'd been urging him to do almost since we'd arrived in 1815, certainly since we'd taken the house on Hill Street and had a fancy address to write from. Liam had kept putting me off, saying that we needed more research. We'd take long walks in the parks or along fashionable shopping streets, go to art exhibits or to the theater, obsessed with studying how the gentry behaved and carried themselves, the words they used and how they pronounced them.

I empathized, in a way. We had one chance to make a good impression on Henry Austen; failure meant losing our best opportunity to meet his sister. In another way, it was making me crazy: there was no time to lose, and Liam was exasperatingly in charge of this part, just by being male. *I* could not write to Henry Austen.

"Good, then." Liam gave me a nod, and only then did it strike me how nervous he must be about this step. Afraid, even.

But there was no time to waste on fear. By mid-October, Jane Austen would be in London with Henry, and events we needed to be involved in would be unfolding; it was like trying to ride a wave, and we were already late.

"It'll be okay. You can do this," I told him. I wondered if he actually could.

WE'D JUST GOTTEN BACK IN THE HOUSE WHEN WE HEARD A SCREAM and a crash. Glancing at each other, we followed the sound up the stairs and into the drawing room to its source: a black cloth hanging in front of the hearth, a bare human foot sticking out. Behind the cloth, I found a little boy, motionless and filthy, and knelt down for a closer look. His breathing was rapid and shallow; he stank of soot. I shook his shoulder.

"Can you hear me?"

His eyes opened and looked into mine. The irises were a warm brown, the whites a startling contrast with his soot-blackened face. "Can you hear me?" I asked again. He nodded and tried to move, but I held him still. "Can you feel that?" I squeezed one foot, then the other. "And that?"

"Yes, ma'am," he said in a strangled tone, and coughed wetly.

"Can you wiggle your toes for me? What about your fingers?"

He could. I felt his vertebrae through his rags, finding no sign of a spinal injury.

I sat back on my heels and studied him, then pulled the bell cord by the mantel. But Jencks was already in the doorway, looking astounded. "Could we have some tea?"

He smirked. "How can there be hot water, with the chimney sweep here, and no fires?"

"I'm starting to see what you mean about him," muttered Liam, who had come behind me without my noticing, then went on, louder: "Jencks! Make it porter. Bring us half a pint. If we've none, go out for some."

"Yes, sir." And he was gone.

The boy had sat up and was rubbing his eyes with his dirty hands.

"Stop that," I said, my tone sterner than I'd intended. He froze, and I held out my handkerchief. "Here, use this. You don't want more soot in your eyes. They will just feel worse."

But he just stared at the cloth. I made my voice even gentler as I went on: "You can get it dirty. I have more. Does your head hurt?"

"Neh."

"What is your name?"

"Tom." It was hardly a breath.

I stood up. "I am Miss Ravenswood. Will you come to the kitchen with me, Tom? Perhaps we can wash you off." I held out my hand, and he surprised me by taking it. When he stood, scattering black dust, he was barely past my waist, and I felt something twist in my heart.

I FOUND MRS. SMITH IN THE STRANGELY COOL KITCHEN, INVENTO-rying spices; Grace, polishing silver.

"I asked for a sweep who did not use a climbing boy." Both women turned shocked glances from Tom to me and back to Tom.

"Miss, I passed on your instructions."

"You can light the fire. We are not cleaning any more chimneys today." Tom's hand transmitted a tiny shudder to mine. "Grace, I will need hot water for a bath."

Her eyes were still on Tom. "I'll bring the tub up to your room?"

A bath was a production, involving a theoretically portable copper tub and many buckets of hot water. "No, leave it in the laundry. It is for Tom here. I think he will feel better once he has a wash and something to eat."

A sound made us turn to see a man who was evidently the senior chimney sweep. Small and wiry, in a fustian suit made for someone larger, he could have been between twenty and sixty; only in comparison to his employee did he look clean.

"What's this?" he growled as his gaze found Tom. He brushed past Liam, stepped into the kitchen, and lunged for the boy, who dodged behind me with a cry. "What's this, now?" As he drew closer, I raised a hand to stop him.

"Here is the problem," I began. Everyone's eyes were on me, and I wasn't sure what to say. Jencks appeared in the doorway next to Liam, tankard in hand, frown on his face. "Your boy has had a fall, Mr.—What is your name?"

"Brown," he rasped.

"Your boy had a fall, Brown, and needs time to recover. Since it occurred on our property, I feel . . . We will let him rest here. We will pay you the agreed amount, but we will not need your services further today." Or ever, I added silently.

No one spoke, and I thought this might work. "Thank you,

Jencks. Can you pay him and show him out?" I held my hands out for his tankard of porter.

Jencks ignored my gesture and looked at Liam. "Sir?" he said. "The job is not done, you understand."

"Pay him and show him out," Liam said in the bored tone he affected with the servants, taking the porter from Jencks.

Brown darted behind me and grabbed Tom's elbow. He whimpered, then let out a cry as Brown twisted his arm, hissing something indistinct but menacing.

"Let go of him!" I said.

"I'm na leaving without the lad." He gave Tom a shake. "Come, then, look lively." Tom's head was down. His expression was unreadable, since his face was covered with soot, but his posture was naked misery, one arm awkwardly extended in Brown's grip, the rest of him curled in on himself, as if trying to be as small as possible, or to not exist at all.

"You have no choice," I snapped. "Just go. Jencks—"

"I paid five quid for this one at the workhouse not twelve months past. Leave him here? Are ye mad?" When he began pulling Tom out of the room by the arm, I stepped into their path. Brown stopped. He was working his jaw and breathing fast but seemed hesitant to shove me aside.

"I will give you five pounds for him," I said. The room got quiet: Grace frozen in front of the door to the laundry, Jencks and Liam in the doorway from the hall. The only one moving was Mrs. Smith, who was starting a fire in the stove, yet I felt her listening too. "Five pounds, and whatever was agreed on to clean our chimneys. You will not get such an offer every day."

Brown stared at me long enough that I had time to wonder what I was doing.

"Ten. I spent a great deal training this one. And eats me out of house and home, he do."

"Six." I crossed my arms over my chest and stared back at him. "Six before I change my mind."

"Seven."

"Done."

He whistled. "Indeed! Fine folks will have their fancies." He released the boy, shoving him a little. "When they toss you to the gutter, Tom my lad, you'll know where to find me. If luck's with ye, I'll take ye back."

AFTER HIS CLEANING, TOM TURNED OUT TO HAVE LIGHT BROWN hair that stuck up like the quills of a porcupine, a sweet, anxious face, scarring on his knees and elbows, bruises all over. He shyly insisted he was ten, though I would have guessed six. We dressed him in one of Liam's shirts, wrapped him in a blanket, and put him in a corner of the kitchen near the stove, where Mrs. Smith gave him porter, followed by bread, milk, and ham. When I turned to go upstairs, she followed me into the hall.

"A word with you, miss?"

We went to the little room where we had our morning conferences.

"What will you do with the lad?" she asked once she had closed the door behind us.

"What would you advise?" She did not answer. "Did I do wrong, do you think?"

"'Tis a parish boy, you know. That's what he meant about buying him from the workhouse. He might be an orphan, a child of some shameful union."

"Which would not seem to be his fault."

"No one said it was, miss."

We stood in silence.

"Let him rest, and then? Perhaps he can stay. We could use another hand, could we not?"

"Very badly. But he is barely past leading strings."

"He will grow. Especially if fed."

"Boys are known for that." Unexpectedly, she smiled.

UPSTAIRS, I FOUND LIAM STANDING BY THE WINDOW IN THE LI-brary, arms folded, apparently doing nothing but waiting for me. "Are you mad?" he demanded in a furious whisper. "Are you stark raving?" Out of words for the moment, I closed the door behind me, walked to the big dark desk, and leaned back against it. I was still trying to come to terms with my own actions, and being scolded didn't help. "Is it changing history you're after?"

"It's not like that."

He was staring down at me, eyes blazing blue, breath audible, face reddening. "And that . . . Brown . . . will take our money, and go to the workhouse, and buy himself another child! Do you think you can save every climbing boy in London?"

"Do you think that's an argument for not saving *one*?" He did not reply, just kept staring at me, but his anger seemed to leave him. He looked stricken. "What was I supposed to do, send him on with that horrible man?"

He turned away abruptly, sat down at the desk, and rubbed his eyes with his palms, then rested his face in his hands, so the next words came out muffled: "What you were supposed to do, was not interfere. As we both know."

The chief danger of time travel, aside from the obvious physical risks to travelers themselves, was of somehow changing the past so as to decisively alter the future you'd come from, setting in motion some version of the grandfather paradox. Opinion at the institute was divided on whether this was possible; previous missions had created ripples of change, but just nibbles around the edges. A statue of the poet Randolph Henry Ash, which had long stood in a traffic circle in Hampstead, had disappeared overnight, along with all records of its creation. A short street of terraced Georgian houses in West London, leveled for a nineteenth-century department store later destroyed in the Blitz and turned into a miniature park, reappeared one winter morning, vacant and run-down but otherwise unscathed. This had to be passed off to a puzzled public as a conceptual art project. Still, the institute could not know everything: what changes might there have been involving not stone and mortar but the quiet facts of people's private lives? This question sometimes troubled me when I lay sleepless in the small hours.

"A year of creosote exposure, a lifetime of inadequate nutrition . . ." I meant that Tom would not live to be old, to reproduce, to leave any trace in this world at all, let alone alter the probability field and change the historical record. But I found I could not say this so flatly; the injustice of it made my own anger blaze up instead. "So what have I changed? Must every day of his short, pathetic life be full of suffering?"

Liam took his hands from his face. "Rachel," he muttered. I waited for him to go on, but that seemed to be all; he looked at me searchingly.

"Well? You could have stopped me. You're the man; you control the money, you could have countermanded my orders.

Nothing would have delighted Jencks more. So why didn't you? You're complicit, too." He said nothing. "Don't pretend otherwise."

"Rachel," he said again, and this time his voice shot a shiver through me, as if my own name were a term of endearment. I remembered he'd been an actor; for a moment I expected a soliloquy. Instead, there was a long silence, in which we did not look at each other. Something had just happened, but I was not sure what.

"Perhaps we should write to Henry Austen," he said.

"Yes."

He unlocked a drawer in the desk and took out a sheet of paper, opened another drawer to find a quill, a small knife, a bottle of ink, and a box of pounce, the sand-like substance for blotting. He arranged these in front of him, picked up the quill and the knife, and began to trim the quill's end.

"I always felt like Shakespeare when we used to practice with those," I said, grateful to change the subject.

"Forever on the verge of writing a sonnet—Oh, I wrecked it."

"Here, here, let me see. Give me the knife."

I took the quill to the window for better light, cut a new channel up the middle, and brought it back. Liam opened the ink bottle, dipped, and began. I leaned across the desk to read upside down:

33 Hill Street, 23rd September
Dear Sir,

He paused; a large drop of ink fell onto the paper, and he groaned. "I never did that in Preparation."

He blew the paper dry and continued in a scratchy burst:

I am emboldened to write to you, a stranger, by the enclosed letter of introduction, as well as by the history of my family's association with the Hampsons in Jamaica, the island of my birth, for I arrive in London with but little acquaintance.

He paused and read it over.

"After the death of my father . . ."

Liam frowned. "I remember." He continued:

After the death of my father, the inheritor of an extensive coffee plantation who devoted his life, his fortune, and his sacred honour to the humane treatment of his slaves and their gradual manumission, as well as to the diffusion of the Gospel among the benighted population of that island . . .

"Will he believe any of this?" I was seized with doubt. "It's preposterous. Who frees their slaves?"

Liam, still writing, did not answer at once. "A great lie is no harder to believe than a small one. It's about utter conviction in the telling."

"I still wonder at their making us slave owners. They stink of blood. Even ex–slave owners."

"As long as you've money, you smell good."

If you should have no objection to receive me into your house . . .

"I always hated that line. Like we want to be reminding him of Mr. Collins." It came straight from the letter in which that pompous clergyman is first heard from in *Pride and Prejudice*.

"He might hope to rejoice in my absurdities." Liam was reading over what he had written.

"But really. Are you sure we want to say that?"

Liam paused and tilted his head at me. "You suggest departing from the script, and sending him a letter of your own?" He asked it mildly, yet with an edge. I felt something shift beneath me, as I realized we had not moved on from the argument about saving Tom, but were continuing it in another form.

"No. I didn't mean that. Go on."

I propose to wait on you on September 28th, at 4 P.M. I remain dear sir, sincerely & etc.

Doctor William Ravenswood

He made two more copies before he was satisfied. Meanwhile, with a different ink and an unusual paper, I worked on our letter of introduction. Like the one to Henry Austen, it had been composed by Project Team members and memorized by us both. It purported to be from Sir Thomas-Philip Hampson, the owner of extensive property in Jamaica, and a distant Austen relative.

An audacious, genius move. The fifth and sixth Hampson baronets had spent most of their time in Jamaica. The seventh, the current one, was born there in 1763, but left for school in England, where he later settled. Times were changing: by the early nineteenth century, owners of large West Indian estates were nearly all absentees. The climate was harsh, the tropical ailments deadly, and the cruelty needed to keep the system running something polite people preferred not to face. But the more conscientious, or avaricious, made the dangerous crossing to see to things, like Sir Thomas Bertram in *Mansfield Park*.

Research had established that the seventh baronet had been in Jamaica several years ago, when he could have met us. Better, he was there now, and would be for months. A letter from Sir Thomas-Philip Hampson was entrée from someone plausible, important, and connected to the Austen family, whom we were in no danger of meeting in England, if all went according to plan.

I had to copy my letter over only once, pleased with my handwriting: spiky, bold, and decisive. Properly folding and sealing it, then enclosing it in Liam's letter, was another adventure. The desk was a battlefield when we were through, dusty with pounce, scattered with ruined wafers, scraps of sealing wax, and discarded copies, evidence to be burned in the fireplace.

A REPLY CAME TWO DAYS LATER. IT WAS PROPPED AGAINST THE coffeepot and waiting for us when we sat down to breakfast: a solid, fern-folded piece of rag paper that we just stared at. More than any moment so far, more than when I had opened my eyes in Leatherhead, I felt the strangeness of what I was doing. We had interfered in history. We'd sent Henry Austen a letter that had never previously existed; he had read it, and sat down to reply, time he would have spent doing something else. Looking out the window on a sunny afternoon? Humming a little song as he studied himself in the mirror? I suspected he would prove vain about his looks; it went with what we knew about his charm, inability to keep secrets, unwillingness to choose and stick to one profession.

I picked up the letter, snapped the wax, and unfolded its crisp, perfect thirds. The handwriting was faultless: no blots, lines arrow-straight, words of unvarying size. We had spent a lot of time on the technical aspects of letter writing, a crucial signifier of belonging to a certain class. While the one that had gone out to him had been good, it had not been like this.

23 Hans Place, September 25

Dear Sir,

  *Your letter of the 23rd being received
with pleasure, I look forward to making your
acquaintance. Will you honour me with a meeting
at my club, on Wednesday the 27th, at 6 P.M.?*

"So he did have an objection to receiving you in his house."

"He probably knows lots of people he would not want in his house."

"He needs to vet you."

"A colonial, a slaveholder, friend of some distant cousins?" He examined the letter. "I hope there are no physicians at his club that I should know from my schooldays at Edinburgh."

"You can fake your way through," I said with more confidence than I felt. "Maybe the years in the tropics have weathered your complexion, and altered your appearance?" I looked at him: skin unlined and pale, with a rosy undertone. "Or something."

ON THE BIG DAY, LIAM TRIED ON EVERY STITCH HE HAD ACQUIRED since we had come to 1815, leaving the rejects strewn around his bedroom and dressing room. He paced the third-floor landing, muttering, going into my room to study himself with dissatisfaction in the house's only full-length mirror, and asking me about each outfit. "I need to seem rich. But quietly rich. A gentleman. But not a fop. What about this waistcoat?"

"I think you need to err on the conservative side."

"You might be right." He disappeared into his room, but I

was soon called in for a ruling on trousers. He had ordered a new wig, which arrived that morning, along with the man to curl and lightly powder it. Wigs had gone out of style by 1815; only very old men and members of certain professions—including doctors—still wore them.

The coup de grâce, a bath. The clean smell preceded him as he came down to the drawing room, where I was sewing a shirt, or trying to; his agitation had infected me and I was incapable of focusing on anything.

"Well?" Liam pirouetted, there was no other word for it, in front of me. After all that drama, his outfit was perfect, flattering his rangy but broad-shouldered frame; he had a presence I had not acknowledged until that moment, as my gaze lingered on him absentmindedly. He wasn't my type, but I knew how it was when people were thrown together in extreme situations. It had happened in the ER, and on my humanitarian missions especially. Before I went to Peru, there had actually been an informational session on the topic, which we joked seemed devised to absolve the married people from guilt about cheating on their spouses. *It's not real, what you're feeling.* Liam was a cold fish, with the formality typical of Old Britons, far away from his own emotions. I suspected he looked down on me as an American, and he seldom got my jokes. He'd be terrible in bed. I put my odds of sleeping with him before the mission had ended at 70 percent.

"Even Beau Brummell would be impressed."

"But not like I am trying too hard?" He adjusted his wig, grimaced at himself in the mirror above the mantel, and brushed something off his lapel. "Brummell never tries too hard. That's his secret."

"Oh, no." I tried not to laugh at his self-absorption. "The look is perfect. But do you know what you're going to say?"

He tore himself away from his reflection to glance at me. Our eyes met; there was a pause as I realized he was every bit as nervous as before, hiding it only slightly better. He rolled his shoulders, took a breath, and exhaled. "I'll think of something." My heart sank.

I WATCHED FROM THE WINDOW AS LIAM STEPPED INTO A SEDAN chair and was carried off, disappearing into traffic. I pictured him arriving at the club, giving his name to a man at the door, and being ushered inside. But I struggled to penetrate to what lay beyond. I sat with the sewing forgotten in my lap, staring at the wall, unseeing.

A dim interior, with dark wainscoting? Smoke and shadows, lit by hundreds of tapers in chandeliers like the shops in Bond Street? Drinking? Cards? I conjured circles of men, roaring with laughter, or toasting the charms of some actress. Henry Austen, in a corner, not alone; such a man is never alone long; Liam is brought to him. They shake hands . . .

I pictured this so vividly my head hurt, but I couldn't see what came next. I wished I could be there; Liam, alone, seemed unequal to it. But the Project Team's guidance had been clear: a first meeting needed to take place between men, who mingled more indiscriminately. If William Ravenswood could pass as a gentleman, his sister might be presumed a lady, worth Henry Austen's knowing; a potential match, even, since I was wealthy and unattached. If he liked us, he might introduce us to his sister. Could, might; would, might.

I sighed, stood up, and walked to the window. The darkness of the room made me invisible, and I could stare as boldly as I wanted: an oyster seller, a lamplighter, a coach rattling past, a blind man with a harp being led by a little boy.

First meetings were brief and ceremonial; I could expect Liam back at any moment, yet the clock struck eight and he had not appeared. In one way, I was not eager for his return; I felt increasingly afraid the meeting would be a failure. As long as he had not come back, he had not failed, but existed in an indeterminate state, like Schrödinger's cat.

The clock struck nine.

Perhaps it had been a disaster, and Liam was wandering around London, reluctant to return with bad news. Or something had happened after he left the club. He'd been hit with a falling object—dropped chamber pot, loose roof tile—and was unconscious in a dirty street. Press-ganged near the docks, his protests of being a gentleman dismissed with rude laughter. Knifed, kicked, robbed, left to die.

No. I was being ridiculous. Henry Austen had been late; he seemed like someone who would be. Or Liam had won him over and they were still talking; it wasn't impossible. He was good with the servants, never betraying that there was anything odd about living with people who cooked his meals, made his bed, or carried hot water up three flights of stairs so he could wash himself. These were things I was still struggling to find natural.

I paced the drawing room, my thoughts chasing each other. If the meeting went as planned, Liam would subtly emphasize our wealth—we'd just sold a large coffee plantation—and need for investment opportunities. Henry Austen should be eager to court rich clients, but it was a fine line. We didn't want to be merely clients; we had to interest him socially, or we'd never get to meet his sister. Also, his bank was going to fail in a few months, meaning whatever money we placed with him was gone forever; we had to give enough to get his attention, but not too much. We'd managed to deposit most of our forged wealth by now across a dozen banks and in investments in government bonds. It should be plenty for our time here, but when it was gone, it was gone.

The clock struck ten.

If this meeting went badly, it would be time for plan B. Leaving London, finding a house to rent somewhere near where Jane Austen lived in Hampshire, easing ourselves into the life of the country gentry, and eventually meeting her. Not impossible—genteel people visited one another in the country a lot, presumably out of boredom—but it had disadvantages. She led a quiet life at Chawton Cottage with her mother, sister, and friend; we might meet her entire country-gentry neighborhood without crossing paths with her. And since she was going to come to visit Henry shortly and stay in London until mid-December, there would be no chance of meeting her in Hampshire before that. By then it would be the dead of winter, the worst time for visits, months wasted in futile waiting.

Not unlike what I was doing now. I returned to the window and stared out, willing Liam to appear. He did not.

But we had to get to Hampshire eventually anyway, because that was where the targets of our mission were. The manuscript of "The Watsons" had to still be in Jane Austen's possession, and where could it be but in her house? Then, there were the letters to her sister, Cassandra. It was the particular wish of Eva Farmer that we get those as well: a priceless trove of gossip and biographical information that Cassandra mostly destroyed before her own death, leaving only a few dozen as keepsakes to some favorite nieces. And for Eva Farmer, it was ask and get; just as Norman Ng had said, she was the presiding genius behind the Jane Austen Project.

I thought back to our one encounter, when she had come to the institute weeks before Departure. It was her affectation to pretend to be like anyone else, so she instructed that no special measures be taken for her arrival; the institute should go about its normal routine. Which was nonsense: how was that possible with Eva Farmer expected? But that was how she happened to show up, tiny and dapper, with a smooth bob of white hair and a small security detail, in the sand room during equestrian practice.

Horses were rare in our world; I'd never gone near one before being chosen for the Jane Austen Project. But by then I was used to the smell and scale of them, so despite my surprise I dismounted from my sidesaddle position with relative grace, handed my reins to my instructor, and dropped a curtsy. We'd been advised to meet her in character; it was how we spent our days anyway.

"Dr. Katzman." Dark eyes took me in, a gaze thorough but approving. "How happy I am to meet you in person at last." Her tone swooped and fell, and she dragged the final word out as if unwilling to let it go.

I felt light-headed. I had never been in the presence of someone so famous, so important, so rich. The energy of the room had changed, drawing everything into a swirl around her, like the aura in a Van Gogh. She had a sheen that seemed partly expensive tailoring and grooming, partly just her.

I wondered if being called by my real name meant I could answer as myself instead of as Mary Ravenswood, the persona I would assume in 1815, but I decided to stick with playing Mary. "The honor is all mine, madam."

"I supported your candidacy almost *from the start*." She had a way of stressing and elongating random syllables, and an Old British accent that I was pretty sure was assumed, since she had grown up a dentist's daughter in Saskatoon, with nothing but the force of her genius and determination pushing her to rise as she had. "I did, you know. Others were less sure, but I was *adamant*."

"For which I am grateful." I made another little dip of my head, feeling both seduced and silly. "Would it be impertinent to ask why?"

"I was *most* intrigued by your biography; your travels, and the lives you have saved." She paused. "And by something you said in your essay, about *repairing the world*." She paused again, and looked at me expectantly. "The phrase is from the Kabbalah, isn't it? Isaac Luria? I've studied it. But it was a long time ago."

I was not sure what to say. Eva Farmer was a rarity in our specialized age, a true polymath: a physicist whose work had led to the Prometheus Server, a tournament-level bridge player, the author of an acclaimed biography of Jane Austen and another book about daily life in the early nineteenth century. She played the harpsichord, and had a noted collection of early musical instruments. But the Kabbalah? Really?

"I think so," I finally said. "But I was using the term in its more general sense, of our obligation to our fellow human beings, to make things better to the extent we can." My words sounded absurd as I stood there in my military-inspired Regency riding habit, still clutching the crop I would never in a million years use on a horse. I had meant those things when I wrote them; I meant them now. But I had provided medical care in epidemic zones, been on the ground days after a catastrophic earthquake. Our world was so full of suffering, and I was going off to 1815 in search of a manuscript and some letters? "Perhaps it has little to do with Jane Austen," I said, following my own thoughts to this apparent non sequitur.

"It has *everything* to do with her," Eva Farmer said, her tone permitting no argument. "And each sentence of your essay was shot through with your love of—it is not too strong to say your *reverence for*—Jane. I knew as I read it that you were the person I could rely upon *to do what needs to be done*." She concluded these words with an abrupt nod and an arch of her meticulous eyebrows. "I think we understand each other, Dr. Katzman."

I thought we did not. But there was no time to ask more: behind me, I heard hoofbeats. Liam, who had been at the other end of the sand room when she and the others had come in, dismounted and made a low bow over her outstretched hand.

"Professor Finucane, a *pleasure* to meet again."

They knew each other? They began talking about some mutual acquaintance, and my audience was over. I was not sure if I was more sorry or relieved.

WHEN THE CLOCK STRUCK ELEVEN, I WAS FILLED WITH THE URGE to do something, but what? I could hardly go searching for Liam; London was chaotic and dangerous, especially for a woman, especially at night. Even a hackney coach was not something I could safely take alone, certainly not at this hour. Which meant—what? Inviting Jencks? No, there was nothing to do but wait. If Liam was not home by morning I would visit the Bow Street Runners, forebears of the Metropolitan Police, or write to Henry Austen myself and—No. If he was not home by morning, he could only be dead. Or press-ganged.

Could he just be on the town with Henry Austen? For a man with money, London's choices were endless: gambling hells, taverns, the theater, bordellos at every price point—No. I refused to accept that Jane Austen's favorite brother, a respectable banker and a future clergyman, would propose a visit to a whorehouse. Nor could I see Liam joining him; he'd blushed and turned away from the sight of me in underwear, our first night in London. Gambling was easier to picture. Though I cringed at it: Jane Austen never having a cent of her own until she sold her first book, while her brother could be driving around London in his curricle, throwing away money at gaming tables.

Yet it was a world run by men, for their convenience and gratification, as I understood better each day I was here. Maybe they had gone to a play, or were still boozing at the club; it was an age of heavy drinking.

Liam had to know how worried I was, how anxiously I was waiting. And yet—

The clock struck twelve as I stared at the dying fire. Time was a rack, and I was being slowly stretched on it.

A PROLONGED POUNDING WOKE ME UP, THEN SHUFFLING STEPS and masculine muttering, slide of bolt, creak of door. Jencks: "Evening, sir."

"William!" I ran to the landing, and down to the foyer, though running down a stairway is never a good idea, especially in the dark, in a long skirt. Near the bottom, I stepped on my hem and stumbled, flailed my arms, and fell into Jencks, nearly extinguishing the candle he held. Shadows leaped as he staggered back. "Jencks! Sorry!"

"Pardon me, madam," he said coldly.

"No, pardon me." Why was he still awake? But, he had to be: his last job of the night was to make sure the doors were secured against burglars, rioting mobs, and whatever else London might bring.

I turned to Liam, who stood just inside the door, swaying slightly. His face and shirtfront were dirty, his wig askew, his eyes glassy. Jencks clucked in an almost maternal manner as he stepped forward, brushing a leafy twig off Liam's shoulder and leaning past him to bolt the door.

"Shall I lead you to your room, sir?" he asked with surprising gentleness. "Lean on me if you need."

I stepped forward. "Thank you, Jencks, but *I* will take care of my brother. I had intended all along to wait up. I am sorry I did not dismiss you sooner. It was thoughtless of me. But—may I have your candle?"

He handed it over, along with a disapproving look, and started up the stairs to his room at the top of the house. "Good night to ye then, sir. Madam."

On closer look, it was mud, not blood, along one side of Liam's face and down his front; he had a scratch on the other cheek that had bled and dried, however. I could smell the alcohol on him. "Where the hell were you?" I asked in an undertone; Jencks was still not far enough away to suit me. "I was worried sick."

Liam lurched forward, into me. Being smaller, I got the

worse of the impact; it was like walking into a wall. I dropped my candle, which went out. "Oh, sorry," he muttered.

I felt around on the floor and found the candle, reunited it with its candlestick, then stood up. My eyes were adjusting; the fanlight above the door admitted a glow from the streetlamps outside that was almost enough to navigate by.

"Here, let's go." I took his elbow and steered him toward the stairs, trying to decide how badly this might have gone.

Liam didn't notice the first step and stumbled onto the stairs, landing on his hands and knees. "Oops." He staggered upright.

"You can crawl if you want. Maybe it's safer. Nowhere to fall."

"Rachel dear, what a disgrace, crawling up my own stair-case." His accent seemed to have shifted: a rising intonation, a softening of vowels. Hadn't he said he was from London? "I'm not so wrecked as all that."

"Fine, hold on to me." I extended an arm; he hesitated but took it.

We started up the stairs in silent concentration. The farther we got from the foyer and its fanlight, the darker; by the third floor, where our bedrooms were, I was feeling my way along the wall. I guided Liam into his room and toward his bed, where he sat down heavily and sighed. I hesitated by the door, wondering if he was coherent enough to provide useful information, dismayed at his having recklessly gotten drunk amid London's dangers, relieved he'd survived them.

"Are you going to be all right?" I asked. "Do you need anything? Some water?"

He leaned forward and rested his head in his hands. "Are

you not going to ask how it went, at all?" He sounded Irish, not that I'm an accent maven.

Amused, I leaned against the doorframe. "Nuuu, how'd it go?"

He sat up again; I could see only his outline in the gloom. "It wasn't the total disaster anyone would have had a right to expect."

"So what happened? What did you do?" Besides drink a lot.

"There was this, this bowl of punch." He paused. "A dangerous substance. Alcohol should not taste good. A few of his friends showed up. Including a physician about my age, who was also at Edinburgh." Liam paused again to let the effect of this sink in. He laughed, long and low. "Who remembered me from anatomy lectures!"

"Wow." I had edged back into the room. "Lucky escape! Was he already drunk?"

"And then someone proposed we all go to the theater. But first, more punch. So much more punch that the air all went out of our theater plans. We talked and talked—and later, I don't know how, Austen and I ended up walking across Westminster Bridge, just talking." He paused before he went on, quieter: "It was so beautiful. The lights of boats on the water."

He fell silent, and I was too, envious at the freedom of men.

"We have to take that walk one night, Rachel dear," he said, and yawned.

"Unfortunately, the only women who get to wander around London after dark are whores."

"Oh. There were a lot of them, now that you mention it."

There was another pause.

"So, what's he like? Tell me everything."

"He's lovely. He's Jane Austen's favorite brother—what can he be, but lovely? But you can decide for yourself, because we are invited for dinner next week."

"Are you serious? Both of us? I can't believe it." Dinner was a big deal; I would have been happy with less: a morning call, an invitation to tea.

"I hardly can myself."

This stopped me. "But it did happen? He did invite you? Us?"

"He did," Liam said, suddenly cautious.

"So why aren't you more excited? I don't understand."

"I *am* excited." He'd started trying to pull off his boots. "So excited that—I can't—even—Jesus—" He stopped trying. "Jencks usually does this."

Unwilling, I moved closer. "Here, give me a foot." I took hold of his boot at the ankle and yanked as he leaned back on his bed. This mixture of servile and intimate unsettled me, because it was Liam; with someone less buttoned-up, it would have been funny. "I usually charge extra for this service," I joked, thinking of myself as a doctor, then realizing that we'd just been talking of whores. His boot slid off all at once, and I lost my balance and hit the floor, still holding it. There was shocked silence before we burst into smothered laughter, conscious of the sleeping house, the servants.

Maybe 75 percent, I thought.

CHAPTER 3

23 Hans Place

THE DAY OF THE DINNER, I HAD A BATH AND SPENT MORE TIME than usual thinking about my appearance, though I did not try on everything I owned. By then I had just three dresses for evening, and only one I liked: white silk with subtle dots, a simple design that I admired in the late-afternoon light bouncing off my dressing room mirror. Thanks to Grace, handy with curl-papers, I had a tidy knot in back and demure corkscrews at the hairline instead of my usual tangle of ringlet. Olive-toned skin, brown eyes under a wide forehead tapering to a narrow chin, mouth generous, nose aquiline. I have always liked my nose, but that afternoon I examined it with tender concern and a question I had never asked myself before: Did I look too Jewish?

More to the point, would Henry Austen suspect? I narrowed

my eyes and looked at myself, trying to see what a stranger would. A Caribbean background was exotic and dubious, a screen on which people could project their notions of the other: Moorish, mulatto, Sephardic, whatever. Continuing to study my image, I reflected that context was disguise, and Liam was providing it. Tall, pale, and angular, he looked British, had already convinced Henry Austen he was a gentleman—we would not have been invited otherwise—and I was being introduced as his sister.

So much depended on this night. A more cautious person would have been frightened, but I was excited. Even if in the course of the day I developed an eye twitch, and the jolty trip west to Chelsea in a hired carriage felt like a ride in a tumbrel to my own execution. Liam was more taciturn than usual, arms folded and expression abstracted as he stared out the carriage window.

"Remember," he said as we turned in to the circle of Hans Place, "be friendly. But reserved."

What did that mean? "Right. I'm on it."

He winced. "And—if you could—stay in character a little more, even when we're alone? It would never do to slip up, if something takes you by surprise. You sound so American sometimes. Like just then."

I studied his long face, trying to fathom the mind that lay behind it. I had the accent cold; if anything defines a doctor, it is being able to memorize and produce on command. I heard Mary Ravenswood's voice in my head, found myself using her vocabulary and her syntax—in thought and aloud—without trying. And the weirdness of this sometimes gave me the urgent need to salt my discourse with medical jargon, an obscenity, an Americanism, or a choice word in Yiddish, the lingua franca of

New York—anything to avoid vanishing into the part of a Jane Austen heroine. "Very well," I said, my diction flawless. "Thank you for recalling me to my duty."

It might have seemed that our conversation the night Liam came home from meeting Henry Austen would have brought us closer. But he never alluded to it again, and I think that things people say drunk should not be used against them—and anyway, what had he said? Nothing important. It was more a feeling, and feelings are wispy things.

HENRY AUSTEN HAD VERY WHITE LINEN, A CRAVAT THAT CRADLED his neck in bleached, pillowy ruffles of textile perfection; as Liam introduced us, I was transfixed by its play of light and shadow. Whether to shake hands is the woman's prerogative, so I held mine out—I needed to be assured of his physical existence amid the unreality of this moment. His skin was smooth and soft, hand pleasantly warm; it enclosed mine with a firm grip, like something it had a right to. A man who knows what he wants, I thought, and felt a warning flutter. Arousal? Alarm?

"I am honored, indeed, to meet you, Miss Ravenswood." He bowed over my hand, redeeming the formality of the gesture with a conspiratorial smile. Medium height, tidily built, exquisitely tailored, with his own hair and the prow-like Austen nose of the portraits, he looked just as I had expected, like he had walked out of my own thoughts. Or maybe even a little better. "After all that your brother told me of your originality and charm . . . But I sense, he did not exaggerate."

He had bright hazel eyes and a direct gaze, and I had an impression of being surveyed—in discreet, gentlemanly fashion, but surveyed—as I replied: "You have the advantage of me then, for he refused to say more than a word of you. For all I begged." The day after their meeting, sunken-eyed and subdued, Liam would say only that they had dined very well—nineteenth century for drinking yourself into a stupor—and repeat that Henry Austen was lovely, and that we were *both* invited to dinner.

Henry glanced at Liam, who raised an eyebrow and shrugged in a way that did not deny my accusation, before he turned away to look into a large atlas that lay open on a table nearby.

"Your brother is the very soul of discretion, is he not? He did not want to tell, though it was the truth, 'Oh, that Mr. Austen, he is old beyond his years, of a crabbed disposition and with one foot in the grave, yet we must humor him, for Sir Thomas-Philip has sent us with a letter . . .'"

"I already see you are none of those things, sir."

"Distingué, let us say. Everything sounds less painful in French."

"You are familiar with France?"

"As much as anyone can be in such days as these. My dear wife"—his gaze, which had been on me all this time, skittered off to the mantelpiece, then returned—"was educated there, and her first husband was French, poor man." At my look of concern, he added: "A count, you know. Guillotined. Dreadful business."

"Oh, how ghastly." I turned toward where his glance had gone, and found a miniature propped on the mantel, between a porcelain spaniel and a candle box. "Is that her portrait?" I asked, though I already knew. Eliza Hancock in her teens: huge dark eyes, wedge of a chin, elfin smile, and a lot of eighteenth-century hair. A lively letter writer and urbane flirt, she was courted in widowhood by two of her first cousins. Henry was eventually successful; his oldest brother, the clergyman James, not so much. Which must have caused some awkward moments, even in a family as affectionate as the Austens.

"She has been gone these two years." He took down the tiny painting and placed it in my hands.

I studied the portrait. "I am sorry for your loss." I looked up at him and sensed from the hasty way his eyes rose to meet mine that he had been studying my chest. Which, in his defense, was hard to miss; décolletage was the focus of fashionable 1815 evening wear, the breasts as usual cantilevered upward by the corset, but unlike in day wear, not modestly concealed by a fichu or a spencer.

Amused but embarrassed, I handed the portrait back with a little bow, and looked around his drawing room, desperate for a new topic. The room that met my eyes was studied shabbiness and leather-upholstered disarray, piles of books and a worn but important-looking Turkish rug. "Your home is charmingly situated; positively rustic." Chelsea, at that time, was more like a village, not really part of London. "Have you lived here long?"

Liam had withdrawn, seeming absorbed in the atlas. From his vantage point behind Henry's back, he chose this moment to look up and nod, smiling. Was he mocking my conversational efforts, or encouraging them? Why wasn't he helping me out?

"A scant two years, yet I am well and settled. I hope I shall not move again soon." Henry had taken this house after the death of Eliza, perhaps to escape the sad associations of his previous address. I knew that he would move again—soon. With his bank collapse, he would lose this house and its contents, leaving London forever. No more dinner parties, theater outings, and visits from his country relations; he would become a clergyman, and always be short of money. It was a strange feeling to know his future: distracting and a little melancholy.

"Ah, the others must be here." He turned at the sound of voices in the hall. "A very quiet party; I hope that will suit. Just Mr. and Mrs. Tilson; they are my neighbors and practically family to me, my London family; my own is so country-bound. Except my sister Jane. She would live here if she could."

"How singular," I said. "And why is that?"

He seemed surprised. "She enjoys observing people. And here there is such a variety."

"Did you ever think of making a home for her here after the death of your wife?" I asked, something I was curious about, but too personal a question for someone I had just met. I added: "But that is presumption on my part; she may well have her own household to look after."

"She is unmarried," he said. "But yes, she lives with my mother and other sister in Hampshire, so she is well settled as households go. I would not think of uprooting her, and they would not stand for it. Yet she comes here quite often; she will be here soon. Perhaps you would like to meet her."

I bowed my head, hoping he meant it, but the Tilsons walked in before I could answer.

ABOUT HENRY'S AGE, THEY SEEMED OLDER. MR. TILSON WAS placid, ruddy, and obese. It amazed me, when we sat down to dinner, how much he ate. One moment, his plate was full and the next empty, but his progress was stately, never hasty or greedy. Mrs. Tilson was lean, pale, and worn-looking, as I knew the veteran of eleven live births. Her youngest would be about two.

At meeting us, they showed neither coolness nor warmth: my first experience with what I would later think of as standard English-gentry manners, my first sense that Henry was not like other people.

He and Liam carried the conversation at dinner. Drawn out by Henry, Liam told self-deprecating stories about our voyage from Jamaica: seasickness, storms, a narrow escape from pirates, our fleecing at the hands of innkeepers on the road from Bristol, where we had docked, our astonishment at the size and magnificence of London. As he went on, relaxed, earnest, almost naïve, yet funny too, I realized how badly I'd underestimated Liam's improvisational abilities.

Dinner was in two courses in the Georgian style, a table full of assorted dishes from which people served themselves whatever was nearest, until they had eaten to a stop. Then the manservant cleared the table and produced another set of dishes, similar to the first, except less meat-heavy and accompanied by white wine instead of red. The only person who drank a lot was Mr. Tilson, though it had no effect that I could see except making him redder.

After the second course was removed, a bottle of port and small dishes of dried fruits and nuts appeared, and we went on sitting. In the middle of a discussion on whether another war with the United States would be necessary—Henry and Mr. Tilson thought so; Liam was arguing against it—Mrs. Tilson gave me a fleeting look and stood up. It was time to withdraw and leave the men with the alcohol.

"We will let the gentlemen determine the course of peace or war," Mrs. Tilson said, inclining her head and gliding out of the room, while I followed in her wake, and we were back in the drawing room, where I had started the evening.

She seated herself on one of the side chairs near the hearth, and I did the same.

The pause that followed felt long. She had said almost nothing at dinner, leaving me with no idea of what sort of person she was, or where I ought to start a conversation. Worse, I had no idea what sort of person *I* was. As Dr. Rachel Katzman, there were a million things I would have loved to ask her about: childbirth practices, natal care, hygiene, pediatric morbidity. As Miss Mary Ravenswood, I sat with my hands folded, all my words dried up.

"Your brother is quite droll, is he not?" Mrs. Tilson said. I wasn't sure this was a good thing, but her little closed-mouth smile reassured me. "I have not been so well entertained since I gave up the theater."

"What do you mean, you gave it up?"

"Simply that I stopped going."

"And why was that?"

"It began to seem too frivolous. Incompatible with my duty as a Christian."

I knew Jane Austen was friendly with Mrs. Tilson, who was a fervent Evangelical; I also knew Jane Austen, though serious about religion, went to the theater whenever possible. "I hope you will not think worse of me, madam, if I confess I am excited about the prospect of a little theatergoing, after so many years without the opportunity."

"Dear Miss Ravenswood! You must enjoy your time in town. To be sure, you must."

"And yet, not neglect my duties to my Savior," I mumbled.

Mrs. Tilson brightened. "We read the Gospel and talk about it, my sisters and my older daughters and I, every week." She added, "Perhaps you would care to join us?"

"Very much." I wondered if she was being polite, or if this would actually happen.

We smiled at each other. Before I could think of how to change the subject, she said:

"Did I understand Dr. Ravenswood correctly, that this is your first visit to England? That you have lived all your lives in Jamaica?"

"It is my first. But my brother studied at Edinburgh, and went to London once or twice."

"Of course, the Atlantic crossing was so dangerous." The long war with France, which had complicated every kind of travel beyond the British Isles, had ended only that summer; people still seemed to be struggling to adjust to the notion of peace. She glanced at me; I felt the unspoken question. "Yet your parents did not think the climate unhealthy?"

"Our coffee plantation was in the mountains; it is temperate." I paused. "Or is it the moral climate you refer to?"

"Miss Ravenswood!" She looked away. "I intended no disrespect."

"I am grateful for your frankness." She had given me my opening. "I must explain. My father, when still a young man, inherited from a cousin little known to him, and set out to see the property. What he saw convinced him to devote his life to improving the lives of those slaves that had fallen to his charge, and to their gradual manumission. It was the work of years. After his death, my brother and I resolved to sell the land and leave. If you know of life on that island, you can imagine my father's efforts did not endear him to the other proprietors."

"Indeed." Her reaction was everything I'd hoped for; she

had grown very still and attentive. "Mr. Austen did not tell us that."

"We have tried to do it as quietly as such a thing could be done. We do not seek the world's notice, nor fear its disapprobation. And yet, such a step—"

She took one of my hands in hers and looked into my eyes. "Miss Ravenswood! I understand perfectly."

The door from the dining room opened and the gentlemen filed in. Conversation became general, and tea soon appeared. Mrs. Tilson, de facto hostess, presided.

"Will you take sugar?" she asked me.

"I have had enough of it for a lifetime."

She put down the tongs and gave me a look full of meaning. Sugar was the primary product associated with the Caribbean; there had been calls for boycotting it, to protest the conditions there.

Henry, who had seated himself near us, turned at this. "Sugar is a vice, I collect," he said. "Yet one I would find hard to live without. But I am a poor weak creature, a slave of appetite, am I not, Tilson?"

"Like Odysseus lashed to the mast," Mr. Tilson agreed.

"Hardly a vice." I'd made a mistake. A dog whistle to Mrs. Tilson, my remark as overheard by Henry was an impolitely direct reference to geopolitics. "An indulgence—a luxury—but not a vice. I was wrong to speak as I did. Do not compound the error by endorsing my foolishness, Mr. Austen."

"You are my guest; I would endorse foolishness far more flagrant." He inclined his head. "How fortunate I do not have to; you spoke only simple truth, a rare enough thing in this world."

I acknowledged this with a nod, outflanked. When I raised my eyes again, he was still looking at me, and Liam had started asking the Tilsons about the part of Oxfordshire that Mr. Tilson was from.

"Miss Ravenswood," Henry said, leaning forward to speak in a low tone, "I hope you soon feel at home in London." I caught a whiff of him, like freshly ironed shirt and something vaguely, not unpleasantly, medicinal. "Certainly it is different from what you are used to."

I acknowledged it was, but that did not make it displeasing. "And my brother and I shall rely on you to be our Virgil, leading us through all this."

He lifted his eyebrows. "I hope you do not equate London with Dante's inferno. Although parts, perhaps, are not unlike. You need to stay out of those parts."

"I already see I shall be much in want of guidance." I tilted my head and smiled at him. Would it be too forward to remind him of his offer to introduce me to his sister?

"WELL?" LIAM DEMANDED IN THE CARRIAGE ON OUR WAY HOME.

"You were amazing! Well done."

"But what did you think of him? Amiable?"

"He is." The brother Jane Austen loved best, he would be irresistibly fascinating only for that. But then, those characters she gave his name to: Tilney, her most charming creation; Crawford, her most ambiguous. "But perhaps in the French sense, more than the English."

"Too smooth and plausible?"

"Maybe." But this wasn't exactly it. So what, then? I thought again of how he had looked at me, a subtle smolder. "I think he must be a practiced flirt," I surprised myself by saying.

"He *is* Jane Austen's favorite brother."

"So you think she will be a flirt, too?"

"Not exactly." But he did not elaborate, just rested his head in his hands and exhaled audibly. "I kind of like him. But it's more important that you do."

"I like him well enough." Well enough, I meant, to play my part of a potentially plausible match for a person who would soon lose all his money and could use the soft landing a wealthy wife would provide. No longer in my first youth, a little questionable thanks to my Caribbean background, I was possibly just about right for a widowed forty-four-year-old banker who had never quite lived up to his youthful promise.

The prospect of being dealt to him like a hand in a game of cards was both chilling and hilarious, like I'd been embedded in a Jane Austen novel still unwritten. This was the idea, why we'd come here in the socially mixable guise of brother and sister: to keep him interested, to have a reason to be around, until we could get to Jane Austen, the letters, the manuscript. Yet I realized, as we jolted home, that I was surprised it was working: so seemingly easily, so fast.

"I'm not much at flirting myself," I admitted, wondering where this need to confess was coming from. The evening had unsettled me in a way I was still trying to figure out. "Too ambiguous. Too miss-ish."

"Don't sell yourself short. You were flirting up a storm back there."

If this was a compliment, it wasn't one I wanted; I realized that my idea of myself was connected to *not* being a flirt, to being a person who was direct in speech and forthright in desires. And right now, I desired a change of subject. "So, Liam, where are you from?"

"London. Why do you ask?"

"You *are* Old British, then? Or are you from somewhere else originally?"

"We are all British now." That was the official line, what everyone said after the Die-off and all that had followed. Britain, better prepared, had become a beacon among nations, a refuge to English speakers everywhere, reestablishing some of its nineteenth-century empire, though in changed form, for empires now were empires of the mind, human ingenuity and imagination the steam locomotives and coal mines of our time.

"But some are more British than others." Also what everyone said; hierarchies had emerged, as they always do. "Are you *Old* British?"

There was a pause. "What makes you doubt it?"

"I've worked with you for over a year now, and it never occurred to me to wonder until recently. Whereas I'm—You talk to me for five minutes, and you know I'm not." He made no reply, leaving me to suspect I'd hit on a sore point. "But it doesn't matter. I was just curious."

"What gave me away?"

"Look, it's not like that."

"Just wondering. What was it?"

He wasn't going to let this go. "That night you came home from meeting Henry Austen, you sounded different, that's all."

We rode on in silence awhile before Liam muttered: "I'm from Ireland. But I left ages ago. I don't really identify—" He did not finish his thought.

"Do I know my accents or what?" I said, hoping to take the conversation in a less murky direction. It made no sense that he was reluctant to acknowledge this, yet he was, and I felt embarrassed for him: for his affectation, for my having found him out. But he'd created such a convincing impression of Old Britishness during Preparation; one strengthened by his girlfriend, Sabina, whom I'd met a few times when she'd visited the institute, all tall blondness and bored, aristocratic drawl. "And there's such a wonderful irony to it. Don't you remember, we read that thing about contemporary views of foreigners, how in 1815 the English despised the Jews and the Irish more than anyone? Even more than the French!" Despite the two-decade war they'd just finished having.

Our hired carriage had two narrow seats facing each other, so shallow that we kept accidentally bumping knees and apologizing. Liam leaned back, and his lips twitched into a smile. "Perhaps it's even why they sent us."

"The diversity candidates?"

"Or something." After a pause he continued: "To show how open-minded they are. The inclusive and high-minded essence of Old Britishness. Merit only."

His tone was so neutral that I could not be sure if he was being sarcastic. There were only two ways to proceed: back off and let him be mysterious, or push past the discomfort of whatever this was about. Like lancing a boil. Once I had put it to myself this way, my choice was obvious. "I'm sorry if I seemed nosy, but I don't see what you have to—It's not where you start but where you end up that counts, and you're doing great, it seems to me." He made no reply. "You wrote a wonderful book, you were picked for this mission, you have a beautiful girlfriend—" He stirred uneasily at this, and I transitioned into "You never told me how you and Sabina met. She's not an academic, right? She's something in an auction house?"

"Ages ago. In high school."

"She's Irish, too?" I resolved to show surprise at nothing.

"Of course not." He paused, and I was about to jump in with another question, but he went on: "We were at Crofton together." I knew this as one of the most elite boarding schools, a bastion of Old Britishness.

"So you were high school sweethearts? How nice." I always wondered about people like that: had their personalities set, like concrete, at sixteen or seventeen?

"Oh, no! She would have nothing to do with me, those days."

I thought this over. "That wasn't very discerning of her then, was it?"

He made no reply. My words hung in the air, and it was not until the coachman called out to the horses and pulled on the reins that I realized we had reached Hill Street and home.

I WOKE UP THE NEXT MORNING WITH A SENSE OF URGENCY, AL-ready midthought, as if I had been working through all this in my sleep. I needed to pay a morning call on Mrs. Tilson. More important, I needed to plan a dinner, to reciprocate Henry Austen's hospitality. And I didn't have much time. But a dinner like he had offered, with its seven dishes in the first course and six in the second, was hard to imagine.

Though I usually met with Mrs. Smith after breakfast, today I could not wait that long. Straight from washing and dressing, I hurried the three flights down, to find her flour-dusted and at work on pies. "Do you want your coffee, miss? Why didn't ye ring?"

It flustered the servants when I appeared belowstairs without warning, but I was always inventing reasons to go there. The kitchen fascinated me, hot and fragrant, site of mysterious, complicated projects.

"How much notice would you need to make a larger and more elegant dinner than usual? For, perhaps, three guests, in addition to my brother and myself?"

Mrs. Smith pursed her lips and looked into space. She had dark eyes, a large, mild face, and the sturdy but short frame of someone who had worked from an early age with inadequate protein. "How many dishes, were you thinking? And what?"

"They are big eaters. Well, one is. At least five dishes per course? I rely on you, Mrs. Smith. What is being served these days?"

She nodded. "Right." She held up one hand, and then the other, extending a finger for each dish as she enumerated it. "A soup to start—mulligatawny, say. Duck with peas, mayhap. A rabbit, smothered with onion. Boiled beef with cabbage, everyone likes that. Beetroot. And for the next, a nice fish in white sauce. Some pudding. A ragout with mushrooms, that is very fashionable now. Salad. Smoked eel?"

"Those all sound good."

Mrs. Smith, out of fingers, was staring into the middle distance, still holding up her floury hands. "Drowned baby! It will be just the thing for the pudding."

"Excellent." I wondered what morbid imagination came up with the name of this dish, a vile, suet-based thing. "How much time would you need to put together such a dinner?"

"Two or three weeks should be plenty."

I looked at her in dismay. In two weeks, Henry Austen would already be getting sick; his sister would already have come to stay with him. "Can it really take so long?"

She drew herself up to full height and blinked a few times. "I am sure it was different in Jamaica. But here, 'tis just me and little Tom pitching in as he can. There's a great deal of work involved, and time, and you can't find everything in the market, of good quality, the first time you look. And the rabbit, you know, has to hang a few days to—"

"What about a week from now? Or eight or nine days? Grace can help, too."

"Grace'll be busy scouring things. And helping you dress." She said it gently, but I felt a wash of shame. Since I had not yet hired a ladies' maid, I'd drafted Grace to help me with my hair and clothes before the dinner with Henry. That she had proved adept did not surprise me: Grace was good at everything she turned her hand to. But I had not thought until now how keeping her busy for several hours on my grooming must have put her behind on everything else.

Mrs. Smith coughed. "Which brings me, miss, to my sister. She is between situations right now, but she is an experienced kitchen maid. She worked under a French man-cook in one of the finest houses in Kent. It would be just the thing, to help me out."

"Your sister?" *Between situations* meant jobless, which no servant could afford to be for long. "If she is at all like you, I will hire her at once. Ask her to come here and talk to me."

"Oh, thank you! I will send word."

"But do you think we can have this dinner in sooner than two weeks?"

She was still beaming at the prospect of her sister's joining her. "Oh, faith, I hope so. I will go a-shopping and see what can be managed."

"Next week? Say, Tuesday? That gives us almost a week."

She hesitated before answering that yes, it probably could be done. I walked back upstairs, fingering the spectronanometer on its chain around my neck and thinking of all I had to do. A footman. We needed a footman.

The breakfast parlor and dining room were both on the ground-level floor of this house, which was a textbook terraced Georgian, three windows wide, four stories high, in addition to the basement level, with the kitchen and other utility spaces. I walked into the dining room and examined it with the judging gaze of my potential guests. A large room, with a plastered ceiling and a long table, sixteen carved mahogany dining chairs. In our first days in Hill Street, Liam and I ate dinners here, but soon we were using the smaller breakfast parlor for all meals. That room's table was better suited to the scale of two people, its location closer to the stairs from the kitchen and easier on the servants.

The dining room table was so long, in fact, that only five people at it seemed absurd. How hard would it have been for the Project Team to provide us with a few more fake letters of introduction, along with all the fake banknotes? We were new to London, but still—not a single cousin, friend of a friend, godparent? Yet I understood. Each contact increased the chances of running into someone actually from Jamaica, and our risk of exposure. We had to encroach on as little of this world as possible.

I folded my arms and thought. Dishes, silverware, linens—was the flatware sufficiently elegant? A dinner like this would take a lot of candles. I needed to order more.

Was it a good idea to reciprocate Henry Austen's dinner with a dinner, or would tea suffice? Briefly I was tempted: tea in the drawing room, cake and fruit handed around, so much less to get wrong. But no. A dinner would prove beyond question that we knew how to behave, belonged in this sphere. Assuming we didn't mess up.

I HAD INTENDED TO CALL ON MRS. TILSON, TO CONSOLIDATE OUR new friendship, but got so caught up in my planning that I lost track of time, and was both glad and mortified when Grace came in to announce that Mrs. Tilson instead had come to see me.

Sitting by the windows in the drawing room, she looked more fragile and pale than she had by candlelight, and I wondered if she was anemic, a common ailment among women who had given birth as much as she had. Probably she'd lost some teeth as well.

"I trust you and Mr. Tilson are well?" She nodded. "And your children. Did I understand that you have the good fortune to have a great many of them?"

"I am mother of eleven."

"You hardly look old enough, madam, to be. They must be very young indeed." She was lucky to be alive; giving birth in this era was like Russian roulette. Of Jane Austen's five married brothers, three would lose a wife to childbirth complications, a tragic but not uncommon ratio.

I fingered the faint bump on my arm where the hormonal implant had gone in, shortly before Departure. I had insisted on the strongest version, preventing not just ovulation but menstruation entirely, which I could not face in a world of thin, light-colored clothing, tragically lacking in tampons. How did women manage it?

"My oldest, George, is sixteen, and little Caroline-Jane just two."

"I give you joy of them. All healthy, I trust."

"William, poor object, we lost to putrid fever when he was six." That was diphtheria, which I had never seen a case of and would have loved to hear more about, but she was continuing: "And little Georgiana lived only a few days, the sweet angel."

"I am truly sorry."

Mrs. Tilson's eyes were moist with tears she blinked back. "But the rest are cheerful things, and sturdy."

"What a merry household it must be," I said.

The conversation stalled. How could I steer it to Jane Austen? "You are long acquainted with Mr. Austen, I collect."

"Oh, yes. Mr. Tilson has the bank with him. They have known each other forever."

"And you are neighbors; how agreeable. Do you know his family as well?"

"His younger sister, to whom we are all very attached, comes to town quite often these days. After the death of his wife, she tries to keep his spirits up." She paused. "Not that his spirits seem so low. His resilience is inspiring. Yet how he doted on Mrs. Austen! And they had no children; very sad."

"Very sad indeed."

We contemplated the sadness of this for a beat. "So this sister—I suppose her unmarried, that she is free to travel up to town as she wishes?"

"Yes. She and her mother and older sister live in Hampshire near another brother, a very wealthy man. It was he who gave them a cottage to live in, and a dear, cozy little place it is, or so I am told."

"I am unfamiliar with the English customs—is that unusual? Ladies living on their own?"

Mrs. Tilson considered. "Not improper; but few have the means. And there is usually a bachelor or a widower in the family who needs someone to keep house, as with you and your brother." She paused. "I think they enjoy their life as it is."

"Indeed?" I tried to look politely interested, instead of madly curious, hoping she would enlarge on this. She didn't. "What are they like? Are they charming, like Mr. Austen?"

Her keen look made me I realize I had said too much. "They are. Though the older sister is more reserved; the younger has something of Mr. Austen's lightness. But you will meet her; she is coming to town soon. A neat little creature, very quick."

"Quick in what sense?"

"In every sense. With a needle, or a pen, or her wit." Mrs. Tilson continued more softly: "She writes novels, you know. It is supposed to be a great secret, and she does not publish them under her name, to be sure. But her brother tells everyone, so no harm telling you. I am no novel reader, but I enjoyed them."

"I wonder if I have read any. How are they titled?"

Mrs. Tilson listed the three that had been published by then. I did not have to feign delight when I said they had found their way to Jamaica, and I had loved them all. "To think I may meet their authoress! Such a thing is more than I dared to dream of, when I resolved to come to London."

"But you must not mention you know this, Miss Ravenswood, do not raise the subject; let her do so, if she chooses, that is my advice to you."

"I quite understand. Is she, I wonder . . . An authoress! Oh, what is she like, madam?"

"Nothing of the scribbling bluestocking about her. She has a great elegance of mind. And is very good with children." A pause. "Her sister, though I do not know her as well—she would be the one you might suspect of writing."

"Why?"

"A more formidable sort" was all Mrs. Tilson offered. "Yet I admire her greatly, too; a very pious lady. Delightful family, all of them. Two brothers in the Navy, you know, another in the church. And the one adopted by his relations, to inherit a fortune." Another pause, briefer, and she reached out and touched my hand. "Dear Miss Ravenswood! How glad I am to have made your acquaintance." She had risen to her feet, bringing me to mine. As I walked her downstairs and out into the hall, I glanced at the clock and saw that twenty minutes had elapsed, the perfect amount of time for such a visit. Mrs. Tilson was turning away and nearly out the door before I remembered to ask her about the following Tuesday.

"DINNER?" LIAM PUT DOWN HIS TEACUP. "NEXT WEEK? ARE YOU sure?"

"Mrs. Tilson has already said she and her husband will come, so it has to be."

"Short notice to plan a dinner."

"That's what Mrs. Smith said, too. But she came around." I resisted observing that Mrs. Smith had to do the work, while Liam was merely raising objections. "We don't have time to lose." He did not reply, a silence I took as assent. "You know what we need, though? A footman. Can you work on that?"

Servants and employers both advertised in newspapers, which was how we had found our first three; there were also registry offices, but they were sketchier. We had worked together choosing Jencks and Mrs. Smith and Grace, interviewing candidates just after we took occupancy of Hill Street, with the furniture still swathed in white cloths against dust. But now that I had grown more familiar with how this world worked, it was clear that there was a division of labor we had ignored. Men hired manservants: grooms and stewards and valets. Women hired housekeepers, kitchen maids, and laundresses.

"I was planning to look into the carriage situation."

"That can wait." Still on the to-do list for impersonating gentry was to acquire a carriage and horses. "But we can't have a dinner without a footman."

"Can't we?"

"With only Jencks serving? I don't think so." Jencks was dour and midsize, with a Northern accent and a disapproving manner he reserved in especially strong form for me. He slowly, grudgingly performed all possible duties of a manservant, from keeping Liam's clothes in order to holding the keys to the wine room. "It takes him forever to clear the table when it's just us. Imagine him with company here, and three times as many dishes." I did not suggest that Grace help; a woman serving at dinner had the flavor of poverty. "Go to that coffeehouse where they have all the different newspapers, and see."

"Hmmm." Liam poured himself more tea.

"Make sure you get a tall one." Footmen advertised themselves by height, a marker of status for their employers. A good-looking pair of matching large size was especially prestigious, though two footmen seemed excessive for the scale of our household.

"Shall I focus on handsome, too?" he murmured, and I allowed that maybe Liam did have a sense of humor.

A FEW HOURS LATER, HENRY AUSTEN SURPRISED ME BY STOPPING in. On his way home from the bank, he explained, and chancing to have a volume with him he thought my brother and I might enjoy—

"How kind of you to think of us. What is the book, sir?"

We were in the drawing room, standing by one of the long windows that overlooked the street. He had found me alone; Liam had been gone so long that I was starting to feel anxious.

"Ah," he said. "It is not so new now; it came out a few years ago. And yet I hoped you had not heard of it, in your Indies, that I might have the credit of introducing it to you."

"You are very mysterious."

It was not improper to be alone together, yet it had a frisson: the air hummed with possibility. He seemed almost shy of me, a contrast to the night before.

"I am the very opposite of mysterious, I fear, rather the simplest of creatures." He had been holding a book behind him the whole time and now put it—medium size, bound in calf—in my hands. "It is only a novel," he said with a little laugh.

"*Only* a novel?" I examined it, debating how to react. "Ah, *Pride and Prejudice*." Should I admit I had read it and ruin his pleasure in introducing it? If I pretended not to have, did I risk later being exposed by Mrs. Tilson as a liar? Was he going to admit his sister wrote it? "But this is only the first volume."

"If you like it, I shall furnish the other two."

"I already know I like it." I looked up at him. "I must be frank, Mr. Austen; I read this in Jamaica." Disappointment creased his face, but vanished as I went on: "And loved it. Silverfish were eating my copy; I had to leave it behind. I am very, very gratified to see this book again. It is like an old friend." I hugged it to my chest; his eyes widened, and I wondered if I was laying it on too thick, but I had gone too far to turn back. "It is so wonderfully clever, so witty, and yet so sound in its moral guidance! I think the person who wrote it must be very remarkable." Henry Austen's eyes were bright; his mouth had dropped open a little. "Tell me, do you think it was really written by 'A Lady'? I trust it is no censure on my own sex to suspect a masculine hand penned this. It has such verve, such majesty, and yet such lightness!"

He was speechless for a moment, but finally managed: "I have it on the best authority that its creator is, indeed, a lady."

"The best authority?" I asked teasingly. "What would that be?"

He hesitated, smirked, colored, but did not speak.

"If you have met her yourself, and discussed the work with her, perhaps I will allow—"

"Do not say more, or I shall be tempted to be indiscreet."

We had moved closer together, like planets drawn into each other's orbits. He brought up a hand, index finger raised, paused like he was about to go on, then, to my astonishment, brought that finger to my mouth as if to gently forbid me from speech. Our eyes met, and I thought that nothing in Preparation had prepared for me for this moment; my close reading of the works of his sister and her novelistic contemporaries was not much help either. Parting my lips, I playfully put the tip of my tongue on his finger.

He gasped and took his hand away, and I thought I'd made a mistake. But when I glanced up, the look in his eyes—amused, hungry—suggested I hadn't. All he said was "Miss Ravenswood! Forgive me. I do not know what came over—"

"There is nothing to forgive," I said, and looked out the window in confusion, just in time to see Liam approaching the front door. "My brother is come. How delighted he will be to see you!"

"Oh! Indeed." And we stood there, properly and quietly but too close, as Jencks opened the door and Liam came up the stairs.

CHAPTER 4

OCTOBER 10

33 Hill Street

IN THE DRAWING ROOM, I WENT OVER IT ALL IN MY MIND. MULLI-gatawny. Duck with peas. Rabbit smothered with onion. Boiled beef. Beetroot.

A vegetable tart. Ragout with mushrooms. Salad. Smoked eel. Drowned baby.

Dried fruits. Walnuts. Olives. Hock. Claret. Port for the gentlemen.

Tea. Cakes.

Wineglasses. Silver. Linen.

Henry Austen. Mr. and Mrs. Tilson. Mr. Seymour. Mr. Jackson, a widower, and his two oldest daughters. We'd met these last four at tea at Henry Austen's three days earlier, and I had invited them as well, thinking of that long table, all those chairs. When

I told Mrs. Smith more people would be coming, she had lifted her eyes in amazement, but said only "We will do what we can, miss." Then she sent her sister out in quest of another rabbit and more smoked eel.

"Are you sure I haven't forgotten something?" I had been pacing the room, fingering my spectronanometer, glancing down into the street, resisting the urge to go consult once more with Mrs. Smith. She'd thrown me out of the kitchen a few hours earlier—polite but firm, exasperated with my meddling.

"You haven't," Liam said, but he was nervous too. He was wearing a new coat and kept looking sideways down at himself as if checking the straightness of his seams. "People have prepared for expeditions through the Amazon with less obsession."

From downstairs, a knock. I looked out to see a carriage stopped below.

THE THREE JACKSONS, THE TWO TILSONS, AND MR. SEYMOUR AR-rived before Henry Austen. As we made small talk in the drawing room, my concern mounting about the duck's chances of ending up overcooked, I was struck by a reserve in how my guests were conversing. It made me suspect that Henry was the thread that linked them, that they had little to say to each other in his ab-sence. Or was this just how people were? Liam was doing his best to keep the conversation alive, but Henry's lateness had become the general topic by the time he showed up, and my concerns had widened from overdone duck to dinner more generally.

He was elegant as ever but ruffled, in clothes and manner. "A tiresome business at the bank that could not be put off; I must beg forgiveness." A look passed between himself and Mr. Tilson before he turned to me and bowed over my hand. "I must beg it of you in particular, Miss Ravenswood." Our glances locked, and I thought of the last time we had met in this room.

"There is nothing to forgive," I said and, remembering I had said just the same thing then, blushed. The way he was looking at me suggested he was remembering it too. "And why distinguish me, when all have been united in concern for you?"

"But the others were not giving their first dinner in London. The others were not anxious that anything should mar the perfection of the occasion or the splendor of the mutton."

I could not help smiling at this. "If I seem anxious, it was only on your behalf. We feared some mischance had overtaken you."

"Precisely why I am so repentant. A hostess has a thousand details to worry her, without her guests adding to them."

"You are here; that is all that matters." I thought I saw a yellow tinge to his skin and to the whites of his eyes, but perhaps it was a trick of the light. "And your health, sir? Are you quite well?"

"You are as much the physician as your brother."

"Even more, perhaps. But you do not answer my question."

"I am well, I thank you" was all I got, and it was time to go in to dinner.

"SETTING UP A CARRIAGE! HOW DELIGHTFUL!" THE GENTLEMEN had many questions, which I was happy to let Liam take as my eyes roamed the faces of my guests, wondering if they liked the food—I was too keyed up to have a sense of taste—and if our new footman, Robert, moved with sufficient grace. Under the judgmental eye of Jencks, who was in charge of the wine, Robert cleared the first course swiftly and put everything for the second just where I had told him it should go, while managing to be both tall and handsome; Liam had hired well. No liquids had slopped onto the rims of the plates; everything was roughly the right temperature and not too badly overcooked, considering. Even better, people were talking more unrestrainedly than they had been before we sat down.

As hostess, I was at the head of the table, and Liam at the foot. Guests chose their own seats, as was the custom; Henry had managed to place himself at my right. The elder Miss Jackson, Eleanor, had taken the seat across from him, which was fascinating and awkward too. Because I knew she would marry Henry Austen in 1820, I could not help suspecting she had designs on him already. I was terrible at estimating ages here, but supposed her to be around my own age or perhaps a little younger, verging into spinster territory. She was attractive, with large dark eyes and a handsome profile that she kept emphasizing by looking sideways at Henry, with the result that she was continually turning her cool stare on me, or else showing me the back of her graceful neck. I got no sense of her personality: all questions I put to her were answered as briefly as possible. Henry, who definitely looked slightly unwell, kept talking to me, then lapsing into uncharacteristic silence as Miss Jackson eyed him sideways.

I glanced down the table in search of relief; Mr. Seymour, a lawyer friend of Henry's, had begun asking Liam about the legal technicalities of manumitting a slave. Liam was replying with an impressive mastery of detail, but was having trouble turning the conversation to something of more general interest, while I could see Mrs. Tilson getting silently pink and annoyed at the very notion of slavery. Her husband was focused on eating. Mr. Jackson, large and genial, was talking to Mr. Tilson about enclosure, while the younger Miss Jackson, Henrietta, a petite woman with red hair, kept casting admiring looks in the direction of Liam and Mr. Seymour, making me wonder if she had resolved to marry one of them, though Mr. Seymour was portly and well past forty, and Liam out of reach for reasons she could not imagine. But how ghastly to be a woman here, I thought, as I realized that even I, who should know better, was thinking of them only in reference to men: those they would marry, or those they might wish to.

Robert was clearing the second course; port and nuts and dried fruit came out. Soon, the moment when I would have to stand and lead the ladies upstairs to the drawing room. I caught the eye of Mrs. Tilson down the table; she gave me a tiny nod and a smile. I stood up, saying: "If you will, ladies," then wished I had said something more memorable, but it worked.

I TRIED AGAIN TO DRAW OUT MISS JACKSON, BUT SHE WAS EVEN more reserved than at dinner, further evidence that she viewed me as her rival. Since I was powerless to reassure her that she would triumph in the end, I gave up and turned to Mrs. Tilson. Suddenly talkative now that it was just ladies, she began telling me about an abolitionist friend of hers who had had the astonishing honor of meeting William Wilberforce, renowned parliamentarian and anti-slave-trade crusader, a few days earlier.

"What was he like then, your Mr. Wilberforce? Would your friend call him agreeable? Or does he exude the air of fanaticism?" I put a hand to my mouth. Wilberforce, like Mrs. Tilson, was an Evangelical, one of the born-again Christians whose zeal often annoyed the less enthusiastically devout. Had I just implied that she was also a fanatic?

Mrs. Tilson only looked heavenward. "Such a man, I can hardly begin to describe. Such amiability, such conversation, and yet such moral seriousness and faith. That is what Mrs. Seagrave said, at least."

"Mayhap you will meet him yourself someday, madam."

"Oh! It would be more than I could contemplate."

AFTER A TIME, WE HEARD VOICES AND LAUGHTER AND FOOTSTEPS on the stairs: the men. My back was to the door, but I sensed the arrival of Henry by the way the gaze of Miss Jackson turned in that direction and then dropped. She was talking with her sister a little distance from Mrs. Tilson and me. Would he approach her?

No; he walked up to me. "I would apologize, once more, for my lateness."

"Pray never mention it again; I have already forgotten it." I sensed Miss Jackson's eyes upon us, but perhaps this was only my imagination; I was not going to look. "I hope all is well at the bank, and whatever is happening there will not interfere with the visit of your sister. She is due in town soon, is she not?"

"How kind of you to remember. She will be here soon." He paused and smiled down at me. "She does not go out into company so much, at her time of life, but I will make certain that she and I come to call on you."

"*I* will be honored to call on *her*." A first visit among new acquaintances is a delicate dance of status; his polite implication that I in some way outranked Jane Austen struck me as absurd. "And what do you mean by 'her time of life'? Surely your sister is not an antique, sir? Is she not younger than yourself?"

"I only meant that she leads a quiet life these days, and is not much in want of new acquaintance. But she will make an exception for you; rely upon it, she will."

"I would not have her do anything she does not wish." He seemed in a hurry to order her around, but perhaps I was overthinking; this was hardly a topic I could be rational on. I needed to stop talking about it before my obsession became obvious.

"Oh, she seldom does, never fear. But what of you, Miss Ravenswood? Have you made any more explorations of London since I saw you last?"

"I am afraid I have been chiefly planning this dinner since then."

"Indeed! Such domestic trials can be all-consuming, can they not? I do not understand how women manage it all; they are truly the stronger sex. Without my faithful housekeeper, Bigeon, I doubt I would eat, or be able to find a clean shirt, after two or three days."

"I am sure you understate your own resourcefulness, sir."

"Maybe only very slightly." He smiled and held my gaze.

WHEN THE DOOR CLOSED ON OUR LAST GUESTS AND LIAM AND I turned to walk up the stairs, I heaved a sigh. I did not want to give a dinner again soon; it had been a success with a high price in stress. I hoped I would not have to, if this one had accomplished its mission of honoring our new friends and showing them we knew how to behave. "It went well, I thought."

"No major disasters." Liam was untying his neckcloth as we returned to the drawing room. "Henry Austen was definitely all about you."

"Is that good or bad?" Two floors away I could hear a faint splash and clatter of dishes being washed, before I closed the door.

"That depends on whether you are Miss Jackson or not."

"So you noticed that. I thought maybe I was imagining things."

We stood in front of the fire. I felt calm and relaxed, as if an enormous weight had been lifted from me. "Your little speech on manumission—I don't think I could have recalled all that on the spot."

"How fortunate you did not have to." He stretched his arms, cracked his knuckles, and rubbed his eyes, as if releasing all the accumulated tensions of the evening.

"Do you ever have the feeling—" I stopped.

"What?"

"It sounds crazy, I know. Sometimes I feel like I am forgetting my own life, entirely. As if it was something that happened to someone else. And that we really *were* in the Caribbean, and came here on a ship, and . . ." I paused. And are brother and sister, I had been about to say, but realized I did not believe that part. I am an only child, but I felt certain if I'd had a brother I would understand him better than I understood Liam, who remained a closed book to me.

"It happens all the time to actors. Even in a normal situation, when you get to take off your makeup and put on your usual clothes and go home between performances." Liam pulled his wig off, dropped it on the mantel, and ran his hands through his short dark hair. "This thing always makes me feel like I have lice. And about twenty years out of style."

"I was in Mongolia for nine months, volunteering after the earthquake. That was the longest. And at the end of it, my own life had come to seem unreal. But not like this."

"You were still allowed to be yourself."

"Maybe that's the difference."

After a pause, he said: "When the ladies withdrew, Henry Austen began trying to interest me in an investment scheme involving a canal in Cornwall. A surefire twenty percent a year, he says."

"So that's what men talk about when we leave, business? Ugh, great. Just don't give him too much."

"No fear."

WITH TWO HANDSOME MATCHING BAY HORSES, A GROOM-coachman, and a secondhand but elegant landaulet, we entered another social realm, of people with nothing better to do than go for drives: for pleasure in the parks, or more purposefully through the crazy streets of London. We'd done lots of shopping here—for cloth, provisions, writing supplies, parasols, reticules, fans, ribbons, a rented house—and it was mostly a source of anxiety, with so many ways to get things wrong. The carriage, though, was all pleasure: I found the blur of motion astonishing in a world where the default speed was walk, the danger scary yet exhilarating.

Servants remained a challenge. For the style we were supposed to be living in, I'd known from the start that we needed more; two women and a man were all the Dashwoods of *Sense and*

Sensibility had when they went into Devonshire to survive on five hundred pounds a year, the emblem of downward mobility.

True, Tom, the ex—climbing boy, had responded to having enough to eat for the first time ever by pitching in wherever he could, helping Mrs. Smith with kitchen tasks like pot scouring and spit turning and helping Grace with everything. But he was a little boy, and Grace was overwhelmed, even so. Apparently she was doing a bad job with the dusting, or so I overheard Jencks telling her in a low but poisonous tone early one morning. Coal scuttles sometimes ran empty; once or twice she failed to make my bed, so I began to make it myself.

I decided to promote her to lady's maid and find another housemaid. I liked Grace, who was hardworking and fastidious, seeming determined to make the best of a grim life: she'd been a servant since being orphaned at eleven. I could not go on trying to dress myself, fix my own hair, and keep my increasing ward-robe in order, and having her help in these intimate ways was better than hiring a stranger. That she had no experience as a lady's maid seemed a plus; she would not be judging me against others with more experience at being a lady. Grace—or North, as I had to remember to start calling her, since a lady's maid got the dignity of a surname—produced her younger sister Jenny as a housemaid candidate. Jenny had previously been a maid of all work at a linen draper's in Cheapside, where she had not been treated kindly, or so North confided.

Mrs. Smith's sister, Sarah, who had come to help with din-ner party preparations, stayed on as housemaid—kitchen maid. The two new manservants, Robert, the footman, and Wilcox, in charge of the carriage and our horses, settled into an uncom-fortable détente with Jencks. He was now the head male servant, in theory primarily the butler, but focusing most on his second-ary job as Liam's valet, leaving the domestic void to be filled by handsome Robert. I was fond of Robert and averse to Jencks, whom I suspected of listening at doors and was certain did not like me. The way he looked, or more often avoided looking, at me, his tone of voice: everything declared me lesser, while with Liam he was respectful and attentive to the point of being servile.

Eight servants, about right for the sort of people we were pretending to be, was a lot. Employing them was like running a small business where the workers never went home. And if there had been little privacy before, now there was none. To talk without fear of being overheard, Liam and I had to speak in whispers, go out for a walk, or take the carriage: to Hyde Park or farther, up toward Hampstead Heath, where London plunged into country. The house was ours but not ours, and sometimes I missed the informality and disarray of our three-servant days, which already seemed to belong to a lost past.

THE DINNER HAD BEEN A SUCCESS, OR SO I HAD THOUGHT, UNTIL Henry Austen dropped out of sight. Before it, he had asked us to tea since his own dinner and had accompanied Liam to Tatter-salls to advise him on horse buying, in addition to the memora-ble afternoon he had dropped by with *Pride and Prejudice*. After, he accepted an invitation to tea and then retracted in a polite letter pleading unexpected bank business that sent him out of town. In that letter, he promised to come and see us soon. He didn't.

Since I knew that he would soon contract a mysterious ail-ment that would incapacitate him for weeks, I began to wonder if he was already sick. Or had we done something wrong, violated some subtle politeness rule? There was no one to ask, and nothing to do but wait; since he had promised to come see us, it seemed a breach of etiquette to go see him first, or so we feared. I reminded myself of a character in a Jane Austen novel, Anne Elliot perhaps, divided from the person I most needed to see, reliant on chance or the actions of others to bring us together. We drank tea at the Jacksons', went for drives in the park, and never ran into Henry Austen. I visited Mrs. Tilson as late in the day as politeness allowed, hoping I might see him coming home from work, but I didn't. I made a point of going shopping on Henrietta Street near Covent Garden, the location of his bank; nothing.

We had made so much progress in 1815, but now all forward motion seemed to halt, and I am not good at waiting.

CHAPTER 5

OCTOBER 16

33 Hill Street

ONE MORNING SO FOGGY THAT THE WORLD OUTSIDE WAS JUST misty suggestion, we were at breakfast when Jencks brought in a letter from Henry Austen.

"We're supposed to talk about that investment today," Liam said, snapping the seal. "I hope he's not canceling."

"Wait. You were supposed to see him? You never said."

"I was sure I had." I was sure he hadn't. Liam was reading. "He won't be at the bank. He's ill." He handed me the letter.

I scanned it, hoping for a symptom, anything. But it took half a page of beautiful handwriting and elaborate phrasing to convey what Liam had said in two sentences.

"We'll go see him anyway, though."

"He's ill."

"That's why we're going." Maybe I'd had too much coffee, but I was vibrating with impatience, a sense of things undone. That the cold damp had kept me indoors for days didn't help. "You're a doctor. You're his friend. You want to help." We were speaking as ourselves, barely audible, heads together across the table. "That was our guidance. We need to go there."

Liam drew himself up and looked at me. "I meant, I'll go. But not you."

I felt a flash of annoyance, though he was right. I was not the doctor here, and nondoctors did not pay social visits to ill acquaintances. I knew all this; just as I knew what the Project Team's instructions were at this stage of the mission.

It was annoying, however, that my first news of this meeting with Henry came in the letter that canceled it. I'd been sitting around for days, puzzling over his absence, while Liam had known something he'd not bothered to tell me. There is a point where reticence starts to feel hostile. It was not just his unwillingness to talk about himself, but also the way he seemed able to produce a new personality on demand, like that first night at Henry's. How he'd implied being Old British but wasn't. He was an actor, or former actor, so maybe I should expect layers of deception. Yet I didn't like it; as his colleague, I deserved a better sense of the person under the act.

"Right, that's what I meant," I said at last. "Just try to notice everything for me. The color of his skin. Ask him about his appetite and the state of his bowels. If he has eaten anything unusual. Check for fever. Listen to his pulse."

And maybe that was another problem. Liam had done a good job impersonating a gentleman of the era, but could he go into a sick man's bedroom and convincingly play a doctor?

People in 1815 knew almost nothing about illness or the human body, so impersonating a physician should be just a matter of looking thoughtful, a little chin stroking, dropping a few relevant phrases in Latin or Greek—as gentlemen, doctors had classical educations. We had learned about the state of medicine at the time, about the humors, the lingering influence of Galen. In theory, Liam was perfectly trained for this stage of our mission; he just had to act doctorly and wait for Henry to recover, as he eventually would.

Which was also troubling: to know that he was going to get very sick and that I would not be allowed to do anything to relieve his suffering.

Liam, who'd started eating ham with a provoking calmness, failed to reply. "You'll remember all that?" I demanded.

"I will."

"Say it back to me."

He poured himself more coffee. "Skin color. Appetite. Bowels. What he has eaten. Fever. Pulse."

"And palpate his abdomen, if you get the chance." Physicians, as gentlemen, were not supposed to touch their patients; using your hands was like work, not genteel. Some more modern members of the profession were starting to challenge this idea, though the real scientific revolution in medicine was just barely getting going.

Liam shot me a look that might have been amused. "I doubt we will achieve that level of intimacy today."

"Something to keep in mind, though."

"And what should an abdomen feel like?"

"Anything out of the ordinary," I said, repressing a sigh. Would it have killed the Project Team to find a doctor with an acting background? "Masses. Tenderness. When you percuss, dullness where would you expect—"

"Percuss?"

This time I did sigh. "Here, I'll show you." I walked across the room and threw myself on the settee by the door, faceup. "Come here; kneel down. Here. No. Wait."

Remembering I was wearing a corset—which you couldn't feel a thing through—I stood up and indicated Liam should lie down where I had been; his eyes widened, but he obeyed. His blue coat fell open, revealing a fawn waistcoat over a chalk-white shirt, as I perched on the edge of the settee and leaned over him, placing my hands on his lean abdomen. It felt comforting to be a doctor again, even briefly.

"Touch everything lightly at first, all over—like this—and then with a little more pressure, lightly, your hands like so. But don't look at your hands. Look at his face. If you touch something tender, the face will show it. If that happens, pay attention to where it was, so you can tell me."

In disregard of my own advice, I had been looking at my hands, but then I glanced up. I noticed tiny flecks of gold in the blue of his irises; I was aware of the width of his shoulders and his faint smell of bay leaf soap, of coffee and ham. He was motionless except for the subtle rise and fall of his breath, expression inscrutable, yet I could sense his focus on me, as women can. I took my hands off him and leaped to my feet, irritated. This day just kept getting worse.

"You probably won't get a chance to do it anyway," I said as I walked to the window. The breakfast parlor was at the back of the house, the view of our scraggly little garden and the backs of other houses.

"Probably not," he said. He quickly joined me at the window, but I did not look at him. Had he imagined I was making some stealthy sexual advance? Trust me, I thought; if I do, you'll know.

"For now, just get a history. Ask him about, oh, night sweats, shortness of breath, tingling in the limbs. Headache, faintness, vomiting, spots in the vision. Pain moving the head or difficulty swallowing. If his urine is unusually dark. If his stool looks any different than usual. And itching! Ask him if he itches."

"What do you think he has?" Liam sounded so alarmed that I laughed. Robert walked in to clear the breakfast things, and our conversation was over.

SHORTLY AFTER NOON, LIAM HEADED OFF ON HIS MEDICAL ER-rand, and I was left to wander the house aimlessly. I had already had my morning conference with Mrs. Smith; my hair and clothing had been worked over by Grace. I had nothing but time, and the unfortunate combination of active brain and idle hands. In the drawing room, staring out at the street, I considered the waste of human capital that I was now part of. Maid, mother, milliner, seamstress, housewife, midwife, fishwife, alewife, barmaid, whore. That was it, except for the odd actress or authoress. Yet intelligent, energetic women had to exist in the same proportion in every era; human nature did not change so fast. How did they manage it, how did so few go insane?

This was a question my time here had brought me no closer to answering. I picked up my sewing and took a seat by the window. Though I would gladly have paid tailors to do everything, perpetuating the illusion of my assumed identity meant a work-basket of sewing supplies and a backlog of projects. Medical training had made me dexterous, but sewing was so boring that I was always setting it aside in favor of a book. We'd read extensively from the period as part of Preparation, but found on arriving here lots of novels that had been lost to history. Often terrible and deserving of obscurity, but fascinating anyway for what they revealed about their time.

So far I had completed two pillowcases, four petticoats, and one and a half shirts for Liam, probably a week's work for a normal woman. I picked up the half-done shirt; the gathered part where sleeve met shoulder was tricky, but not beyond me, if I paid attention. Heaving a sigh, I threaded a needle and got to work.

HENRY AUSTEN, HIT BY HIS MYSTERIOUS AILMENT IN THE FALL OF 1815, was out of commission for weeks, unable to negotiate on his sister's behalf with John Murray, soon to be the publisher of *Emma*. Probably his illness also caused him to pay less attention to the bank of Austen, Maunde and Tilson than he should have at this critical time, with banks failing all over England, a result of economic shocks connected to the end of the war with France.

What I knew came from my study, in Preparation, of Jane Austen's letters written to her sister in mid-October from Hans Place. One tells of "a bilious attack with fever" that had sent Henry home early from the bank and to his bed, adding, "He is calomeling & therefore in a way to be better." Calomel, or mercury chloride, is a purgative in small amounts; the Georgians loved dosing themselves with mercury. It did not help; as the letter continues the next day, he is still in bed: "It is a fever—something bilious, but cheifly Inflammatory." The apothecary had already come twice, taking twenty ounces of blood each time; bloodletting was another popular remedy.

His illness was, in a way, not important: he would recover. Yet if we could manage to become part of his life, Liam trusted as doctor and friend, we would then be in position to observe when, in early 1816, Jane Austen would start showing symptoms of whatever would kill her a year and a half later. Our other major goal was to figure out what that was. You could argue it was irrelevant, centuries after the fact, but her early death has long tormented her biographers and her fans. The hunger to answer this question was why the Project Team had needed a doctor; it was why I was here.

Henry's illness was the opening, the reason we had been sent at this moment, in this guise. But could we make use of it?

I JUMPED UP AT THE SOUND OF A KNOCK TO FIND OUR CARRIAGE stopped below and Liam at the door. "I thought we might take a ride," he said to me from the bottom of the stairs. I grabbed my spencer and was out the door in time to hear him sending Wilcox back to the stables. Liam driving himself meant we could talk freely. Which meant he had something to say.

"Well?" I demanded. We were seated on the box and had reached the relative calm of Hyde Park.

"He said he's been having some kind of attack. But no details. 'A violent bilious attack, my dear fellow,' he kept saying."

"Which probably means vomiting. Did he mention that? How did he seem?"

"Weak. Yellowish."

"Was he in bed?"

"He talked of getting up later."

"Did he say whether his skin itched?"

"He said it did. He seemed surprised to be asked."

"Does he drink a lot, when the ladies withdraw?"

"No more than anyone else."

"But you both drank heavily, that night you first met."

"Uncharacteristic. We were having such good talk—one bowl of punch led to another."

"So, occasional binge drinker."

I was merely thinking aloud, but Liam said: "You make it sound pathological. This is just life, as they live it now."

"Was his urine darker than usual, did you ask?"

"I did not."

"I suppose he had a fever? Was he hot to the touch?"

"I did not touch him."

"Well, did he appear feverish?" Liam didn't answer. "He might have looked sweaty, or flushed. The eyes can look strange, too. Glassy."

"Perhaps he was a little flushed," Liam muttered after a pause. "He was so yellowish, hard to say."

"What about his bowels? Were his bowels very disordered?" Liam said nothing.

"And how does his stool look, did you think to ask?"

Another silence followed, a long one.

"It isn't a thing I felt comfortable asking a gentleman," Liam said at last. His voice was quiet, but there was a hostile edge to it. "That is to say, I forgot item eleven on your extensive list of questions. But even if I had remembered, I would not have asked him." After another pause, he added with more of an edge: "So there you are."

We had been inside the park, headed north, but at the next opportunity, shortly past the Reservoir, Liam turned left, then left again. I registered this without reflecting on it, lost in my own thoughts, which were divided between trying to diagnose Henry Austen's ailment secondhand and wondering about Liam. Quiet people; you never knew about them. Then I looked up, surprised to realize we were leaving the park, but on the south side. Liam took the left at Knightsbridge and then turned onto Sloane.

"Isn't this the wrong direction?" I asked. The park is a more pleasant place to ride than the streets. Past Sloane Square, the area grows desolate: there is the Royal Military Asylum, the orphanage for children of soldiers killed fighting Napoleon; then a large gloomy hospital with a graveyard conveniently nearby; then Ranelagh, the former pleasure garden now shuttered and abandoned. It was a long trip back to Hill Street. "Why did you go this way?"

Liam made no reply, but I got a clue when we turned in to the circle of Hans Place. "Surely you're not headed back to Henry Austen's?"

"It appears I am."

"It's too late for visiting—it must be nearly five. And you were there already." Liam did not look at me or answer, but I sensed anger in the set of his neck, his jaw. The thought struck me that if he should decide to commit me to a lunatic asylum, lock me up at home, or beat me, the law was on his side, and all our money in the bank in his name. Not that I believed he would do any of these things, but that he *could* sent a chill through me, that I was in a place where such things were possible. "Hey, look at me." My voice shook. "What are you, crazy?"

We were already outside Henry Austen's. Liam pulled the horses to a stop and finally turned to face me, his expression not angry, as I'd expected. He seemed to be having trouble finding words. Finally he began: "The thing is—we've got to be on the same side here, Rachel, because—"

He stopped. And in that pause, something happened. Looking back, I would say it was the moment I first saw him clearly. Not my idea of him, not the various selves he had on offer, but what was: his shyness, his odd charisma. What had possessed me to needle him like that?

"I know," I said. "We do. I'm sorry. The main thing is to cultivate him, to make him trust you. And you've been doing that. I shouldn't be so—"

The front door opened to reveal Henry Austen's manservant, Richard. "Dr. Ravenswood!" He seemed delighted. "The lad will see to your horses in a moment. I'll ask if the master is at home." Beaming, he disappeared again. Yet I doubted our visit would be welcomed by his employer; a doctor might plausibly call again at this hour, saying he'd forgotten something—but what was my excuse? I felt myself grow cold all over, then hot with anticipated embarrassment.

"My vails must be too generous," Liam said. "I thought he was going to kiss my hand earlier when I slipped him some money on the way out. Has he been watching the street all this time, praying for my return?" Despite everything, this made me laugh. "And now I can never give less—he will hate me."

"That's the least of our worries. What are you going to say to Henry Austen?"

"I'll think of something."

ALL I COULD HOPE WAS THAT HENRY WOULD NOT BE "AT HOME," but Richard ushered us into the empty drawing room, assuring us the master would be down immediately. We stood by the hearth like two people facing the firing squad. How was I going to get through this?

I heard Liam's faint gasp and looked up. Henry stood in the doorway, yellower than I could have imagined and wearing a banyan, a more elegant iteration of a bathrobe, over shirt and pants. Behind him was a slender woman, on the tall side, in a lace cap with a few curls spilling out. She had his nose, hazel eyes like his, and a quizzical expression that seemed right. Yet I could not believe it, until Henry came into the room and said:

"Doctor, I am honored indeed by your second visit today—Miss Ravenswood, by your first. And my sister, Miss Austen, having expressed the wish to be introduced to you—"

"The honor is all ours," Liam said, stepping forward and putting out his hand, then, remembering that shaking was the lady's decision, jerking it back. "I am—that is—your honored, er, humble servant." He bowed, turning a deep scarlet.

Jane Austen studied him, expression unreadable, and did not offer her hand. She inclined her head slightly and looked at me. Her eyes were bright, her gaze direct. I thought of meeting Eva Farmer: I had the same sense of being in the presence of a formidable intelligence, of feeling the air around us warped by the force of it. After a moment of silence that seemed to stretch and stretch, I managed to squeak, "How d'ye do?"

"Please," she said. "Sit down. So good of you to come." Her voice was husky, as if she were getting a cold, with a drollness that seemed to give her commonplace words an extra spin. Liam and I sat as abruptly as marionettes, and a longer silence ensued.

Henry came to the rescue. "My sister has been here just these few days. I was not fit to go out, or we should have called on you before now, Miss Ravenswood, as I promised. I regret the omission."

Jane Austen smiled at her brother. "You need not apologize. One would think, to hear you, that they are come to town with no other design than to meet me." She turned her smile on us. "But that is Henry. He never thinks but of how to promote my happiness."

"So you have not been in town long?" I winced at the banality of my own remark.

"Just since Friday."

"And your journey, uneventful, I trust?"

"Quite." She paused. "A part of one hopes for banditti—an overset—if only for something to recollect later in tranquillity—"

"Jane!" Henry protested. She gave him a look that excluded outsiders. Since it was well past the hour when mere acquaintances dropped by without warning, and they had surely been having a good time alone together, catching up after months apart, I wondered why he'd let us in, why she'd come along to be introduced, and if she was now sorry. We weren't offering much in the way of witty conversation.

"You are a quite frequent visitor to town, I think your brother said?" I asked.

"As frequent as I can be."

There was another little silence. Liam was no help; he was just staring at Jane Austen, eyes wide, biting his lip.

"You are new to London, Miss Ravenswood. Do you find it agreeable?"

"Very much. Though I have heard so much of the beauty of the English countryside, that I confess a longing to see that, too."

"It is hardly a matter for confessing to, as if in shame. If I may ask, what stops you?" I hesitated, since I could hardly admit the truth she had already jokingly guessed, that I was in London for no reason other than her. "There is not want of money, or leisure, I trust?"

These words seemed to rouse Liam from his trance. Springing to his feet, he said: "If the ladies will allow, I must speak to Mr. Austen in private. I came with the view of making another particular inquiry into his health, and I do not propose to trespass on his hospitality for a second time today longer than necessary."

Henry looked up. "I hate a fuss. I am feeling better. And is it something we must go to another room for?" I had hardly noticed him, I had been so distracted by his sister, but now I took a good look. Though as put together as ever, freshly shaven, with gleaming linen, he looked tired, in addition to seriously jaundiced.

"Let us adjourn, sir, and I will allow you to judge."

Henry frowned and hesitated, but politeness won. "Then, if you will—" He stood up and waved a graceful hand toward the door. Liam led the way into the passage, and I was left with Jane Austen and my own sense of disbelief. How long had I anticipated this day, worked toward it, longed for it? And what I mostly felt was fear; I would have given anything to be at home reading one of her books instead. How can you possibly impress Jane Austen?

As I sat paralyzed, she took a handkerchief from her sleeve

and wiped her nose, which was a little red. I realized though I was likely to fail with conversation, I was certain to fail with silence. I took hold of my courage and said:

"To answer, I think my chief difficulty lies in not knowing where to go first. What do you advise? The Lake District? Derbyshire?"

She tilted her head thoughtfully. She seemed less playful, and I realized her real audience was her brother; he was the one she was trying to get a laugh from. "Kent is very beautiful. After my own country, it is the place I know best."

"You have a brother there, I think?"

"Yes." She offered no more on that. "Or you might try Lyme Regis, on the Dorset coast."

"Why?" I wondered if she had yet written the part in *Persuasion* where her characters go there. Maybe she was working on it now.

A lift of her eyebrows suggested my question had been abrupt. "It is very picturesque."

A pause. "I shall take your advice, then, with pleasure. But, October, is it too late for a trip to the seacoast? Should it wait until spring?"

"Some find autumn the most beautiful time there. But it is colder." She paused. "The daylight dwindles."

I bowed my head. "A more melancholy time, to be sure."

"Henry merely said you are new to London. Where do you come from, that all of England is strange to you? From Ireland?" Her nostrils twitched, as if in delicate distaste. Or was she thinking of Thomas Lefroy, the law student from Limerick and future lord chief justice she had famously flirted with in 1796? Did she think of him much?

"We are from Jamaica. In the West Indies." I stopped, mortified. "But forgive me, Miss Austen, I am sure you know where that is; I do not need to furnish a geography lesson."

For the first time she looked at me with a gleam of amusement. "I do. But you are right not to assume. Have you met many people here yet, ignorant of where it lies? Do not answer; it may not be a credit to my countrymen and women. I met a young lady in Alton last week who was certain that Elba was in the Red Sea. I cannot think how she acquired this idea." She paused. "But you did not grow up on Jamaica."

"It grieves me to contradict you, but I did."

"Your father was in colonial government?"

"He inherited a coffee plantation from a distant relation."

"I see."

"But, you must understand, he was no friend to the slave trade, no more than my brother and I, his heirs. We have unwound our interests there, and shall not return."

"Indeed?" Her gaze had a disconcerting intensity. "And are you homesick?"

No one here had asked me such a thing. What answer would make her think I was a good and sensitive person? She wrote movingly about attachment to location, suggesting she knew homesickness herself. But the West Indies—louche, blood-soaked, full of tropical diseases like the one that had killed Cassandra's fiancé in San Domingo in 1797—was it acceptable to miss somewhere like that?

"One does not love a place the less for having suffered in it," I began cautiously.

"An interesting notion." She continued to study me. "And— forgive my questions, they are impertinent, but I cannot help myself—was he English, your father?"

There was a little silence as we regarded each other. "Since William the Conqueror," I said, wondering again if this was the right answer. Perhaps something exotic would have made us more interesting. Huguenot, like Thomas Lefroy. Descendants of aristocratic refugees of a Polish uprising. I would have been whatever she wanted, if only I knew what. "Do I strike you as foreign, Miss Austen?"

She did not smile, but she brightened. "Thank you. A direct question is the best way to repulse an impertinent one. Henry has a wide circle of acquaintance, as you know." I was amused at how she had praised my question without answering it. From the hallway, we heard Liam and Henry returning. She went on: "I hope we can talk again. I would enjoy learning more about the life there. I have traveled rather little, and do not expect to do so in the future."

I bowed my head. "The pleasure would be mine."

CONVERSATION ON THE RIDE HOME WAS DISJOINTED; LIAM AND I were as giddy as drunken goats.

"What did you talk about? What was she like when it was just you?" Liam demanded.

"Well, you know. Terrifying."

"I know, I couldn't—I was just—"

"You were speechless. I never saw you like that."

"Are you saying I talk too much?"

"No! You always say the right thing in company. A one-man schmoozefest. Except for just then."

"Oh, mother of god, it was humiliating." He paused and

added: "And, that thing he was wearing? I want one. I am going to the tailor's *tomorrow*."

His digression into fashion amused me more than I let on. "The banyan? It was nice. But, more to the point, you sly dog, did you *know*? Did you know, when you went back there—"

"That I was taking us to meet Jane Austen?"

"Exactly."

He did not answer right away. "Something Henry said earlier made me know she was in the house. But if you are asking if I expected *that*—no."

"She said she wanted to talk to me again. But I don't know if she meant it." I paused. "Do you think she suspects . . ." I stopped, thinking my question would just sound crazy to him.

"That we are time travelers from the future? No."

CHAPTER 6

OCTOBER 17

33 Hill Street

WOKE UP WITH A SORE JAW, LIKE I'D BEEN CLENCHING MY TEETH in my sleep, and a memory of a dream about Isaac of York, the emotionally overwrought moneylender in *Ivanhoe*. I did not have to work to understand: Isaac personified my anxiety about what I'd decided against asking Liam on the way home. But would they even recognize a Jew? I wondered, eyes still closed. Or would they expect the hook-nosed caricature of satirical prints? Chances are Jane never saw one before, up close. But Henry. Could you work as a London banker in 1815 and never—

But I had more immediate problems. Yesterday, meeting her had loomed as a huge achievement; today, it made me realize how many hurdles remained. We had to devise a reason to be in Chawton, and a way not just to be invited to her house, but to get into the very bedroom of the two sisters, the probable location of the letters and "The Watsons." To earn her trust, and to know her so well she would confide details of her illness. Yet it was clear she did not like people easily or right away, unlike her brother, and had no motive to cultivate them for business reasons, as he did. How to make her like us? It seemed hopeless. What did I have to offer? My starstruck adoration would only scare her. My knowledge of her future, post-humous fame—but what use was that; how could I leverage it?

Perhaps, in superior understanding. What I love about Jane Austen has never been the marriage plot; the quest for a hus-band in her novels struck me, even when I was younger and more susceptible, as a MacGuffin, or at least a metaphor. I have always suspected this is how she meant her books to be read. Many peo-ple from my world find it strange, even tragic, that the author of such emotionally satisfying love stories apparently never found love herself, but I don't.

For one thing, she was a genius: burning with the desire to create undying works of art, not a cozy home for a husband and children. For another, she wrote the world she knew, and what she felt would appeal to readers. The marriage plot is interest-ing mostly for how it illuminates the hearts of her characters, what they learn about themselves on the way to the altar. She concerns herself with bigger questions: how to distinguish good people from plausible fakes; what a moral life demands of us; the problem of how to be an intelligent woman in a world that had no real use for them. If I could get to the point of talking about her books with her, and make it clear I understood this—maybe then she would see I was not like everyone else, and I would not need to steal "The Watsons." She would share the manuscript with me of her own accord.

I was consumed with curiosity about this book; what did it reveal about her, that she felt the need to destroy it?

THE FIRST FIVE CHAPTERS, ALL THAT SURVIVED IN MY TIME, TELL the story of Emma Watson, nineteen, brought up by her wealthy, affectionate aunt and uncle in refined comfort and expectations of a tidy inheritance. When the action opens, her uncle has died, her aunt has remarried unwisely, and Emma has been cast out penniless, to return to brothers and sisters she barely remembers, and a kind but ailing father, whose impending death is certain to make the four unmarried sisters' precarious financial situation even worse.

Why Jane Austen supposedly never finished it is a question that has long tormented scholars. James-Edward Austen, the nephew who would in his old age write the first biography of his aunt, snobbishly speculated she had made a mistake in setting the novel among people too lowborn. Others have argued that its depiction of the brutalities of class and money was too painfully realistic for her to continue with. But I never believed that, even before the discovery of the Anne Sharpe letter. *Sense and Sensibility* has an equally grim opening of disinheritance and a slide down the economic ladder; if we did not know its happy ending, we would think of it differently.

LATER THAT MORNING, WHEN I ARRIVED TO VISIT MRS. TILSON, she greeted me with "Miss Ravenswood, such good news: Mr. Austen's sister is come to town!"

"Yes. I went to Number Twenty-three with my brother—

which is how I missed your call yesterday—and there I had the pleasure of meeting her."

"So you saw him? Mr. Tilson says he is excessively ill, and has not appeared at the bank for days."

"My brother was concerned about his health, and stopped to inquire."

"And?"

"And there we had the pleasure to meet Miss Austen."

"Oh, she is a delightful creature! But, what of Mr. Austen? Is he really very ill?"

I hesitated. "My brother expects him to make a full recovery."

"The poor man, he has suffered enough. The loss of his wife—"

"Yes, very sad." I was trying to decide how to direct the conversation back to his sister when I did not have to: the servant appeared to announce her.

That morning Liam had decided to go see Henry again, while I'd come along to Hans Place but had gone next door, to Mrs. Tilson, whom I owed a visit. I hadn't felt ready to see Jane again so soon. Despite being what I had come to 1815 for, it had been overwhelming; I needed to process the experience, maybe think of some suitable conversational topics I could produce with the appearance of spontaneity the next time we met. That she might show up at Mrs. Tilson's was a possibility I should have anticipated, but hadn't.

She was wearing the same light blue dress as on the previous day and a warm smile that dwindled as she walked into the room and realized Mrs. Tilson was not alone. She doesn't like me, I thought, my courage failing. And why should she?

"Dear Jane!" Mrs. Tilson stood up to take her hands and give her a kiss on each cheek. "How is your brother? Better today, I hope."

She took a moment before replying, still holding Mrs. Tilson's hands. "He says he will go to the bank, though he has not actually gone yet. He sends his best love." She acknowledged me with a quick look.

"Miss Ravenswood tells me *her* brother is confident of his speedy recovery."

Jane gave me a second look. "Is he? A comfort indeed."

"I am not sure he said 'speedy.'" I felt pedantic correcting her, but Liam's medical reputation was at stake. "He is certain recovery will be complete. But it may be slow."

"Your brother is kind to take such a lively interest in someone he has known so short a time."

This stung, though I wasn't sure it was meant to. "Mr. Austen's warmth and candor make him seem a far older friend than he is," I replied. She inclined her head to acknowledge the truth of this. "Does he seem better this morning?" I went on. "Less yellow?"

She frowned. "He was not so *very* yellow, surely."

"Yellow?" Mrs. Tilson brought a hand to her mouth. "You did not mention he was yellow. It cannot be yellow fever, can it? Ought you to be visiting a house with children?"

"I had no thought of such a thing—" Jane began.

"He does not have yellow fever," I interrupted, before this could go any further.

They both looked at me. "How are you so certain?" Mrs. Tilson asked.

"I just am." This did not seem to satisfy them, so I went on:

"I have seen yellow fever in Jamaica; that is not what Mr. Austen has. And even if he had it—*which he does not*—we would not fear contagion from him."

"Why not?" Jane demanded.

I hesitated. People got the disease from mosquitoes, but no one knew that in 1815. "It is contagious only in the tropics. The few, rare cases seen in temperate climates have never displayed this characteristic."

"You seem very sure of this." Mrs. Tilson sounded doubtful.

"I often assisted my brother in the infirmary, madam, that we established on our plantation."

"Ah, indeed?" Mrs. Tilson said. "You were a true Lady Bountiful, then. I hope you may find similar opportunities for good works in London."

"From what I have seen, there is no shortage of wretchedness and despair to relieve." I glanced at Jane, who was suppressing a yawn. Mrs. Tilson would be inviting me over again to read the Bible if we went on like this. "But I do not mean to hug myself as some plaster saint, Miss Austen, do not misunderstand me."

"What an alarmingly Papist metaphor. I should hope not." Her eyes brightened with amusement, though. "Henry has assured me you and your brother are both very agreeable, and a welcome addition to his circle. Though *he* had little to say for himself yesterday. Is the doctor usually so disinclined to speech?"

"Not in the least!" Mrs. Tilson said.

"Perhaps he was overset by meeting you," I offered.

She looked blank for an instant; then she smiled. "You are cruel. Whether I ever in my life struck a gentleman dumb with admiration, I leave for others to determine. But I shall surely never do so again."

"Ah, Jane!" Mrs. Tilson surprised me by laughing while I was still extracting meaning from this tangle of words. "Miss Ravenswood, upon my word, she was a great beauty—"

"And an outrageous flirt," Jane added.

"—and broke hearts by the dozen, in her day. And I happen to know she still—"

"Soft, no more!" But Jane was laughing too.

I had been there twenty-five minutes by then, bordering on too long, so even though this was just getting interesting, I prepared to make some polite remarks and leave. Before I could, the servant came back into the room.

"A Dr. Ravenswood, madam," he said to Mrs. Tilson. A look of surprise crossed both women's faces; morning calls were mostly the realm of women. I was surprised too, since Liam and I had agreed to meet at the carriage outside, where Wilcox waited, when done with our respective visits. Perhaps Henry had mentioned his sister had come here, and Liam had decided to seize the opportunity to make a better impression on her than he had yesterday. I hoped he could; I felt nervous for him just thinking about it.

The moment Liam entered the room, expression meek but posture confident, I saw he had assumed yet another persona for the occasion, and was determined not to be intimidated. He shook Mrs. Tilson's hand, nodded to Jane, and folded himself into a chair with an air of humility. "I would not intrude, Mrs. Tilson," he began, "had I not wished to reassure Miss Austen that her brother seems to me much improved this morning."

"I suspected as much myself," Jane said.

"Your medical acumen, madam, puts my own to shame," he

murmured. "But I am not confident he is entirely out of danger. I must ask you to keep a close watch on him, and try to help him avoid excess fatigue. His nerves—Mr. Austen does not strike me as a nervous man in general, but he has lately been under some considerable strain, has he not?"

His voice was soft, his tone confiding, and as he gazed earnestly at Jane, I feared he was too insinuating, that he would annoy her with presumption of an intimacy they had not achieved. But I was wrong; it seemed to be working. She tilted her head slightly and blinked rapidly a few times. Was it possible she was blushing? "So fortunate that you are here in town with him now," he continued. "I know he has the very highest regard for your cool judgment and strength of understanding." Shameless flattery, innocent delivery; could she possibly have her head turned so easily? If she was laughing at him, though, she hid it well, but then I would expect nothing less from her. "May I return tomorrow, madam? Just to see how he fares?"

She was silent a beat too long. "We had invited some friends to tea, before this recent episode. Please join us, sir, if you are at liberty." Her eye fell on me, as if she was suddenly remembering I was there. "And you, of course, Miss Ravenswood. About seven, if you will."

AT HANS PLACE THE FOLLOWING EVENING, IT WAS A SIZABLE PARTY: the Tilsons; Mr. Seymour; the Miss Jacksons with their father; a French émigré whose name I never got; a nautical friend of one of the sea captain Austen brothers. Jane, expression dutiful, was presiding over the tea table, and Liam stationed himself near her, holding cup and saucer with a negligent grace, giving her serious, sideways looks, and now and then saying something brief. They looked, from my perspective halfway across the room, awkward, at least at first. Then their upper bodies began to incline more toward each other; I saw her smile, and push a loose curl out of her face. Their remarks lengthened.

I was tempted to go over and join their conversation, but feared jinxing Liam; if he was flirting as openly as he had been the morning before, I might be in the way. Besides, there was Henry to think about. He had greeted me warmly on arrival, and though he circulated among all his guests, he returned to me, a favoritism that made Miss Jackson resolutely turn her back on us. I thought he looked improved from when I had last seen him, but still not well. His eyes had a worrisome glassiness, and the whites remained faintly yellow. He'd impressed me with his perfect tailoring, the night we first met; now his clothes hung on him as if he had lost weight. I tried to notice these things without being obvious, but visual survey is crucial in diagnosis. I could only hope that my discreet appraisal struck him as admiring, not odd. Yet it was admiring, too, I realized as my eyes lingered on him with pleasure as well as professional interest; a handsome and clever man who makes no effort to conceal his admiration is never a bad thing.

He'd picked up the thread of our conversation from a few days ago, about travel, and was full of ideas about where my brother and I needed to, or should not, go.

"No one visits Bath anymore except gouty retired admirals and entrenching dowagers. But Cheltenham—it is worth seeing, delightful, unspoiled. I have some thoughts of going there myself for a few days, if we can get a party together."

"That seems an excellent plan."

He moved a little closer and said in a lower tone, "Perhaps you and your brother will join us."

A strangely intimate offer from someone I had not known long, but maybe polite people proposed this sort of thing without meaning it. "I should be delighted. It is a spa?"

"Its waters are famed for their restorative powers."

"So perhaps it can help you."

He frowned. "I am fully recovered. Cheltenham has many attractions beyond those for invalids."

"To be sure—and none would call you an invalid, Mr. Austen." He bowed. "Yet my brother and I both worry about your health. I hope you will allow him to continue to visit you often."

"I am always pleased to see both of you. But not to fuss over me; I am fully recovered."

"I hope. Yet there is something in your countenance that troubles me." I dropped my gaze; I had been studying him too openly. "Forgive me for speaking so frankly. It is only out of concern."

"Your kind concern does you honor. It is such as is seldom met with in this world, where I fear people think chiefly of themselves."

"Are you a cynic, Mr. Austen?"

"Not if you mean by that one who does not acknowledge the reality of human goodness," he murmured. "I have evidence of it before me." His gaze took me in, warm, mild, and innocent. No, not innocent. I had a sudden idea of how he'd be in bed—playful, fearless, ready for anything—and blushed hotly at my own thoughts, at my suspicion of his. "Are you enjoying *Pride and Prejudice*?" He had sent over the other two volumes soon after our conversation.

"Perhaps even more than the previous times."

"Yes, it bears up well under rereading. And do you still think a man wrote it?"

Our glances went toward Jane, who continued to talk with Liam, more animated now. "Your argument was so compelling. I find myself . . . swayed."

He gave me a look full of meaning, and it struck me that maybe flirting was not so hard if you were doing it with the right person.

"WELL?" LIAM ASKED ON THE WAY HOME; WE WERE INSIDE THE carriage, Wilcox driving. "Henry Austen seemed quite glued to your side. That's good. He asked all sorts of promising questions about you this morning when I saw him at the bank." They'd met there to follow up on the Cornwall canal investment—five hundred pounds we could say goodbye to forever.

I was disconcerted by the notion of them discussing me, though I knew I shouldn't be; this was how it was supposed to unfold. "Like what? What did he ask? What did you tell him?"

"You are virtuous and wealthy and unencumbered. Isn't it all truth?"

Liam politely parried my efforts to learn more until I gave up. "And your conversation with *her*?"

"Not an utter disaster, thank god." His tone was so serious that I laughed, and he looked at me in alarm. When I forget myself I have the laugh of a madwoman, a cackle that goes and goes. I'd worked on modulating it in 1815, but laughs are like sneezes, not entirely controllable. "What?"

"You are a shameless flirt. At least you were yesterday, so

I'll assume you were tonight, though I couldn't actually hear you."

He looked at me, thinking this over. "I did my best," he said, and this time I did not let myself laugh.

"What did you talk about?" I asked instead.

"Books, mostly."

"Hers?"

"Among others."

"How did you dare do it?"

"I did not admit to knowing she wrote them, which made it easier to talk about how wonderful they are. It was a natural transition from Fanny Burney and Samuel Richardson. Realism, comedy, the marriage plot."

I considered this, trying to decide how I felt about it. On one hand, his success was my success. On the other—why did this appear to be so easy for him? It did not seem fair.

"I guess you couldn't get the conversation around to 'The Watsons.'"

"And how would *you*—" he began, and then, realizing from my face that I was joking, smiled. "I'll work on that next time."

MOSTLY I AM NOT GIVEN TO REMEMBERING MY DREAMS, OR FINDING them very interesting when I do; usually I am stitching up an endless series of trauma patients or staging futile searches for important lost objects. But arriving in 1815, and meeting Jane Austen, had apparently done something to me. First there was the one about Isaac of York, who had urged me to try to blend in more, as he never could in 1194, and then, the night after that tea, one about Henry.

I am with him in his curricle, the two of us riding through Hyde Park on a strangely sunlit morning. I should be enjoying myself; instead I am puzzled, thinking, *This can't be right. I don't belong here.* And then the scene changes: we are no longer in the manicured environs of the park, but in a craggy landscape out of an Ann Radcliffe novel. A wooded hillside, a rushing waterfall. The road ahead curves out of sight, but the grade is alarmingly, cartoonishly steep. Henry seems unconcerned, holding the reins loosely and smiling sideways at me, dappled light of the sun through leaves flashing past us.

"Do you not think," I say, "we should get out and walk? The road—the horses—"

We're picking up speed. It's too late; there'll be no stopping until we reach the bottom, a long way down. I am filled with fear, or maybe it's desire, and I think: Is it possible that I never met the right man because he died centuries before I was born? But I dismiss this as nonsense, even as he says in his pleasant, ironic voice: "An excess of caution, Miss Ravenswood, can be more fatal than its opposite."

I OPENED MY EYES TO THE FAINT LIGHT OF DAWN AND THE SOUND of rain: I'd left my window open, letting in cold air and the smell of coal smoke, the sounds of London waking up. My dream— Henry Austen, a carriage, a waterfall—was slipping away, and with relief I let it go. It's true though, I thought, still half asleep, as if answering a question or justifying myself to some imaginary listener, Jane herself perhaps. I've never been in love.

I don't want to settle, or lie to myself, to dwindle into the compromises of coupledom, chasing an illusion of happily-ever-after. My parents' marriage was a happy one until my father's untimely death, so I can't be said to lack role models.

I've been intrigued, in lust, craved unsuitable men, been bored by the attentions of differently unsuitable men, had sex as often as I could. Silly crushes, torrid affairs, tedious boyfriends, and close male friends, with and without benefits: elements that never coalesced.

Maybe I've never met the right person; maybe I never will. It doesn't mean there's anything wrong with me.

CHAPTER 7

OCTOBER 21

33 Hill Street

MY MOOD AFTER THAT TEA AT HANS PLACE WAS WARY OPTIMISM: Henry was attentive; Jane, if not exactly won over, seemed to like us a little. The next morning, Liam wrote to him, repeating his promise to come and inquire after his health whenever asked. Forty-eight anxious hours passed without a reply.

"Is it possible the letter was lost?" Liam said. He was making slow circles around the library, pausing to look out at the gloomy day. I was supposedly sewing a shirt, but I kept forgetting and stopping. "Or we've offended him. I did something wrong."

"Enough," I said. "Order the carriage. If he's well and he's already left for the bank, we'll see her, is all. And that's worth doing, too."

I HAD A SENSE OF WRONGNESS AS SOON AS I WALKED INTO THE house. Richard, happy to see us as ever but looking tired, showed us into the drawing room.

Jane was alone, standing, twisting a handkerchief in her hands. "Oh," she said. "I am very glad you are come, Dr. Ravenswood." She acknowledged me with a look, and turned back to Liam. In dress, she was as tidy as usual, but her eyes were red-rimmed, with new dark circles under them. "My brother was so much better, the night you came to tea, and he has grown sensibly worse ever since. I have been quite distracted."

"Too distracted to ask for aid?" Liam asked gently. "I would have come much sooner. Why did you not send word, Miss Austen?"

"May I impose on your good nature, and ask you to go and see him? He has not left his bed since the day before yesterday."

"It will not be an imposition but an honor." He bowed.

"You are kind, sir. Richard will show you upstairs. Richard?" He appeared from the hall to lead Liam off, and Jane turned to me with a weak smile. "He is very good, your brother. But I do not need to tell *you* that."

"Come and sit down," I said. "Forgive me, but you look tired."

Looking surprised, she obeyed. I sat down, too, and gave her a long look. "Have you been sleeping properly, or have you been up half the night nursing?" Her expression was answer. "And eating? When did you last have a proper meal?"

"I have been—"

"But you must eat, and you must sleep. You will do your brother no good by falling ill taking care of him." I touched the bell. "Have you had breakfast yet?"

"I cannot think about food at such a time."

"I take that to mean no." When Richard appeared, so quickly I supposed he must have been out in the hall listening to us, something to keep in mind, I said: "Could we have some tea?" I turned to her. "Or do you prefer coffee?"

"Tea," she said faintly.

"And . . . something. Whatever the kitchen affords. Is there any cold meat, Richard? Perhaps the cook could make Miss Austen a roast beef sandwich? Could we prevail upon her to boil her an egg? Is there any cake?"

Richard's startled gaze went from me to Jane and rested there. She gave him an almost imperceptible nod. "Very well," he said, and vanished.

We looked at each other for a moment. "Forgive me, Miss Austen, one more question. Have you washed your hands since you left the sickroom? That is very important, though not a thing people are always aware of."

Her eyebrows lifted. "You are quite decided in your opinions today."

"It is only out of concern for you."

"I shall go and wash them."

Alone in the drawing room, I stood up, more restless than usual, and made a circuit of the room, noticing in a corner a portable writing desk—a sort of small box with compartments— sitting open on a table. *Hers.* I had last seen it behind glass at the British Library, along with her wire-rimmed glasses and a manuscript chapter of *Persuasion*, the one she ended up not using. I stopped and stared. Of all the amazements of 1815, this struck me the most: her actual writing desk. A few sheets of paper were partly under it, one covered with her unmistakable handwriting, tiny but precise: perhaps one of the letters to Cassandra I had come to steal. Hearing footsteps approaching, I whirled away and sat down where I had been, just in time, as Jane returned.

"So kind of you to come," she said in a newly formal tone, sitting down. She picked up a piece of work from her sewing basket nearby, glanced at it, and let it fall. "Not necessary, but kind. I am sure he will improve soon. The apothecary was here yesterday, and he took some blood. That has to help."

"Oh, immensely." I was unable to keep the irony entirely out of my tone.

She gave me a sharp look. "He has a sound understanding of the case." I heard a knock, and then Richard's steps, headed to the door. "That may be him now; he said he would come back today. Mr. Haden. So conscientious."

She held up a hand in apology and disappeared into the hallway, from where I heard the soft murmur of her voice and a man's but could distinguish no words, then footsteps going upstairs as she came back into the room.

Mr. Haden, clever and agreeable, became a fixture at Hans Place during Henry's illness and recovery. At least one biographer suspected Jane of a flirtation with him, though he was a decade younger. Others contend that if any flirting took place, it was between Mr. Haden and Fanny Knight, a niece of Jane and Henry's. In either case I had been curious to meet him. Well, Liam would get to.

Jane sat down, saying, "I have some thought to write to my sister and brothers to inform them of Henry's condition, yet I do not wish to alarm them needlessly." She stood up again and made a circuit of the room.

"Why not see what my brother has to say?"

"Yes, perhaps I should." She sat down. "You are full of helpful ideas this morning, Miss Ravenswood."

A servant I had never seen before, a youngish woman with a doleful face, staggered in and put down a large tray with tea things and more: bread, butter, a plate of thinly sliced meat, a hunk of seedcake. Jane looked at it with a frown. I poured a cup of tea and put it in her hands. "Here," I said. "Let me give you a bit of this cake, it looks excellent."

"I am not hungry." She took a sip of tea.

"Yet you must eat," I said, adding impulsively: "You want to disregard the body, perhaps; you consider it a bit beneath you, slightly coarse, even to have one. But think about this. Where do you suppose reason and imagination dwell?" I put a slab of cake on a plate and passed it to her. "If the weather improves tomorrow, I would like to take you out in our carriage. You need air. Will you promise to come?"

Her eyes had grown wider at this speech. "I promise to consider it," she said, and took a bite of cake, then another.

Nearly finished by the time we heard footsteps coming down the stairs, she wiped her mouth and stood up.

"Dr. Ravenswood," she said as he walked in, her expression a question.

"You are right. He is worse. But I am confident of an eventual, full recovery. At present matters approach a crisis. The liver is much disordered." I repressed a smile at the conviction with which Liam delivered this line.

"Should I write—if you were in my situation—that is, do you think it advisable to summon my sister and brothers, if there is the slightest danger that he—"

To my surprise, Liam reached out and touched her shoulder for an instant. "Ah, Miss Austen, how brave you are! You cannot carry all this alone. 'Twill be a comfort to have them here, will it not? Do not hesitate; write to them."

"I shall, if you think it advisable, not alarmist. If you will excuse me, I shall do so at once."

She went to the table, pulled up a chair, and sat down in front of her writing desk. I tried not to stare as she took out a new piece of paper, opened her ink bottle, examined two quills before choosing a third, dipped it, wrote a line, quick and sure, and stopped to look up at Liam. "Mr. Haden continues with Henry?"

"He will be down presently. We exchanged some thoughts on the case; he will share them with you. I do not want to impose; he is in command of your brother's care. I merely seek to advise."

I wished Liam would take command and put a stop to the bloodletting and doses of mercury; a doctor outranked an apothecary. But this answer seemed to please Jane, who gave him a look warmer than any she had ever given me as he continued: "And if there is anything, anything, I can do, do not hesitate to summon me, at any hour." He bowed. "We leave you to your letters."

"WELL?" I ASKED ONCE WE WERE HEADING HOME. WE HAD LEFT Wilcox behind again today, so we were free to talk.

"He looks like hell. Much more yellow. Complained of nausea and vomiting. He said he has kept down nothing but tea and barley water since that other night, when we saw him. And you will rejoice to hear that I got a look at his chamber pot." He paused, as if hoping to increase my suspense. "Very dark urine."

"Everything points to the liver. Wash your hands thoroughly when we get home. If it's a hepatitis strain transmitted by the oral-fecal route—"

"I've touched nothing fecal." Liam looked worried.

"Just keep your hands away from your mouth and your eyes until you can wash them. We can't afford to get hepatitis."

THE NEXT DAY, THE SUN HAD COME OUT. WE RETURNED TO HANS Place, where Liam was immediately led upstairs, as if this had already become a routine, while I was shown into the empty drawing room but told Miss Austen would be with me soon. My eyes returned to her writing desk, but it was closed up tight this time. Focused on sitting quietly, properly, not to be caught in some wrong attitude if she walked in unexpectedly, I found myself looking at my hands, strong though small, which once stitched up patients, now reduced to sewing shirts. I thought how our cells are constantly dying and being formed anew, and that the longer I stayed here, the more I was becoming a product of 1815. At least, on a cellular level; I did not think my thoughts and feelings had changed. But would I know, necessarily?

After ten minutes or so, as I was starting to wonder if there had been some misunderstanding, footsteps coming down the stairs announced the arrival of Jane Austen.

"Miss Ravenswood," she said, and for the first time she took my hand, saying, "Do not fear, I washed it. I beg your forgiveness for making you wait. I was talking to your brother."

"You can atone by coming for a drive with me. The day is fine, and you seem to me in want of an outing." She looked better than yesterday, though still tired. At my words she smiled faintly.

"I cannot think of it at such a time. My brother—"

"Is in the capable hands of *my* brother. Do come. Today I have with me not only the coachman but my footman, so we can ride in state."

"Your footman! Indeed." Footmen were luxury goods; Henry himself did not have one.

"He had many errands and did not want to accompany us, but I insisted, because it was my wish to take you out, and I knew you would not, if there was no footman. See, he is outside, looking melancholy." I had drawn her to the window with my prattling nonsense; I could not let Liam be the only one who could act his part with such an appearance of ease.

"A very handsome equipage," Jane said, and I knew from her tone she was coming.

I HAD HAD SOME THOUGHTS OF TAKING HER SHOPPING; COULD anything match being in a bookstore with Jane Austen? But in the end we stayed in the park, enjoying the rare sunlight and the people-watching from the carriage, which had its top retracted to maximize our pleasure.

"There is the notorious Mr. Manwaring, in that gig," Jane said. "I know him from Henry's parties. He is looking—he is looking at me, but he cannot understand how I could be riding in such a fine carriage, with a lady he has never seen and a footman—there, I shall nod to him, too late for him to react—that will give him something to think about."

"Do you enjoy your brother's parties? He had left me with the impression you were more fond of quiet."

"I am old now." I rejected this with a shake of my head. "And Henry, too, is not as he was. When his wife was still living—those were parties. With musicians, and ices, and quantities of French émigrés, each one with an improbable story of escape. Those days are gone, Miss Ravenswood." If her words were nostalgic, her tone was brisk and her glance amused as she looked at the sunlit landscape ahead of us. "But one cannot live in the past. Nor would I want to. I sometimes feel the most interesting part of my life has started only now."

Her words chilled me; I knew how little of it she had left. "Why is that, do you imagine?"

She gave me an enigmatic smile but did not answer.

"Perhaps," I hazarded, "your literary success affords you some gratification?"

I tried to catch her eye, but she had turned away, seemingly studying something off in the distance where green park gave way to gray city. Finally she said, "Oh, Henry never could keep a secret."

"In truth, it was Mrs. Tilson," I blurted out, and Jane laughed, a throaty, wicked chuckle.

"Even better! I must give over always suspecting him. But it *was* amusing, that other night, hearing your brother go on about my work, with such an air of innocent admiration." She shrugged. "Suspecting he knew—and suspecting he knew that I knew that he knew . . . He is quite a practiced flatterer, is he not? Forgive me, that is not a thing I should say to you."

I assured her it was exactly a thing she should say to me. "But I hope you do not take him for some sort of coxcomb."

"I? Oh, no."

THE SAME DAY SHE'D ASKED LIAM'S ADVICE ABOUT IT, JANE WROTE
to her sister, Cassandra, as well as to her brothers James and
Edward, telling them of Henry's illness in terms that must have
been dire, for it brought them hurrying to London. *Hurrying* being a relative term.

The first day after that was the sunny one of the carriage
ride, when she admitted to being the author of her novels. The
second day was overcast, but she came out with me again anyway. We went to Hatchards, where I bought several books she
had expressed an interest in, and then to a pastry cook's for ices,
where I insisted on paying. The third day it rained and we did
not go anywhere, just stayed in the drawing room, talking and
laughing while Liam and Mr. Haden attended on Henry, whom
Liam reported to be about the same, maybe slightly better.

Jane was starting to be comfortable in my presence by then,
though it was clear, when Liam came down at the end of his sickroom visits to brief her and bid her farewell, that she preferred
him. When we were all three in a room, it was he who held her
gaze, his words she hung on. I tried not to mind this; he and I
were a team, after all.

On the fourth day, Richard did not take Liam to Henry at
once, but showed us both into the drawing room, where Jane
stood, looking out the window. She greeted us warmly, but
seemed troubled.

"I think he is better today," she said, looking from me to
Liam and keeping her eyes on him. "I wonder if you will agree,
Doctor, or think it merely a sister's disordered fancy."

"I am sure you are an acute observer."

"I will ask you to go there in a moment and be the judge, but
there is a delicate matter I must address first." She looked up

at him through her eyelashes, tilt of the head, a trusting gaze. "My brother Edward arrived in town late yesterday and was so alarmed at the sight of Henry that he insisted we call in a physician he knows. I explained to him that we are already consulting *you,* as well as Mr. Haden, but he was adamant."

"Nothing could be more natural." Liam's tone was soothing. "Perhaps this one comes recommended by your brother's friends?"

"Oh! Indeed. Dr. Baillie attends on the prince regent himself. To my mind not a recommendation at all, but Edward feels differently."

"Consult him to be sure, if it will put your brother's mind to rest."

"You will not be affronted? Henry feared you would be; he grew agitated and even snapped at Edward."

"Miss Austen, agitation is what he must avoid of all things."

"It is not intended as a slight to you."

"I am not known in London; nothing could be more natural than to consult someone who is." He paused. "But you will, will you not, let me continue to monitor him? As a friend? In an advisory capacity; I should not presume to interfere with any course of treatment that Dr. Baillie might advise."

And if Dr. Baillie advised increasing the bloodletting? Mercury, opium, and snails? I sighed before I could stop myself, but neither of them noticed.

"You hardly need to ask, as if it were a favor to be granted. Your kindness . . ." She turned back toward the window, then hurried over, looked out, and rushed into the passage. "Richard!" she cried. "Richard, hurry! They are come!"

I went to the same window to see a carriage stopped outside.

A pale face looked out from the gloom of its interior, but no one moved, except the coachman, who left his seat to pull two trunks from the boot and drop them, from a height, onto the street. Richard scurried outside, opened the door, and helped two people alight.

The lady, wearing a brown pelisse, was tall and solidly built without being fat; on her face was an impassive expression, on her head a frilly lace cap. She was up the stairs and out of my view before I could notice anything else. From the hall, I heard:

"My poor dearest one!"

"How good you are come, at last. How was your journey?"

The man, who wore the black coat and distinctive neckcloth of a clergyman, stretched his limbs and rubbed his eyes. He dropped a coin into the outstretched hand of the coachman, said something to Richard, and started into the house. I turned from the window to find Jane reentering the room, arm in arm with the new arrival. "Miss Ravenswood, may I present my sister, Miss Austen. Dr. Ravenswood, my sister."

Cassandra Austen inclined her head without a hint of warmth and said nothing.

"Dr. Ravenswood has been extremely helpful," Jane was explaining as the second passenger walked in. Taking no notice of anyone, he shouted down the hallway: "A glass of water, if you would be so good. I am choked with dust."

James Austen, as it could only be, flipped the tails of his coat out of the way and threw his long limbs into a chair. Leaning back, he closed his eyes. "The last five miles are always the longest, or so 'tis said, but I never fully felt the force of that threadbare aphorism until today. Dear Jane, but I forget myself. How is Henry? Is Edward come? What of Fanny?" He had a pleasant, melodious voice I imagined his parishioners appreciated when listening to his sermons.

"Edward is here, but Fanny must stay in Kent for now. I hope she can come a little later. Edward went out on business he could not avoid, but he will return. As for Henry—"

"They are not with him in the sickroom?" Cassandra demanded. "You have not left him alone, given your alarming report of his condition?"

"Only for an instant; I came down to greet the Ravenswoods."

"I would be honored to go and see Mr. Austen now," Liam said. Cassandra looked him over with a quick but thorough gaze.

"You shall go there without delay," Jane said, which was not quite true, as she then introduced James Austen to us. Sighing slightly—we seemed to be one more inconvenience in a day full of them—he stood up and went through the motions.

"The doctor and his sister are but lately come to town," Jane explained. "Henry had met them shortly before his illness, and Dr. Ravenswood has been most helpful. They are from Bermuda, and know our Hampson cousin there."

"Jamaica," I said, quietly hoping it was audible only to her.

"What did you say? Do not mumble! I deplore mumbling," James said, though in a slightly friendlier tone.

"We are from Jamaica, not Bermuda—does not signify—a mere trifle," I said.

"Jamaica. My wits desert me today." Jane shook her head and brought her fingertips to her forehead.

"I very greatly doubt they ever do," Liam said.

This earned him another stare from Cassandra. "If they were from Bermuda, Jane, they would know the Palmers." Her speech was different from her sister's, slower and crisply enunciated.

There was something hostile in her precision. "But perhaps they know them anyway?" she finished, fixing her gaze on me.

"I do not have that pleasure." I knew who she meant. Charles, their younger sea captain brother, had married a daughter of John Grove Palmer, former attorney general of Bermuda. She had died the previous year of complications following the birth of their fourth child.

"Where is my water?" James asked, and yanked the bell cord.

"Jamaica and Bermuda are not so very far apart," Cassandra observed. I sensed an implied reproach in our failure to know the Palmers, but before I could respond, Jane said:

"Over a thousand miles."

"What is that? Not a week's sail on a swift cutter with favorable winds." I couldn't decide if they were sniping at each other, or if this was how they joked.

"Cass. You must be weary. Would you not like to wash your hands? Perhaps some tea? We have some very agreeable tart Henry has barely been able to touch."

"I must see him!" Cassandra said, walking out of the room and up the stairs.

James had sat down again and thrown his head back. "I begin to despair of my water. Pray, Jane, what sort of people does Henry keep in his employ? Do you know where he finds them? Do you have the slightest idea where he finds them?"

Jane was still standing in the middle of the room, as were Liam and I. She turned pink and seemed about to say something, when we heard a rattle from the hallway. A servant I had never seen before hurried in, carrying a tray with a single empty glass and a pitcher of water. She was nearly as short as I, her face lined but her body slender as a girl's. She had purple ribbons in her lace cap and brought a whiff of lavender; her plain black dress was elegant in its simplicity.

"Et alors!" she cried, putting down the tray. "You are here, Monsieur James! I knew you would come!" To my astonishment, James stood up and hugged her.

"How is Henry?" he asked. "I count on the unvarnished truth from you, Bigeon." Of course: the longtime housekeeper, first working for Henry's wife when she was still Eliza de Feuillide, then for the couple, now just for Henry.

"Monsieur Henri, hélas," she said, shaking her head as James poured himself a glass of water and drank it down. "He must be seen to be believed. I will be looking for a new situation soon."

"Madame Bigeon, for shame," Jane said.

"Mademoiselle Jane, you know I am not one to mince the words."

In the silence that followed, Liam and I shot a glance at each other, then he turned and looked at Jane.

"Might I see him now?" he asked. "It is my heart's wish to put you at some ease on this."

Surprising me again, James finished a second glass of water and stood up. "Let us go then, Doctor, and see for ourselves, shall we?" He held up a hand to his sister. "Jane, stay. You have been his nurse long enough; you are limp as a rag. Cassandra is here; she can take over." He stood back with a supercilious flourish to let Liam exit the room first, and they were gone.

Madame Bigeon gave Jane a shrug, picked up the tray, and left too.

Jane let out a small sigh and sat down in a chair by the window. She hid her face in her hands and began shaking—with silent laughter, it took me a moment to realize. Getting herself under control again, she lifted her gaze to meet mine.

"Ah, Miss Ravenswood," she said. "How seldom things ever go as we expect them to. And how tedious existence would be if they did."

"Yours is a philosophical disposition today," I said, taking the seat next to her.

"Certainly, the irony in longing for the comfort of one's dearest—in summoning them of your own accord—and then, when they arrive—" She spread her hands. "I think Henry is better today, upon my word, I do. But I have created such a crisis now—everything in a stir, everyone's peace cut up—now he must be sicker than ever, to justify their pains."

"But think how you would feel, had it turned out differently. If you had not told them, and he—"

"You have nothing but logic and sense on your side, two things I cannot abide." She was smiling. "Do not suppose I regret of my actions; I rarely do." She paused. "It is amusing, that is all."

"SO HOW WAS HE?" I ASKED IN THE CARRIAGE. WE HAD AGAIN LEFT Wilcox home, and were taking the long way back through the park, for though the wind was cold and the air damp, there was much to discuss.

"She's right. He is better. Not great, but I see a difference. And he was able to keep some food down."

"What did you think of Cassandra and James?"

"Did you see that look Cassandra gave me? Like I was something she'd found stuck to the sole of her shoe."

"Do you suppose Jane had mentioned us when she wrote?" This gave me a chill; how would she describe us? It was too metafictional that we might appear as characters in the same letters we had come to steal for scholars of the future. For Eva Farmer.

"I was thinking they were annoyed to see outsiders at such a moment. But that's an interesting idea." There was a pause as we looked across the park: dead leaves swirling in the open stretch of ground under a sullen gray sky, only a few intrepid horsemen pursuing their exercise. "What could she have said, to put Cassandra on her guard so?"

"Or maybe 'on guard' is just how she is."

"But we must win over Cassandra. She's crucial; she has the letters."

At that moment I thought of them—and the manuscript—as I never had before: not just the fruit of Jane Austen's passing thoughts and enduring genius, but physical artifacts, with bulk and solidity. Did Cassandra keep the letters in a locked desk drawer? In a strongbox, under her bed? The Georgians liked locks: tea and sugar, not just money and silver flatware, were valuables they secured, and lock picking had been one of the arts we had learned in Preparation.

I shivered. Liam was continuing: "And anything that's helped us with Henry and Jane—money, in his case; a certain charm, I suppose, in hers—our exoticism, say—won't help. On the contrary, it doesn't seem the sort of thing she likes at all."

"So you need to figure out what she does like. You need to be the Henry Crawford here, working two sisters at once." Henry Crawford, the clever and charming villain of *Mansfield Park*, is one of Austen's most confounding creations; you feel as if he almost could be good, as if in the writing she was trying to make up her mind about him.

Liam gave me a sideways look, a flash of startled blue. "Is that how you see me? A cold-eyed cynic?"

"I didn't say that! He was all about acting, you'll recall."

"I do recall."

We went on in a silence that lasted so long I began to wonder if I had offended him; there really was no figuring him out.

"Why does it surprise you?" I finally said. "We're a little like Henry and Mary Crawford, don't you think? Barging into their lives, with our money and our alien notions, stirring the pot? Trying to seduce them? Of course, with nobler motives."

Liam gave me a look: long, amused. "It hadn't occurred to me, no."

"I always used to think," I began, "if there was ever any clue at all to Jane Austen the person hidden in her work, it's in *Mansfield Park*. In that duality between Fanny and Mary. Dutiful and humble, or witty and amoral—it's like the struggle that was taking place inside her."

"And now that you've met her?"

"Now I am more confused than ever."

Another silence fell, more comfortable. "We've just got to get Cassandra on our side," I said at last. In that moment it did not seem impossible; we'd done so many hard things already. "I think Jane likes me a little by now. And she definitely likes you."

This was truer than I wanted to admit. I thought of the trusting gaze she'd turned on Liam as she explained the awkwardness surrounding the Dr. Baillie problem; it was like I was not even in the room, the way they had been looking at each other. Perhaps biographers would never puzzle over her flirtatious asides about

Mr. Haden in the letters from this period, because they would no longer be there. Maybe the letters would tell instead of one Dr. Ravenswood, and his conscientious attendance on Henry during his illness.

"Does she, do you think?"

He sounded so solemnly unsure of this that I could not help myself: I laughed. For once unafraid of being overheard being unladylike, I threw my head back and roared. The release of tension felt so good I couldn't stop; one laugh caused another. I snorted and gasped, my face contorted, until my stomach hurt, and until Liam, who'd first looked at me in dismay, was laughing too.

CHAPTER 8

OCTOBER 26

23 Hans Place

USHERED INTO HENRY'S DRAWING ROOM, WE FOUND JANE THERE with one more brother for us to meet: Edward, now surnamed Knight, because inheriting the fortune of the rich, childless relatives who'd adopted him required taking their name. I've always been intrigued by this: a boy removed from his parents and elevated in rank, like Frank Churchill in *Emma,* and curious about how his siblings felt. Happy to have such an important brother, or envious at not having been chosen? Did they cry for missing him, when he was gone? Did he for them?

After the reception from Cassandra and James the day before, I was ready for the worst, but Edward Knight surprised me.

"Miss Ravenswood, I am delighted to meet you at last!" I found my hand in his—how had that happened? He was blond, pink, and beefy, seeming from another gene pool than the olive-toned, sharp-nosed Austens I'd met so far. "Jane has told me so much of your kindness to dear Henry during his illness." His blue eyes were soft; they looked into mine as if, for this moment at least, no one else existed in the world. I began to understand why the Knights had picked him. "And the good doctor—charmed, charmed," he said, turning to Liam. "I must thank you for all your trouble, your solicitous care."

"'Tis nothing, sir, I am happy to do what I can."

"Do not take offense at my urging to call in Dr. Baillie. He saved the life of a friend of mine a few years ago, snatching him from the very jaws of death. Since, I have maintained the highest opinion of him, and when I heard Henry was so ill I could not—But it is not intended as any disrespect to you."

Liam inclined his head. "And not taken as such. I am sure we will find we are in accord. Has the doctor been here this morning?" he asked Jane.

"He is there now. Along with Mr. Haden and my sister, and my brother James. The sickroom can barely accommodate the patient. Will you join the crush?"

"How is he?" Liam asked her.

"He continues better. It is almost a social occasion—a levee—and Henry fits the role of the Sun King as if born to it."

"Jane, what nonsense you do talk sometimes. Our new friends will think you serious."

"They know better. Will you join them there, Dr. Ravenswood?"

"If you wish it." Their eyes met, and he stood up. "I am yours to command." With a bow, he left the room.

There was a moment's pause as we three looked at each

other, and then Jane said, "Wait, I forgot—if you will forgive me, Miss Ravenswood—" She rose and hurried out of the room after Liam, leaving me alone with Edward Knight.

He gave no sign of there being anything odd about her abrupt departure, merely smiled and said: "Jane says you grew up in the tropics. What a change you must find London!"

"An agreeable one, though." I studied this example of the landed gentry, thinking I might not get another opportunity. Edward had in one sense made his sister's literary life possible, since he'd provided the cottage in Chawton where she now lived. It was Jane's first permanent home after an unsettled, impecunious decade of moving around with her parents and sister in the wake of her father's retirement, and later his death: a season in Bath, stays at the seaside, long visits with friends and relations, not a life conducive to writing. Once established in a routine, she made up for lost time, though I'd always wondered why he had not done something sooner. "Have you traveled much yourself?" I asked him.

"Oh! When I was young. Now I have too many responsibilities to venture far from home."

James, looking no more pleased with his life then he had yesterday, walked in, sank into a chair, glanced over at Edward, and gave me a nod. "Miss Ravenswood." His sharp brown eyes took me in, up and down; I had an impression of being examined as if I were an exotic creature at Astley's Amphitheatre.

Cassandra, just behind him, greeted me less curtly than James had, if no more warmly, and said, "But what of Jane? Was she not here?"

"She was," I said, since no one else seemed inclined to answer.

"She is unaccountable," Cassandra said, sitting down and looking around the room, her air as dissatisfied as her brother's. "Have you been in London long, Miss Ravenswood?"

"Since September."

"And you aim to settle here?"

"I am sure I cannot say yet, madam."

"Perhaps you have some family you will need to visit elsewhere in England?"

Having no reply to this, I merely inclined my head. The barrage of abrupt questions was rude, as we both knew. James looked maliciously amused, while his brother was harder to read.

"I think—" Edward began, but Cassandra was continuing:

"Jane was not able to tell me much about your family."

"What would you like to know?" It was not a friendly question, but it had not been a friendly remark.

"Cass," Edward said, soft but decisive. I don't know what would have happened then if Jane and someone I had never seen before had not walked into the room, midconversation. He was an older gentleman, who, with his grave expression, old-fashioned black suit, distinctive wig, and silver-headed walking stick, could only be Dr. Baillie. He looked exactly like a physician, in short—unlike Liam, who after meeting Jane had stopped wearing his frizzy doctor's wig and started growing sideburns.

"It will be an honor," Jane was saying, her face pinker than usual. "Please tell Mr. Clarke I am home most days. But he will write, I expect, before he appears."

"You will find him a man who stands upon ceremony." Dr. Baillie smiled a little and nodded to the rest of us.

"Will you sit awhile, Doctor?" Jane asked. "Perhaps you would like some tea?"

"You are kind, but the press of my business, madam—perhaps another time." He bowed, looked around. "I am glad your brother is feeling better. Good day to you all, then."

And he was gone, leaving silence in his wake. "Well," Jane said, sitting down next to me and looking around at all our faces. "It seems I am to be invited to tour the royal library at Carlton House." She laughed her wicked little chuckle. "Not when His Majesty is at home, fortunately. It emerges that he is an admirer of my work—"

"Perhaps we should discuss all this later," Cassandra said with a glance at me.

"Oh, Miss Ravenswood knows," Jane said; I could have hugged her. "She is quite one of the family by now. Certainly more than Dr. Baillie, to whom Henry managed to reveal I am an authoress. Then, when Dr. Baillie told the prince that his new patient was the brother of the lady who wrote *Pride and Prejudice,* the prince said—" She shrugged and smiled. "His librarian will call on me soon, I am told, to arrange the visit."

"Most condescending!" James said, looking more cheerful. "Truly a mark of favor." I remembered learning that he had once been considered the genius writer of the family, penning verse for all occasions and starting a magazine with Henry at Oxford.

"But you must be polite to him, Jane, and not reveal what you think of the prince," Edward said.

"She would not be so foolish as that," Cassandra said, not sounding convinced.

"It is an honor," I said, "but no more than you deserve. Your work has given great pleasure to many people, and will to even more in the future, I am confident. And the prince has aesthetic discernment, whatever else we might regret about him." The prince regent, later George IV, was notoriously gluttonous and debauched, by 1815 a monument to excess of every kind.

Into the little silence that followed my speech, which I feared had been too earnest, there came the sound of footsteps descending the stairs, and Liam walked in and sat down next to me. My rush of relief surprised me; facing all these Austens by myself had been unnerving. His eyes traveled over everyone and came to rest on Jane.

"We were just discussing my coming visit to Carlton House," she said to him. "I mention this only so you understand what sort of exalted company you find yourself among, to what manner of rank and consequence you must grow accustomed."

I glanced at Cassandra, whose face was impassive; only a slight narrowing of her eyes hinted at feeling.

Liam bowed his head. "You will be an ornament to that establishment, madam," he said, his tone of gentle mockery matching hers.

After a pause, Cassandra said: "Since we are so openly airing your private affairs, Jane, may I ask what has happened with Mr. Murray since you wrote him last?" As far as I knew, John Murray and Jane Austen were still trying to come to terms on publishing *Emma,* a negotiation that had been interrupted by the drama of Henry's illness.

"Oh! A rogue, as I have said. But a civil one. He has agreed to call in two days' time, and I hope we can settle the matter then. Henry insists he *will* rise from his bed and help me talk to him." She paused. "But I do not think that is necessary. I feel quite equal to Mr. Murray."

"I can help," Edward said. "Can selling a book be different than selling barley or pigs? We must insist on a fair price and hold to it. I am a man of business, Jane; I understand these things. Let me treat with him."

"I am not entirely persuaded that selling a book is like selling a pig," said James. "For one thing—"

"Perhaps we can conclude this discussion at another time," Cassandra said. "It must be vastly tedious to our guests."

It wasn't, but her meaning was clear. Liam and I exchanged a glance and stood up at the same moment. As we made our goodbyes, Jane looked worried, but she made no effort to stop us.

"I ALWAYS SAW CASSANDRA AS JANE'S DEFENDER," LIAM SAID. IT was late; the din of London outside was subdued by a cold, steady rain. After a depressing dinner of pigeon pie and boiled potatoes, we were sitting over the claret, discouraged and slightly drunk, talking in tones so hushed we had to lean across the table to hear each other. "She stood between her and their mother, whatever was going on there. Not just their mother. The world. Everything. Cassandra's the one with influence with Edward—she got him to let them use the house in Chawton, so Jane could live in one place and work on writing. She runs the household, so Jane doesn't have to. But now—" He stopped.

"Now?" The wine had made Liam more talkative than usual; it was making me logy.

"Jane doesn't need her anymore. She has something all her own, doesn't she? Her books, her London life with Henry. Can Cassandra feel unappreciated, left behind? Envious, even?"

"You think?"

"Her own sense of right and wrong, her love for her sister, won't let her resent Jane, so she resents everything else. What takes Jane away, what distracts her. London. Henry and his worldly friends. Random people one knows nothing about."

"Like us?"

"Exactly."

I refilled our glasses. "What did she run after you to tell you?" Liam looked at me. "You left Edward and Jane and me in the drawing room to go see Henry. Then she hurried out of the room, I assume after you. Did she say something?"

"Oh." He rested his chin on his hand. "Not to be afraid of Cassandra. Not in so many words, but that was the sense of it. That she would take care of Cassandra."

"Meaning what?"

He shrugged. "When I got to the sickroom—she did not join me, she went as far as the door and then went somewhere else—Cassandra and James were standing in one corner, whispering. They gave me the most disapproving stare and kept on whispering."

"Awkward."

"Henry at least seemed happy to see me." He was silent for a moment. "But no. They don't scare me. James doesn't matter. Cassandra could be an obstacle. But we'll think of something." He sounded like he was trying to convince himself of this.

"The worst is," I began. "No, it sounds ridiculous."

"What?"

"The feeling I get, that they look at me and they *know*."

Liam, who had been staring down at the table, lifted his gaze and studied me. "The main thing is, show no fear. Give away nothing. Never grant them an opening."

In a flash of insight, or at least its illusion, one of those muddled leaps of logic that alcohol offers, it struck me that he was talking about himself: not just on the mission, but in general. "Was that how you did it?"

"What?"

"Whatever you did. To so convincingly pose as Old British."

I'd expected Liam to follow his own advice and give away nothing, but he leaned back and smiled at me, folding his arms. The dim flicker of firelight gave a sculptural quality to his craggy features, and I realized I liked his face; I'd grown used to its unbeautiful angles and planes. "I'm so happy you found it convincing."

"Maybe you shouldn't put too much weight on that. I'm American; what do I know?"

I thought back to our earliest days at the institute, and how I had seen him then: his way of speaking, his reserved formality. And then, that girlfriend. Had Sabina been with him, the first time we'd met at the institute, before the interviews and the psychological testing and the role-play exercises that had narrowed down the handful of final candidates to two? A strange thing not to be able to remember, but all my memories of the institute felt vague, rusty with disuse. I was left with an impression of cool, patrician tallness and yet unable to recall particulars.

"Sabina," I said, and he stopped smiling. "She's Old British, though, isn't she?"

"Very."

"I think that helped persuade me, too."

"Halo effect?"

"She seems like a lovely person." Which she didn't. "So you

met her at school?" I wondered why I was asking him this; Sabina was the last thing I wanted to talk about. "And how did you end up there, anyway? It can't be easy to get into. Especially—" I stopped; I had no tactful way to finish the sentence.

"If you're no one, from nowhere in particular?"

"I didn't say that; you did."

"I passed an exam."

"Just like that? You passed an exam?"

"It was a very hard exam."

A section of coals in the fire, burnt through, collapsed with a gentle hiss. I could hear the cry of a night watch outside, the rattle of a distant carriage.

"It was one teacher I had; he encouraged me to try for an impoverished scholars spot, he knew a little about how it worked. He saw in me the thing I'd always felt in myself, that I didn't fit, in that godforsaken town, in that random family. And to everyone's amazement, I passed."

"And you went off to England. You were all of what, fourteen?"

"Thirteen." He divided the last of the wine between us.

"And found somewhere where you fit."

"Mother of god, no." He rested his forehead in his hand. "I've never found that. Perhaps here in 1815? I like it; there are rules, and you follow them. I'll miss being Dr. Ravenswood when it's over. I've no knack for being myself."

"You'll be different when it's over," I said, disconcerted by this confession. The notion struck me that maybe this, too, was an act; that he was playing some part for me. But why should he bother? "You'll be important. Finder of 'The Watsons.' It'll be great."

"Right," he said, in his old tone of polite neutrality, and it was like a door had closed in my face, one I realized I wished to open again but wasn't sure how. Then he cleared his throat, looking awkward. "Just before Departure, Sabina—We got engaged."

It took me a moment before I raised my glass. "Congratulations! That's wonderful." Sabina had sent a chill through me in the few times I'd talked with her, an impression more unfavorable in retrospect, as my sense of Liam had shifted. They'd seemed perfect for each other then. But now? I felt obscurely disappointed in him. "I'm sure you'll be very happy."

Gazing down at the table, he didn't look especially happy, but then he never did take much delight in his own triumphs. Why he'd chosen this moment to share his news was another mystery. Perhaps simply because we seldom drank this much; he'd grown confiding. And I had raised the topic.

If he'd just beamed and thanked me, like any normal engaged person, we could have moved on, but the silence lengthened. I've never been married; I've never been engaged. I'm not opposed to committed relationships in theory, but I guess I am in practice. Maybe I like freedom more. A memory of Sabina at the institute came back to me: standing next to Liam at a little celebration of the end of Preparation, shortly before we left for 1815. She was nearly as tall as he was, had her hand on his arm, was finishing his sentence for him. What had the conversation been about? I couldn't remember. What had left me with such an unpleasant impression of her? Something about her long, graceful limbs, her supercilious expression. "I hope you'll be very happy," I said, and realized I'd just said much the same thing.

"I hope so too," he muttered. "Her family will have some time to get used to the idea at least, while I'm gone."

"What's the problem with her family?" But I had a suspicion already.

"You know. They have money. But it's not the money, so much." He waved a hand vaguely. "It was like walking into a story, the first time I went to their house. I didn't understand that people actually lived like that, outside of books. With oil paintings of their ancestors, and furniture someone bought in 1800."

So maybe you fell in love with a house, I thought. Maybe you fell in love with an idea. But I didn't say that; what do I know of love? Yet I felt again an obscure disappointment in him: maybe he was like everyone else. This surprised me, for I hadn't realized I'd thought he wasn't. I twisted a curl around my finger and tried to think of a tactful response. "They'll come around, if they understand it's what Sabina wants. And if they don't—well, to hell with them."

"That attitude, right there, is exactly why people love Americans."

"Do people, actually, though?"

"If they have any sense."

WE CONTINUED TO VISIT HANS PLACE ALMOST DAILY, HENRY slowly improving, though it would turn out to be nearly two weeks before he was well enough to come downstairs.

Cassandra took over as his principal nurse, which kept me from having to see much of her, and freed Jane for other things. Like negotiations with John Murray. One day I was shown into the empty drawing room, noticed a stack of paper on the Pembroke table, and risked a closer look, suspecting page proofs, for it was type, not handwriting. *Emma Woodhouse, handsome, clever and rich . . .* was all I dared read, but it was enough: *Emma* was going forward.

Then there was the royal librarian, James Stanier Clarke. Jane Austen's life was surprisingly constricted considering the hugeness of her subsequent fame. She never sought to meet or correspond with other writers, and her visit to Carlton House was her closest brush with history with a capital H. It intrigues her biographers and also frustrates them, because no written account survives: what she saw and thought, either of the fulsomely opulent palace or of Mr. Clarke, whose subsequent letters to her established him as a comic monster of self-importance, a real-life Mr. Collins.

One morning Liam and I had gone to Hans Place, as we did most days, to see how Henry was doing, and found Jane alone in the drawing room, wearing a dress I'd never seen before. Since I knew her wardrobe well by now—it was not extensive—this seemed worth noting. "Oh!" she said. "It is you."

"Were you expecting someone more *formidable*?" Liam asked with mock gravity and the French pronunciation, taking her hand and kissing it. Though their flirtatious banter was an established thing by now, it still amazed me. The assurance with which Liam carried on was a tribute to his acting skills, but what was she feeling? That was more of a riddle.

"Merely my niece, Fanny Knight. Edward went back to Kent to fetch her, and they have been in town since yesterday. She is dear to me, yet no one would describe her as *formidable*—though she is very accomplished. But no"—she looked from Liam to me with an arch smile—"I fear you have missed the important visitor of the day. Mr. Clarke, the prince's librarian, left only a few minutes ago." She paused. "A man of such parts is met with but rarely . . . Is that a carriage stopping outside, is that what I hear?"

Liam went to the window. "Your acuteness is astounding. Mr. Knight and a young lady, getting out of a chariot."

The account of the royal librarian's visit had to wait while we greeted Edward and were introduced to Fanny, his oldest child. She was blond and pink, a daintier version of Edward, with a dignified air that made her seem older than twenty-two, which she was. She'd been just fifteen when her mother died of complications after her eleventh time giving birth. Edward never remarried, leaving Fanny effectively the woman of the house from then on, with many servants to command and lots of little brothers and sisters to worry about. It would prove good training for her subsequent marriage to Sir Edward Knatchbull, a widower with six children, to whom she'd give nine more.

Fanny embraced her aunt tightly and greeted us coolly, but Edward was as friendly as ever. "Well, Jane," he said when we had all settled ourselves, "and what of the prince?"

Her eyes were bright with amusement. "Mr. Clarke came to call this morning, Ned, you have only just missed him. I entertain the highest hopes of Mr. Clarke. Such self-importance, such solemn nonsense! It is fortunate I received him alone; I would have been unable to keep my countenance had you all been here."

"What did he say that was so comical?" Fanny asked.

"It was not so much the words, my dear, as his manner of conferring them on me. Each sentence polished to a lapidary gleam and measured out like gold on a pawnbroker's scale."

Edward said: "Jane, have you ever been to a pawnbroker?

Unless you are leading a more dissolute life than we think when here in town with Henry, I cannot imagine such a thing."

"It is the pernicious influence of Mr. Clarke; that gentleman has overthrown my seat of reason, and my metaphors are rioting like Luddites in Lancashire."

A stir of air made me turn to see Cassandra standing in the doorway. "Ah," she said, her gaze surveying us all and pausing on Liam. "Dr. Ravenswood, you *are* here. Henry was hoping so. Will you go up and see him?" Her tone, if not warm, was at least polite. She acknowledged me with a curt nod.

Liam stood up at once. "I am come with no other design, madam; take me to him."

"I think you know the way to his room by now. I shall test your powers of navigation," she said with an ambiguous smile, sitting down in the chair he had been occupying. Liam bowed and started upstairs, as I tried to decide if this familiarity was insulting or a sign she was warming to him. Liam had seen more of Cassandra in recent days than I had, since they were both often in the sickroom with Henry; something he'd said yesterday suggested she was perhaps becoming less hostile.

With a start, I realized Cassandra was speaking to me, in the same coolly civil tone she'd used on Liam.

"Henry says he is feeling much better. If he continues to do so, he would like to leave his bed and see you tomorrow. Will you and your brother be able to come for tea?"

"Nothing could give us greater delight." Seeing a look pass between the two sisters, I wondered if one had originated the invitation, and required the other to deliver it. This reversal in what I thought to be their usual chain of command was interesting. Seeing Henry, after all this time, would be interesting too.

CHAPTER 9

NOVEMBER 7

23 Hans Place

AT TEA THE NEXT EVENING, WE FOUND CASSANDRA, HENRY, AND Jane; Edward and Fanny Knight, and Mr. Haden, the apothecary often mentioned in her letters from this time. Mr. Haden was nearly as short as I and slightly built. This, along with his remarkable eyes—so blue they were nearly violet, with the longest eyelashes I'd ever seen on an adult man—gave him a boyish quality. There was something awkward in his bow to me, but his manners were gentle, his eagerness to please evident. He was attentive to Fanny, but not flirtatious; maybe biographers had gotten that wrong. I also thought he and Jane showed no special signs of favoring each other—she was flirting only with Liam. Could our arrival have prevented that friendship from deepening?

Henry kissed my hand with a quiet intensity that made me blush and look around, but no one was paying attention to us; Liam had gathered everyone else around the large atlas on the table and was explaining something about the West Indies.

"Miss Ravenswood," Henry said in a tone that was likewise quiet and intense, without its usual irony. "How good to see you again. I have missed you."

His skin and the whites of his eyes were only faintly yellow, but his eyes were too bright, his face drawn. He looked twenty pounds lighter and ten years older than when I'd seen him last. "I am glad to see you feeling better, sir. You have given us all a fright."

"One must do something to attract the notice and sympathy of the ladies, after all," he said, sounding more like himself. His gaze dropped to my chest, as if this were a sight he had resolved not to deny himself; he looked into my eyes again, smiled, leaned in a little closer, glanced down once more and back up. I inhaled his clean-linen smell and felt warmth spreading through my body, origin between my legs. I'd last had sex the night before I left for 1815, with Ezra Inverno, one of the coders on the Prometheus Server. More than two months ago or centuries in the future; by either reckoning a long dry spell. But then, no one had said time travel would be easy.

"This something of yours was a bit extreme." As I studied him in the candlelight, I felt horniness giving way to compassion. Recovered from a dangerous illness, he could not know all that would soon go wrong: the collapse of his bank, the loss of his money and his home.

"Nothing risked, nothing won." He paused. "How have you passed your time, since I saw you last? I expect you have found much to do in town, and made many new friends." *Male friends* was the unstated subtext, or perhaps this was just my imagination.

"None I like so well as the old new ones, like you and your sister."

"You are far too generous; you say only what I wish to hear. But do tell me, has my family been kind to you? Have they treated you as you deserve?" His glance went to Cassandra, who was talking with Edward by the window that looked down onto the street.

Only one answer was possible, and I gave it. "Oh! To be sure."

But it was a strange question; I would have turned it over in my mind more, except that it was driven out by stranger things that happened later.

TEA AND SEEDCAKE AND MUFFIN HAD GONE AROUND, AND WE were talking about the theater. Somehow, *Lovers' Vows*, which figures prominently in *Mansfield Park*, had come up, and Fanny, with more animation than she had shown before and a piece of seedcake in front of her, was making fun of a particularly over-acted version she had seen in Bath. She was waving her fork in the air and declaiming: "I am well, only weak! Some wholesome nourishment!" when she fell silent and dropped the fork. It hit her plate with a clang.

"What is the matter?" her father cried. But she did not speak. Her eyes grew wide, and she brought her elegant hands up to the white column of her neck.

"Fanny!" Cassandra cried.

My eyes were on her upper thorax, which as fashion demanded was exposed, her breasts pushed up by her corset, making respiration easy to see. Fanny was not breathing. I observed this for what seemed a long time, until satisfied it was true, then I stood up.

"I am going to come behind you, and—and help. Do not be afraid." She had stood too; she would be flinging herself around the room in a vain quest for air in a moment.

I struck her on the back several times with increasing force but no effect. Someone was screaming, "Fanny!"

I brought my arms around her torso, formed one hand in a fist just above the umbilicus, wrapped my other hand around the fist and jerked my hands up and back. The surprise of it sent a shudder through her frame, but the obstruction stayed. I did it again. Nothing happened.

Once more I pulled up and in, harder—I had feared hurting her, for she was insubstantial under the floaty muslin, and I had not allowed for how her corset, like body armor, was deflecting my force—and this time it worked. A piece of seedcake flew out of her windpipe and landed near the hearth. She drew a ragged breath and coughed into her handkerchief, tears filming her eyes. I patted her on the back, gently this time, and sat down, feeling dizzy.

Red in the face, she wiped her eyes, heaved a sigh, and sank into her chair. After a long moment, Cassandra poured her some more tea. Cup and saucer clattered in Fanny's hands as she took a sip.

Finally Henry said in a low tone: "You saved her life. How did you know to do that? Truly, you are even more remarkable than your brother said."

"It would have come out. I just helped."

"No, but really," Mr. Haden said. "I never learnt such a thing, Dr. Ravenswood. I should like to. Once, a cottager died before my very eyes, choking on a piece of turnip; I could have saved him, had I but seen this first! How ever did you learn it? Will you show me?"

He was addressing Liam, though *I* had performed the life-saving procedure. I sat in silent indignation for a moment before I noticed Jane, who was looking at Mr. Haden. She glanced at me—an eye roll, a sarcastic twist of her mouth—for only an instant, but it was enough. To survive as a woman here and remain sane, it was essential to have a healthy sense of the ridiculous; that was the thing she had grasped before even out of her teens. I was way behind her, but then, weren't we all?

"Later," Liam said. "We will be happy to show you, but not at tea. It is enough excitement for one day."

"But, Miss Ravenswood, tell us," Cassandra said. "Where did you learn such a thing?" With that, everyone was looking at me, the same question in their eyes, except Liam, who seemed unsure where to look, and decided on the floor. I hesitated. Where could I have?

"My old nurse," I began, "performed this on me once, when I was about ten and had inhaled a sugarplum. Do you remember that, William?"

I saw relief in the smile Liam gave me. "How could I forget? Later, you would not rest until she taught you—she said it was a secret of her Ashanti people, along with a charm for ensuring that the goat's milk would not sour—"

"That one did not work very well, though—"

"And the cure for broken hearts," Liam said, and I feared our improvisation had gone too far.

Jane broke the silence that followed. "Were you able to try that one, sir?"

"Never," he said, and the conversation resumed more normal channels.

BUT I FELT A DIFFERENCE AFTERWARD. MAYBE MERELY IN ME; that finally, after weeks of sewing shirts and drinking tea and watching Liam flirt with Jane, I had done something useful. To my amazement, Cassandra sat down next to me on the other side from Henry and began telling me in a low tone about the challenges of keeping Madame Bigeon in line, and how hard Jane had been driving herself on the proofs of *Emma*. In Cassandra's telling, she herself was the only thing at Hans Place standing between moderate disorder and utter chaos. I smiled and agreed with every word of it, as Henry watched us with a satisfied air.

Edward, who had seemed almost in tears after what happened, took Liam off in a corner for a long talk, which looked serious and ended in a vigorous handshake.

"SO WHAT WAS EDWARD SAYING TO YOU?" I ASKED ONCE WE WERE in the carriage and on our way home.

"Well," Liam began with the hushed caution of someone delivering bad news, "it seems he has asked us to be his guests at Chawton Great House."

I shrieked with glee and bounced on the seat. Liam winced and pointed toward Wilcox, outside on the box. "But that's great. When does he say we can come?" I asked in a whisper, then paused. "Or was he just being polite?"

"He said he would call soon and we could discuss the details." Liam, resting his head in his hands as though worn out from his labors of impersonating Dr. William Ravenswood, went on, "He wanted to give you a horse."

I felt a gush of laughter welling up within me like a sneeze, like an orgasm, and choked it back, mindful of Wilcox. "He wanted to what?"

"He was a long time after explaining he had a handsome mare that he thought would be suitable for a woman of your size." I thought Liam might also be trying not to laugh.

"It was a Shetland pony?"

"I told him we were set for horses, but we had never seen anything of England and would like to get out of London—if he knew of anyone with a house to let in some pretty part of the country he could recommend. So at that, he insisted that we come to Chawton, and if we liked Hampshire, he would help us find a place of our own, but that we would be his guests for now."

"So we will be just down the street from Jane Austen."

And the letters. And "The Watsons."

I was still taking this in when Liam said, "He was wild to find some way to thank you for saving Fanny's life." There was a pause, as the horses clip-clopped down Sloane Street, which was fitfully lit by flickering lamps and oddly quiet, considering it was not so late. "You did, didn't you? She would have died, had you not been there?"

I looked at him in dismay as I realized where he was going with this. How had I avoided seeing it myself? "Impossible. She marries a baronet, and has nine children, and lives to 1882."

"So she would have saved herself, without your help."

"She would have to have," I said slowly, picturing Fanny at

the moment she had held her hands up to her throat. "You have another theory?"

"Perhaps our being there at tea caused her to choke. We made her self-conscious."

"So we were both the cause of the problem and its solution?"

"That would be tidy." He paused. "I don't believe it, though."

"You're saying we've disrupted the probability field."

Liam rested his forehead in the heel of his hand. "It seems like it, doesn't it?"

I stared out the window, at London bumping past, seeing again in my memory the steel-gray corridors of the Royal Institute for Special Topics in Physics. How excited I had been to be there, how amazed to be going to 1815. Had I considered that this could happen? I'd thought so, but now faced with it, I realized I really hadn't.

UPSTAIRS, NORTH HELPED ME INTO MY NIGHTGOWN AND DRESSED my hair, braiding the back sections loosely for night and rolling the front into curlpapers. I usually enjoyed this private, indulgent part of the day and North's calm presence. But she must have sensed I was tense; she asked me if something had happened.

After I gave a brief account of Fanny's choking, she clucked her tongue. "So you saved her life, miss! That's two for you that I know of." We were in front of the glass as she worked on my hair, and our eyes met in the reflection, my face a question mark. "*Tom.* What would've been his lot, if you'd not bought him from that man? How long do you think they last, climbing boys?"

I looked away.

When North finished and left, I sat at my dressing table for a long time. I thought of Fanny as she had looked when she couldn't breathe, Tom the morning I had found him in the drawing room. Those coins stolen from my bag, my first day in London. Money had velocity; how many hands had it passed through by now, how many lives had it altered?

But the intervention need not be so dramatic. We had shifted the current of events just being here: hired servants who would have found different jobs or gone hungry; occupied a house that would have been rented by someone else or stood empty. Common sense suggested that such small things should not change the course of history, yet surely they could, through some course of causality impossible to trace back. Mission intensity, and likelihood of probability field disruption, was measured according to the three major variables: how far in the past, how long spent there, and the degree of involvement needed to accomplish the project goals. People had traveled much further back than we had—but they never stayed long in the remote past, and they rarely did more than observe cautiously. Our mission was 8.5 on a ten-point scale. I had known this; yet my knowledge, until now, had been abstract.

I looked into the mirror at my scared face. In the weak light from the dying fire, my head bristling with curlpapers, I was like a vaguely familiar stranger: the same dark eyes and wedge-like chin, but altered. What am I going to do, I asked my eerie reflection. What am I going to do?

I pulled off the counterpane and wrapped it around me, picked up my candle, and tiptoed out into the hall, floor icy against my bare feet. I hesitated before Liam's door, then eased it open like a housebreaker, slipped in, and closed it behind me.

I whispered: "Are you awake?"

His room was darker than mine and colder, a barely open window letting in a waft of night air. I heard a rustle and a creak, a quick intake of breath. "Rachel?"

I lifted my candle for a look around. "I wanted—" There was a Windsor chair in the corner; I moved it closer to the bed and sat down. The room smelled of night, and something else vaguely familiar, like bay leaf soap and wool, earthy but pleasant. "I wanted to talk to you."

He had sat up, rubbing his eyes with the heels of his hands. His gaze paused on my curlpapers. "What's happened?"

"I just needed to talk for a minute. Did I wake you up? I'm sorry."

Tousled and blinking, but alert now, arms wrapped around his knees, he inclined his head with the hint of a smile. "Don't worry."

"I knew I wouldn't sleep—thinking about what you said—"

"There's a difference between us then. I couldn't see how lying awake would change it."

"I can't fall asleep on cue. The mind doesn't work like that."

"Oh, but you have to train it."

"Can you do that?" I was intrigued, despite myself. "You'll have to show me sometime."

"I can show you now."

"You'll probably tell me to *breathe,* and think about something nice. It's time to panic."

Liam laughed, long and low, somehow secretive, and I felt better. Unlike me, he did not have the laugh of an insane person. "Very well. You first."

I leaned back. My feet were cold; I tucked them under me.

"What I recall, our mission had a point zero-zero-three chance of 'significant' probability field disruption, which would mean a disruption of more than five percent of the field at any given point."

"Does that number comfort you?"

"That's not your recollection?"

It was a moment before he answered. "It seems so far away, doesn't it? Like something that happened to someone else. The institute, all of it." He was right, but I didn't want to admit that we both thought this, and he went on: "And what does it mean? Five percent of the billions of, I don't know, colliding quarks that make up an average day in 1815?"

"It would be something macro." I looked around the dim room, asking myself what I was doing here. If I'd woken up to find Liam standing in my bedroom, I would not have taken it as calmly as he had. "Like a person choking to death who is supposed to live to 1882."

"But she didn't. So maybe it's as they said. The probability field is like a mesh net; it's elastic. She chokes, but she doesn't die. Equilibrium restored."

"How can you be so nonchalant about this?"

"Because it's useless to worry about things you can't control?"

I did not agree, but this was a philosophical labyrinth I had no wish to step into. "What about Tom? You told me it was a bad idea to try to help him. Maybe *that* was where we went wrong." Cramped from my pretzel pose, I stretched my legs out and put my feet on the bed.

Liam said after a pause: "You think Fanny Knight choked on a piece of cake because you saved a climbing boy?"

"I'm not saying there's direct causality. But if the field is dynamic—and it is, action at a distance connecting in quantum, unpredictable ways?"

There was another long silence. Two flights down, the clock struck twelve.

"You were right to do what you did that day."

"But even if—"

"Someone rescued me once. They'd no reason to do it, except human decency, and my whole life was different because. If that's where we went wrong, with Tom—too bad."

"How did they rescue you?"

He ignored this, going on with increased energy: "And I don't believe it. One climbing boy, more or less—people like that don't change things. If we'd run over Wilberforce in our carriage, maybe." I shivered, recalling my first morning in 1815, when I'd nearly been mowed down myself. "Little people don't matter. Except in the aggregate."

"They like their lives as much as the great ones."

"I mean, they don't change things."

He said this with such assurance that I was silenced for a moment, wanting to believe him. But finally I had to say it, what I realized I had come to his bedroom and woken him up for: "If we have really disrupted the probability field, what happens then? And we come back, and the world we know is gone, and we have to be rectified, and forget who we are?" Only the nonconforming memories, I reminded myself, but this was no comfort.

It was Liam's turn to go silent. At last he said: "We took that chance, didn't we? Along with everything else. Are you sorry you did this, now?"

The sleeping house was still, but outside I could hear wind

in chimneys, the cry of a night watch, horseshoes on cobble-stones a long way off. It was as if a thought passed between us, quiet as a sigh. "No," I said. "I'm not. Despite everything."

"And what do you mean, then, by 'everything'?"

"If everything's gone. We go back and—I don't know—" I stopped. "It's unknowable, though, isn't it? What would it even be like? Like trying to picture the world going on without you af-ter you're dead. You know it has to, but—" I stopped, not pleased with where my train of thought was taking me.

"Does that scare you?" Liam murmured. "I don't know. I've always rather liked the idea of the world going on without me. I suppose it's why I was so taken by the idea of time travel. Our world is going on without us now, and we're none the worse."

"That's because we're alive, silly."

"I suppose we are." He laughed quietly.

I considered again that he had a nice laugh. It was of a piece with his versatile voice, his graceful walk, his breadth of shoul-der and way of holding his long head sideways as he held my gaze. His eyes.

Which were fixed on me, glittering in the semidarkness, a look on his face like he'd just thought of something. Uncomfort-able, I dropped my gaze and found myself staring at his hands in-stead, which were still wrapped around his knees as he sat up in bed. It was not much help; they were strong-looking, with knobby knuckles and long fingers. His sleeves, pushed back past the el-bow, offered a view of forearm I never got by day: milky pale, with visible musculature and sleek, dark hairs that I resisted the urge to reach over and stroke. They would have a soft nap, like velvet.

And just like that, I didn't know what to do. My heart was racing and I forgot to breathe; I tried to twine a curl around my finger and felt curlpapers. I'd come here in curlpapers? Mother of god, as Liam would have said.

I took my feet off his bed, which now struck me as suggestive, one step away from climbing under his covers, and stood, a stranger to my own body, legs obeying mind's command, but awkwardly. I picked up my candle.

"I'd better go. Thanks for letting me vent. Sorry I disturbed you."

For what if I did pull back the covers and slide in next to him, close enough to smell the salt on his skin, to hear his breath quicken? *Just to get warm,* I would say. *Let's talk this over in a little more detail.* He would not resist me because men, in my experience, can't. Or don't. A direct approach, managed right, rarely fails.

But I couldn't do it. I was paralyzed.

He peered up at me. "You didn't." In the chiaroscuro of my candle's light he looked puzzled and innocent.

"I was—I feel better now that we talked, though. Thanks. Good night!"

My mouth was dry and I got these words out with difficulty, then turned so fast I extinguished the candle and had to feel my way toward the door. It should have been a relief not to see or be seen, but the darkness felt more intimate, knowing he was in it.

"Good night then, Rachel dear. Come back anytime." There was a creak and a rustle as he settled back down, and my blind hand found the doorknob.

WHEN I OPENED MY EYES TO WATERY NOVEMBER SUNSHINE, EV-erything that had happened the night before was still in my mind, but I was no longer stunned. It was as though in sleep I had adjusted my thinking to contain these ideas, the way scar tissue might grow over a small foreign object in the flesh. Probability field disruption. An invitation to Chawton. And Liam. I stared out at the patch of sky I could see from my window and let my mind play over these things.

No one had ever believed that we could travel to 1815 and change nothing. Yet Liam was probably right: history consisted of big events and larger-than-life characters. Waterloo and Trafalgar and Borodino, Napoleon and Nelson and Kutuzov. Jane Austen. The rest of us contributed to history in our little ways, as drops of water make up an ocean: collectively powerful, meaningless alone. That Fanny Knight had nearly choked to death was not important, in this view. She hadn't; that was the main thing.

And now her father had invited us to Chawton. This was huge. It probably never would have happened otherwise; that is, if she had not nearly died. I felt a chill pass through me as I considered this. It was as if *something*—the world, the future—had needed her to do so, in order for the next domino to fall. As if our arrival in 1815 with a mission had set something astir that had previously been quiet, altering the energy of the world and the outcome of events. This line of thinking was making my head hurt, so I turned to what I did know.

Edward's main property was in Kent; the Chawton estate in Hampshire was smaller, not a place he spent a lot of time. But in 1809, when he'd offered his mother and sisters a choice of two possible houses, they'd picked Hampshire over Kent, for it was more like home: Chawton was near the vicarage at Steventon, where all the children except Edward had grown up, where

Mrs. Austen had been a busy clergyman's wife, with a herd of dairy cows, a large garden, and a houseful of boys the Reverend Austen was schoolmaster to. The cows and the boys were gone, Mr. Austen ten years dead, yet in many ways the life in Chawton of the three Austen ladies and their unmarried friend Martha Lloyd was a return to that earlier time: calm and self-sufficient, growing their vegetables, making spruce beer, and keeping chickens. The world beyond their village, with food riots and textile unrest, might almost not exist, or so I imagined. It would be fascinating to get out of London and see. And how would Cassandra react to us being Edward's guests? She would have to accept us; indeed, it had seemed last night that she was starting to.

But there remained the Liam problem. What had happened, where had this come from, to catch me so off guard? I'd walked into his room with no other thought than a need to talk: looming insomnia, the wish for a friendly ear. I'd walked out with an overpowering wish to sleep with him.

And yet I'd done nothing about it, another puzzle. I am straightforward; my needs are simple. I like having sex, preferably with men, though I don't rule women out. No one needs to be tied up or spanked, and no one needs to be in love. I've found this approach of not overthinking to work well. What I should have done was sit down on the bed, give him a long look, take one of his beautiful hands in my own, and let events unfold naturally. What I'd done instead was stammer like a teenager with a crush and run away. Inexplicable.

True, we were stuck in the early nineteenth century until next September and the Opportunity of Return, posing as brother and sister. Living as we did, there was risk of being caught in flagrante by a servant. And there'd be no getting away when things went south if he turned out to be one of my mistakes—gloomy, withholding, dysfunctional, or complicated. This did not seem impossible. Then, too, he was engaged. A man in love.

All good reasons to hesitate, but they felt after the fact: last night none of them had occurred to me. What was wrong, then? He'd never shown much sign of being attracted—maybe I wasn't his type—but this was not a disqualifier. We were only human. I doubted he'd reject an unambiguous advance; and even if he did, I'd be no worse off than I was now. So why had I run away instead?

I saw again in memory his face as he had looked up at me, just before I'd fled the room. There had been something so guileless in his expression that I'd felt ashamed of my own desires. The Old British are prudes, I reminded myself—forgetting for a moment he wasn't Old British, merely pretending. He'd not had the experiences I'd had of working in remote locations and extreme conditions, did not understand how it affected a person. Maybe, in that way, he was a little naïve. Or maybe he had religious scruples, not that he ever spoke of religion. Or maybe he'd been saving himself for marriage?

This idea of my colleague as a thirty-seven-year-old virgin struck me so forcibly, sad and yet funny, that I gave a snort of laughter and felt better. I rolled onto my stomach and ranged under my nightgown, enjoying the warmth and smoothness of my skin, the soft resilience of my flesh. I imagined his hands on me instead of my own, and let myself forget, at least until I was done bringing myself off, that I had not really solved anything.

A FEW DAYS LATER, WHEN I HAD BEGUN TO WORRY THAT LIAM might have misunderstood, or that that the master of Chawton House had had second thoughts, Edward stopped in when we were still over breakfast to repeat his invitation. His business would keep him in town longer, he would need to be in Kent for three or four weeks, then he would be in Hampshire through the new year, on and off. We were welcome to come as soon as next month, though perhaps we would prefer to wait for spring, a more agreeable time there.

December, we said: we wanted to be in the country as soon as possible, to breathe the clean air and shake off the corrupting influence of London. Liam expressed himself with such warmth on this point that Edward looked taken aback, and suggested a week in Cheltenham or Weymouth—it would do us no end of good. Which we then had to promise to consider.

"I MUST GO TO THE TAILOR." LIAM WENT TO THE WINDOW FOR A look into the street, at Edward Knight getting into his carriage. "Surely there will be shooting. I need outfits."

"What a clotheshorse you are. Were you constantly shopping in our own time too?" I had resolved to treat Liam exactly as before, to take a leaf from his playbook and give away nothing. So far, it was going well. "I suppose you were."

"I never had any money."

"Oh. Great, so you can indulge your pent-up demand."

"My long-suppressed desire to be Beau Brummell?" Liam murmured. "Sometimes 1815 does seem like an endless fancy-dress ball."

"Or to be a gentleman."

He gave me a sharp look. "Do you want to come to the tailor's with me? I was thinking we could go for a walk, after. It seems a shame to waste the day."

WE WERE IN HYDE PARK, THE UNSEASONABLY MILD WEATHER having held, when I saw Jane Austen at a distance. "Over there," I said, trying to indicate without pointing, "at the edge of that group of people? There—don't stare, but by that weeping willow, with two other women?"

By the time he saw her, she had noticed us too. She bade farewell to the women she had been walking with and came over. We asked after Henry's health.

"He is very well. So well, I have left him on a bench—he insisted on coming out—so I could take a turn with Miss East and Mrs. LaTournelle. Will you join me in returning to him?"

The wind had picked up; it felt like November again. Jane put herself between us, and we were off. She began telling us about the new book they had started reading in the evenings: *Guy Mannering, or the Astrologer,* by the author of *Waverley,* which she feared no one would like as well as *Waverley.*

"How far away did you leave him?" I finally asked.

"Somewhere over here." And then I saw him. He'd been joined by a heavyset gentleman in a blue uniform coat and a big hat, with a weather-beaten face and a blond ponytail. Henry saw us and raised a hand; the naval officer bowed, shook Henry's hand, and was off.

"Did you find them in the park, Jane? How enterprising of you!" Henry was cheerful, but I thought he looked tired.

He stood up, and we made our way, more slowly, south toward Sloane Street and Hans Place. We began four across, but Jane and Liam, heads together and talking earnestly, were faster; Henry and I fell behind.

"Were you ready for an outing of this duration?" I asked. "We could stop and rest. Look, here is a bench."

"Miss Ravenswood, I fear you must think me a confirmed invalid."

"I am only too accustomed to saying what I think, without studying how it might appear. You must think *me* a savage."

"Not in the least." He smiled down at me. "I admire an open, warm, ardent temperament. A person too cautious ever to risk putting a foot wrong—I have no use for such a character."

"You are charity itself to put such an interpretation on my lack of tact."

"I wish to correct your impression, though, as to my health. I am daily improving, and expect to be fully restored to myself within weeks."

"I give you joy of that."

Ahead of us, Liam and Jane, too far away to be overheard, broke stride for a moment, turning toward each other and back to look at us. They both had the same cool, assessing gaze of people trying to make up their minds. Then they turned and went on.

"But if I may speak frankly, as a friend—"

He took my gloved hand and pressed it to his heart, which made my own heart give a lurch. "I would not have you speak any other way."

"I would urge you to be temperate in both eating and drinking. Not that I am suggesting you are, now, *not*—but the liver has suffered an insult. It will be a weak point for you always. Take fatty meats, spirits of every kind, and wine, in strictest moderation."

I glanced sideways to see how he was taking this. But I might as well have told him to tie a string around his big toe, or to drink a potion of crushed pearls and snails; my medical advice surely seemed just as random, particularly since I was female and by definition could not know anything. I wished there was something I could do that would actually help him. He gave me the impression of a man walking cheerfully at the edge of a cliff, and I felt again that mix of compassion and desire that had puzzled me the evening I had saved Fanny from choking.

He gave me a mischievous smile. "What about tea?"

"Harmless. Beneficial."

"That means I can in good conscience invite you and your brother to join us in drinking some on Tuesday. Cassandra is going into Hampshire with Edward that morning, so the sad little remnant of our party will need cheering."

I WAS GLAD OF THE INVITATION, BUT ITS EXCUSE SEEMED PARTICularly flimsy once we arrived: No one at Hans Place lacked cheer. Jane and Fanny were sillier and more animated than I had ever seen them, sitting on either side of Mr. Haden with Liam across from them, and conversing in low tones, breaking into laughter, leaning over and nearly touching their noses together like ponies before galloping off into some fresh conversational extravagance. I overheard only scraps, but suspected they were talking about Mr. Clarke, and Carlton House; Jane had finally made the promised visit there.

I was wedged in a corner, Fanny's rented harp on one side,

Henry on the other. We'd landed on the subject of the fabulous party at Burlington House, thrown by White's club to celebrate the end of the war with France. In 1814, a year early, as it turned out. That Henry had been there I knew already from Jane Austen's letters.

"I read in a newspaper that it cost ten thousand pounds. Is that true?"

"Oh! I have no idea; I am grieved that the account focused on such a vulgar aspect."

I thought it odd that a banker would consider the price of *anything* a vulgar question, rather than an interesting one. Maybe this explained some of his business problems.

"What I remember was, I had never seen so many happy people in one place at one time."

"Rightly so. To defeat Buonaparte, it was the work of a generation, was it not? Yours."

"I can claim but little credit; it is my two brothers who are sea captains."

"I hope I can meet them and thank them for their services to king and country."

"You will meet Frank; he is at Chawton. You will have a wait for Charles." He paused. "Would it sound ungracious to say I miss him already?"

"Your brother Charles?"

"Buonaparte."

"Not ungracious. Perhaps unpatriotic."

"But I would never wish him back—escaped from exile, once more at the head of an army—oh, no."

"Not even the French could stand more of such excitement."

"Yet Frank and Charles are already longing for a new war;

there are so few opportunities to advance in peacetime, even fewer to take a prize."

"People ahead of them on the lists do not die quickly enough in peacetime?"

He laughed. "Miss Ravenswood! You are worse than Jane!"

"I could only wish to have half her wit."

"She is one of a kind." He glanced over at her. "But you are correct. The secret of advancement there lies in surviving what kills others. And luck, to be sure, especially with one's patrons." He looked around the room; his bright eyes came back to rest on my face. "And it is equally true in civilian life, in less dramatic form. One does not come home with bullet holes and cutlass wounds. At least, not the visible kind." He fell silent again, glancing around once more; it did not take great insight to speculate that he was thinking about his bank.

"Indeed. A peace so longed-for; yet adjusting is not easy. If you consider what has happened to the price of wheat—" I stopped. Ladies probably did not talk about commodity prices.

He gave a sigh. "My affairs are quite involved." His affairs? Why would he discuss his finances with me? Was this leading up to a request for a loan? But surely that was something he would ask Liam. "The situation looks grave right now, but I am confident there can still be a good outcome."

At the bank? It was my turn to sigh. Poor Henry. Poor doomed, cheerful Henry.

Unless. I had saved Fanny from choking. Maybe I could save his bank. A bank failure often hinged as much on a loss of confidence as on the reality of its financial state; a timely infusion of liquidity might make all the difference. The bank collapse meant not only Henry's personal ruin, but also the loss of every-thing his brothers had invested with him. Their support kept Chawton Cottage running, so the crash reverberated through Jane's life too; it is one of the stresses thought to have contrib-uted to the onset of her fatal illness. Maybe helping out his bank would buy her a few more years, even if it meant I could never diagnose her disorder. Enough to finish "Sanditon"? For if we had disrupted the probability field, maybe it would be better to make the best of it: we could be a force for good, and heroes to the entire Austen family.

He was continuing: "I hesitate to speak, with this sword of Damocles hanging over my head. And yet, knowing you will leave London soon, I must."

But he did not. He fell silent long enough for the conference on the sofa to break up and for Fanny to yield to the requests of Jane and Mr. Haden, and sit down at the harp.

"There is a new song I have been working on with my music master," she said. "I play it remarkably ill."

"You will let us be the judge," her aunt said, and Fanny struck the harp, accompanying herself vocally. She had a pleas-ant if forgettable voice, on key at least.

I was not really listening; I looked back at Henry. I felt his awkwardness and pitied him—it's embarrassing to ask for money. "Please, do not hesitate to speak of whatever troubles you."

"I think you cannot fail to understand what troubles me," he finally said, so quietly I had to lean in a little to hear him. Our eyes met. "You, with your remarkable penetration."

I stared at him as he went on, still quietly, but speaking

faster: "I do not dare to ask if the feeling is returned; this would be the height of presumption. I would ask only, can you give me leave to hope?"

He wasn't asking for a loan. I stood frozen, mouth open slightly, as self-satisfaction with my own intended generosity faded to astonishment. Our plan had succeeded too well. What was I going to do now?

"May I call on you tomorrow?" he whispered.

"Yes" came out before I could think better of it.

CHAPTER 10

NOVEMBER 15

33 Hill Street

MY THOUGHTS KEPT ME AWAKE UNTIL DAWN. WAS IT POSSIBLE I'd misunderstood, and Henry was going to ask for a loan? Or could it be something else I hadn't even thought of? In Preparation we'd devoted surprisingly little attention to the possibility of a proposal, despite the emphasis on my playing a role in which this would seem a risk. But then, we'd been chosen, among other things, for our ability to improvise. It was time to show what I was made of.

After I finally fell asleep, I woke up late and devoted special attention to my hair and clothing. Downstairs I found the breakfast parlor empty, one place set, and summoned handsome Robert to request coffee and rolls.

"Has my brother gone out?"

"He called for the carriage and left a short while ago."

Perhaps just as well; another problem I'd not resolved was whether to tell Liam what had happened. "Do you know where he went?"

"He did not tell me, madam. I can ask if Jencks knows."

I had a brief pang at the freedom of men to go where they wanted, without notice. "Nay, do not trouble yourself."

I GOT THROUGH BREAKFAST, THOUGH MY MOUTH WAS DRY AND Mrs. Smith's rolls, normally delicious, might have been sawdust. Back upstairs, I brushed my teeth with my marshmallow-root stick and coral tooth powder; the last thing I needed was bad breath.

In the drawing room, I forced myself to work on a shirt, trying to match my breathing to the in and out of the needle, and to empty my mind. I'd never taken Liam up on his offer to show me how to train my thoughts so as to fall asleep—a skill that would have been handy last night. Only last week I'd barged into his room, but already it seemed to belong to a lost world, filed under things I'd never do again, for I was on my guard now always. Giving away nothing. Was this how he went through life, then? How could he stand it?

From downstairs, I heard a knock on the door, but even before I looked to see the familiar curricle stopped outside, I knew it was Henry.

HE WALKED IN LOOKING SERIOUS. "MISS RAVENSWOOD."

"I am afraid you have missed my brother, sir; I expect him back shortly."

I had put down my sewing and stood up when he came in; we were in the middle of the room, closer than normal social distance.

"It is principally you I am come to see. I think you cannot fail to understand that." His hands were clasped; he brought them up to his heart. He was looking down at me, hazel eyes bright and for once without the slightest glint of humor. "Nearly from the first moment I met you, I felt there was something—something different about you, unlike anyone I have ever known. You must allow me to tell you how ardently I desire and love you."

I felt dizzy; my heart was pounding so madly that I had a sense it must be visibly throbbing. I could not resist glancing down at myself, to find the spectronanometer on its silver chain resting quietly between my breasts. My ticket home.

"You are silent," he said, taking my hand in two of his. "May I take that to mean"—to my astonishment, he dropped to one knee—"that you will consider making me the happiest of men?"

I stared down at him. Time seemed to expand, the light in the room to acquire weight, as if we'd stepped into a Vermeer painting. I wondered if Jencks might be listening at the keyhole, or what would happen if Liam should come home and walk in. Then I stopped wondering those things as something shifted inside me like a slow grinding of tectonic plates, but scarier; I felt the role I was playing take over and swallow me. I was having the conversation that could determine the course of my life: whether to take this man in holy matrimony, hand over to him my fortune, my fate. It was terrifying. What if he actually loved me and was not merely after my money, what was my responsibility then? What was I to do? How did people *know*?

"You must give me time to think," I tried to say, but my words came out in a whispery gasp. Still holding my hand, he leaned in, pulling me closer.

"I did not hear you, sweet angel."

"You must give me time to think," I repeated. As he was still on one knee, my neckline was at his eye level; I wished he'd stand up, but he seemed in no hurry to do so. Maybe the man did not rise again until you said yes. "This is an important decision in a lady's life, as I am sure you understand."

He looked up at me. "I do understand." And then he was speaking in a rush: "Though, please, be merciful, do not take too long. You have made me feel like a young man again, Miss Rav—Or may I call you by the name I call you in my heart? May I call you—Mary?" He went on without waiting for an answer: "Yet as the poet said, 'But at my back I always hear, / Time's wingèd chariot hurrying near—' I am as ardent as any man of one and twenty, but I am—and my health—my prospects are—I am—Perhaps I can talk to your brother—I—"

His head was practically in my chest, so I pulled him in the rest of the way, anything to stop this torrent of words. His nose found harbor in the cleft next to the spectronanometer; his moan of pleasure vibrated through my rib cage as he wrapped his trembling arms around my waist.

"Mary," he said. "Oh, Mary."

We stayed like that for a while, our breath coming fast. The moment felt deceptively peaceful, like something had been resolved. But when he turned his head and began to nibble along the top of my dress, bringing his hands up to untuck my fichu and then to try to ease my breasts out of the confines of my corset and toward his mouth, I realized we were not at Mansfield Park, and I had to make a decision fast.

"Mr. Austen!" I cried, pushing him away and jumping back, my outrage partly genuine, but also fighting down a laugh. Had I expected him to show the restraint of one of the heroes in his sister's novels? "Is this how you offer your hand?"

It took him a moment to regain his balance before he stood up with remarkable dignity, everything considered, pulling down his waistcoat and smoothing his trousers. His face was flushed; he shot a quick glance at me and then away. "Miss Ravenswood, forgive me. You have made me forget myself."

"Perhaps you had better go." His use of my first name had seemed presumptuous, but switching back to my last felt cold. He had the shamefaced expression some men get after sex when they want nothing more to do with you. "I will think, hard, about what you have said."

An amused look came into his eyes for the first time in this conversation, and with a tiny smile he stepped forward and bowed over my outstretched hand. "I leave you to your thoughts, madam." And with one more conspiratorial glance, he was gone.

I sank into a chair and covered my face with my hands. I sat for a while, very still, eyes closed, trying not to replay what had just happened; I would think about it all later. Then I heard footsteps coming up the stairs.

"Was Henry here?" Liam asked, walking into the room. "I thought I saw him in his carriage just now, but he didn't seem to—" He stopped. "What's wrong? Has something happened?"

I looked down to find I was still holding my fichu. "Um," I said, going to the mirror over the mantel and tucking the length of fabric back into place. "Yes, he was here." My face was flushed, my hair in more than usual disarray. As I tidied it, I looked from my reflection to Liam's. He'd followed me to the mirror, staring at me in what looked like horror.

"Are you all right? Did he—did he do something?" I turned from the mirror to him as he held his hands out, like he was about to touch me reassuringly, but couldn't decide where and then thought better of it. He took a step back, still looking down at me, wide-eyed. "Did he do something to you?"

"I'm fine." I nodded toward the open door and put a finger to my lips. "Let's take a walk."

IT WAS NO WEATHER FOR FRIVOLOUS OUTINGS, THE AIR DAMP AND the clouds thick, threatening rain at any moment, and I shivered despite spencer and shawl as we turned in the direction of Berkeley Square.

"He asked me to make him the happiest of men," I said without preamble.

"Did he really? Amazing." Liam's tone was low and cautious, and he kept shooting sideways glances at me. "What did you tell him?"

"Your amazement is a little unflattering. It's like I've never received a proposal of marriage before." In fact, I never had, but now that the shock was wearing off, I felt my spirits rising; I could not suppress a grin of triumph.

Liam gave me another quick glance as if assessing my sanity. "Amazing, as in—grand—brilliant. It means we've succeeded in convincing them that we—But what did you *say* to him, Rachel dear?"

"I told him I had to think it over."

"And how did he take that?"

I paused, recalling the enjoyable sensation of his nose in my cleavage. "As well as can be expected."

"He didn't ask to talk to me?" Henry would need to have the money conversation with the male relatives of anyone he hoped to wed; marriage was as much about property as love. What he could offer, what I brought to the table, terms of the settlement.

"I think he said something about talking to you. We didn't really get into it."

"He was too busy removing articles of your clothing?" Liam demanded, his voice rising. I blinked; had he just said that? "Whispering sweet nothings? Pledging his undying love?"

"Have you lost your mind?"

He turned his head away and did not reply for a long moment. I looked down the street, a tunnel of terraced houses bristling with ironwork and watchful with windows. And at the end, Berkeley Square opened up to swirling gray clouds behind bare tree shapes, like a promise of freedom.

"I'm sorry. I've no right to ask about anything that happened between you and him. Except as pertains to the mission."

His words were formal, his tone careful. Could he be jealous? I felt a flutter of hope, also amusement. "There's nothing to—"

"Of course you're attracted to him. He's a compelling—You just have to be careful, that's all, we both have to be careful, this—You don't want to change history, is what I'm saying. At least—at least not more than we apparently already have." He fell silent, looking miserable. "He's the sort of man one can't help—But just be careful, Rachel. This is not our world."

"You don't imagine I feel anything for him? I'm playing a part. Remember?"

"I see how you look at each other," Liam muttered. "I don't judge, but I see. You've not acted before, you don't know; it happens before you know it's happened, when the feelings you feign become the feelings you—" He stopped.

I thought of the sensation that had overtaken me when I was with Henry, of vanishing into the role. As we reached the square and stepped in under the bare trees, the sky had grown darker; a drop of rain plinked onto the brim of my bonnet, then another.

"I'm not going to fall in love; it's not the sort of thing I do." This sounded so unintentionally melodramatic that I was embarrassed, and felt the need to laugh and add, "Nor am I going to sleep with him. Not that I'd mind, if he weren't a research subject."

Liam stopped walking and gazed down at me, blushing, hesitating. I marveled at how I'd ever found him homely, for even his flaws now charmed me: his slightly crooked nose, his excess of chin, the habitually gloomy expression in his beautiful eyes. The rain had passed the drops stage, was more of a drizzle, but we ignored it.

"What? I'm just being honest. He's handsome and he's funny and he's Jane Austen's brother. Sure I'm attracted. Is that so terrible? I have no tender feelings for him. I don't do tender, either."

"All right then," Liam said, taking his eyes off me with what seemed an effort and starting to walk again so abruptly that he disturbed a knot of crows; they scattered, fluttering and shrieking, from a loaf of bread they'd been working on. "Is there anything else I should know, while we're exploring the subject?"

I took a breath. Maybe this was my opening. "Is there anything else you want to know?" I asked playfully, putting a hand on his arm.

"Rachel!" he began, turning toward me again, now with the same look of dismay he'd worn back at the house. "You are heartless, aren't you?"

"What do you mean?" I let my hand fall away.

"Don't—just don't—I'm not—Don't mock me. Please."

"Who was mocking you?"

But the rain could no longer be called drizzle; the sky opened up. We wheeled and started back at a brisker pace, too late. Before we reached home we were running and breathless, sped on by gusts of wind that flung sheets of rain at us. Water squelched in my half boots, my shawl was sodden, the lower half of my dress clinging suggestively and weighing me down, my bonnet a wreck. Jencks and North, with towels and assurances we'd catch our deaths, hurried us off to our separate rooms and into dry clothes.

WHEN WE RECONVENED IN THE DRAWING ROOM, I HAD THE SENSE of a danger averted. We drank tea and said nothing that could not be overheard; I had no proof, had never caught him at it, but I felt that Jencks listened at doors. It was a way he had of seeming busy in the hallway when I sometimes came out of the drawing room stealthily; he would be straightening a picture that always hung crooked or running his finger along the wainscoting in search of dust. Nothing a servant might not reasonably do, yet why just then?

Liam, reverting to his old air of formality, looked anywhere but at me, which was something of a relief. I was mystified by exactly what he'd said on our walk, yet its general sense was clear: he was warning me off; he had some scruples, perhaps connected to his fiancée. I hadn't given up hope, but I needed to rethink my approach.

We discussed the Henry Austen problem, elliptically.

"It's awkward," I said. "A definite no will close doors with the sisters. But something must be said. Sooner or later. How long do I get, to think?"

Liam, staring into the fire, shook his head. "Take as long as you can, is my advice. But once the thing with the bank happens—" He did not finish his thought.

"I wish I'd managed to forestall this. I shouldn't have let myself be alone with him."

His eyes met mine for an instant before he dropped his gaze and muttered: "Maybe I should talk to him. Tell him you're thinking. Have the money chat."

I was briefly tempted; it would appear to move things forward, without the need for me to face Henry.

But then I shook my head. "I need to do this myself."

If Liam talked to Henry, Henry would know I had told him what had happened. But could he imagine that I would have told everything: my own indiscreet behavior, his eager response? Impossible, yet the idea gave me a chill: the two of them talking about me, one knowing what the other merely suspected.

THE WET WEATHER CONTINUED FOR SEVERAL DAYS, GIVING ME AN excuse to stay home from Hans Place. Liam went, reporting that Henry's health was continuing to improve, that he had said nothing about wishing to marry me, and that Jane sent her regards.

Then one morning she came to visit, a thing she'd never done before.

"Henry left me here," she explained. "I told him I would catch up to him in Henrietta Street; I must do some shopping and then we will go home; he is not yet strong enough to spend a full day at the bank."

It was an honor but a surprise too; I knew she had to be busy with the proofs of *Emma*.

"I shall order the carriage; I can take you to Henrietta Street myself. Or perhaps you prefer my brother as escort; or we can all three go. He is still upstairs dressing; he will be down soon."

"Does he take longer to dress than you?" She looked amused. "But it is as well; I am always happy to see him, but it is agreeable to have a quiet coze with you." There was a pregnant pause as I debated whether Henry would have told her he'd proposed. "You are not affronted that Henry did not stop in but merely left me here?"

"Not at all. He has a bank to run."

"He does." She paused again. "He did not wish to seem to tease you."

"Oh, he would never do that."

He must have told her, then.

She studied me with her bright eyes, so much like her brother's. "If there is anything I can tell you, Miss Ravenswood, to set your mind at ease, please do not hesitate; ask me." A creak of footsteps came from the floor above. "Your maid has the dressing of your hair?" she went on quickly, and I nodded, whipsawed by this abrupt change in subject. "She must be more than usually gifted, for I always think you have the most en-chanting curls, so natural-looking. How does she contrive to make them so springy and variegated?"

"Nature, madam, made them so." I was disconcerted; in her world personal compliments are rude, except among the closest of friends. This newly intimate tone meant what?

"So it did! I see now." She leaned closer for a look. "I was mis-led, for your brother's hair, though equally dark, is so straight."

At that moment, to my relief, Liam walked in.

CHAPTER 11

DECEMBER 1

En Route

FROM HILL STREET TO CHAWTON IS ABOUT FIFTY MILES: MUCH OF one short winter day and part of another. The weather had turned cold: ruts had frozen solid, and ice puddles shattered under our wheels like glass. I had long since stopped hearing the roar of London, as I realized only when the city was already behind us, along with its scruffy outskirts: brickworks, bleaching fields, shambles, tanneries. It all gave way surprisingly soon to stubbly harvested fields bordered by hedgerows. The sky was gray, and there seemed to be a lot of it.

I'd been busy: organizing and packing and choosing things to be sent ahead, because cargo space in the landaulet was minimal. Deciding who would come along—Wilcox, for the horses; Jencks to be Liam's valet; North to be my maid—with the rest to stay in London on board wages, looking after the house. There had been tradesmen's bills to pay, take-leaves of our new friends. The enforced inactivity of travel felt strange after all that. It was too bumpy to read the novel I had brought, so all I could do was stare out the window, remembering my previous long carriage ride, to London in September.

My sense of apprehension was nearly as great now, even if I was more used to this world. Being a houseguest had etiquette perils that grew more vivid as our departure for Chawton loomed, costing me sleep as I lay awake thinking of all the ways we might be exposed there. Also wondering what I was going to do about Henry: how long I could put him off and what would happen once I finally said no.

Though she never stated it openly, it became clear from Jane's manner both that Henry had told her of his offer and that she was in favor of it. She'd been friendly before, but grew warmer, almost confiding; the strangely personal remarks about my hair were just the start. She kept up her flirtation with Liam, but he was no longer so obviously her favorite, the focus of her attention. Instead, I seemed to be.

Impossible not to be seduced by this; impossible not to feel its danger. We had gone to Hans Place a few times before leaving London, including the night before we started our journey. Henry was circumspect around other people: the Tilsons, the Jacksons, Mr. Seymour. If not for the subtle smolder in how he looked at me sometimes, I would hardly have suspected it myself. But then, he had contrived to take my hand and lingeringly kiss it after helping me into my pelisse as our carriage stood at the door, the other guests gone, Jane halfway down the stairs distracting Liam with a story about a quarrel between Madame Bigeon and the butcher's boy.

"You are thinking about what I have said?" he murmured, eyes meeting mine.

"I think about it day and night." I felt his hand tremble slightly as he pulled off my glove, kissed each knuckle in turn, and continued to hold my hand. My mouth had fallen open; my chest was straining against the prison of its corset.

"Precious Mary," he whispered. "I will come down to Chawton as soon as I can. You will have mercy on me then, will you not?"

EVEN THOUGH THERE WOULD BE FEW OPPORTUNITIES TO SPEAK privately or as ourselves once we were staying at Chawton House, Liam and I said little as our journey got under way, except to marvel at the sights outside the window. A new constraint seemed to be oppressing us in recent weeks; Liam had grown more silent than usual, but so had I. My mind returned more than once to our conversation the day of Henry's proposal, inconclusively, as if mining it for clues and not finding the answer I wanted.

Finally I said, "The Tilsons seemed to be having a very serious talk with you last night." At Hans Place, they'd ended up in a corner with Liam, from which he threw a glance at me from time to time, as if pleading for rescue, while I sat on a sofa with Jane, she telling me in a low tone things about my future neighbors in Chawton that she felt I might need to know.

"It seems they are thinking of moving to Canada, and they wanted my advice."

"Why would they think you know anything about it?"

"More about the Atlantic voyage, what it was like. If it was as terrible as they'd heard."

"What would they do in Canada? With all those children?"

"Whatever people do there. Fur trading?"

"You think it has to do with the bank collapse?"

"They have some sort of cousin there. He's encouraging them."

The Tilsons did not go to Canada. Mrs. Tilson would die in 1823, age forty-six, in Marylebone, where they moved after the bank collapse. Her daughter Anna, fifteen, died a few days later, so some contagious illness must have struck the household. Mr. Tilson would outlive her by fifteen years, moving back to his native Oxfordshire.

Unless we'd changed history, and this was one more sign of how. I looked at the wintry landscape outside the carriage window and shivered.

"You tried to talk them out of it?"

"I told them Canada was very cold."

A silence fell, but I sensed we were both thinking about the probability field, a suspicion confirmed when Liam went on: "There's no reason they couldn't think about it. It doesn't mean they are going to go."

"I am sure you were persuasive in your case against it."

"I did my best." Looking gloomy, he rubbed his eyes. "And what about Henry? Was he pressing you for an answer?"

"Not annoyingly. But I'm sure he wants one." Liam did not answer, and I continued, "I've been thinking." I paused, unsure how to go on, but finally said: "What about a long engagement?" Apart from a sudden intake of breath, and a certain intensity of gaze, he showed no reaction, and I went on. "It would give us an excuse to lend him some money, and try to save his bank. Because I keep thinking, if we've messed up history, why not do something useful? We know that the stress of the crash may have been part of what brought on Jane's illness. So what if we could . . . postpone it?"

Liam looked away from me and out the carriage window. "A very generous notion," he said at last. "I admire its audacity. There are so many things wrong with it, though, I don't know where to start." He fell silent.

"Well?"

"Well, like that research was unable to determine exactly what happened with the bank. We might give him every cent we had and it would still fail."

"We'd need to keep enough till we go back. But they sent us with more than we could really spend, as far as I can tell, only for masquerading as gentry and impressing Henry. And since we've done that . . ."

Liam leaned forward, asking in a whisper, "But if something goes wrong? And we can't get back?"

In theory, the wormhole can collapse, rendering it unusable, whether because of probability field disruption, or something else. There's no way of knowing what happened to the three teams that never came back, but this is one possibility. I looked at him and could not speak as everything seemed to tilt slightly, rearranging the landscape of the familiar, stranding me in an alien land.

"I always thought it was why we were sent with such a lot. Just in case."

"Just in case," I managed to say.

"Or, it's possible only one of us could get back. We have to consider that. I've no useful skills; I'd be dead in a year without money."

"I could work as a midwife." I thought of all the lives I might save; for a crazy moment the vision tempted me.

"If only one of us could go, I certainly wouldn't let you stay here." He sounded nettled. He added, looking out the window: "Unless you want to marry Henry, and be Jane Austen's sister-in-law. As you say, if we've messed with the probability field, why not do it properly?"

"Are you out of your mind?" I demanded, realizing we both were, a little. Before I thought better of it I leaned across the seat and took both his hands, looking into his eyes. "Liam! We're not going to be stuck here, so stop talking like that. But you're right; we need to be careful. We can't give away all our money." I paused. Our gloved fingers were entwined; I was close enough to see the flecks of gold in his blue irises. He looked, I thought, terrified. "But maybe there is still some way we can help them. We have to think how."

Liam's nostrils flared as he took a breath and stared at me, squeezing my hands for an instant so hard I yelped and he let go. "You're a very good person." He fell back against his seat and closed his eyes. "I wish—"

"What?"

A pause. "Let's say, I wish I'd met you sooner. Like, when I was seven."

I smiled. "I would have been three. We wouldn't have had much in common."

He opened his eyes and seemed to consider this. "Do you mean we do now?"

I was puzzled by his teasing tone, but grateful. "Would I have to have grown up in your town, to accomplish this? Where in Ireland did you say it was?"

"No, no, I would have—Where did you grow up? In New York, then?"

"In Brooklyn."

"In Brooklyn. And what was that like?"

"Nice." I tried to think how to sum it up for him. "We lived in an old house. My parents and I, I mean, and my grandmother." For an instant it all rose before me in memory: the worn stone steps at the front, the faint smell of old wood when you stepped inside, the slant of sunlight on the stairs down to the kitchen, which was on the lowest floor, like in our rented house in London. "It would have been built not so long after when we are living now. We had a garden in the back, where my friends always came over to play because they mostly lived in apartments. My mother had a studio on the top floor, with skylights, and it always smelled wonderful, like paint. *Has*, I mean, she still has." I stopped, seeing it too clearly now and suppressing a sudden wish to cry. I thought of the world as it had seemed in my childhood and how I'd felt then, warm and safe in my family's love. "I miss her so much."

"Do you?" I thought he sounded puzzled. "So she's an artist?"

"She would set up a little canvas for me next to hers and have me do projects." I smiled as I thought of this. "And they were always taking me to museums and concerts and things, well before I had any idea of anything, except that it was extremely important. I remember first going to the opera when I was six. With my father. *The Magic Flute*."

"Did you like it?" His tone was cautious.

"Actually? I loved it. It was like the music picked me up and body-slammed me—" I looked out the carriage windows to see we were approaching a town. "Do you think this is Guildford? It must be, right? It's getting on toward dark."

That was the midway point where we'd arranged to spend the night: Jencks and North had traveled ahead of us by mail coach to smooth our way, making this arrival at the Angel far different from the night we'd walked into the Swan to be insulted by the innkeeper. Having been shown up a dim, creaking flight of stairs to find our rooms waiting, our things unpacked, the promise of dinner in the best private parlor, I washed up, my mind not on the challenges ahead but on the world I had come from. I seldom allowed my thoughts to stray there, and now I understood why: a rare mood of homesickness had overtaken me with the vision of my mother, painting in the attic, wondering if I would be all right.

I drank too much claret at dinner, and talked too much about my childhood, as if by talking about it I could live it again. "My father taught me to play chess," I explained. "It amazes me, when I think of it; he was a cardiologist, and he taught at a medical school, but I always felt like he had time for me. Like I was the most important person in the world, to him. I suppose, though, memory—there had to have been times—I remember when I was little, having to go to sleep before he was home, and being so, so disappointed." We were done picking at the duck, still sitting over the plates, room half in shadow. Liam's eyes were fixed on me; it was hard to say with what emotion. "He died suddenly, five years ago. I miss him every day. He had an undiagnosed heart problem. It's ironic, right? He would have been quite fascinated by his own condition." I pushed my plate aside and put my head down on the table, fighting back tears. Had I ever been quite this drunk in 1815? Or maybe it was just emotion. "I miss him every day." Liam reached over and patted my shoulder tentatively. His touch sent a jolt through me, and I sat up. "I'm sorry." I tried to laugh. "I'm wallowing."

"Wallow away, Rachel dear. We'll be at Chawton House soon enough, and on our best behavior."

"I've gone on and on about myself, and asked nothing about you."

"Don't worry."

I stood and immediately felt dizzy. "We'll be making an early start, I suppose."

"Breakfast at half-seven, the man promised me."

I turned to go and then turned back. "Liam. Will you give me a hug? I need a hug."

He got up without hesitating and came around the table to enfold me in his long arms. It was a better hug than I'd expected, not perfunctory; but then, he'd been an actor. We did not, as so often happens, carefully keep our torsos apart; there was an illicit thrill in this as I rested my forehead on his neckcloth and inhaled the aromas of bay leaf soap and coal smoke and carriage interior and linen and Liam. He swayed slightly, like a birch tree in a breeze, and stroked my hair. I felt his breath on my scalp, and then, as I moved in closer, felt the flutter of his erection stir, grow, and solidify against me.

We stayed like that a long while, saying nothing, breathing harder. I lowered my arms from where they'd been chastely around his shoulders, admiring the musculature of his back on my way down, and pulled him tighter, eliciting a groan. His hands slid down past my waist to seize my butt and lift me up, pushing us together with such force that the air left my chest as my feet left the ground. Surprising, but not unpleasant; he stuck his tongue in my ear, nibbled at my earlobe, and blazed a wet trail of kisses down my neck, breath hot and fast. "Oh my god," he whispered. "Rachel."

Then he let me down and stepped back.

"I'm sorry," he said, gaze on the floor. "I'm sorry. I shouldn't be doing this."

"Yes you should." I moved toward him, but he quickly put a chair between us, and I stopped, surprised and humiliated.

He covered his eyes with one hand as if to shut out the sight of me, his arousal still evident in his pants. "You're vulnerable; you can't consent. You've had too much to drink. You'll hate me later. I'm not such an animal, to take advantage—"

I laughed—not because this was funny, though it was—but in confusion, and he winced. Grabbing my shoulders, he spun me around and pushed me gently yet decisively toward the door. "Off with you now. I'm not made of stone, you know. Sleep it off." In the doorway, we paused; the hall was empty, dim with too few candles in sconces along the walls. I thought he might close the door behind me, but he continued to steer me toward the room I had been assigned. I put my hand on the doorknob, remembering I'd been given a key. And where was it now? Oh, yes, my spencer had a pocket. I fished it out and unlocked the bulky, old-fashioned mechanism on my first try, thinking I couldn't be really drunk if I'd managed this complex task with such ease. And since I wasn't really drunk, consent was not an issue. Opening the door, I turned to share this insight with Liam. Before I could speak, he shoved me into my room, using not just his hands but his whole body, an opportunity to kiss the nape of my neck and thrust a still-notable erection into the small of my back. Both at the same instant, and just for an instant; then the door clicked shut and I was alone, off balance and staggering in the darkness.

What the hell had just happened, did not seem an unreasonable question. I lurched toward where I correctly estimated the bed to be and fell onto it, my eyes growing accustomed to the dimness and starting to distinguish vague forms in the room. Then I heard footsteps in the hall, a knock followed by a door opening, a clatter of dishes, a murmur of male voices. Jencks! Taking away the dinner things. If this had gone on as I'd wanted, we'd have been caught for sure.

I'd dodged a bullet, but lucky was not how I felt. I rose to my feet and felt my way back to the door; when I heard Jencks emerge, I looked out and asked him to send North to me. By now I could see enough in the gloom to distinguish a candle on a table, which I lit from the nearest one in the hall before returning to my room and settling down to wait for North to come help prepare me for bed.

"LOOK," LIAM SAID IN A LOW TONE. "UP AHEAD, THERE."

Amazing and deceptively ordinary, Jane Austen's house: squat, brick, close to the road, with a low wall around it. In our own time, it is the heart of a complex covering several thousand acres devoted to the author and her era, offering a surreal mix of the scholarly and the frothy. There is an unrivaled library of early women's writing, thanks to Eva Farmer, and a re-creation of the Assembly Rooms at Bath, where dancing lessons take place daily. A guillotine donated by the French sits incongruously in the middle of the green in nearby Alton, a town entirely sub-sumed by Austenworld, where costumed visitors can pay to im-merse themselves in the lives of a textile worker, a dairymaid, a member of the landed gentry. This hunger for all things Austen, however tenuously connected to her, was an aspect of my own world I'd taken for granted, but now it seemed both touching and demented. What was it that people wanted so badly from Jane Austen anyway? What did I myself want, for that matter?

It was midday as we neared Chawton. I'd slept unchar-acteristically well, waking up refreshed, not at all hungover, and very puzzled. Why had I behaved so impulsively? And why had Liam rejected me like that, contradicting the evidence in his own trousers? His so-called explanation was absurd. No, something else was at work here, something murky, which made staying away from him a good idea. In truth, he had done me a favor last night. But when I remembered his body pressed against mine, our two hearts pounding, the smell of his skin, it did not feel like a favor. It felt like something I wanted to never think of again.

That morning, I had dawdled over my hair and fussed un-necessarily with my clothes but finally had to walk down the hallway to where breakfast was laid out for us in the same private parlor as dinner the previous night. This time, its door stood open, as if the room itself were insisting it had no secrets. Liam, sitting at the table, looked up and gave me a nod and a quiet good morning; he had the grace to blush. I sat down and poured my-self some coffee.

"I'm sorry if I made you uncomfortable last night. It wasn't my intention." I would have done well to stop there, but I took a sip and continued in a tone impossible to keep free of irony: "Clearly you are a man of honor. Your devotion to your principles—and your fiancée—is admirable. Let's move on and pretend this never happened."

Liam had sat with his chin propped on his fist throughout my little speech, staring at the table. He lifted his eyes to meet mine and looked away. "Let's" was all he said, and in that moment I felt such a passionate hatred of him, such a wish to throw my coffee in his face and storm out, that it should have told me something. But I swallowed my anger, along with some toast, and we prepared to continue on to Chawton.

AFTER JANE AUSTEN'S HOUSE, PAST THE INTERSECTION WITH THE road to Winchester, there followed more cottages, smaller than hers and in worse repair. Beyond them, I saw sheep-dotted fields and, briefly, Chawton House, square and dark against the pale sky at the top of a hill, before we turned and it was hidden by trees. We passed barns and a stone church before the house came into view again: a long driveway leading up to a circular sweep, gables and chimney pots, a figure in black standing outside.

When the carriage stopped, the figure in black, who proved to be the housekeeper, greeted us, apologizing that sudden business had prevented Mr. Knight from being here to welcome us personally. He would be home for dinner and looked forward to seeing us then. Captain Austen and his wife would be there, as well as Miss Austen, Miss Lloyd, and Mrs. Austen, along with a few select neighbors; something in her tone hinted that this was all slightly unusual, and all in honor of us. Dinner would be served promptly, as every night, at 6:30. She hoped this was not too early for people of fashion such as ourselves; with an amused look, Liam assured her it wasn't.

While telling us these things, she'd led us through a stone entryway and into a large room. As my eyes adjusted to the dimness, I saw dark-paneled walls enlivened by a few mounted antlers, an unlit fireplace big enough to stand in, and a massive, graceless staircase. The smells were of old wood and dampness, and it was cold enough to see my breath. I shivered. I felt I had once more traveled back in time; this room could not have looked much different in the reign of Elizabeth. We stood still for a moment, stunned into silence, before the housekeeper, while giving us a brief history of the house, led us on, along a badly lit corridor, up a short flight of stairs, around a corner, down a shorter flight of stairs, around another corner, and finally into a room on a more human scale than the entry hall.

The walls were paneled in dark wood here too, and latticed windows with bumpy glass looked out on a gentle hill that ended in a coppiced wood. One end of a long table was laid with cold meat, bread, and wine. Did we want tea? There was only one answer to this question, I knew by now. Waiting for it to arrive, I looked out the window again and saw it had started to snow.

IT SNOWED ALL AFTERNOON, ON AND OFF, ENOUGH TO DUST THE rooflines and bare trees and palings and grass stubble. Despite taking more care than usual as I thought of all the new people I would meet, I was done dressing well before 6:30 and unsure what to do next. I dismissed North and paced in the bedroom I'd been given, looking out my window and wondering if I dared wander around the house, or if I would get lost, ending up somewhere I should not be: the kitchens, say. So I was delighted when a maid showed up with a message from my fellow houseguest Mrs. Frank Austen, wife of the sea captain: she was in the second-best parlor, and would be honored to meet me before dinner, if I wished it.

Would the maid be so kind as to lead me to the second-best parlor? She would: to a pleasant room with faded pink tapestries and a modern-style Rumford stove.

"Miss Ravenswood, forgive me for taking the liberty." A plump woman with tired eyes and a lace cap put down her sewing, rose from a chair near the window, and came forward to greet me, stretching out her hands. "I was most eager to meet you, and I knew it would be a crush at dinner. The excitement of a new arrival in such a small village, in the winter no less, cannot be overstated. And I have been a great deal at home, of course."

"I understand you have a new arrival of your own, madam. I give you joy of that."

Smiling, Mrs. Austen lifted a finger to her lips and led me back to where she had been. A sleeping infant not more than a few weeks old, wrapped as tightly as a chrysalis, lay in a small basket beside her chair.

"Herbert-Grey," she said. "I find him perfection, but perhaps I cannot be objective." Her complacent look contradicted her qualification.

"He is beautiful." I leaned over to see him more closely as we sat down on either side of the basket. Mrs. Frank Austen, like Mrs. Tilson, was one of those prodigies of fertility that the era abounded in; at thirty-one, she had been married nine years and Herbert-Grey was her sixth child; she would have five more, dying soon after the eleventh, in 1823. It staggered the imagination. "Is there anything more miraculous? That new-baby smell, those perfect little ears!" I sensed my best chance at winning her over lay through her children. "But how are *you* faring, madam? It is not easy to be a mother so many times over."

I touched the bump on my arm, now hardly the memory of a bump, where the hormonal injection had gone in, and reflected that freedom from unwanted pregnancy was not just a lifesaver and a convenience; it put an unbridgeable divide between me and the women of 1815. This realization made me sad, despite my not having the slightest wish for children of my own.

"Never better, I thank you. I am feeling very well. Quite an old hand by now."

"Will you have a wet nurse, or . . ." I paused to think how to phrase it delicately. "In the Indies, it is common to—But what is the custom these days, in England? I am most curious."

She widened her eyes, but answered without hesitation. "Indeed. I feed him myself. Things were different in the age of our parents, but to consign your own darling little one to an unknown . . . woman, of unknown habits . . . it is not to be thought of." She looked at me more closely. "But I should not talk of such things to unmarried ladies, Miss Ravenswood. You will forgive me."

"It is I who raised the subject, madam. You must forgive me, then."

"But perhaps you will be married yourself soon," she went on dreamily, and I gave her a sharp glance, wondering if this was just a general good wish, or based on something she'd heard. Would Henry be so indiscreet? Would his sister? How awkward it would be then, when I finally said no. My mind returned to the long engagement. I had intended to discuss this with Liam yesterday as a serious possibility: if it might be dared, how it might be managed, the opportunities it would afford for getting closer to the sisters, and for what we had come to do. Instead, our conversation had quickly veered off course, into topics we should never have touched on. I retraced how this had happened, and considered once again the possibility of sexual jealousy: Liam's, toward Henry Austen. But it was impossible. I'd thrown myself at him last night, and—I needed to stop thinking about this.

"You grew up in the Indies, then? Captain Austen tells me it is a most beautiful land, but barbarous."

"He is right," I said, and we began to talk about Jamaica.

IN THE DRAWING ROOM BEFORE DINNER, I DISCOVERED THAT LIAM had gone to call on Cassandra that afternoon, and had already met Martha Lloyd and Mrs. Austen; he introduced them to me with an air of thinly veiled triumph. Apparently, Jane had given him a letter to give to Cassandra that last night we had visited Hans Place, so he had walked to the cottage despite knowing he would see her that evening at dinner. This was all vastly polite and Mr. Knightley–like: the short period of time between his arriving in Chawton and paying a visit; doing her this honor despite the status gap between a wealthy gentleman and an impecunious spinster; that it had been snowing.

"Why did you not say you were planning to go, William?" I asked in mock indignation, which was actually not mock. "I would have very much liked to have come as well." Staying at home made me appear, by contrast, cold, lazy, and indifferent to the people I most needed to impress.

"The idea came to me only after luncheon, and I did not know where to find you in this enormous house," he said, making Martha Lloyd laugh. Her eyes were dark and prominent; they sized me up shrewdly from under her lace cap of spinsterhood.

"And of course, no one can ask a servant to send word," I said.

"The Chawton House servants can be quite terrifying," Martha said dryly. "We should not wonder your brother feared to trouble them, on only his first day here."

"Are you libeling my servants, Miss Lloyd?" Edward Knight asked, appearing next to us. His face was pinker than usual; he looked cheerful and relaxed, country gentry in his element. "You must not give Miss Ravenswood such nonsensical ideas; what if she does not have your sense of humor and takes you seriously?"

"She might perish of cold before she summons the courage to ring and ask for a fire," Martha murmured, and Edward laughed, then turned to Liam.

"Dr. Ravenswood," he said in a low tone, "may I impose upon you for a moment? There is something . . ." I could not hear any more; he had taken Liam's arm and led him off, leaving me in a circle consisting of Cassandra, Martha, and old Mrs. Austen, who was appraising me with a look so thorough it verged on rudeness.

"So you know dear Henry from London, is it?" Her accent was different from her children's: plummier, old-fashioned. Stooped yet tall, she was an imposing figure despite being largely toothless, with an impression of vitality that belied her age. "I am sorry for ye, being from London. I cannot imagine, to be consigned to such a Bedlam, able to do one's duty to neither God nor man. How Henry endures it, I cannot say. But he is here quite often—his other bank is in Alton." I nodded. "Your brother said his health is mending after this recent attack. Can I believe him?"

"He is a doctor, madam," I said, amused by her frankness. "You must believe him. And how is your health?"

"I am seventy-seven, you know, so I must not expect much. I think Death has forgotten me. I do not know what else to think."

"Astonishing. Are your people long-lived, as a rule?"

"The Leighs enjoy life. They do not hasten to leave it." She looked at me with more interest. "Forgive an old lady, your name again?"

"Ravenswood, madam."

"An unusual one. I do not know I have heard of it. What was your mother?"

"A Massie, of the Derbyshire Massies."

"I do not know the branch. Have they any connection to those in Norfolk?"

"Perhaps a distant one."

"Or those of Sussex?"

"I think not, no."

It was a nightmare version of Jewish geography, minus the playful sense of mutual discovery that usually accompanies that game. I was holding my breath; Mrs. Austen was looking thoughtful. "And where are *you* from? Not from London originally, to be sure."

"The doctor and his sister are from Jamaica, Mamma," said Cassandra, who had been observing us with a little frown. "They are connected with the Hampsons there."

"Ah. The Hampsons." I exhaled, impressed that she seemed to immediately know who Cassandra was talking about, though they were cousins of her mother-in-law. If she ever met these distant relatives, and the record is silent on this, it would only have been shortly after her wedding in the 1760s. "The Hampsons," she repeated. "Then you own property in Jamaica. But you do not live there. No one does."

"We have sold it and moved away."

"A happy day for you. Did it go all ill after the end of the slave trade?"

"Mamma! Do not assume they were slaveholders."

"What can anyone of property there be, else? It is all built on slavery, is it not?" In London everyone we had met, except Mrs. Tilson and her abolitionist friends, avoided the dangerous conversational shoals of slavery as if by instinct.

"Mamma," Cassandra said again, shaking her head.

"Indeed," I said. "That is why we surrendered our interests there and came to England."

A pause followed this. "Surrendered, I see," Mrs. Austen said, in a tone suggesting she didn't but was too polite to ask more.

"That was very obliging of you," Martha said. "It takes the demands of being a Christian to a rigorous extreme indeed." I inclined my head in acknowledgment, unsure if she was mocking me, or if this was just her usual face.

Martha seemed poised to ask me more, but Cassandra said: "I had the whole story from Mrs. Tilson in town, so I beg you, do not quiz her, Martha. They manumitted their slaves little by little and then sold the land. Wilberforce himself could not ask for more. So—"

The two women exchanged a look, and Martha nodded and smiled at me. "Forgive me, Miss Ravenswood. I have grown too accustomed to saying whatever comes to my mind. It is the privilege of old spinsters, you know, and nearly our only one. But I blame Cassandra; she has been most mysterious on the subject of Edward's newest guests." She was studying me as closely as Mrs. Austen had been. "Do you and your brother aim to settle in England?"

"He hopes to find a house to let, in some pretty place, and live quietly. If we can find something to buy, we shall." They were all looking at me as if not satisfied with this answer, and I wondered if I sounded naïve. "I realize suitable properties do not come on the market every day." There was another pause. "You will let me know, however, if you hear of anything nearby?"

The ladies laughed politely, as if I had made a joke, but not a very good one.

CHAPTER 12

DECEMBER 19

Chawton House

I SETTLED INTO LIFE AS A HOUSEGUEST BETTER THAN I'D DARED hope, with my worries about exposing myself through some subtle country-house etiquette blunder proving groundless. Edward Knight was concerned with our comfort, but not smotheringly so, and so were his servants, whom I was careful to tip well and often. I was no longer in charge of managing a household; my main tasks were to show up properly dressed and on time at meals, and to be agreeable to everyone. I could do this.

Sitting around with Mrs. Frank Austen and her children, I also got a lot of shirts made. I'd started to find sewing less boring: there was something satisfying in a perfect row of tiny stitches, in completion. It was even a little erotic, contemplating the work of my hands next to Liam's skin, though I tried not to think about this.

Days went by when he and I saw each other only at meal-times, which was good, for despite the debacle at the Angel I remained strangely attracted to him. Not the kind of attraction when you want to see the person; more the kind when you wish to forget about them and can't. Our bedrooms were in opposite wings of the house, our activities divided by gender. Liam and Captain Frank Austen, a compact man with the Austen nose and the unpretending friendliness of a naval officer out of *Persuasion*, went hunting a lot, heading out in the morning darkness and not being seen until dinner. Edward never joined them; he was back and forth to Kent and busy even when he was around, out on estate business or holed up with paperwork.

It was a few days before Christmas, Mrs. Frank Austen and I in the second-best parlor with her youngest and oldest children, Herbert-Grey and Mary-Jane, when the servant opened the door to Cassandra and Jane, newly home from London.

Mary-Jane's plain little face underwent an extraordinary transformation. "Aunt Jane!" she screamed, leaping from her hassock and running to tackle her aunt as she entered the room.

When Jane stood up from greeting her niece and gave me her hand, I was startled. She was thin and drawn, yet her skin was as bronzed as if she'd been under a tropical sun.

"How was your journey?" I asked, trying not to stare. "Did you come down with your brother?" Ladies did not travel solo; she had to have been accompanied. I meant Henry, but felt strange saying his name. We could not in propriety write to each other, and it was appropriate for him to leave me alone while I was thinking over his offer. Yet we'd been in Chawton nearly three weeks; his silence was becoming mystifying. Couldn't he have found a reason to visit his bank at Alton by now, or to write to Liam and ask after me?

"Richard was sent with me as far as Farnham, and then my nephew James-Edward came up from Winchester, where he is at school." She studied me. "Henry sends his best love. He is consumed with the bank these days, and still not perfectly well."

"I am sorry to hear that."

She gave me another look, more penetrating and thoughtful. "He will come as soon as he can."

"Did you get here only yesterday, Jane?" Mrs. Frank Austen asked. "How good of you to come to see us."

"I could not wait, my dear, to see little Herbert-Grey, and to be able to send word to Henry of his new friends' not having perished in this shocking weather, accustomed as they are to the Indies. And to see Mary-Jane, I would trudge through snowdrifts far deeper than these."

Mary-Jane giggled appreciatively, and we pushed Jane into the best chair by the fire, where she was briefly allowed to admire Herbert-Grey and then questioned: London, Henry's health, Fanny, the road from London, the weather on her walk from the cottage. Despite looking ill, she seemed relaxed, less wary than she had been in town, as she described an outing to the theater with Henry, Fanny, and Mr. Haden.

"Mr. Haden accompanied you to the theater?" Cassandra asked. "Henry's apothecary?"

"I told you, my love, he is not an apothecary. He is a *Haden*—something between a man and an angel." She looked at me. "Is it not the case?"

"He does have gentle manners. And the most extraordinary eyelashes."

Cassandra, unsatisfied, looked from me to Jane and back. "But you do not think that Fanny—"

"Fanny will be certain to bestow her affections rationally. Unlike most nieces of my acquaintance—present company excepted, Mary-Jane! Which reminds me, what of Anna?" That was James's oldest daughter, married the year before and now a mother at twenty-two. "What of her little Jemima? I long to see them. Why is Wyards so far off?"

"But it is not, really, is it?" I asked. "Is it not upwards of a few miles from Chawton?"

"Not as the crow flies," Jane replied. "But we are not crows. And worse, have no carriage; we live in a very small way. In better weather, I could take Mother's donkey cart, but in winter it would not answer."

"Mr. Knight's carriage is at your disposal, it is not?" I could not imagine it would not be. He was so kind to everyone. Had given them a place to live. And she was Jane Austen! *Everything* should be at her disposal. That I was thinking this way only showed that in my excitement at seeing her again I had temporarily lost my mind.

A little silence followed before Cassandra answered: "To be sure, in case of need—Edward is the best of brothers, and would never refuse us. Yet we do not impose on his good nature." I remembered learning how Cassandra would spend months at a time at Godmersham, the Knights' estate in Kent, after the birth of one or another of the many children, helping out with the older ones or with whatever needed to be done. A maiden aunt, one might say, had nothing better to do. But Mrs. Frank Austen, despite six children younger than eight, did not seem to expect her sisters-in-law to be her unpaid servants.

Feeling less delighted with Edward than before, I said, "Then I hope you will consider our carriage as your own, for even the most frivolous of outings."

Everyone laughed at this, even Mary-Jane. "You are very kind, Miss Ravenswood," Mrs. Frank Austen said, "and very free with your brother's carriage."

"Is it not as much mine as—" I began, and stopped, realizing my mistake.

"We must put Dr. Ravenswood among the first rank of excellent brothers," Jane said quickly. "I am not sure that even any of ours can compare, Cassandra. And that he drives a landaulet, as opposed to a curricle—this says everything one needs to know about that gentleman's consideration for his sister, and indeed for anyone else within range of his benevolence." She had begun this speech with her usual mock gravity, but grew earnest midway through, almost dreamy, as if a new thought had struck her.

"You puzzle me," I said, grateful for how she had turned the conversation. "Why does a landaulet make him a better brother than a curricle would?"

"A curricle is a selfish vehicle, when we consider it closely. A carriage for a gentleman, but only for him. A lady can go out alone in a landaulet in complete propriety and comfort."

"Vastly practical," Mrs. Frank Austen said. "Particularly when one's husband is away at sea for years at a time." She gave a little sigh.

"He will make someone an excellent husband," Jane continued. "If I were of a matchmaking turn of mind—But fortunately for you, Miss Ravenswood, my imagination is channeled in other directions, and he can continue to be your most excellent brother. His new wife will not turn you, penniless and shivering, out of her opulently furnished home on Berkeley Square, or wherever she might find it incumbent to live." She surprised me with a wicked smile, and I realized how much I had missed her.

"I should like to see her try!" I said, as Cassandra gave her sister a warning shake of the head.

"But of course you have an ample competence of your own," Jane went on, looking dreamy again. "More than ample, perhaps?"

"Jane!" Cassandra said.

Just then, Herbert-Grey woke up, screaming inconsolably and ending that particular line of inquiry as we turned to admiring his lungs.

CHRISTMAS TO TWELFTH NIGHT PASSED IN A FASCINATING BLUR OF feasting and wassailing and Yule log lore and mummers before life settled into the quiet routine of a rural winter, but two things troubled me. We could not live at Chawton forever; although Edward insisted, in his quiet way, that we were his guests as long as we wished, there's oppression in being a houseguest, even in the friendliest house. We needed a place near enough to visit Jane and the others easily, but nothing seemed to be available. Edward kept assuring us he had his ears open, that it would all work out, and anyway we were welcome.

And then there was the problem of winning over the ladies at the cottage, to find a way to the letters and the manuscript.

Progress felt slow, particularly before Jane's return from London. I'd called on Martha and Mrs. Austen and Cassandra several times in those weeks, and was received with more formality than warmth; I sensed they did not know what to make of me. The wealth that had gotten Henry's attention made us almost too grand for them; this might have been making them uncomfortable. Yet it was irritating to notice how they'd seemed much happier the few times Liam accompanied me. He was better with the banter; I'd resigned myself to that. Worse was my suspicion they considered him more important merely by his being male. A widespread attitude in 1815, but to find it at Jane Austen's house, of all places, was disturbing.

MARY-JANE, AGED SEVEN AND A HALF, ENJOYED SPILLIKINS, which I also turned out to be good at, and sewed faster and better than I. She liked to question me about Jamaica, showing lively curiosity but a grasp of geography strangely weak for a sea captain's daughter. With Jane back, she had new enthusiasm for visiting her aunts, and I often accompanied her. I grew attuned to the rhythms of that household, learning not to call too early, when Mary-Jane and I would be in danger of finding Martha Lloyd and Cassandra busy at some household task and Jane at her little table in the front room, putting away pen and paper and looking up at us with a strained smile. An hour or two after noon was best; weak winter light streamed into the parlor and everyone sat down to sew, the talk flowing more freely when it was just women: village gossip, family gossip, discussion of whatever book was currently being read aloud in the evenings.

Jane's return, and her obvious warmth toward me, seemed

to have reassured the others. My sense of becoming closer to them all had limits, though. I was no nearer to the letters or "The Watsons"; I had never gained access to the bedrooms upstairs, where they presumably were. One day I'd chanced to find myself alone in the front room with her writing desk sitting temptingly open, papers arrayed around it covered with tiny lines of her beautiful handwriting. I'd just stared at it, fascinated but un-willing to come closer, not sure even in that moment if it was fear of getting caught or the dishonor of the act that stopped me. Perhaps one need not exclude the other.

WHILE JANE AUSTEN WAS IMAGINING THE FAMILY OF UNMARRIED Watson sisters left in dire financial straits by the death of their father, her own father died. Like the fictional Mr. Watson, Mr. Austen was a retired clergyman, kind and intelligent. Like the Watson women, the Austens were left to manage on a painfully meager income, but were richer than their fictional counter-parts in brothers. Without James, Edward, Henry, Frank, and Charles, Jane would have ended up like the Brontës, a governess or a schoolteacher; it is the dreadful fate that lurks offstage in her work. And perhaps it is no accident that it was her friend Anne Sharpe, long-suffering former governess for Edward Knight's children, to whom she confided she had finished "The Watsons" but would never try to publish it. "It turned out, my dear Anne, to have shown far too much of my heart," she explains in the Croy-don *Ivanhoe* letter.

"Poverty is a great evil; but to a woman of education and feel-ing it ought not, it cannot be the greatest," earnest Emma Wat-son says in "The Watsons," adding: "I would rather be teacher at a school (and I can think of nothing worse) than marry a man I did not like."

To which one of her sisters replies: "I would rather do anything than be teacher at a school."

OUR WALKS TO SEE JANE AND THE OTHERS DELIGHTED ME NOT ONLY because of the destination: Mary-Jane outside was even more entertaining than Mary-Jane inside. Tutored by her father, she knew a lot about nature, not just for a little girl, but for anyone. We took the long way, through the woods, where even in their leafless state she could identify every tree I asked about, as well as point out the burrows of various animals.

"A fox lives there," she said, pointing to one. "Or, he used to. I hope he moved away. They hunt them, you know. I think it is horrible."

I did too, but I was wary of agreeing too readily, as if I might betray myself as alien. "But they eat the chickens. That is not good."

"*We* eat the chickens. Why is that better? The fox has to live, too."

"Mary-Jane, you are wise beyond your years. What is that tree?"

"For shame, 'tis a hornbeam. Everyone knows that. And look there—"

I looked where she pointed, but saw nothing.

"An owl! In the hollow of that tree, there."

Then I saw it: a spookily pale heart-shaped face looking at us, large eyes and no visible beak. "What kind of owl is he?"

"Barn," she said pityingly. "You don't know anything, do you?"

"Do you know the names of all the plants, too? Will you teach me, when they start to come up?"

"I don't know the names of *all* the plants," she corrected. But she promised to teach me what she knew, and when spring came, she proved true to her word.

MARY-JANE AND HER FAMILY HAD MOVED OUT OF CHAWTON HOUSE by then, to the place in nearby Alton that they had arranged to rent. And so had Liam and I, with surprising ease considering all the energy I'd put into worrying about it. Edward had assured us that he would be the first to hear of anything suitable, but in the end it was Jane who saved us.

"I had it from old John Waring, who delivers milk for the Prowtings, who heard it from the carpenter there," she told me one day in early January. "They had found a new tenant for Ivy Cottage, had even made some repairs, which it badly needed, but now it's all gone awry." She looked up from her sewing. "You have said you are looking for something, so I thought I would mention it. But Ivy Cottage is very humble. Probably it will not answer."

"Is it one of those brick thatched ones, beyond the turning to the Winchester road?"

"Not the one that looks like a strong wind could bring it down at any moment, the other one." She paused. "It is even smaller than this house. I should not have mentioned it, only—"

"No, I am very glad you did."

I WAS GRATIFIED NOT ONLY BY THE PROSPECT OF LIVING SO NEAR, but also that she had told me about it; this meant she was willing to have us there. When I raised the subject with Edward at dinner, he looked surprised, then doubtful.

"I knew about that. But it isn't the sort of place you would want to live in, I assure you. Very small."

"We have no need for a palace," Liam said. "It sounds charming. I shall write Mr. Prowting at once."

"We can go call on him tomorrow," Edward said, still looking doubtful. "I have a free morning, and I am sure he would be happy to—But you will not—Well, you will see."

IVY COTTAGE WAS SURROUNDED BY A LOW BRICK WALL AND A THICK hedge of boxwood. I liked it even before I stepped inside, to be met by the smell of old wood and beeswax. A front door opened to a hallway and a steep, narrow staircase, to four little rooms on the first floor and four above, while another staircase, more of a ladder, led to two attic rooms with sloping ceilings. The rooms were dim and furnished in a style that might have been popular fifty years earlier, the windows small and the timbered ceilings low; Liam had to duck to go through doorways. Mr. Prowting's steward proudly pointed out the recent replacement of the thatch, the newly installed pump in the primitive kitchen, and less proudly the privy in the back, one of several outbuildings down a path through a kitchen garden, with fruit trees and a tidy well and fields beyond sloping to a pond. It emerged there was the possibility to rent further adjoining land as well, and Liam began asking the steward about pasturage, soil types, water meadows, and haying cycles, while I listened in silent amazement. We had studied farming of the period in Preparation, but not in such detail.

Edward seemed silenced too. Finally, when the steward had gone to the gate to speak to a passing tenant, he said:

"You cannot mean to live here."

Liam and I glanced at each other; after a moment Edward continued, as if he'd found some answer in our expressions: "You would want to whitewash everything, to be sure and have it all thoroughly scrubbed. It is not as bad as I feared. You will want to stable your horses at the Crown; they are the best for that." He paused. "Or do you mean to give up your horses?"

He must have thought we'd lost all our money. Or that we never had any; that we were only posing as wealthy people and were now reverting to our true level. Living in a cottage voluntarily had to be incomprehensible to a person like Edward Knight.

"We shall do no such thing," said Liam, shocked. "We wish to live simply, Mr. Knight, but not in abject poverty. We have not lost the use of reason." Edward brightened as Liam went on: "I think with the improvements you suggest—and a few more I have in mind—it can be very pleasant. You will see. Come and eat mutton by our fire, and you shall see."

WE CAME TO TERMS TO TAKE THE HOUSE FOR A YEAR, AT A PRICE A fraction of the Hill Street rent. But we would not stay a year; we would have to vanish one day, to return to the portal in Leatherhead, and leave everyone wondering. No, that would not do; we would need a story. An impulsive tour of the Lake District, maybe. But how was it that I had just stopped agonizing about finding a place to live, and now I was anxious about my exit plan?

It seemed a flaw in my character, this constant requirement of a worry to feed on. Then I realized, with an intuitive lurch, that my real problem was not how to leave the house, but how to occupy it, living in such a small space with Liam.

"You were asking him a lot of questions," I said as we walked back to Chawton House alone, business having sent Edward Knight to Alton. "I don't know if he was impressed, but I was." A bantering tone seemed safest. "How do you know all that stuff?"

"Edward has a lot of books about agronomy."

"Are we seriously intending to take up farming?"

"No point in moving into a house with so much land otherwise."

"I don't know the first thing about it." Food in our world was made in 3-D printers, using laboratory techniques refined over the years since the Die-off to maximize nutrients and minimize waste. It was good, resembling in flavor and appearance whatever it was a simulacrum of—or so I used to think, until I had gotten to 1815 and had real food.

"It will give us the perfect excuse to visit the Austens. All those things they do—brewing spruce beer, growing potatoes, making bread, keeping chickens—we will need to watch, and ask questions. Be around."

"Clever! I'm game. But no pigs. I draw the line at pigs."

"One must draw the line somewhere," he agreed gravely.

THE NEXT DAY WHEN I SHARED THE NEWS, JANE SEEMED PLEASED but almost as surprised as her brother. "You really mean to take it, then? Martha, you owe me a shilling."

"You are a gamester? You bet on what we would do?"

"Only a friendly wager. She does not have to pay me. And I am sure she will not, since honor means nothing to her."

"But I will never hear the end of it if not," Martha said, looking up from her knitting. "How many servants will you keep, Miss Ravenswood? You will not have much place to put them. But perhaps you can find people from the village."

I had been thinking about this as I lay awake the night before, wondering what I had gotten myself into, sad about the need to dismiss servants I had mostly been so happy with. Mrs. Smith probably would be horrified by the primitive smallness of Ivy Cottage after Hill Street. I would miss her pies and her calm steadiness. North might stay; she liked me, but what about her flightier sister Jenny? Wilcox was out of a job, given the lack of stables at our new home, but country air would be good for Tom, who had developed a worrying cough. I hoped this would be an opportunity to get rid of Jencks.

"This is quite a change for you, from what you told us of your life in Jamaica," Cassandra observed. "Will you not find it all rather mean?" She was no longer hostile, as she had been at first in London, yet I always had the sense of her not being entirely sure about me.

"I like the idea of leading a simpler life."

"Sometimes the idea is better than the reality," Jane said. "Will you keep your house in town?"

"I do not know that we have decided. Do you think we ought to?"

She laughed her throaty chuckle. "That is the sort of simple life I like, when you may ask yourself such questions."

There was a knock before the maid, flustered, showed in Henry Austen and Liam.

"Look who I found," Liam said. There was an astonished hush, and then Jane jumped up and embraced her brother, followed by Cassandra and Martha. I rose too, unsure what kind of greeting was appropriate.

He finished embracing his sisters and Martha, then turned to me. A thin layer of dust coated him, and a strong tang of horse came from his traveling clothes: a many-caped riding coat, rough buckskin trousers tucked into tall boots. We paused for an instant; everyone in the room was looking at us. I held out my hand and he took it in both of his.

"You have just come from town, I collect?" I asked.

"The only explanation for my bedraggled appearance. Your brother saw me and hauled me in—but I shall go to the Crown in an instant, and make myself decent."

"You are not proposing to stay there?" Jane asked. "Do not be absurd! You will stay with us."

"Let me tell Betty to get the room ready for you," Cassandra said, hurrying out.

"I can help," Martha muttered and followed her.

"Dr. Ravenswood," Jane said, going over to Liam and taking his arm, "let me borrow your strength for a moment. There is a jar in the stillroom that none of us have been able to open—" And they were gone, Henry and I left alone with a theatrical suddenness. I couldn't help admiring how smoothly everyone had managed it. Only, what was I going to do now? We were standing by a window, our hands still clasped.

"How are you, Mr. Austen?" I asked inanely. He looked down at me; his eyes were red-rimmed and there was a strange brightness in them, an intensity that made me think he might be feverish again. "I have been thinking over what you have said with great care."

He squeezed my hands. "I must be truthful. I am come to my bank in Alton on painful and urgent business. I am optimistic by nature, but I fear the worst. And in that case—I will no longer be a man in a position to—That is, my offer—You understand." He stopped. "Indeed, that is why I have not spoken to your brother, as I should have, outlining my—Everything has happened so quickly, Miss Ravenswood, so quickly and yet so slowly. I cannot say from one day to the next what my true financial state might be. It has been agony."

I looked up at him, disarmed by his forthrightness. Feeling some inner fortification crumble, like a wall coming down in a shower of bricks and dust, I shivered with fear, or gladness. "You cannot suppose it is about money? That *that* is why I hesitate?"

"My dear, it is always about money. We live in the world, after all."

"You know that I have some of my own, do you not?"

"If you take me for a fortune hunter, I must tell you that you are quite mistaken."

I squeezed his hand. "Henry. If I may call you that?" The effect of my words was startling; a tremor passed through his body as he stared down at me. "I will marry you. But I think we must try to save your bank first, shall we not, before we tell everyone?"

AND THAT WAS HOW I ENTERED INTO A SECRET ENGAGEMENT, A thing you are never supposed to do, for reasons *Emma* and

Sense and Sensibility make clear. Yet even from the start it wasn't entirely a secret. As soon as they'd come back into the room, I felt Martha and Cassandra suspected something, while for Jane it was more than a suspicion. Her gaze went first to Henry. His expression and his manner seemed to give away nothing, but somehow she knew. She smiled at me and pressed my hand when Liam and I left.

"My dear Miss Ravenswood," she said with an arch look.

Since the whole idea was to get money to Henry, which I could not do on my own as a woman, I had to tell Liam. I did so in as few words as possible, once we were out of earshot of the cottage.

I was shaking as I began; we had not discussed this—or for that matter, really any serious subject touching on the mission—since we'd traveled down from London, weeks ago. Which was crazy. True, the house was big and we were divided by our gender-specific activities, with little privacy. True, I'd been avoiding him—more than I'd acknowledged until this moment. The incident at the Angel, weird and awkward even at the time, had assumed greater ghastliness in retrospect. But still. It was undignified to sulk over a rejection; beneath me, as an admirer of Jane Austen novels and as an independent woman. Why should I grant him such power? Before I was done speaking, I'd started to feel better, almost defiant.

Liam said nothing for a long time. We had turned from the lane onto the drive that led to the Great House, and were approaching the church halfway up the hill. When he finally spoke, he kept his eyes fixed on the landscape around us and his voice calm.

"It's bold," he said. "But maybe that's what we need to be,

right now. You've not made any progress, have you, with getting upstairs to look for the letters, or with asking her about 'The Watsons'?"

"Not yet." I was stung by this implied criticism, though he'd delivered it in a mild tone. But before I could defend myself, he was continuing:

"I'll talk to Henry. Maybe tonight. Perhaps I can travel with him when he returns to town—Did he give you any idea how much money he might need?"

"We didn't actually talk about it."

"Perhaps not a subject one discusses with one's intended," Liam said with a small smile, finally meeting my eyes but not holding the gaze. "Oh well. I'll talk to him."

"You're not angry?" My mind returned to the unfortunate encounter at the Angel; with an effort I put the memory away.

He looked at me sadly but said nothing.

"I mean, that's good. I'm glad you understand this was necessary."

"Just be careful."

"I always am."

CHAPTER 13

JANUARY 24, 1816

Chawton House

LATE ONE AFTERNOON, NOT LONG BEFORE WE WERE TO LEAVE ED-ward's house, I was alone in the library, which was large and impressive as a room, less so in books. There were lots of bound volumes of *The Spectator* from the middle part of the previous century—exciting only in comparison to all the books on agronomy. I probably should have been reading one of those, but I'd come looking for a novel. Not a particular one, though I knew the sort I wanted: something like *Memoirs of Miss Sidney Bidulph*, ridiculous yet entrancing. Edward Knight did not seem to have any novels, strange for a brother of Jane Austen; I could not even find hers. The titles were getting hard to read, with the room growing darker; I was in its dimmest corner, far from the fireplace. I was thinking I should get a candle from the mantel when the door at the other end of the room creaked open and two men walked in, midconversation: Edward Knight and Frank Austen.

". . . expect me to rescue him this time!" Edward said. "He has lived beyond his means for years. He is an opportunist, not even an effective one. And with the lawsuit oppressing me—he cannot think that I will rescue him."

"He has no unreasonable expectations, I am sure, Ned. What does the letter say? Can you show me?"

"As fine a piece of self-justification as I have ever seen in written form! Here, feast your eyes."

There was a pause, which was when I should have revealed that I was there. I had not been trying to spy, and while I'd heard things I should not have, they were nothing terrible. But I was too surprised to react, and then it was too late, as Edward went on:

"And that hint he drops at the end—about an opportune marriage—has he lost his reason entirely?"

"Nothing wrong with marrying an heiress, if one can manage it. You did."

"That is not the same at all. I was of independent means. And she was of a known family of long-standing respectability— if he is referring to the lady I suspect, we know nothing of them, nothing . . . slaveholders . . . this queer business with moving into Ivy Cottage . . ."

His voice dropped lower and I could not make out the rest. By then I was on my hands and knees behind a sofa. My heart was banging in my chest; I felt sure they must hear it, like something from a Poe story. And what would I say, when they found me?

"They have easy manners and a great deal of conversation. But these days, that means nothing—still, you invited them to be your guests. You put the imprimatur of approval on them, more than Henry. How was he not to think—"

"She saved my daughter's life! An invitation to my house is nothing, to that. I take no exception to them—as acquaintances, as guests—but to ally yourself that way?" He paused and barked an unhappy laugh. "But I shall write to Sir Thomas-Philip, once I have a free moment, and we will learn all. Of course, being Henry, he probably will have wed her before word comes back."

Silence followed, Frank Austen presumably still reading Henry's letter. I was face to the floor, breathing carpet dust. Terrified of sneezing, I covered my nose with my hands.

"So he is finished."

"What do you think I was telling you? How much had you invested?"

"How did this happen? Can you—you are a man of business—can you explain?"

"The usual way, I suppose. Loans on easy terms, to the likes of Lord Moira, gentlemen who regard seriously only their debts of honor—and when you are an opportunist, a blockhead, and apparently, a fortune hunter—by God, were I not—what I . . ." He broke off as the door creaked open, adding in a different tone, "Dr. Ravenswood."

"Forgive me. I was looking for my sister. They told me she was gone to the library."

"She is not here," Edward said. There was a pause.

"I did not mean to interrupt, sir. I will go."

"No. No. There is no need for apologies, or use in concealment. You will know all soon enough. Our brother—your friend—is undone. His bank is ruined."

There was a silence, and then Liam said: "Alas, I knew it was coming. There was nothing that could be done. I went up to town last week, to offer him a loan, but he refused."

"Indeed?" Edward sounded surprised. In fact, Liam had gone to London not to offer Henry a loan but to make one: thirty thousand pounds, half of the amount we'd come to 1815 with. And to judge from what I'd just overheard, it had not been enough; and now it was gone. I felt a thrill of fear at this prospect, even as I told myself I was being ridiculous. We had plenty for our remaining time in the past. "He refused, did he?" He sighed.

"It was noble of him, but I still wonder if it could have helped."

"No use asking such questions, Ravenswood," Edward said. "It has happened, and we must all make the best of it. If you will, I have some letters to write before dinner—"

There was a pause, and after a moment, I heard the door open and close again. Another long silence followed. Had they all left? Was it possible?

No. "Sometimes, sir, one longs to be at sea. If the Admiralty would give me a ship right now, I should ask no more. She could be a leaky brig, and my heart would be light. But forgive me, I forget myself. This sad business has set us all ahoo."

"I quite understand."

"If I might ask—I suppose, if you were able to offer my brother—I must presume you were not much invested in his bank, then?"

"Only in a very small way."

"Very prescient of you." Frank Austen sighed. A pause.

"Captain! Would you join me on a walk? I must go to the stables to see—I fear my horse has taken lame."

"I should find my wife and tell her the dreadful news. This house is too big; we are forever losing each other."

"I saw her in that pinkish room, not long ago."

"Thank you, sir."

The door opened and closed, and the room fell silent. My legs were falling asleep, and my neck hurt, but I feared getting up; what if someone had forgotten something and came back? Face to the carpet, I closed my eyes, willing time to pass. Then, to my horror, the door opened again; footsteps approached me and stopped. I lifted my head. Liam.

"How long were you crouching there, you poor object?" His hands felt cool and strong as they raised me up and briskly skimmed my hair, my forehead, my nose, my shoulders—"You're all dusty!"—our first physical contact since the debacle at the Angel. As a painful wave of lust coursed through me, I collapsed on the sofa, unable to look at him.

"I can't believe they didn't see me. You obviously did immediately."

"Mrs. Frank Austen told me you had gone to look for a book. So I suppose, when I walked in—You weren't exactly invisible back here, but they were distracted."

We stayed in silence for a while, I on the sofa, he standing nearby, arms folded. I tried not to recall the feeling of his hands on me. Or to admire his shoulders.

"So, our money seems not to have helped," I said at last.

"So it would seem."

"So you were right and I was wrong."

"Don't put it like that. We both agreed to try, and it didn't work. We've still enough to live on." *As long as we can return to our own time and are not stranded here forever* was the unspoken end to his thought; I felt the thrill of fear again. "Especially if we give up the house in town. Which we clearly should, now."

"I'm kind of outraged he told Edward before us."

"I suppose he was ashamed." He paused. "He must be miserable. He was a wreck when I saw him last week. And then he still had some hope."

"But why did you tell Edward that you tried to offer him a loan?"

"I think I was thinking—I was trying to make Edward see me differently. It's like Mr. Darcy, patching up Lydia's marriage. We're practically members of the family, we're helping out." I had to admit this was clever; that Liam had a kind of intelligence completely different from my own. "A truly gentlemanly gentleman would never have revealed it, but ever since the thing with the cottage, I get the sense Mr. Knight is not so sure of me, so I haven't lost much." He paused. "You think I should have told him the truth, that I actually gave him money? I nearly did, but something stopped me."

"What he was saying before you walked in is that he's going to write to Sir Thomas-Philip Hampson and make inquiries."

Liam smacked his forehead with his palm. "That'll be the end of us, then."

"It gets worse. What's motivating him to write, you might ask. Apparently Henry made some reference in his letter to marrying me."

"Mother of god." Liam packed a lot of feeling into four syllables, adding after a moment, "How long do you suppose we have, if Edward writes to Jamaica?"

Wind and currents make the length of Atlantic crossings unpredictable, but this much we knew: a letter and its reply could make the round trip before September and the Opportunity of Return, assuming both people were prompt in their correspondence. I could only hope Sir Thomas-Philip was the sort of person who let unanswered mail pile up on his desk.

"Not long enough."

A FEW DAYS AFTER THAT, LIAM WENT TO LONDON ONCE MORE, TO break the lease on the Hill Street house and to settle things with the servants. I said it made no sense for me to go, that my time would be better spent overseeing the work at our new home. In reality, I could not imagine being stuck in a carriage for hours with him, or spending another overnight at a coaching inn.

"But Henry will be there," Liam said, as if this were an argument for going, instead of another reason not to. I was not sure how I felt about Henry just then, except not in a hurry to see him again. It was certain to be a painful scene, with the lost thirty thousand pounds between us, and my need to assure him I still loved him and wanted to marry him, only not yet, and that we still needed not to tell, even though the point of secrecy was far less clear now that we'd failed to save his bank. I did not feel up to all the duplicity required.

Instead, I wrote him a letter trying to say some of this—I could do that now; we were engaged—which I gave to Liam, not yet sealed.

"Read it so you know where we are with him," I said. "I have no secrets from you." We were in the library again, a rare moment alone.

He gave me a look. "Everyone has secrets."

"Okay, but none I put in this letter."

"I don't want to read your letters to Henry!"

"Can you just tell me if you think I've expressed myself properly? It's kind of tricky."

"Only if you insist." With a frown, he started reading.

THE MORNING AFTER LIAM WENT TO LONDON, MR. PROWTING'S steward stopped by Chawton House with a large key and a message: the work was complete, and the cottage ours whenever we were ready to move in. I grabbed my pelisse and headed down the hill, eager to see the place again and to try to imagine my new life there. I'd felt uneasy around Edward Knight ever since the conversation I'd overheard, but the thought of moving to Ivy Cottage, living in such a confined space with Liam, was disconcerting too.

Pausing at the gate, I saw a woman down the lane heading my way: Jane.

"Ah," she said when she drew close, her gaze traveling from me to the key. "So it is yours? How delightful. Have you just been inside?"

"Not yet. Will you join me?"

I managed the key with difficulty, pushed the heavy door open, and stepped into dimness, smelling limewash and old wood. Next to me, Jane looked up and down, nose twitching discreetly, taking everything in.

"Not as bad as I feared," she said at last.

"It makes me think of what the Dashwood ladies must have felt when they arrived in Devonshire to their new home."

"You are kind to think of my work."

"I nearly always do."

"But you have not, like the Dashwoods, lost—That is, I hope—" Unexpectedly she took my hand and squeezed it. The hand that wrote *Sense and Sensibility* was larger than mine, shapely and cold, and like her face, oddly bronzed. "Henry has told me what happened. That you and your brother gave him money, and that now it is gone. I hope it was not—I hope it was not more than you can afford to lose. I could not bear to think that, after everything else that has gone wrong."

"Do not trouble yourself." My hand squeezed hers back as we went into one of the front rooms. The walls were fresh and white; the floors sloped a little, but the wide boards were clean. Two comb-back Windsor chairs sat on either side of a sturdy round table. With a shudder I anticipated the awkwardness of sitting here alone with Liam.

"We must get more chairs," I said. "Then we can invite you for tea. I wish I could offer you some now, but there is no teapot. Nor tea. Do you buy yours around here, or in town?"

"Do not change the subject. I have asked you a serious question and I want the truth. Even if I fear it."

"We gave him nothing we could not afford to lose." I wondered if Henry had revealed the amount; thirty thousand pounds was a staggering sum. "Please stop thinking about it."

She sat down, leaning forward. Her wince caught my notice. "Does your back pain you?"

"Oh, a little. I am rather old, after all."

I sat down, too, and studied her. "Is the pain constant? Only when you move in certain ways?"

She ignored my question. "May I be quite honest? I am so happy you are going to be my sister. We knew Henry must re-marry eventually; he is ill-suited for the life of a bachelor, even

244

if he was one for so many years while trying to win Eliza. But I was afraid that—I am so very glad it is you." She looked into my eyes, smiling but serious too, and I felt a thrill of shame at my own deceit.

"He must have loved his first wife very much. I cannot expect to take her place in his heart. Or in your family." I paused. "Do you think Mr. Knight will be very shocked, Miss Austen?" I wondered if he had written his letter to Jamaica yet.

"Edward must not think he can command everyone's life." She paused. "We will be sisters soon enough. Do you think it would be too hasty—Shall we, then, use our Christian names?"

She paused, as if really concerned about what I might answer, as I concentrated on trying to look happy but not excessively so, when I wanted to jump up from my chair, throw my head back, and laugh. This was a far bigger triumph than a proposal of marriage.

"Jane," I said, trying it out. Leaning over and kissing her on the mouth would not have felt more intimate, or more daring. "I would be honored."

We sat in peaceful silence for a moment before she said: "In general, Mary dear, secret engagements are wicked things, though when it comes to the particular, I find it hard to disapprove of Henry. And there is a certain delight in being in on the secret, I must confess."

She spoke kindly, but I felt a cold sensation wash over me. "Yes" was all I could say.

"I understand a need for discretion, so soon after the bank crash. Who knows if his creditors might not go after you, if they thought the alliance had already been contracted?"

In my wildest flights of worry, lying awake and thinking of

things that could go wrong, this one had never occurred to me. "Would they?"

"It is not likely, but it is better to be cautious. Still." She reached out and patted my hand. "Do not wait too long to tell, or scenes might arise unpleasant to everyone."

I didn't want to talk about this. "You show the dangers of this very well in *Emma*."

"I had not realized you had read it already."

"Did I not say? I loved it. Your best work yet. It is marvelous, how you hide the truth in plain sight."

She blinked. "An interesting way of putting it."

"Is that not what you did? The secret engagement—Emma's unrecognized love for Mr. Knightley—it is all there."

"But I did not expect people to see it, so easily. Perhaps I am sadly transparent."

"No, no," I protested. Though I could hardly admit to my numerous rereadings and a thirty-page paper I'd written as an undergraduate, I said: "As soon as I had finished, I read it again. This time, knowing what was coming and looking for the clues."

"Did you really? I am all astonishment. Henry has chosen his wife well indeed, if I am always to have such flattery close at hand."

LIAM RETURNED WITH A LETTER FROM HENRY AND LOTS OF HOUSE-keeping news. Breaking the lease had been easy, and he had overseen the packing and removal of those possessions we'd acquired in London that might prove useful here; they would make a slow and expensive trip by wagon to Chawton. Mrs. Smith and her sister had declared they were happy to move to the country, a pleasant surprise; it turned out they had grown up near Basingstoke and had family nearby. Jenny, as I had expected, wanted to be paid off and try her luck elsewhere, while handsome Robert, to my disappointment, did too. This meant Jencks would again be our only manservant except for the ex-climbing boy Tom.

"Jencks says he wants to garden." We had taken a walk so as not to be overheard discussing all this: it was an early February day of weak sunlight and dramatic clouds. It was cold, there was still a little snow on the ground, yet something about the light was different; I sensed the world moving toward spring. "That he knows everything about gardening, and he did it in Scotland."

"Is that where he's from?"

"Yorkshire."

"Does he know the plants are different here?"

"He seemed to really want to stay."

"How is he going to garden and be your valet at the same time?"

"We'll figure it out. Maybe it will be good for him. He will be too tired to listen at doors." I had never voiced this suspicion and was surprised to realize Liam shared it.

"I wish you could have managed to get rid of him and keep Robert." Liam did not reply. "There's something about Jencks that worries me. I think he's got a crush on you."

"I'm sure it's not that."

HENRY'S WAS A GOOD LETTER, FULL OF FEELING AND INFORMAtion; I felt myself growing fonder of him as I read it. He was headed to Oxford, where he would stay with an old friend for the next few months while preparing for his ordination. Edward had promised him the curacy at Chawton once that happened; it was a small income but better than nothing. With the money I brought to the table, however, we would have enough to marry on. I admired the politic delicacy with which he expressed all this, but felt a little less fond of him after getting through that part of the letter. He concluded by promising he would come to Chawton to see me as soon as he could.

"So you talked to him about money?" I asked once I had finished and given the letter to Liam. "What *is* the size of my fortune, anyway? Did we ever decide on that?"

"Fifteen thousand seemed right." He was folding and unfolding the sheet of paper but showed no hurry to read it.

"That's all?" It was a lot of money for a woman to possess, yet it seemed small considering how wealthy we'd been pretending to be. "Was he disappointed?"

"It's a bit more than half of what we have left. It seemed fair." He added: "He's doing very well to marry anyone of any fortune at this moment in his life. If he was disappointed, he didn't own it." His eyes met mine; we had stopped walking without intending to.

My question had been joking. *What fortune are we pretending I have?* His reply unsettled me, with its implication that our pretense could assume reality, that the portal might fail, and Liam give me half our money and send me off to marry Henry Austen. But he could not have meant it to come out like that. If I had to spend my life here, it would be bearable only with Liam, I realized, and put this thought away as the dangerous thing it was.

"How are we going to manage all this?" I asked. "If I can only somehow get to the letters and the manuscript in time to break off the engagement before Henry moves to Chawton and takes up the living."

And before a letter comes back from Jamaica. And in time to get to the portal.

I'D DREADED LIVING IN SUCH A SMALL HOUSE WITH LIAM, AND IN some ways it was just as unnerving as I'd feared. Our bedroom doors faced each other across the narrow hallway; if I tried, I could hear a creak as he got into bed at night, or splashing as he used his washbasin in the morning. Though I mocked myself for it, I always went out to the privy, no matter how rainy, late, or cold it was, rather than risk being overheard peeing into a chamber pot.

Planting started in the kitchen garden under cold frames. We acquired chickens and two Jersey cows, which Tom was given charge of. A tiny cat, black except for one white front paw, made herself at home, first in the outbuildings, eventually insinuating herself into the house. I did not want to name her, for then she would be ours, but she was soon known as Alice B. With the help of Sarah and Mrs. Smith, I learned how to make butter and soft cheese, to distinguish weeds from seedlings, and to brew beer. Several dresses, among the first I had acquired the previous fall, were downgraded to work wear. I was occupied from first light until dusk, and I was strangely happy. Too tired for insomnia, I seldom lay awake thinking of all my problems, and of Liam so provokingly near.

In London we had taken no notice of the Sabbath, but here

we had to in order not to stand out, attending morning and afternoon services at the church down the hill from Chawton House. "Observing Protestants in their natural habitat," Liam called it, but I liked the way the church smelled: musty, like time. I enjoyed studying the dim interior, the stained glass, thinking about Cranmer, and Henry VIII, and Thomas Cromwell, turning over in my mind the archaic, resonant phrases from the Book of Common Prayer:

See then that ye walk circumspectly, not as fools, but as wise. Redeeming the time, because the days are evil. I studied my fellow churchgoers' fashion choices, pleased whenever I was able to recognize a hat from a previous week disguised with new ribbons. *Then said the king to the servants, Bind him hand and foot, and take him away, and cast him into outer darkness; there shall be weeping and gnashing of teeth. For many are called, but few are chosen.*

THE OTHER DAYS OF THE WEEK, I WOULD OPEN MY EYES WHEN THE bedroom was still dark, with a sense of anticipation, dressing by feel. Downstairs, Sarah would be reviving the kitchen fire that was banked overnight and Mrs. Smith rolling out dough or grinding coffee. Tom, who had grown several inches since the day he fell out of the chimney, would duck his head to me and smile shyly on his way out to the livestock.

"Awake already, miss?" Mrs. Smith said, as if surprised every time, and I would pause to enjoy the smell of the coffee; always wishing to drink some right then, but it was not made yet and would taste even better after a couple of hours' work. The sun was coming up, mist was rising off the pond, the chickens were awakening.

AM I MAKING THIS ALL SOUND LIKE A RURAL IDYLL? IT WAS NOT.

The farming was fun, but something of a disaster. Only the cold frames saved us. The garden struggled because of abnormally low temperatures due to volcanic ash in the upper atmosphere after an enormous eruption in the Dutch East Indies the year before. There would be crop failure and famine in much of Western Europe and North America in the years following. If we'd actually had to live on what we produced, as many people did, our diet would have been inadequate at best, but having money, we could send Mrs. Smith to market days and often did, as well as count on the arrival of steady deliveries of coffee, wine, and other luxuries, which we shared with our friends at the cottage as much as they would allow.

We got more chairs, and invited them over often on those cold evenings. Even old Mrs. Austen, who seldom went anywhere, often came, Ivy Cottage was so close. Gathered around the big, primitive hearth in the front room, firelight flickering as we laughed and told stories and read aloud, I felt at those moments I could not wish for anything more. If not for a few nagging worries, it might have been Arcadia after all.

CHAPTER 14

APRIL 3

Chawton

'D BEEN STRUCK BY THE CHANGE IN JANE WHEN SHE RETURNED from London near the end of the year: by her weight loss and the strange hyperpigmentation, the bronzing. And then there was her back, which seemed to continue to trouble her.

In the first weeks after our move to Ivy Cottage, we saw her a lot. She and the others came by many evenings, and I continued my habit of visiting in the early afternoon, joined not by Mary-Jane anymore but by Liam. His idea of seeking their advice on gardening and animal husbandry was a good one, for there was no end of things to ask about, yet the visits took on a different tone with him there. A gentleman is a disruptive element in a household of ladies, and they did not seem at first to know what to do about him, earnest though he was in his questions about farming. That particular flirtatious focus he'd shown toward Jane in London was less visible now, pinned as he was under the watchful gaze of Cassandra, Martha, and Mrs. Austen, yet I still had the feeling of something between them, which was less a matter of words than of silences, more of glances than of laughter.

Then, toward late March, Jane began to stay home when the others came over, and to be absent when we stopped by; she was "resting," they explained. One afternoon, the third time in a row we had failed to see her, Martha had said as we left: "Jane will be excessively sorry not to have seen you." Commonplace words, and her edge of irony made me doubt everything she said. But she paused and added: "Come back this evening, for tea, if you like. I hope she will feel better then."

WHEN WE SET OFF FOR A SECOND TIME THAT DAY TOWARD THEIR cottage, the wind had risen; clouds were sailing across a dark blue sky in which the first stars were showing up.

"Do you think she's writing?" Liam asked. "Is it her way of not wasting time on us?"

"She doesn't have much to waste."

"True." The night sky was something I had never gotten used to here. I stared at it as I breathed in the cool air, which smelled of damp earth and new leaves. It was early April; early September was the Opportunity of Return. That is, assuming it still existed. And, if not, what then? I sneaked a sideways look at Liam, who was gazing up at the sky too, with an expression that struck me as wistful, and I had a sudden picture of the little boy he might have been: smart but already gloomy, earnest but lacking the armor needed to survive. That would have to come later. "Or she doesn't like us anymore."

"She likes you, Liam, I know she does."

"Oh, but she likes you better."

We exchanged a conspiratorial smile. Maybe it will be all right after all, I thought, not sure even at that moment quite what I meant by "it."

"I AM VERY GLAD TO SEE YOU ONCE MORE."

Jane was unusually serious as she greeted us, giving her hand first to me, then to Liam. She had stood up when we came in, rising from one of the mismatched pink chairs near the fireplace and walking to the middle of the room. Too few steps to be sure, but I thought she limped. And was that a walking stick by the chair she had just vacated?

"Have you been unwell?" Liam asked her in a low tone, leading her back to her chair and sitting down in its counterpart. "You can tell me. You must, you know." On our walk over I'd urged him to try to assess her health, but I had not expected him to act quite this fast. "Have you any pains or aches?" he went on, so softly I strained to hear the words. "Night sweats?"

"Sickness is a dangerous indulgence at my time of life." Her voice was just as quiet. "I am feeling much better."

She's the stoic type, I thought. Or she's lying; maybe even to herself.

"What about this?" He held up the stick. "Is it you using this, or your mother?"

I looked away to find the eyes of Martha, the only other person in the room, on me. "He has been put straight to work, has he not?" she said. "How we do abuse his good nature."

"He is happy to be of use." We took a few steps farther away from the two at the fire as I asked in a lower tone, "Has she been ill, really?"

Martha looked sad. "She does not like to complain, but she is worse. In another person, you would hardly notice, but she has always been such a great walker. And now she is not." Her eyes followed mine back to the conversation at the fireplace. "Perhaps it is just age. None of us are becoming younger." Her tone suggested she didn't believe this; at fifty, she was ten years older than Jane and showed no sign of slowing down.

"Does she have trouble walking? Or is it that she tires easily?"

"She says her joints pain her. And she does not have the stamina she did. She wanted to call on you, one day last week, and we set out, but had to turn back. You know that is not far."

"Indeed, no." As I was thinking what to ask next, Mrs. Austen and Cassandra appeared. Both greeted me and turned, more eagerly, to Liam.

"I have been waiting for Dr. Ravenswood to listen to my cough," Mrs. Austen said. "It is worse since the morning."

"And I have been at pains to convince my mother that the doctor is here for tea, and does not want to hear about people's ailments," Cassandra added. Neither Liam nor Jane could have been happy to have been interrupted, but they did not show it; he surrendered his chair to Mrs. Austen and insisted he was ready to listen to her cough at any moment with complete delight.

As Mrs. Austen began coughing experimentally, Jane rose, made Liam take her chair, and joined us, saying to me: "Your brother cannot help it. He brings out the valetudinarian in everyone. Even my mother."

"Even?" Martha murmured.

"It is something in his doleful countenance; it makes one long to confide in him." She continued, gaze on me: "A hasty person would say the brother and the sister are not at all alike, Martha, but we are not such dull elves. I begin to discern it, though he is so tall, and she so little, and his eyes so blue, and hers so"— her own eyes bored into mine for an unsettling instant—"dark, and as for their features in general, barely a point of similarity can be traced—"

"Where do you begin to see the resemblance, in such a case?" Martha asked, amused. My heart was pounding and I did not know where to look.

Jane said: "Both have an air of having fallen to earth. One can tell at a glance they are not truly English. They are so correctly, so perfectly English."

Too horrified for speech, I bowed. I felt the eyes of both women on me and could not meet them; instead I looked across the room to where Mrs. Austen had stopped coughing and Liam was leaning in, questioning her. I longed for some way to warn him that she was on to us, but there was none.

"Jane, you are merciless." Martha touched my forearm gently. "You know, Miss Ravenswood, do you not, that she quizzes only people she likes? She regards it as a mark of distinction." I looked up, surprised by her words and her expression, kind without a hint of irony.

Before I could think of a response, Cassandra said: "I am

sorry. My mother sometimes claims the privilege of age over-much. Let me see what is become of the tea."

WHEN THE TEAPOT WAS EMPTY AND THE SEEDCAKE SEVERAL SLICES smaller, conversation slowed, and I began to think of leaving. But then Martha asked Jane about a new piece of music Fanny Knight had copied and sent from Kent, and Liam encouraged her to play it. Soon we were all around the piano, Liam appointed to turn pages. Though the tune was simple and too sweet for me, her fingering was good and she played with a precise intensity that fit her character.

I said: "You are a true proficient. Will you play us another?"

"You are kind. There is nothing else fit to hear." But she made no move to get up; the room seemed to echo with her song.

"Perhaps you would play us something," Cassandra said to me. "Jane mentioned there was a pianoforte in your house in town—are you not a musician?"

"I would not give myself that distinction." I wanted to avoid being observed; I was still smarting from *so correctly, so perfectly English*. Teasing or not, it pointed to a flaw in our presentation, one I wanted to go away and think about. At the piano, Liam had picked up a piece of music from the neat pile and shown it to Jane, asking her something. She nodded and played a phrase; they conferred, and she played another.

"Give us that one!" he said. "'Tis a favorite of mine."

"Is it, sir? I am sorry then, for I barely remember it." She played a few more notes, and as Liam followed them with his voice, unexpectedly resonant and tuneful, she looked up in surprise, which I shared. The long hours I had spent on music during Preparation, he had been off shooting or learning to drive a carriage; these were hard to master and essential to impersonating a gentleman in a way that music was not.

"I will play it only if you will sing." She lifted her hands off the keyboard and looked around the room for support. "You see, the words are all here, if you need them."

"I am sadly out of practice."

"Oh, please do," Cassandra said. "Since Charles went back to sea, we have not heard any singing worth the listening. Henry claims never to be in voice, and as for the younger Digweeds—" She left this thought unfinished.

Liam hesitated and glanced at me. I gave a tiny nod, thinking he had gone too far to politely back down. He turned back to Jane, saying, "I can deny no wish of yours," studied the sheet a few moments, humming quietly and following the notes with a finger, then put the music back on the piano, nodded at her, and took a step back, rolled his shoulders, and took a breath. They began.

HE HAD BEEN AN ACTOR; IT MADE SENSE THAT HE HAD VOCAL training. He had good range, excellent breath management, and a surprising ease, an absence of affectation, as if singing were as natural as talking—but it wasn't just that. The rough texture of his voice gave the song, a sad one about love gone wrong, a melancholy ferocity; it was like someone had opened a window and let in the Brontës. Cassandra, Martha, and Mrs. Austen were staring at him with the surprise that I was trying to conceal, while Jane lost her way and stopped playing after a certain point, so that he had to finish unaccompanied, intensifying the effect.

O, the rain falls on my heavy locks
And the dew wets my skin,
My babe lies cold
Within my arms
O Gregory, let me in.

When the song was done, no one said anything. Then Jane stood up and shook his hand vigorously, as a man might. "You astonish me, sir, you astonish me," she said, and her eyes were shining. "Thank you."

She hurried out, limping slightly; there was the creak of quick footsteps headed upstairs, a sob, the slam of a door. We remaining five looked at each other, stricken. As they will when she's dead, I thought. Soon.

"I am sorry to distress your sister," Liam said to Cassandra, and the familiar sound of his speaking voice brought me partway back to reality. "Were there some painful associations with that song? I could not have known."

Cassandra just shook her head.

"Perhaps I should go to her," I said. They all looked at me. "Make sure of her," I added, and turned and hurried upstairs. I had to get out of that room. I thought I understood why she had fled, because I had felt it, too, what I saw in her face.

I paused at the top of the stairs, confronted by a dark, narrow hallway with a window at the end, several closed doors, and a lump in my throat. Then I realized I had been here; we had toured the house museum in my own time, as part of Preparation. If historians got it right, her bedroom, which she shared with Cassandra, would be the first one, just ahead of me. I stepped toward it and knocked. "It's me, Mary. May I come in?"

I did not wait for permission. Opening the door, I stepped into the deeper darkness of the room to see a pale shape lying on one of the beds. The curtains were open, offering a square of night sky as I felt my way to a chair near her bed and sat down. When my eyes had adjusted to the dimness, I saw she was face-down in a pillow, hands clasped at the back of her head. After a time, she turned to look at me, but said nothing. It was too dark to see her expression.

"I wanted to be sure you had not been taken ill."

"I had not," she said, adding after a pause, "I only felt an ir-repressible desire to be alone."

"I needed to also, but I would not disturb you. Shall I go out in the hall?"

I heard amusement in her voice as she said: "Perhaps we can be alone together. If we do not talk."

"Yes."

The silence that followed was strangely comfortable, and it lasted so long that I began to wonder what they were doing downstairs. Probably I should rejoin them. I was about to stand up and say so when she spoke.

"I shall not come back down tonight; it would be too much of a spectacle. Please tender my excuses to your brother for run-ning away."

"*You* do not need to make any excuses," I said, a little more vehemently than necessary.

"You are charming in your quick sympathy, but also myste-rious. What do you imply by that singular emphasis?"

"You may claim all the privileges of the artist. Including that of being whimsical."

"The artist?" Again I had the sense of a laugh held back in the way she said it.

"Was the word ill-chosen? I think not."

She adjusted her position to lie on her back and look at me. "Forgive me if I injured your feelings earlier, Mary." I was on the verge of denying she had when she went on: "Martha is right, you know. I feel such an affinity for both you and your brother, for all that I have known you such a short time." She paused. "Though in novels, such an immediate intimacy is generally not to be trusted."

"Like Isabella and Catherine in *Northanger Abbey*," I said, and caught my breath in horror as I realized my mistake, adding hastily, "I mean, the way Elizabeth and Wickham talk so unguardedly, the first time they meet in *Pride and Prejudice*."

"*Northanger Abbey?*" she repeated, sounding puzzled, as well she might. That novel had come into the world titled "Susan," after the original name of its heroine, and was sold to Crosby and Co. for ten pounds in 1803 but languished unpublished, for reasons lost to history. It was not until she finally had money of her own from writing that she was able to ask Henry to go and buy the book back for the same sum, not mentioning until afterward that it was by the author of the successful *Pride and Prejudice*. I like to imagine Henry casually revealing this on his way out of Crosby's office, manuscript in his arms. But I also wonder: couldn't her brothers have pitched in to come up with ten pounds a little sooner, so she could try her luck with another publisher? Was this not seen as important, or was she too proud to ask?

"*Is* there such a novel? I do not think I have heard of it. I would remember such a title. And characters named Catherine and Isabella?" She would later change Susan to Catherine, or maybe had already done so; the book would not be published until after her death.

"I was mistaken," I said, hoping the dimness of the room would hide the confusion on my face. "I was thinking of something else, another novel—"

"So Henry has told you of my misadventures with that book." A statement, not a question, and I exhaled in silent relief. "He never could keep a secret. But it does not matter. We are nearly sisters by now." She paused. "Still, I urged him, in my last letter, not to keep this engagement concealed much longer, and I shall tell you the same."

I had no reply to this. I did not want to alter history any more than I already had; a mysterious person agreeing to wed Jane's favorite brother and then vanishing would surely become part of the Austen family lore and be irresistibly fascinating to the same biographers I was trying to aid with the rescue of the lost letters to Cassandra. It was all too meta. Also, it would be apparent to those at the institute, back in my own time, that I had done this, something I absolutely should not do. "Is there a reason for your wishing to keep it a secret?" she asked, not accusingly but so gently I felt ashamed. "You can tell me, you know. Unlike my brother, I am vastly discreet."

"It seems too soon after everything with the bank," I said. This did not strike me as particularly convincing, but it was the best I could come up with. "There is what you have mentioned— the risk of creditors coming after the money I would bring to the alliance. And even if that is unlikely, to lose the money of so many people—and then to immediately turn around and wed a

West Indian coffee heiress—it might strike the world as lacking in repentance."

"You are right, of course; I had not seen it in quite that light." She paused. "We need to marry your brother off first; then your own wedding can pass almost unnoticed." It was hard to know from her tone if she was joking. "But why is he burying himself in the country, in this case? It does not seem the right way to go about the thing. What is his age, Mary?"

"Seven and thirty."

"I think I understand why he did not marry in the Indies. But what, do you suppose, is holding him back here?" She considered this problem as dispassionately as if Liam were a character in a novel. "Was that not his design in coming to England?"

"His and my design in coming to England," I began slowly, "was first, to move to a more temperate and civilized land where we were not confronted daily by the moral horror of slavery. Second, with the dream of meeting the author of my favorite books in all the world." She laughed. "I hope I have known you long enough that I can say this and you will not think me a lunatic. From the first time I read your works, I was amazed. They are witty and sparkling, but with such a deep understanding of human nature. I was consumed with curiosity about the person who could write like that." I paused, feeling light-headed. "Of course, my highest aspiration was to perhaps meet you once. Not in my wildest flight of ambition would I have aspired to call you by your Christian name and sit in your bedroom." She was silent; I feared I had said too much. "Do not think me a lunatic, I beg you."

"I do not." But her tone was different, warier.

"You do not want to be known, to be a public figure. I understand that. Yet you must reckon with the consequences of your own genius."

"And they are what?" she asked, sounding amused.

"That everyone will want a piece of you. Think of Mr. Clarke, the prince's librarian. Now imagine a world full of people like him, but less polite. More demanding."

"Mr. Clarke is an excellent argument for remaining as anonymous as possible."

"And I will make of myself another, and ask you something I long wanted to know but feared to bring up."

"An alarming introduction. What is it?"

"Your brother told me that the two books you published first, as well as 'Susan,' were the works of your early adulthood, completed before you were five and twenty. Did I understand him correctly?"

"That is something close to the truth. But why—"

"And you wrote nothing else, between around 1800 and a few years ago? Such a long silence, from such an inventive mind, I confess myself at a loss to understand."

She said nothing for a moment. "I suppose I was at a loss as well."

"Did you really not write, in all those years?"

"Is that what Henry told you?"

"Perhaps I misunderstood."

"I wrote; how could I not? I revised and edited those three, of course. But mainly—" She stopped. "Perhaps I had lost faith in myself. The life I led in those days was not suitable to composition, but that is hardly an excuse. If I had wanted it enough—But that is not it. I did. I wanted it so much, it was all twisted in my heart." She paused and added: "Mostly, I burned what I wrote. A costly waste of paper."

"Oh, that is tragic," I said, before I could stop myself. "Even though I had suspected something of the kind, to hear you say it like that, so calmly—"

"I assure you, they were better off burned."

"But you did not destroy everything?"

There was a long pause before she answered. "No, not everything." She sat up. "Perhaps we have shared enough confidences for one day, Mary. I would like to rest. Will you apologize to all of them downstairs for me?"

AS WE WALKED HOME, THE WIND HAD STILLED AND THE CLOUDS had gone, exposing the stars in their unruly brightness. I was roiled by the conversation I'd just had and by the music, my thoughts like a tangled skein of yarn I could not find the end of.

"What was that song?" I finally asked; it seemed like the simplest question.

"It's called 'The Lass of Aughrim.'"

I puzzled over why the title was familiar. "Oh. That song in 'The Dead,' am I right?" How had James Joyce gotten mixed up in this? Who would be next, Samuel Beckett?

"I'm impressed you know that."

"Surprised, you mean."

"At the improvement of your mind by extensive reading? Never," Liam said in his best Dr. Ravenswood manner before going on as himself. "I presented a paper about it once, in the course of which I also learned to sing it. When I saw it at her piano, it was like an old friend. But I should not have sung. It's only dodgy men in her novels who are musical. It was a mistake."

"A mistake? I don't know. They may all fall in love with you now, which might be awkward."

"That's right atop my list of worries."

"Liam!"

"What?"

"Sing something else?"

After being convinced I meant it, he began a song, I think in Italian, that I had never heard before either, while my gaze rose to the stars and my worries, at least for that moment, were silenced.

We are just vessels. The art is eternal.

As we neared home, we stopped walking and he stopped singing. We paused at our gate for a moment, as if waiting for something to happen. I had the urge to pull his head down and kiss him. Instead I said: "Maybe let's just walk for a while. It's so beautiful."

Without answering, he turned away from the house and we continued the way we'd been going. The lane wound past the turning to the manor house and led through fields bordered by hedgerows; I used to walk there in the winter, but lately I had been too busy with farming.

"Why didn't you tell me you could sing?" I asked, conscious again of not asking the question I really wanted to ask. Which was what? It fluttered around the edge of my tangled thoughts, just out of reach. "You never even hum, for god's sake. And yet you have the most beautiful voice! And I'm so envious of people who can sing."

"Perhaps that was why. I didn't want you to be eaten up with envy," he offered.

"Ever the gentleman."

"What did you talk with her about, upstairs?"

"Lots of things."

"'The Watsons'?"

"I was getting around to that. Then she sent me away." I gave him the outline of what we had discussed, adding: "You would have done a better job getting her to talk about it."

"Don't be so sure."

We walked on for a while in silence, listening to the odd scratchings and rustlings, the sounds of the night going about its business. I could see very little and yet I felt confident; it was as if sight was a function not just of my eyes but of my entire body. I had the sense, always there but seldom noticed, of feeling the dark world around me: the movement of air on my skin, the ground under my half boots. I was about to comment on how odd this was when Liam said:

"I wanted to apologize for something. It's been on my conscience."

"What's that?"

We walked on a little longer before he finally muttered: "For that night at the Angel."

"Oh." I feigned a laugh. "Are you still thinking about that?"

"Tell me you aren't," he shot back, seeming no longer at a loss for words. "Look me in the eye and tell me you aren't. Thinking about *that*."

It was too dark to look him in the eye. "From time to time." By which I meant, often. "You don't have to apologize. There's no law that says a person has to fuck you, just because you want to fuck them." I heard his intake of breath; had my verb choice appalled him? I hoped so. "It would be nice to know why you— But actually? I don't need to know that. People are complicated. They're full of contradictions." *Especially people like you,* I was tempted to add, but didn't: it was mean, not necessarily true, and more to the point, risked betraying too much feeling. Which was a real danger, alone in the dark as we were, for once with no fear of being overheard.

"You'll never forgive me, then."

"What? Don't flatter yourself. Do you think I attach so much importance to . . . *that*?" Yet my tone revealed I did. How had he maneuvered me into this? It was like verbal aikido. "If it's forgiveness you want, you've got it."

There was a pause before he said, "That isn't actually what I want."

My heart started pounding, but I was determined not to make this easy for him. Not too easy, anyway. "So, what then?"

We'd stopped walking. He turned to look at me, his face a pale outline in the dark. He hesitated, cupped my chin, and lifted my face up. After seeming to think about it, or waiting to be stopped, he kissed me, tentatively and then with more assurance. His mouth was muscular, his breath like tea. I could smell his skin, like salt and soap and the tang of earth from the garden.

Then he buried his face in my neck with a groan, hands pulling me against him, following the line of my corset down my back, and coming to rest where it ended. "I'm sorry, I can't help it, I'm distracted. I'm a lunatic," he whispered into my neck. "I can't stand it any longer, I must speak. Knowing you are there— just across the hallway—"

"You don't have to speak," I said, enjoying being pressed against him. Soon enough I would be fumbling for a way into his pants, but why hurry this moment? His johnson would still be there; at least, I hoped so, that this time he would not turn skittish on me. "Your actions speak for themselves. Fluently."

My admiring hands moved down the lean length of his back and flipped the tails of his coat aside in quest of his ass, firm yet squeezable, exceeding expectations. It really had been too long since I'd had sex. But this was like being so hungry you would eat anything and finding yourself at a banquet; I could not believe my luck. What has changed in him, though, I wondered as we stood there in the dark for a long time, holding each other and breathing fast. What has happened? I thought again of how he had sung for the ladies of Chawton Cottage; maybe something had been shaken loose inside of him.

He had backed me up against a stile, the wooden stepladder-like construction that gives access over a fence; climbing the first step brought me up to about his height. How different the world must look, from up here. What has changed in him, I wondered again, with an apprehension I tried to ignore as I nibbled on his neck and enjoyed the smell of him.

"I'm driven mad, Rachel. From the moment I saw you, I was done."

I think that's what he said; I was at work on his trouser buttons, which were resisting my attempts. There wasn't much give in the buttonholes, and less than usual with the state of things in his pants.

"Dammit," I muttered, and paused to wonder if this was a good idea. Not the thing itself, but our setting: a muddy lane, hedgerows, starlight. I stopped to listen: could anyone be around, another person who liked to take late-night strolls? Hearing nothing other than the usual sounds of the night, I turned again to the trouser problem. "Help me out here."

Taking me by the wrists, he pulled my hands away. "You're wonderfully direct," he murmured, falling silent as he took my earlobe in his mouth, doing something with his tongue that shot a tremor through me. "It's lovely, but can I just enjoy you for a moment? I didn't mean for it to happen like this. You deserve something statelier." He released one wrist to bring his hand up to my chest, encountering mainly corset. "They are sort of imprisoned in there, aren't they?" He brought the other hand up in further study of this issue, and I shivered with delight.

"Set me free," I said, untucking my fichu, throwing off my shawl, and arching my back, straining against the corset and getting partway out. I yanked at my neckline until my breasts fell out of my dress. Cool air shocked bare skin before Liam gasped and buried his head in my chest, seizing me by the waist to lift me one step further up.

"Rachel dear, I would love you forever for that alone," he managed to say before taking me in his mouth as I writhed in pleasant agony and sought his trouser buttons again, now too far below me. I squirmed to reach a top button and flicked it open with one hand. Encouraged by this success, I took a step back down the stile.

CHAPTER 15

APRIL 4

Chawton

THE NEXT MORNING, I WOKE UP EARLIER THAN USUAL, BUT WHEN I looked across the hall, Liam's door stood open; his bed was unmade and empty. Dressing fast, I went downstairs and out the back door into the kitchen garden and the foggy dawn with a strange urgency.

It seemed that everything depended on this moment. Our lovemaking in the lane had been better than I could have imagined; we had giggled back to the house, conspired to behave normally in front of Jencks—who had waited up for us as always—and parted in the upstairs hallway like old friends. But it all could still go south in any number of ways, and I felt that this was when I would know, when I saw him again.

I found Liam crouched in the area we'd been told was the asparagus bed, examining some green spikes that had emerged since the last time I'd looked at it. When he glanced up and saw me, he rose to his feet. He held out a hand, seemed to remember we could not count on being unobserved, brought the hand back down, and stood looking at me.

"Oh, Rachel, it's you" was all he said, but with such quiet intensity, such a light in his beautiful eyes, that I remembered, belatedly perhaps, that I was dealing with an actor.

"Is the asparagus up, really?" I squatted down for a closer look, and as he did too, I added in a lower tone, "I'm glad you're not sorry about what happened."

"Are you stark raving? *Sorry?*"

"I wasn't sure if you might not be." He seemed to have nothing to say to this, and I went on: "Because there's just one thing I wonder, and then I promise to stop talking about this." He tilted his head in inquiry. "What's changed between December at the Angel and now?"

"Nothing! That night, that's what I'm sorry for. I was sorry even when it was happening." He laughed quietly. "I thought, What an idiot I am. I thought, This is how the species dies out. I thought, I am disproving the theory of evolution." He put his head down and laughed more, long and low, but I didn't get the joke.

"So, why?"

"Let's say, I didn't see the possibility that you could like me a little."

I thought back to that night, wondering if it was possible to make a more direct advance than I had. But all I said was "And now you do?"

"And now I do." A sideways glance, smiling but shy, like a child with a secret.

"Well, good." I paused. I'd hit a fork. I could ask, because I wondered, *So what made you figure that out?* And we would go down a rabbit hole of analysis and speculation about who thought what when, and where it was going, and what it meant. I asked instead: "How are we going to manage this? Without the servants figuring out?"

"We have to be careful is all." A pause. "There's not anything else you want to know?"

I felt the prickle of apprehension again. "Like what?"

"I'm breaking my engagement, the instant we are back. But maybe that's too obvious to need saying?"

And then I understood what I had been worried about. Sabina.

With a sense of him hanging on my words, I hesitated. "You don't have to make promises." It came out kinder than I'd hoped. "Things might look different when we get back. Generally, I don't go around stealing people's fiancés."

There was long silence before Liam said, "I'm not anyone's property."

"I only meant, let's not worry about things in our own world right now. We have enough worries here."

"If you like me a little, it's a start. I am not worthy, but give me the chance to try to be." His expression grave, he met my eyes. "But perhaps there is someone. You never said. Yet how could there not be, lovely as you are?"

Even so adroitly framed, this is a question I hate. I shot back: "If there is, I wouldn't tell you. Because I'm not anyone's property either."

"Touché." He smiled again, and I felt he saw through me; there was no *someone*. How would there be, considering the person I am, and the way I have lived my life?

AS I BEGAN MY MORNING'S WORK IN THE GARDEN, I WAS THINKING hard. Maybe he was the kind who needed to imagine himself in love before he could make love. This somehow fit with him: the constant trying on of roles, the shame about his origins. I liked this theory better than my alternate, which was that he'd resolved to conquer my heart as a performative challenge, the way Henry Crawford does with Fanny Price in *Mansfield Park*. A third possibility, that he might care about me, I mean, more than what two colleagues on a challenging mission would naturally come to feel for each other, passed through my mind but found no hold. He had professed too many things, too skillfully, for me to give this one special weight.

Yet I shivered as I thought of something that had happened the night before. Spent, sticky between the legs, I was finally feeling the cold as we put our clothing back in order, readjusting to being again contained within ourselves. He had reached down to twine one of the curls above my ears around a finger, gently pulled it out, and marveled at how it sprang back into place. "I've wanted to do that for such a long time," he whispered, and I felt something catch in my heart, at the smallness of this wish.

AT BREAKFAST A FEW HOURS LATER, THE NEWS CAME IN THE FORM of a servant from Chawton Cottage carrying a sealed scrap of paper for me with a few words on it in Cassandra's firm, even writing. Jane had taken very ill in the night. Could they trouble my brother—

Liam was draining his coffee, wiping his mouth, pulling on his coat. "It might seem weird for us to go together. But you must follow quickly. Don't leave me alone there. What if she's dying already?"

"She's not dying. Just try to make her comfortable. I'll be there soon."

CASSANDRA CAME DOWN THE STAIRS, BLANK-EYED, TWISTING A handkerchief in her hands. "Ah, Miss Ravenswood." She gave me her hand. "It is good of you to come as well."

"I could not stay at home, wondering. What has happened? Please tell me."

"She was taken ill a few hours after you left last night. A violent bilious attack."

"Nausea and vomiting, you mean?" Cassandra looked at me oddly, but nodded. "Had she eaten anything different from the rest of the household?"

"Why would she?"

"But are you certain?"

She gave me another sharp glance. "We all ate the same thing: some green salad from the garden and a beautiful piece of venison haunch from Edward." Her voice broke on the last syllable and she went on in a gasp: "Your brother was very kind to show up so promptly. Yet I fear there is nothing anyone can do." She turned away as a sob, then another, shook her.

"Miss Austen," I said, touching her shoulder cautiously. "You must not say that. Do not abandon hope."

She took a deep breath, and when she turned back to me her expression was blank. "Yes. I must surrender myself to God's will. Thank you for recalling me to my duty."

I could not think of anything to say to this. "Might I see her?"

"You hardly need ask." She turned and headed toward the stairs, and I hurried after.

SHE LAY IN ONE OF THE TWO SINGLE BEDS, HALF-PROPPED UP WITH pillows. The room was clean and full of weak daylight, yet my nose detected urine and vomit, despite the open window. Liam was hunched in a straight chair next to the bedside, chin on his fist. He sprang up when Cassandra and I walked in. "Oh, thank god," he whispered to me. "Here, sit here."

I squeezed his hand in passing as I sat down on the chair, still warm from him, and turned to Jane.

"I am grieved to hear you are ill," I said. Her hair clung to her scalp with sweat, her eyes were glassy and sunken. Her face was as oddly bronzed as ever, but her lips were pale. She gave me a little smile, though, and held out her hand. The other one, I noticed, clutched her side.

"How is the female Asclepius?" she rasped.

"Now I know how you talk about me when I am not here." Keeping hold of her hand, which was hot with fever, I inverted it for a look at her palm. It was tawny, as tanned as the back of her hand, except it wasn't really a tan, of course, not in the Hampshire of 1816, where it rained nearly every day and ladies, if they worked in the garden, covered up.

"Have you taken up palm reading in addition to your other acquirements?"

"I see in your hand you will be a famous writer," I said, trying to match her tone. "Generations to come will mention you in the same breath as Shakespeare."

"Shakespeare? But what about Maria Edgeworth?"

This was so unexpected that, despite everything, I had to choke back a laugh as I continued to pretend to study her palm. "These lines promise to eclipse Miss Edgeworth."

No one said anything as I took her pulse and felt the sides of her neck, observing no swelling in the lymph glands. She leaned back and closed her eyes.

"Tell me how it began," I said. Jane glanced up, and my gaze followed hers to where Cassandra and Liam stood by the window, separately gloomy. "Miss Austen, you might take a rest. Let me sit with her a bit." I gave Liam what I hoped was a meaningful look, combined with a nod in the direction of the door.

"Yes," he said, turning to Cassandra, "you must be weary. You were sitting up with her all the night, were you not?" As she murmured assent he was already guiding her out of the room. "And your mother, this morning? Is she in health?" I heard, then the door shut.

"How long have you been feeling badly?" I asked her. "Weeks, or months?"

"Like this?" A wave of her hand took in the bed, the horizontal position.

"No. I mean, not yourself."

"I hardly know." A pause. "It came slowly. I hardly know. In town, in the autumn, it was so exciting, even after Henry got sick. Meeting Mr. Murray, visiting Carlton House, having Fanny there. But I was often tired. I thought it was just the excitement, and I would feel better once back at Chawton. I did not."

"What sent you to bed? The vomiting? Or is there a pain somewhere?"

"There is a dull pain here, which comes and goes." She indicated her right midsection near the bottom of the rib cage. "It has been my faithful companion these many months. But sometime in the night, a new pain made me forget about that one." She released and clutched again the place she had been holding one hand against. "At times it is unbearable, at others merely agonizing." She winced. "I have never felt anything like it."

"Did they give you laudanum? Is there any in the house?"

She slowly shook her head.

I went to the door and opened it, to find Liam sitting on the top step with his head in his heads. Hearing me, he looked around and stood up. "Laudanum," I said. "Ask if they have some. If not, send to the apothecary." He nodded without a word and turned down the stairs as I returned to my patient. On my way back into the room, I noticed the chamber pot under her bed and gingerly pulled it out for a look, finding a small amount of urine, cloudy and faintly pink.

I sat down in the chair again. "Do you mind if I—" But I had pulled back the sheet without permission. *I am palpating Jane Austen's abdomen.* I was so dizzied by the strangeness of it that at first I could not concentrate. Then I decided her liver was swollen. I kept my hands there, as if the answer lay beneath her skin. Which it did, but not in a way that could help me. "That is the location of the dull pain, approximately?"

"Yes."

"And the sharp one?" I touched where her hand was. "Somewhere there?"

"Somewhere there." She winced again, and closed her eyes.

"Do you perspire heavily, at night? I mean, usually. I can see you are feverish now."

"No."

I took my hands off her liver and felt her neck again, and all around the throat. "Do you have any pain elsewhere?"

"In my knees. At my hips. In my fingers. Sometimes it is hard to hold the pen. To walk."

"How long?"

"I cannot recall exactly. Some time now."

"Do you—" I realized I had no vocabulary for this, a puzzling oversight of Preparation. I did not know the terms polite people used; I did not know the vulgar terms. And since I was spared it myself, the issue had never come up with my servants. For a paranoid moment, I thought how suspicious they must find this: no indisposition, no bloody rags. "Your bleeding—you know. Is it normal?" She stared. "Does it—come every month as usual?"

"Oh!" She looked toward the ceiling. "That has stopped."

"How long ago?"

"This twelvemonth at least, I should think." She looked at me. "May I ask to what these questions tend? Do you know what is wrong?"

I hesitated, but she was continuing: "You and your brother are so very clever. No one has forgotten the evening you saved Fanny from choking. I am confident that you—or your brother, for who is the guiding intelligence of this concern, Cassandra and I continue in some doubt—can effect a cure." She paused, and moved restlessly, seeming distracted, less present. "For despite my sedate time of life, I sometimes feel I have only started to live." She closed her eyes, grimacing, then gagged and retched as I dived for the chamber pot.

The material that came up offered no indication of internal bleeding; good news. It looked bilious, however, and there wasn't much of it, despite the effort the vomiting had cost her. I wiped her face and neck off with a damp cloth Cassandra had left; Jane leaned back and closed her eyes.

"Strange how one feels better, just after," she murmured.

"Not strange at all. It's a simple physiological—" I stopped myself.

She opened her eyes. Studied me. Closed them again. We sat in silence for a while like that, as I stared at my patient, thinking.

A KNOCK AT THE DOOR; LIAM, HOLDING OUT A SMALL BOTTLE AND a spoon. "Excellent, thank you." I took them and paused. "Can you possibly find the housemaid?" I asked in a lower tone. "The, uh—"

Following my gaze, he came into the room, reached under the bed, and picked up the chamber pot with a nonchalant air, as if this were nothing unusual for a gentleman. "Back soon."

As the door closed softly behind him, I turned back to the bed to see Jane's eyes open again, and wide with surprise. She said nothing, however, as I sat down and opened the bottle of opium solution.

It worked fast; within minutes I saw the tense lines of pain in her face smooth out and her eyes, growing glassier, droop a little. "Did Dr. Ravenswood really just carry my chamber pot away?" she asked, her words slow and dreamy. "Or did I imagine that?"

"Try to sleep a little." I patted her hand. "He will return it before you need it again."

"The world is an even stranger place than I have imagined, Mary dear."

"I know. I know."

MY EXISTENCE CONTRACTED TO HER BEDSIDE. I STAYED BY IT THE rest of that day, the hours sliding like shadows as I held her hand, wiped her forehead, gave her as much opium as I dared, and encouraged her to drink the barley water Martha supplied at regular intervals with trembling hands and a worried look. Cassandra disappeared for a while to sleep. Liam looked in from time to time, but mostly sat on the stairs just outside in case I asked for something, sometimes going down to talk to Mrs. Austen, who had spent the day gardening, as if a gravely ill daughter were nothing out of the ordinary. I had been appalled by her coldness, but when she came into the room at last, sat down, and looked at her daughter, something in her expression made me forgive her.

Jane was able to keep down the barley water, or most of it; her fever was not better but seemed no worse. Slightly loopy from the laudanum, she remained oriented. As darkness was stealing into the room, Cassandra, who had come by several times already offering to take over, finally insisted strenuously enough that I stood up, kissed my patient on the forehead as I had wanted to do all day, and promised to return in the morning.

"WHAT DO YOU SUPPOSE IS WRONG WITH HER?" LIAM ASKED WHEN we were outside.

I hesitated, as every feeling I'd resisted all day seemed to catch up with me: uncertainty, sadness, dread. "It seems possible that there are two things going on. Whatever has sent her to bed with pain and fever. And whatever she's had all this time, that's been turning her odd colors and causing the joint pain and fatigue. Of course this might be an acute presentation of the same underlying ailment, but—I don't know." Liam said nothing, just looked at me sideways, worried. "I'm actually praying it's a kidney stone. She'll feel like hell for a couple of days, and then she'll be better. If it's, say, appendicitis—" I stopped.

She'll die. I could not say it.

"But she doesn't die yet. It's only 1816," Liam said.

The thought of the probability field, and what we might have done to it, hung in the cool evening air, present but unmentioned. After a long silence that brought us nearly back to our own house, he said:

"And the chronic thing? Do you think it's what they thought she had? Addison's?"

"Possible."

Primary adrenal insufficiency, named after Thomas Addison, who would first describe it in the middle of the nineteenth century, is caused by the destruction of the adrenal cortex by the body's own immune system. It is rare; a physician could spend a career without seeing a case. Her malaise and nausea could have been caused by the resulting lack of stress hormones—but by many other things too.

The hyperpigmentation, though, was interesting. A comment in a letter to Fanny Knight in March 1817— . . . *am consid-*

erably better now, & recovering my Looks a little, which have been bad enough, black & white, & every wrong colour—had prompted Dr. Zachary Cope, writing in 1964, to propose the diagnosis of Addison's.

Lab tests could have determined the levels of stress hormones in her blood. An MRI might have revealed bilateral enlargement and calcification of the adrenal glands. None of which did me any good here.

"What can you do, if it is?" I realized Liam was asking.

"Do? If it's Addison's? Nothing. I can advise her to avoid stress, which tends to make it worse. Advise her about diet. Malnutrition can kill her eventually with untreated Addison's." I contemplated this, my sense of gloom deepening.

AT HOME, WE HAD A SIMPLE DINNER AND WENT TO SLEEP EARLY, worn out by the day, clasping hands in the upper hallway before we went to our separate rooms.

I woke to realize I was not alone in my bed. Perhaps I had caught the smell of him in my dreams, or felt the warmth of him near me; I opened my eyes in the darkness without surprise, only delight and a thrill of danger. We embraced wordlessly and set to work on the problem of how to make love with the least noise possible.

My sheets, I remember thinking at one point later, alone again and at a contented midpoint between sleep and waking. I will have semen on my sheets. Will I be undone by that? Washing is backbreaking work, between the water hauling, the soaking, the boiling in a large kettle, the mangling, the ironing; there was no plausible way of doing it myself. The best was to be so rich in linen that the job was necessary only every few months, and in fact we'd done no laundry since moving to Ivy Cottage, though we'd have to soon. I'd been planning to bring in a laundress and detach Mrs. Smith's sister, Sarah, from her usual duties to help—but suddenly sending the laundry out, to Alton say, where it could be more anonymous, seemed a better idea. I need to ask someone about this, I thought, and then I was asleep.

CHAPTER 16

Chawton

IT PROBABLY WAS A KIDNEY STONE. AFTER TWO AND A HALF DAYS of agony, Jane felt better, recovering her appetite and insisting on getting up. Within a week, she was back to normal.

Except, I couldn't help noticing, normal was worse. Her liver was still swollen, her skin odd colors, sometimes bronzed, sometimes grayish. Her joints pained her, she admitted, and she continued to lose weight. As that cold, wet spring turned to cold, wet summer, she declined; it was not linear, but it was inexorable. There were days she did not leave her bed at all; at first this was unusual, and then it wasn't.

At times, though, she was almost her old self, taking an outing to the garden—she no longer went farther than that—or going to the parlor to sit at her little table and write. She was lucid and cheerful. She talked of what she would do when she recovered.

Did the others realize what I did? Martha, perhaps; I saw it in her face sometimes when she thought no one was observing her.

But she was busy running the household, taking over the jobs Jane could no longer manage and those Cassandra had no time for; we did not talk privately. Mrs. Austen continued to be consumed with her gardening, her preserving, and her own ailments, seeming unconcerned with those of Jane. Biographers have puzzled over the relationship of Mrs. Austen and her second daughter; seeing it up close did not make it any less of a riddle. They were never openly hostile, yet they spoke as little as possible, like two people trapped together who have agreed to ignore each other.

Cassandra could hardly pretend things were fine with Jane, yet she betrayed no further emotion, at least not to me. She, like her sister, talked about the future as if it were waiting for them both, planning a trip to Cheltenham, for the waters, in the fall.

She spent the bad nights sitting up with Jane, and by June there had begun to be more bad ones than good. In the daytime, I insisted that she rest, and often spent the day with Jane myself, sometimes joined by Liam, whom all the ladies had grown more comfortable having around. After that night he sang for them, something like what I had predicted in jest happened. Mrs. Austen was even more relentless about recounting her ailments; Martha often made him a particular cake with rose-hip jam after he had praised it once; Jane made him sing; and even Cassandra seemed softened. It was as if they had finally decided what to do about him: count him as an additional brother or son, one who did not have to be deferred to but could be ordered about, sent on small errands, good-naturedly quizzed. Perhaps it helped that there was a dearth of actual brothers and sons around just then: Edward had gone back to Kent, and Henry was at Oxford. Captain Frank Austen, though in Alton, was often busy with household projects at his new home, and James, though not far away in Steventon, seldom visited and brought little cheer when he did.

I HAD AN EXTRA MOTIVE IN MY BEDSIDE VIGILS: THE LETTERS AND "The Watsons." I remained persuaded that the bedroom was the likeliest place for them, but searching it was something I'd not dared so far. Despite all the time I spent there, I was never alone, and Jane did not sleep so much as doze fitfully. Those kidney-stone days, when she was doped with opium, would have been ideal, as I realized only later; at the time, her letters were the last things I was thinking of.

Then one day in early June, Jane, who had stayed in bed that morning, complained her joints were paining her more than usual: could she have some laudanum? It worried me she'd asked—laudanum is highly addictive—but I also realized this was my chance. That the doctor in me and the spy were in conflict worried me too, a sense of disquiet I tried to ignore as I gave her a dose from the little bottle, along with an admonition about the dangers of becoming too fond of it.

"You give your opinions so decidedly on medical topics, Mary," she said with a teasing smile. "As much the physician as your brother. Are you sure you did not attend lectures along with him in Edinburgh?"

"I made him tell me everything he learned. I would read his books."

"Remarkable." As her expression relaxed, became dreamier, I had the sense of her ferocious intellect, under the influence of the narcotic, no longer contracted on one point but diffuse, spreading and stretching, finding unexpected connections between things.

"One day perhaps it will not be," I suggested. "Men and women will be free to pursue the same fields of activity. Perhaps it is only lack of education holding us back, as Mary Wollstonecraft suggested."

"Do you mean to say the writings of that person penetrated to the Indies?"

"I had heard the name, but I was not able to find her works until I got to London." I paused. "Do you agree with her? I do not ask about her own scandalous life, but her ideas. What do you think of them?"

She stared at me and then laughed her low chuckle. "She said only what everyone already knows," Jane began, and yawned. "Yet if she was expecting men to snap our chains, I cannot but regard her as vastly naïve. Why would anyone ever willingly surrender such advantages as birth and nature have bestowed on them? You might as soon ask me to go down into the offices and insist that my housemaid let me scrub the floors."

She closed her eyes and settled herself more comfortably, stretching and fidgeting and then growing still. "Mary Wollstonecraft, indeed," she said in a tone that suggested a private joke, and fell silent. Her breathing grew slower and deeper, until I was sure she was asleep.

Motionless in my straight chair next to the bed, I surveyed

my surroundings. If I were a collection of letters, where would I be? There were two small closets in the room, whose doors stood partly open, affording glimpses of clothes neatly folded on open shelves, other clothes hanging on hooks; some shoes on the floor. A dressing table, with a drawer too shallow for anything like letters, held the usual array of dressing table items.

With another glance to make sure she was really asleep, I dropped to my knees for a look under Cassandra's bed, where I saw a rectangular box of an encouraging size. Moving around to the opposite side of the bed, where I would be less visible should Jane open her eyes, I pulled it out.

The box was made of dark wood, smoothly finished, closed with a metal fastening, but not locked. With a wild glance at the door—which remained closed—I lifted the lid.

Sheets of paper folded into squares, tied together with black ribbons in a dozen or so bundles, bore the unmistakable hand-writing of Jane Austen, addressed to "Miss Cassandra Austen." Feeling my heart speed up, I closed the box again, pushed it under the bed, and leaned back on my hands. I just knelt there awhile, focusing on my breath, before I dared to peek over Cassandra's bed for a look at Jane. But she was still asleep.

I realized, the way the obvious can lie in plain sight and yet ambush you, that I hadn't the slightest desire to see those letters. She was Jane to me now, my brilliant sardonic friend; not a historic figure, not a research subject. What she wrote to her sister was none of my business, and reading someone's mail was a deeply dishonorable act. The idea of it filled me with shame.

But this was what I was here for. I thought of Dr. Ping's words: *You must resist the temptation of involvement.* I hesitated, speared on the horns of my dilemma, then pulled the box out again, grabbed a bundle at random, and shoved it down the front of my dress, scratching tender skin with sharp edges of paper as I pushed it past my breasts, the way I had traveled with my forged fortune all those months ago. Would it stay? My corset was confining, yet there was nothing below it to catch the letters, and I had a nightmare vision of them falling out at my feet as I was saying goodbye to Cassandra or Martha on my way out. I closed the box and put it back under the bed, returning to the chair next to Jane. But from then until I was safely home, I kept one hand demurely on my belly at all times, like the bride in *The Arnolfini Portrait*.

THERE WAS STILL DAYLIGHT COMING IN THE WINDOW OF MY bedroom—the days were long, if mostly gray. I closed and locked the door behind me, pulled the bundle of paper out of my corset from the bottom, and put it on my bed. For a moment I was afraid to look, as if the letters had some malevolent power representing my betrayal of Jane. Then I untied the ribbon, trying to memorize how it was knotted, and fanned them out, counting thirteen. I carefully unfolded each, looking only at the dates on the top right corners. They were all from 1800; I knew there were only five extant letters from Jane to Cassandra from that year. I unhooked the chain around my neck and lifted the spectronanometer up to the light, trying to remember the sequence of squeezes to activate its camera functionality.

Our guidance had been to make a physical copy of each letter, using the contemporaneous technology of paper and ink, and to scan them as backup. The compromise I had reached with myself was that I would do only the latter; that way, I did not have to read them. When I returned to my own time, the letters would be stored in the memory of my spectronanometer, Jane would be long dead, and they would be someone else's to render, read, and transcribe. I had only to successfully steal and return them without being caught.

"IT'S QUITE A HAIRSPLITTING DISTINCTION," LIAM SAID LATER. We had gone for a walk in the long, lingering summer twilight. "Talmudic, even; I love it. But how will we know it's recording the images properly?"

Back in our own time, the spectronanometer would have to pair with a device that would extract its data; there would be no certainty until then. Yet it was a robust technology, not new. There was no reason to think it would be squirrelly. "The main thing is, do you agree with me? About not wanting to read the letters?"

Liam, looking off down the lane, toward where the sun was setting in a tangle of tree and hedgerow, did not answer right away. "No mission ever stayed in the past as long as ours, or tried to immerse themselves quite so much. I wonder if they will ever let anyone do it again, once they realize what it does to a person." He paused. "But maybe they won't realize. We will pretend there, as we pretend here, and that will become our reality again." He glanced sideways at me. "You think?"

"Meaning, we will present it as a logistical problem, not a moral obstacle, why we didn't physically copy the letters?"

"Something like that."

"It would be hard to explain otherwise, wouldn't it?"

"Impossible." He rubbed his eyes, and I felt with a sudden sharpness the enormous gap between this world and that one.

STEALING, SCANNING, AND RETURNING THE DOZENS OF LETTERS was a delicate task that took patience, cunning, and the better part of the summer. Jane continued to have ups and downs; fairly often she got up for the day, sitting at her writing table or in the garden, meaning no access to the bedroom at all for me. And even on the days she felt worse and stayed in bed, she had heeded my advice about laudanum and asked for it rarely. When she wasn't drugged, she seldom slept deeply enough to make me feel like I could go into the box under her sister's bed.

What we did instead was talk.

I told myself I had no need to read her letters because I was learning, more directly, answers to many questions we had come to 1815 with. About Thomas Lefroy—she had been drawn to him, she confessed, as he to her; he was by far the wittiest man she had ever met, and the brightest who was not her father or one of her brothers, the handsomest too.

"But it could not be, and we knew it. That was the entire beauty; that it could not last."

"So it was almost as if you were imagining yourselves characters in a story."

"Oh! All the time."

"A remarkable degree of detachment for such a young woman, I should think."

"What did I have else, but my intellect, and the cool judgment to use it?"

"You say that, too, like it is nothing remarkable."

She gave me a droll look. "Mary. How long have we known each other now?"

ANOTHER DAY I ASKED HER ABOUT EDWARD. "WHAT WAS IT LIKE, when he left to go and be adopted by the Knights? What did the rest of you think?"

"I was young then, perhaps seven or eight. I thought nothing in particular at the time. The house was full of boys coming and going—those were the years my father started taking in boarding pupils. Later, of course, I wondered about it. We all did." She paused. "Henry was furious, for many years, that it was not *he* who was picked. But you must never tell him I said that." She paused. "I think the Knights made the right choice, overall; Ned does seem the one born to be a squire."

"But perhaps he grew into the role, once it was imposed upon him."

"And perhaps there is no separating the one from the other."

"Still, it did not strike you as peculiar—one boy selected, like a puppy from a litter?"

She laughed. "Life is full of such oddities, is it not? How did Mr. Darcy happen to fall in love with Elizabeth Bennet, when he could have had any lady in the kingdom?"

"Because you made her so lovable?"

"Oh, yes; perhaps that was why."

IT ALL WENT SMOOTHLY, UNTIL ONE DAY IN EARLY AUGUST.

I had nearly finished the letter project, with the second-to-last bundle to return and the last to remove, and glad of it.

Henry, taking a break from his ordination preparation, was expected for a visit any day now, which would be disruptive. Even
if he did not stay in the cottage, as he had the last time, but in
the Great House, he would be underfoot, interfering with my
ability both to get into the box of letters and to talk to Jane as
freely as we did only when alone. I was so close to being able to
ask her about "The Watsons"; I had nearly done so several times
and then lost my nerve, or decided I needed a smoother segue.

And then, I hadn't seen Henry since I'd started sleeping with
Liam. It wasn't that I thought he would intuit it. Yet I dreaded the
moment when I would find myself again in the company of both
at once, officially sister of one and secret fiancée of the other.
I longed to break the engagement; it was one complication too
many, but ending things with Henry might make me less welcome at Jane's house.

I couldn't risk that. I had to get the rest of the letters and
"The Watsons" first, and I wanted to continue monitoring Jane's
ailment, even though that was increasingly despair-inducing
work, as a worry that I kept trying to dismiss kept coming back.
She had another ten months to live, but she seemed to decline
a little every day. There were no indications that *Persuasion* was
finished, and few signs of it being worked on; on the days that
she came downstairs to her table, she seemed to be mostly writing letters, to judge from the piles of them I would later see on
the table near the door, waiting for the servant to take them to
off to be mailed: to Anne Sharpe in Yorkshire, to Fanny Knight
in Kent, to her brother Charles at sea, to Henry in Oxford. That
we could somehow have altered the probability field so much as
to make her die off early was a possibility I hated to entertain.
But increasingly, I found myself doing so.

SHE HAD SEEMED ASLEEP THAT DAY; I WAITED A LONG TIME UNTIL satisfied that she was, before I stood up and went to the other side of Cassandra's bed to pull out the box and extract a bundle of letters from under my dress. I had turned away to do this; as I finished pulling my corset back into place and smoothing my various layers of skirt, I heard a rustle and turned back, letters in my hand, to find Jane not just awake but sitting up in bed, staring at me.

"What are you doing?" she asked. It was not one of her good days; she'd complained of pain and had taken a small amount of laudanum. Not enough, apparently.

Numb with horror, I dropped to my knees, replaced the letters, and pushed the box back under the bed. Then I stood up again and tried to look innocent.

"What were you doing with those letters?"

First rule of lying: evade the question. "Did you dream something?"

She paused for so long I began to hope this might work. Then she said: "I know what I saw. Do not insult my intelligence, I beg you."

This hit me in a soft point; who would dare do that? I stared at the floor. Then I looked up at her, but found I could not speak.

"Who are you, really?" she demanded, her eyes narrowing to suspicious slits. "There is something uncanny about you, Miss Ravenswood. If that is really your name. You know things you should not know, and you display an unusual interest in my family. Are you some sort of spy? Are you *French*, perhaps?"

I stared at her, still wordless.

"You will tell me what you were doing with those letters."

"Jane, I—"

"Do not use my Christian name. Friends do not behave as you have. You will explain your conduct, truthfully and in plain words, or you will leave and never be received in this house again. I shall tell Henry—" She stopped, perhaps struck by how much I was already enmeshed in her life. "Who are you?" she asked again, this time with a helpless note that made my eyes fill with tears.

I came around to her bedside and fell to my knees. Shame washed over me—not just about the letters, but about all of it. What was I doing here? What kind of maniac travels in time? However I am punished, I thought, I will have deserved it.

"Forgive me," I said, stretching my hands out toward her and hiding my face in the coverings of her bed. "Forgive me. Oh, please forgive me. The truth, Miss Austen, is so strange and improbable that I fear I cannot utter it."

"You had best take your courage in hand, then."

A sob shook me, and I sniffled, finding my handkerchief and wiping my eyes. Then I resolved to stop crying. "You will think I am lying, or out of my senses."

"You will let me be judge of what I will think."

I dared a look at her. Her face no longer cold with anger, it seemed to me stern and suspicious—but also curious. That she might think there could be an explanation for my conduct—and want to know it; that despite damning appearances, she had not given me up entirely—filled me with a reckless courage, like that of people who go into battle outnumbered and outgunned, preferring to die fighting.

"I come from far away," I began slowly. "From a different place. And as it happens, I know the future. In the centuries to come, you will be acknowledged as one of the greatest writers the world has ever known." Still sitting up in bed, she had wrapped her arms around her knees and was staring at me. "Not merely among the first rank of female writers, or writers in English, or nineteenth-century writers, or whatever. You will be immortal. That is why we are here. For—for research."

A long silence followed my remarks, with which, as hardly needs saying, I had just violated a basic directive of our mission. Jane continued to stare at me, eyes bright, expression unreadable.

Figuring I had nothing left to lose, I went on. "But fame has its disadvantages. In the centuries to come, they will want to know everything about you. Everything! They will debate whether being farmed out to a nurse when only a few months old did permanent harm to your relationship with your mother. They will speculate about what was really wrong with your second-oldest brother, George, the one sent away that no one ever talks about." I heard her sharp intake of breath, but plunged on. "What made you change your mind overnight, in 1802, when Harris Bigg-Wither made his offer of marriage, they will ask. Was Mr. Darcy inspired by a real person, and did you love him? Did your aunt Leigh Perrot in fact steal that card of lace from the store in Bath? Why did you choose never to publish your novel about the Watsons?"

Another long silence followed this. Jane's mouth had dropped open slightly. "Miss Ravenswood," she began, and stopped.

"You are correct that that is not my real name."

"To whom, then, have I the honor of speaking?"

Strange, after all the improper disclosures I'd made, that I should hesitate at this. As I paused, there was a vigorous knock on the door.

"Miss Austen? Is my sister in there? I have a surprise for you both."

Liam.

I rose to my feet, my heart pounding like mad; we stared at each other, and she shook her head. "I can brook no more surprises today. Leave me. Let no one in."

"I am sorry," I said. "Will you ever forgive—"

"I beg you. Go now."

I went out into the hall so quickly I nearly walked into Liam and Henry. I closed the door behind me and leaned against it, summoning all my reserves of acting talent.

"I am delighted to see you again, Mr.—Henry." I gave him my hand. Casting a look back at the door, I said, "She is very tired right now, and does not wish to see anyone."

The expectant smile on Henry's face faded. "Is she, then, so very ill? They have told me—But I must see her, Mary, surely she will see *me*?"

"I am sure she will want to. Later."

Liam looked from me to Henry and back, his blue gaze watchful. I felt he knew something was wrong, but this might have been my imagination; I attributed all sorts of powers of intuition to him at that time, which was related to the oddity of our having sex as often as practical but rarely talking, at least out of character, so the simplest exchange—a word, a look, a gesture— could acquire dizzying weight. It was a situation perfect for an actor, I often thought, and indeed he seemed to revel in this role. But what I did not realize until later, until they were gone, was how happy I had been in those days as well.

"Later," I said again, since Henry was still standing there unmoving. "Let us give her a chance to rest." I linked my arm in his and pulled him away from the door and down the stairs. "Are you just come from Oxford? How was your journey? Are you very fatigued? Let us all take a walk, and take advantage of the fact it is not raining, for once. For myself, I have been sitting by the bed all morning—a little air would set me up forever."

Cassandra and her mother and Martha must have been dispersed on their various household tasks; I saw no one but the housemaid as we went outside to the garden. The air was moist and still, the sky full of dramatic clouds. I paused and took a breath. "So beautiful," I said, conscious that I was acting crazy, unable to stop. "Shall we not take a walk?"

Henry, arm still in mine, assented with a puzzled nod; Liam, who had followed us down the stairs, hesitated. "Perhaps I should stay—" he began, before I grabbed his arm with my free hand and started down the lane.

I feared he would go up and try to see Jane. Rationally, this was not likely, yet it could happen. I had to warn him first, which there was no chance to do with Henry there.

But if I left Henry alone, he, too, might try to see Jane. And then what?

I was thinking all this rapid-fire, walking fast, pulling the two of them along and talking nonstop. Henry's journey from Oxford—his progress toward ordination—the unusually low summer temperatures—Cassandra's concern about their donkey's lameness—an expected visit yesterday from James Austen and his wife that had not, in the event, materialized—there was nothing too random or trivial for me to mention.

And this was not the worst. As we continued down the lane, I dropped Liam's arm to focus more closely on Henry, the immediate source of danger; I began to flirt outrageously, as I never had in my life. I leaned on his arm and lavished an adoring gaze on him; I asked about where we might live when we would be married and he the curate of Chawton, a few months from now. I mentioned, with unnecessary suggestiveness, that I was hard at work on my trousseau, as if inviting him to envision night-gowns, petticoats, and marital sheets.

I was conscious of Liam as a brooding presence behind us, but I could not look at him, any more than I could stop what I was doing. I feared once I let silence fall, something terrible would happen. And if "something terrible" was as simple as turn-ing and going back to Jane's house—and the events that would follow—then perhaps my actions weren't so irrational.

Continuing our speedy walk, I realized we had reached the spot where Liam and I had first had sex, several months ago now. I'd been there since, but today was not like other days. When I reached the actual, historic stile, I rested my free hand on it, and then my head. I had black spots in my vision and had a sense of sound fading in and out, but did not immediately draw the proper conclusion from this.

"I think this is the most beautiful field in all of Chawton," I said to Henry, taking a step back from the stile.

"So do I," Liam said in a strangled voice.

"A sweet view," I went on. "Sweet to the eye and the mind. English verdure, English culture, English comfort. . . ."

As I quoted these lines from *Emma,* I had the sense of wrong-ness, of Henry looking at me oddly. He seemed to be speaking, but I heard nothing except a roaring in my ears, and then the world went black.

CHAPTER 17

AUGUST 6

Chawton

OPENED MY EYES, FLAT ON THE DAMP GROUND, GRASS TICKLING the back of my neck, the worried faces of Liam and Henry looking down at me. Liam had fingers at the side of my neck, taking my pulse, though not in the right place. Mortified, I closed my eyes again.

"There, you see, her eyelids fluttered," he said. "She is perfectly well. Her heart is strong. She only must rest. I think the nursing of your sister has taken a toll."

"Ah, indeed, poor Mary," Henry said in a tender tone, cupping my cheek. On the other side of me, Liam's hand went away; I heard the rustle of fabric as he stood up and moved off. "How hard you have been driving yourself! Cassandra has written to tell me of all you have done." There was a pause before he went on: "But we should get her home. It is not good to lie in the damp. Let me help her sit up at least—"

He came from behind to pull me up by the shoulders. I felt his hot breath on my neck and knew it was time to stop feigning unconsciousness. I had to get through this moment, and to whatever lay beyond it. Yet I could not seem to make myself open my eyes.

"Do not elevate her head too suddenly or she will faint again," Liam said, an edge to his voice. "Just let her be. She will be—"

"We must get her home, sir. She cannot lie here in a field like this. It is not only damp, it is improper. And I think it is about to rain." A pause. "Do you not think—"

Henry, putting one arm under my knees and the other under my back, lifted me with a faint grunt of exertion. As he took a few tottering steps, I opened my eyes to find his face next to mine, aglow with excitement. But if he was aroused by the idea of carrying me off like a trophy, I wasn't. I shied and stretched, falling out of his arms and to my feet in one graceless motion, stumbling into him. He took the opportunity to kiss me on the forehead and furtively squeeze my left breast before he stepped back and twined his arm in mine.

"Mary, what a turn you have given us!" he said. "Are you truly able to walk?"

"I am quite well, I assure you." I was focused on standing, not ready to attempt another step; this was a faster return to upright than I would have chosen.

Liam stood watching us with his arms folded, expressionless.

"We must get you home," Henry said, looking down at me,

a hungry gleam still in his eyes. "Are you able to make it there, do you think? Here, lean on this stile for a moment. Perhaps you should go get your carriage to fetch her," he suggested to Liam. "I will stay here." He squeezed my arm. "She will be quite safe."

"I assure you, I am well able to walk." I pushed myself off the stile and started back the way we had come, not waiting for either man's arm, although Henry caught up to me and insisted on giving me his. "I am entirely recovered."

I held out my free arm, hoping Liam would take it, but he did not, walking alongside me and looking at the ground. We continued back, this time in silence; my temporary insanity had passed, and I no longer had the heart for flirting or chatter.

Getting caught by Jane now seemed absorbed into the fabric of reality; whether she would tell Henry was not something I could control. I wanted to go home and quietly think all this over: what had happened, what I would do next. More than that, I wanted to get away from Henry and stop playing the ridiculous role of fainting fiancée. And most of all, I wanted it to be night, so I could lie next to Liam, smelling his skin, feeling the gentle rhythm of his breath.

"SO I TOLD HER—" I PAUSED. WHAT, EXACTLY? "THAT WE WERE NOT who we claim to be. That we were from another world."

It was later, finally almost dusk. We'd gotten rid of Henry politely and staggered into Ivy Cottage, where we'd called for tea. What I had to say seemed too explosive for indoors, where we could be overheard, but Liam had rejected my proposal of another walk.

"You'd better rest," he'd said, running a quick eye over me

and then resuming his study of the floorboards. "Are you really all right?"

I assured him that an isolated presentation of syncope in response to a stressful event was normal and probably not the symptom of any serious ailment. That it was also annoyingly clichéd, like I was turning into the languishing heroine of a nineteenth-century romance, seemed too obvious to mention. I managed to persuade him to come outside, behind the house, to a little bench at the far end of the kitchen garden. There, I told him what had happened.

Liam listened without comment or show of emotion, other than a deepening of his gloomy expression. "So," he said finally. "So."

"We're toast," I said. "I'm so sorry."

"It doesn't seem like you could have done anything different than you did." His words were reassuring, but his manner was remote. As chilly as he'd been when we first met, tone formal, eyes refusing to meet mine.

"I could have not gotten caught."

"That would have been ideal, true."

I resisted my urge to lean in and smell him, to take hold of his head and pull him down for a kiss. The wish to be close was like a physical pain, but if we were safe from being overheard, we could not assume we were invisible. I contented myself with sliding a little nearer on the bench so our thighs brushed; with an almost imperceptible movement, he shifted away again so they did not.

"I'm sorry about Henry, too," I said. Liam sat up straighter.

"Sorry?" he muttered. "For what?"

"That brazen flirting? I don't know, what had just happened with Jane made me lose my head. I wasn't . . ."

"No, no, you need Henry in your corner." He paused, looking around the garden, off at the pink light of sunset at the horizon, anywhere but at me.

"I don't want Henry in my corner. Or in any other part of me." I meant it as a joke, but Liam winced. "She's going to tell him what I told her, and neither of them will ever speak to us again."

"I don't think she will tell." He paused. "Did you mention time travel? Or you just said we were from somewhere else?"

"I said we knew the future. How would we, unless we were from it?"

"How would an intelligent, educated person in 1816 understand this, assuming she did not immediately dismiss it as a lie, or insanity?" His gaze landed on me, and this time he did not look away. "Something biographers have always wondered about, too, is her religiosity. Might she imagine us angels, who chose to take human form? What *is* the Church of England's position on angels?" Seeming entertained by his own idea, he looked slightly less gloomy. "Or demons, come to tempt her, could we be now?"

"I'm having trouble fitting this in with my idea of Jane Austen. I give you points for creativity, though."

"When we go back there tomorrow—"

"We might well be refused entry."

"—let me talk to her first."

"Without me there, you mean?"

"Yes."

"What are you going to say?"

"I'll think of something."

INSOMNIA HAD NOT TROUBLED ME IN MONTHS, BUT THAT NIGHT I lay awake, looking at the nearly full moon through my window and thinking about the disaster that had befallen us. Probably Jane would never speak to me again; we would have to leave Chawton from the awkwardness of this, and wait somewhere for the Opportunity of Return. Would she tell the others? I supposed it didn't matter, that she was the one who counted, yet the thought of Cassandra and Martha and Henry despising us as well made me sad. We would have most of the letters, but not "The Watsons," and I would never diagnose her mysterious ailment. Not to mention that we might have shortened her life. Over all, we would return to our world stinking of failure.

But maybe Liam could rescue the situation somehow; maybe that was why he'd wanted to speak to her alone. Perhaps he could persuade her that I was insane, and that was why I'd done it. That would be legitimate reason to break the engagement with Henry, which would be a relief. Liam could somehow remain friends with Jane, and get "The Watsons," even if it required me to feign madness and pretend to be locked up, like Bertha in Rochester's attic. It was an audacious plan, but it had merit. It was the sort of thing he might think of.

Adding to my list of woes, he stayed away from my bed that night, a first. Maybe he was getting bored of me; my hunger for him was too evident, too scary. Or maybe he was angry about the Henry thing. He'd seemed stricken at the time, indifferent when I brought it up later. Or was that a pose? Maybe he was offended, waiting for me to make a move, and I should go to his room. I willed myself to rise from my bed and steal across the hallway, but I couldn't do it.

So, was I turning into a woman of the nineteenth century, fainting from an excess of emotion and lacking the courage to sneak into my lover's bed? Impossible; yet something was wrong. Something had happened.

I considered that I'd possibly let myself grow too fond of him. For me, having a lover or a boyfriend has always been about mutual enjoyment: a pleasure borrowed, not possessed. I've never liked the idea of shackling myself to one person for life, and I've always made that clear. Except maybe this time.

I thought again of things Liam had told me that night under the stars, the next morning in the asparagus bed: words I'd classified as the verbal flourishes of an actor playing a part. So why had they stuck with me?

He had not meant them. I did not want him to have meant them. Yet I found myself regretting he'd gotten engaged, so shortly before leaving for 1815. Sabina, in her tall blond hauteur, was not right for him; I was sure of that now. If only we'd been a little friendlier in Preparation, perhaps he would have realized this and not committed himself. Why had he, anyway? I tried to imagine the dynamic between the two of them, and failed.

But this was crazy. He is not mine, I reminded myself: I don't want to possess him, or anyone. And maybe it was better that he stayed away from my bed, at least now and then. I needed to practice, for when we returned to our own world and our real lives, and he would stay away from my bed always. With this depressing thought, near dawn, I finally fell asleep.

I WOKE UP LATER THAN USUAL, AND SKIPPED ANY PRETENSE OF garden work, instead calling for my breakfast as soon as I was dressed and downstairs. My brother had already breakfasted and gone, Jencks informed me with a sneer. He always took advantage of Liam's absence to be particularly rude to me, but in a passive-aggressive way that was hard to pin down, and I regretted again that we had kept him on while losing handsome Robert.

"Where did he go, Jencks, do you know?" I assumed it was to Jane's, but wished I'd seen him first.

"I am sure I cannot say, miss," he said, his tone suggesting he knew perfectly well but wouldn't tell me.

THE MORNING WAS SUNNY FOR ONCE, BUT COLD, FORETASTE OF AUtumn in a summer that had never quite begun, and I was shivering by the time I got where I was going. I knocked on the door and pulled my shawl tighter around me, wondering what kind of reception I'd get.

To my surprise, Henry opened the door. "Forgive my informality, but I was passing by the window and saw you coming down the lane, and the maid is busy elsewhere, so I took the liberty." I stepped in, and he leaned past me to close the door, beaming down at me, wrapping an arm around my waist, and pulling me close for a moment, purring: "And I take another! Oh, how I have missed you at Oxford. You are even more delicious than I remembered. Are you quite recovered from your swoon? Please tell me you are. We need no more invalids in the house." He had released my waist but kept a hand on my arm just above the elbow as he guided me down the hallway; I resisted the urge to shake it off. "But in truth, Jane is remarkably well today." He opened the door at the back, which led to the garden and the kitchen and stables beyond, gesturing for me to go first.

Jane and Liam were on a bench under a tree, heads together like conspirators. They looked up as we approached, and Liam rose to give me his seat, meeting my eyes with a look that seemed to be trying to tell me something, if only I knew what. I sat down next to Jane, who gave me a smile and squeezed my hand, and I understood that I had been forgiven, but could not imagine what Liam might have said to make this possible.

And we were not going to discuss it in front of Henry, who stood talking to Liam about a horse he was thinking of buying. How could he do that? He'd gone bankrupt a few months earlier. Perhaps the prospect of a curacy—or a rumored marriage to a wealthy woman—was something he could borrow against.

Not wishing to think about Henry any more than necessary, I turned to Jane, who was wrapped in a thick shawl, more like a small blanket, against the morning's chill. Her eyes shone bright hazel in her bronzed face. "How sorry I am to hear you fainted," she said. "We must bar you from taking care of me for a while. But you see, I am feeling much better today."

I stared at her, struck by a new idea. How, in all the weeks I'd spent sitting by her bedside, turning over possible diagnoses, had this not occurred to me before? It was not much, but it was something. A possibility. "Jane. They do not bleed you, do they?"

"Mr. Curtis did not think it advisable in my case." He was the apothecary in Alton who looked in on her, although I—or officially, Liam—had mostly taken over her care. "Why?"

I turned to look at the men. "William," I said to Liam. "If you are going to go look at this horse of Henry's, please leave word with Mr. Curtis. He should come here as soon as possible."

A pause followed my words as I realized I had spoken too decisively, not as women do. Jane was staring at the ground and Liam looking at her, as if gauging her reaction. Henry seemed startled, then amused.

"Your word is law, madam," he said, and then, turning to Liam, "It is on our way. If *you* think it advisable."

Liam's eyes met mine. "Mary would not have suggested it on a whim. Let us go there at once, Austen. Are you ready?"

"I? To be sure."

AFTER THEY SET OFF, JANE AND I REMAINED OUTSIDE. LOOKING across at the garden and the outbuildings beyond, she was silent, and so was I. I needed my words to match what Liam had told her, but first I needed to work out what that possibly could have been.

Finally she turned to me. "Your brother has told me a most remarkable tale . . ." She frowned. "But, he cannot be your brother, can he? That would explain why you look nothing alike."

"What did he tell you, exactly?"

"That you, and he, using a miraculous sort of engine, had traveled here from the future. I doubted, as you may imagine, but then he told me things about my current novel that I have not even written yet. That were only in my mind, that I had told not a soul. Not even Cassandra."

"And this persuaded you of the truth of his words?" I felt a stab of both envy and admiration. Why hadn't I thought to try this?

"In part."

"And what else, then?"

"There was always something odd about you two. In your manners; in how you appeared at this decisive moment to Henry; seemed without connection to anyone or anything. It is a most irregular explanation, yet I am inclined to accept it, for nothing else makes sense either. He is very persuasive, your— But I keep forgetting, he is not your brother." She stopped and put her bronzed hand on mine. "You are husband and wife?" She looked concerned, as well she might if this were true. "I did not have time to ask everything I wished to, because Henry and Cassandra walked in."

"We are colleagues."

"Colleagues? But how could you travel together—and live in such proximity, a gentleman and a lady? It seems a situation where impropriety would naturally arise—he is not, I am sure— Yet appearances must be against it—" She stopped.

I was amused. "Our age does not place such limits on the freedom of women as yours does. For us, there is no—That is, it is not improper." But I felt myself blush, thinking of the impropriety that had naturally arisen.

She studied me. "He told me you are a physician. Remarkable, yet not surprising."

"What is surprising is how calmly you are accepting all this."

"Is it?" She was still staring at me, her eyes bright. "Perhaps you fail to credit my imagination sufficiently. *There are more things in heaven and earth, Horatio*—but tell me, what *are* your names? What sorts of names do people of the future have?"

"Rachel." I said it hesitantly, remembering a letter to her

niece Anna Lefroy, the novel-writing one with the stormy romantic history. Jane and Anna had an ongoing joke about names; they collected funny ones, from fiction or real life, to share. In the letter, Jane had written, in an aside on a novel they were discussing, *And the name "Rachael" is more than I can bear.* She'd not made it clear why; did she think it ugly, or melodramatic? "Rachel Katzman."

"Rachael," she repeated, beaming. "Cats-man? A man who looks after cats; how singular. Is it an English name?"

"It is not."

"Where are your people from?"

"I was born in the city of New York, in America." To forestall further discussion of my people, I added, "And Liam is from Ireland. That is his name. Mr. Finucane."

"Another extraordinary name. Yet it suits him, does it not?" She was still regarding me thoughtfully. "Are such journeys undertaken often? How did it fall out that you came here, to me?"

"Oh, my dearest Jane." I could not resist; I leaned over and hugged her, making her go rigid with surprise. "I do not think even your imagination can grasp how famous you are. But the shortest answer is, we came for 'The Watsons.'" She stared in undisguised astonishment as I told her how only its first few chapters had survived, passed down through the family. Split up in the twentieth century, one part ending up in the Morgan Library in America and another in the Bodleian—

"At Oxford!" she interrupted. "My manuscript! Why would they want it?"

"I keep trying to explain, you are immortal. So, everyone thought those first few chapters were all there was. Then came the accidental discovery of a letter, long-lost and unknown to scholars, which you had written to Anne Sharpe. Finding any new letter from you would be amazing, so few survived, but this one stated clearly that the novel had, in fact, been finished."

I stopped and waited for her to absorb this, curious what she would find the most amazing. Telling the truth to Jane felt wonderful, a mix of pleasure and relief from unbearable tension, not unlike the first time I'd had sex with Liam.

"Do you mean to say that people in the future *read my letters*?" I realized I'd made a mistake. "My personal, private letters? What gave them the right?" I stared at the ground. "So that was why you were in Cassandra's box? You were *reading* them?"

"No. We have a device that can capture the images on the paper." I refrained from pointing out the obvious: that someone in the future would read them. That once you are dead, you no longer have any privacy. "You must understand, they are one of the most important sources of biographical information about you. Because you were not famous in your lifetime, your life was not well documented. Therefore—"

"Why was I not famous in my lifetime?" she demanded. "If you claim I am so marvelous and such a giantess of English letters? This defies reason."

"Fame is fickle," I began, wishing Liam were here; I'd let this conversation get away from me. "Perhaps your genius was not properly appreciated—"

"What you mean is, I died too early," she interrupted. "When do I die? If you are from the future, you know that. Tell me."

For a moment I could not speak. "Ask yourself if this is something you truly want to know," I finally managed. "Once you know, you can never not know."

"I do not fear the truth." Her eyes bored into mine for a

painful moment, and then her gaze softened. "Ah, but you do. It must be very bad indeed, then. I surely finished the book about the Elliots, for your—Dr. Ravenswood—Mr. Finucane—was able to cite it. But perhaps there was not another one after that. Is that right, Rachael Cats-man?"

We stared at each other.

At last I said: "If you give us 'The Watsons,' we will take it back with us, and then there will be another. No one who ever knew you will ever read it. I think that was what you feared, that it revealed too much of yourself?" As soon as my words were out, I regretted them. She was facing the prospect of her imminent death, and I was angling for a manuscript. Could I possibly have been more tactless?

But Jane, looking off into the distance, for a long time made no answer other than a heavy sigh.

"I am not ready to die. I do not fear death—as a Christian, why should I? But I must own to you, I am not resigned. Not yet. And that, I know, makes my faith imperfect." She paused. "Take me with you."

"What?"

"If you can take a manuscript, you can take me. Perhaps they can cure my ailment, and I can return. An age of miracles like yours should have no trouble with so trifling a request."

"It doesn't work like that," I said sadly. "I wish I could, and let you see our world. I doubt you would like it, but you would find it full of surprises."

"Women are free to pursue all professions and I am cried up alongside Shakespeare. Why I would not like it?"

I tried to describe my world. But I had trouble settling on its salient features: what would be most interesting to her? I talked about the Die-off, the resurgence of Old Britain, the advances in supercomputing and energy generation that made time travel possible. I talked about the destruction of species and habitat, about rising ocean levels, yet I kept feeling, as she looked at me with a skeptical smile, that I was missing the point.

MR. CURTIS SHOWED UP A FEW HOURS LATER, ACCOMPANIED BY Liam. The apothecary was a pockmarked man in the garb of a Quaker, middle-aged, with a wooden box of remedies and a kind but worried face. Henry, with some more friends to see, had stayed in Alton.

The day had turned colder by then, sending Jane and me inside, where we joined the other ladies in the sitting room and stopped talking about the world of the future. As the apothecary sat down with them, I took Liam by the arm and pulled him into the stillroom, closing the door behind us.

"Listen," I muttered, going on tiptoe to talk more directly into his ear, "have him bleed her. Twenty ounces today, and the same weekly until I see improvement."

Liam looked amazed. "Are you not the person who kept telling me how terrible it was to let Mr. Haden bleed Henry?"

"I'll explain later. Just tell him that. And for god's sake, make sure he sterilizes the instrument. Make him hold the blade in a flame, at the side, not the top, for at least sixty seconds."

He stared at me. "She's so thin. Can she lose so much blood?"

"We have to try. I'm not sure it's going to work. But if it doesn't—" I stopped. *She'll die anyway,* I could not make myself say. But Liam understood, or I thought he did. He nodded slowly.

JANE WENT UPSTAIRS TO HER ROOM FOR THE PROCEDURE, WHILE Martha, Cassandra, Mrs. Austen, and I stayed in the parlor, talking and laughing as the daylight faded in the garden outside. I refused an offer of tea, then met Mr. Curtis and Liam coming down the stairs on my way up to say good night to Jane. Liam and I left the house with warm handshakes all around and a promise to come back tomorrow and see how she was.

There was nothing special about that visit except in retrospect; it was the last of its kind. On our short walk down the lane toward home, Liam and I heard rapid hoofbeats and turned to see a rider, not bothering to dismount, pound on the door of the house we'd just left and hand the maid a letter. Express. We exchanged an uneasy look, then a worried one as the rider flew past us and pulled up at Ivy Cottage.

CHAPTER 18

AUGUST 7

Chawton

TOM HAD ACCEPTED THE LETTER AND PAID FOR IT; HE HANDED it to us wordlessly and we hurried to the front room, which had the best light. Liam snapped the seal and stood, back to the window, as I leaned over his arm trying to read upside down. He got through it fast, or didn't bother to finish; after he handed me the paper and left the room, I heard his hasty steps on the stairs.

It was from Edward Knight, as I'd feared, and polite considering its contents. Having written to his relative in Jamaica and learned that no one there had ever heard of anyone by the name of Ravenswood, he must consider his acquaintance with us at an end. He could hardly force us to leave the neighborhood—"I am sure he could," I muttered when I got to that part—but hoped we would leave of our own accord, as we must understand. He deplored the prospect of informing his brothers and sisters what he had learned, but concluded it was incumbent upon him to do so.

He closed by thanking me for saving his daughter's life.

I threw the letter in the flames and watched it curl to ash. We're done for, was my first thought. But at least Jane will understand, was my second. My third was to wonder what Liam was up to.

I found him in his bedroom, his trunk on his bed, standing in the middle of the room and pulling on his hair in an exaggeratedly agonized attitude that made me think of a Kabuki actor in a woodblock print.

"What's wrong?" I asked, walking over to him and putting a hand on his shoulder. Being close to him still sent a thrill through me like a zap of electricity, but Liam did not have sex on his mind.

"Tell Tom to go to the Crown and have them get our horses and carriage ready. We must leave tonight." He whirled and stalked back to his linen press, whose doors already stood open. He pulled out a drawer and stared at it, took an armful of shirts and threw them into the trunk. "Or I must, at least."

"What's wrong?"

"Don't you understand?"

"I understand we've got a problem, but—"

He'd turned back to the linen press and pulled open another drawer. "Go and tell Tom to run to the Crown."

"But I don't see—"

He glanced at me, wild-eyed. "How much cash is there in the house?"

"I don't know, I'll look in the strongbox. At least fifty pounds, because—"

"So never mind that right now. Run and tell Tom."

"But I don't see why—"

"Mother of god, I'll tell him myself, so I will," Liam said, pushing past me and thundering down the stairs. "Tom!" I heard him call. "Tom, where are you, lad?"

I arrived downstairs in time to see Tom, wide-eyed, on his way out. "But I don't understand," I said again. Liam was standing in the middle of the front room, staring blankly at the fire.

"Don't you? Don't you? *They found us out.*"

"I realize it's a problem, but—"

"It's more than a problem, if Henry Austen—Don't you see?" He left the room and ran upstairs. I followed, increasingly concerned about his sanity.

"If Henry Austen, what?" Finally realizing we'd been talking too loudly and sounding like ourselves, I closed the bedroom door behind me. "Liam," I said in a lower tone, "pull yourself together. If we ever suspected Jencks of listening at doors, we're giving him a lot to work with today. Please tell me, in simple words, what's wrong."

"I'm wrong," he said, grabbing a handful of stockings and throwing them, all in a jumble, into the trunk. "How could they ever have thought I would get away with this? What were they thinking, to send *me*?" He hurried to the window. "Moonlight, thank god, at least it's moonlight." He came back to the linen press and seized a heap of neckcloths. "Tomorrow, pay off the servants and arrange to get rid of the animals. Jencks can . . . the next market day at Alton . . . I'll write to the house agent, and break the lease." He threw the neckcloths into the trunk, and pulled his hair again. "Oh, Jesus."

"Liam!"

He shuddered and seemed to see me for the first time. "Will you be all right here? No, maybe you should come tonight. We can leave instructions with the servants and arrange it all by letter. Like it matters," he added gloomily. "Yes, yes, you should come. But you're losing time. Go and pack!"

"But where, in such a rush?"

"It hardly matters! Somewhere else. Toward Leatherhead, I suppose. Lie low and await the Opportunity of Return is all we can do." He turned toward his trunk, toward the linen press, back toward the trunk. His confusion would have been comical if he'd looked less anguished. He examined his collection of waistcoats as if he'd never seen any of them before, then threw them in the trunk, turning back to add a couple of coats. He picked up his dressing case and closed it, adding that to the top, and closed the trunk. "Enough," he said in a doubtful tone. "Unless—No." He shouldered the trunk and began downstairs. "Start packing!" floated up the staircase behind him.

Instead, I followed him downstairs, where I found him looking out the front window, apparently already anticipating the arrival of Tom and the horses and carriage, though it could not possibly happen so soon. In the kitchen, Mrs. Smith, Sarah, and North were huddled together and whispering. They wheeled around guiltily and stepped apart at my arrival.

"We have received bad news," I said. "My brother must set out tonight. Can we get some tea and cold meats before he starts his journey?"

IN THE FRONT ROOM, LIAM HAD UNLOCKED THE STRONGBOX AND was counting money. "Sixty-two pounds and change," he said, looking up. "We can't assume Edward won't spread his news among Henry's banker friends—we can't assume we'll ever see any more money than this before the Opportunity of Return. Assuming the portal even still works, that is." He sat down and buried his head in his hands. "Oh, Rachel. I'm so sorry. This is all my fault."

"What are you, crazy?" I stood over him and ran a hand through his hair, admiring the sweet, clean line of his neck. "You've been amazing. If Henry hadn't told Edward he was planning to marry me, none of this would have happened."

"If I'd been more convincing, it would never have occurred to him to wonder."

"You were very convincing. It's Edward. He's cautious."

"I've done everything wrong from the start."

"Of course you haven't. Don't be silly." I wanted to take him in my arms, take him in my mouth, anything to cheer him up. If we left together tonight, perhaps we could finally make love with our clothes off and without fear of making noise. I pictured rumpled sheets in a coaching inn's bedroom by the raking light of a single candle; the vast darkness outside, the whinny and stamp of horses below in the yard. Lying naked next to each other as long as we wished and talking freely, as ourselves. "I'm serious. Look at me." Taking his hands away, he raised his face to mine, expression solemn. "You've been amazing. I've never met anyone like you." I hesitated, took a breath. *I love you* was what I wanted to say, but the words stuck in my throat. I'd never said them; if I did, what might happen? Instead I leaned down for a kiss.

There came the creak of the door opening, the grating voice of Jencks: "Mr. Henry Austen."

I jumped back, and Liam stood up as we turned to face the door with guilty abruptness that was possibly worse than our original pose. Jencks stood in the door, eyes fixed on us with a ferrety sharpness, Henry just behind, looking horrified.

Jencks moved aside and gestured for him to step in. "As I thought, sir, they are at home."

The door closed behind Jencks, and Henry stood, hands behind his back, speechless, pink, and very straight. The silence lengthened. Finally Henry moved into the room, gingerly. He kept shifting his gaze from me to Liam and back, as I wondered what he had seen, and how it might have looked to him.

Liam stepped forward and held out his hand, oddly normal. "Austen! Did you reach a price on that horse in the end?"

Henry did not take his hand. "I come, I fear, in response to a startling letter from my brother Edward." He glanced at me and away. "In hopes of some explanation."

There was another long silence, and in a flash, an idea came to me.

"Will you have some tea?" I heard myself asking; my voice trembled. "We were about to. My brother was feeling faint, and I was searching for a pulse. The shock of Sir Thomas-Philip throwing us off like this has been devastating. We can only suppose that, after we left Jamaica, someone was spreading lies against us which he had the misfortune to believe." I sank into a chair, trying to look fragile. "As you know, our manumission project did not make us popular there. But I never imagined it would come to this: outright slander, and betrayal by one we considered a friend." I felt a sob rise in my throat.

"Mary!" Henry looked at me again, confusion in his face and voice.

"You see our difficulty," Liam said, taking a turn around the room, gloomy. "To seek to defend myself is to impugn the honor of Sir Thomas-Philip. It seemed, in such a case, best to preserve a dignified silence. But—"

"He has impugned *your* honor. You cannot let this pass unchallenged."

Liam was silent. I had another inspiration.

"I will not let my brother—He fought so many duels in Jamaica, for the planters are quick to anger, and every time I had to fear for his life or his freedom. I will not endure another. And Sir Thomas-Philip is there, and we are here, so it can hardly be arranged."

Henry looked amused. "Forgive me, Mary, but this is not a subject on which ladies need have an opinion." He turned to Liam. "You must write to him, at once, and demand satisfaction. The thing may take months to arrange, yet it must be done."

"You are all enthusiasm to send another man into the line of fire," I said before I could stop myself, nettled by his patronizing reply to me. "And consider this. If anyone has insulted my brother, it is Mr. Knight. He did not take your word about who we were, but went behind your back and spread Sir Thomas-Philip's calumny without concern for its truth. He imagines himself above reproach, yet I must think this very badly done." Both men looked at me in astonishment. "If my brother should send a challenge to anyone, it is Mr. Knight."

A huge pause followed; I had gone too far. It was as if the temperature in the room had dropped. Liam, arms folded across his chest, was staring at the floor. Henry grew pale, his expression masklike in his effort to suppress whatever he was feeling, his eyes narrowing.

"Women are easily led astray by their feelings, so I take no offense at the insult just hurled at my brother," he finally said in a dangerously quiet tone. "Yet you do not correct her—you are silent. Do you concur in this view of your . . . sister's?" He paused and added, taking me in with a glance, "And indeed I cannot but wonder, in view of what I had the misfortune to walk in and witness tonight, if she in fact *is* your sister?"

Liam had turned scarlet. "I implore you to think very seriously of what you are saying."

But Henry was too angry to be wise. "Or perhaps that sort of thing is common in the Indies." For once at a loss for words, Liam glowered at Henry, who went on in the same sneering tone: "But I forgot; you are not really from the Indies."

"I beg you, sir, go at once. I will not be insulted in my own home. Let us part as friends, and pretend this conversation never was."

Henry stared back at him, and there was another long silence. The posture of each man had subtly altered: shoulders squared, nostrils flaring, one foot slightly back, hands clenching and unclenching. Were there going to be fisticuffs, right here in the front room? My heart pounding, I moved a little closer to Liam.

"I have been imposed upon very badly, it strikes me," Henry said at last, with another glance at me.

"I am sorry, Austen, that you feel that way," Liam said, his voice calm, his eyes murderous. "Please accept our heartfelt apologies, and go—"

"You have made of me a laughingstock, in front of my entire family and my London acquaintance. And you are *sorry*?" His voice rose at the end. "I came in hopes of finding you a gentleman, at least, that I might demand satisfaction. But I see even *that* is to be denied me—"

Too fast for me to react, Liam cuffed Henry backhanded, sending him stumbling sideways into a chair and knocking it over with a crash. "You want satisfaction? I'll give you satisfaction!" He had raised his fists and was moving toward him. "Not a gentleman? Fuck you!"

I darted between them, arms outstretched, and braced my palms against Liam's chest.

"Please!" I said. "Please."

For a moment I feared Liam was going to shove me aside, but he froze, breathing hard, his expression growing calmer. When he let his arms fall to his sides, I risked a glance back at Henry, who was also hyperventilating, arms still bent at the elbow and fists clenched. He was staring at the floor. A line of red was rising on his cheek where Liam's knuckles had landed.

"Thirty thousand pounds we gave you, gone forever," Liam finally said. "And this is my answer." Henry looked up, expression icy, and swallowed hard. "But it is a relief to know what you really think."

"Dr. Ravenswood." Henry raised a hand as if to urge him to say no more. "I shall make the necessary arrangements. Expect to hear from my second in a day or so."

With a cold nod, he left the room.

"I shall be looking forward to it!" Liam shouted at his retreating figure. The door slammed behind Henry.

We sank into the chairs at either side of the hearth, and turned toward a sound from the hall. A rattle of china: Sarah, with the tea things.

"I don't mean to disturb," she whispered, eyes large.

IT WAS CLOSE TO MIDNIGHT WHEN THE KNOCK STARTLED ME; I WAS sitting in the front room, too agitated to consider sleep, though I'd sent the servants to bed. I went to the window for a look. Seeing a familiar figure in a cloak, clutching a bundle, I pulled open the heavy door.

"Jane!" I was delighted—and surprised. She had not left her own house in weeks.

She pushed back the hood of her cloak, accepting my offer of a chair by the almost-dead fire and placing her oilcloth-wrapped bundle on the table without comment. Though it was the size and shape of a manuscript, I refused to let my hopes run wild: I put some more coal on and poured her a glass of Constantia. And then one for myself.

"I am sorry for the lateness," she said, looking serious. "But I had to come in secret, as you may well understand." She reached out and put a hand on mine. "Henry gave a most alarming report of his visit. I had tried to stop his coming here, but he was adamant." She studied me. "I can only suppose, then, that we may no longer look forward to calling each other sister." She raised an eyebrow, suddenly droll. "I should have realized that earlier, but there has been a great deal to think about today."

"It was wrong of me to deceive him. Yet my intentions were good—I wanted to give him money to help his bank; we thought he would not take it otherwise. Later, I should have broken it off, but I was afraid you would no longer want to be friends."

She patted my hand. "You should have more faith in me. A lady can always change her mind. As I did, with Harris Bigg-Wither. And his sisters forgave me. It was awkward, but such things always are."

"I am sure you did not flirt with him shamelessly for months, as I did with your brother."

"Why are you sure of that?" She laughed her wicked chuckle. "Why do you suppose he offered?"

"Apologize for me, if you think it will make any difference."

"Oh! Henry will survive; men do not die of broken hearts." She paused. "But sometimes they do in duels. Tell me they are not really going to fight. He insists they are."

"Liam is gone. He set off soon after Mr. Austen left."

"I am glad of it." She took a sip of her wine.

"We lack this idea about honor in our time, that it is best preserved by two men taking shots at each other." Though to my stupefaction, Liam had wanted to stay and duel with Henry; it had taken me some time to make him see reason.

"I should like that about your world." She looked into the fire for a moment. "So he is gone. I am sorry I did not get to say goodbye."

"He was too. But it was safest for him to leave at once. I will follow in a day or two, when I finish some things here."

"Did he go back, then?"

It took me a moment to understand what she meant. "There is just one Opportunity of Return; we must wait for it, and be in the right location, at the portal site."

"And if something happened, and you could not be there?"

"We would never return." I tried not to think about the possibility of wormhole collapse.

"Oh!" She was silent for a moment. "It does seem a perilous business, does it not?"

I leaned forward. "One thing. You must have Mr. Curtis bleed you regularly. Twenty ounces, every week, until you begin to feel better. It may take months, but if I am right about this, you will start to. Your skin should stop being that odd color, you should feel less fatigue and joint pain. Then, do not stop the bleeding entirely, but gradually decrease the frequency, until it is only every few months. You must do that for the rest of your life. Will you promise?"

She gave me a long look. "Are you suggesting this will cure me?"

"It is only an idea, but it seems worth trying." I paused. "And make sure he sterilizes the instrument. Make him hold the blade in a flame, at the side, not the top, for at least sixty seconds. Liam explained this to him today, but you must emphasize it again."

"Sterilize? What do you mean?"

I offered a brief account of germ theory, which she listened to with a furrowed brow and a doubtful smile.

"I was intending to ask you how time travel worked. But after that, I think I shall not." She patted the bundle that sat on the table. "It is 'The Watsons,' of course, as you are too polite to ask. I read it over occasionally, each time wondering if something could be saved, made into a novel the world would be amused and edified by reading. The answer is always no. Yet I cannot bring myself to destroy it, for the same reason I hate it: too much of myself is there. But if people of the future took such pains on my account—" Pushing it across the table to me, she finished her wine and stood up. "I beg you, do not think less of me when you read it."

"I will never think of you with anything other than admiration and astonishment." I rose, too, and she held out her hand. I started to say more but could not, as the reality sank in: I would never see her again.

"And affection, I hope," she murmured. "As I of you." The moment teetered on the brink of heartbreak, but then she smiled. "And your—your colleague. Mr. Finucane. You must convey my regards." She frowned, looking at me more closely. "But are you not—You call him by his Christian name."

"That need not imply the same degree of intimacy, in the world we come from."

"Oh." She seemed unconvinced. "But when you return to where you came from, will you not marry?" My face must have showed my surprise, for she went on: "It only seemed from how he spoke of you, when we talked yesterday, and *he,* so absurdly, apologized for flirting with *me*—Am I wrong? Are his feelings not returned?"

"I am warmly attached to him," I finally came up with. "But in our world, you must understand, women have many other choices in life besides which man they marry."

"I can see they do."

"Anyway, he is to marry someone else." Did I believe this? I wasn't sure. There's a way you can hold two opposing ideas at once, and perhaps it was convenient for me to think Liam had been, if not exactly lying, maybe carried away with his own enthusiasm that morning in the asparagus bed.

She put her hand on my arm, eyes widening.

"He has entangled himself unwisely? Like my Edward Ferrars?"

"She is a far better match than your Lucy Steele."

"But she is not you."

"She is richer, and more elegant. And with her help, he will rise and rise. He is an ambitious man, you know, under his pose of diffidence." I had never consciously thought this about Liam.

Yet as the words came out, something about him that had not made sense suddenly did, and I felt a chill pass through me.

"Perhaps." She looked thoughtful. "He spoke only of you."

I was tempted to ask what he'd said. But pride defeated curiosity, and I congratulated myself on my restraint as I saw her out and said goodbye once more, not starting to cry until the door had closed behind her.

CHAPTER 19

AUGUST 10

Leatherhead

I WOUND UP THE HOUSE IN TWO DAYS AND A FURY OF PHILAN-thropy, helped along by the discovery of several ten-pound notes I'd hidden in the lining of a rarely worn spencer for my journey from London in December and forgotten about. I wrote glowing characters for the remaining servants. I gave our chickens to my favorite neighbor, a widowed cottager named Betsy, and entrusted her with the care of Alice B., the cat. Mrs. Smith and Sarah got their wages for the rest of the year and the contents of the pantry to take back to their family in Basingstoke. Tom, to whom I gave the cows, and North, to whom I gave most of my clothes, were also paid off, with their last job being to accompany me to Leatherhead, since ladies do not travel alone.

Jencks was already gone. Liam had taken him with him when he left, ostensibly as his valet, with the plan to fire him once he got to his destination for letting Henry Austen walk into the room without first checking if we were "at home." Which he'd clearly done on purpose, though whether with the aim of blackmailing us later or just of causing trouble was unclear. But it was obvious in retrospect that Jencks must have figured out what Liam and I were up to and had been saving this information until he could use it.

Seeing Liam set off in the middle of the night accompanied by this sinister creature had been one more source of unease in a day full of it, but what could I do? I did not want him in the house with me, and we feared if we fired him immediately he might come back with mischief on his mind. It occurred to me more than once in the time I was alone in Chawton that Jencks could simply kill Liam on the road; take possession of the horses, the carriage, and its contents; and head for Yorkshire and a new life. He'd get away with it too; who would ever notice Liam was missing, except me?

So it was with trepidation that I pulled into the yard of the Swan in our hired post chaise, late afternoon of a gloomy day, to be helped out of the carriage and pay off the driver. While North and Tom dealt with the logistics of arrival, I looked around, hoping to see Liam, and instead seeing the man who'd denied us lodging on our first night in 1815. I recognized him at once, though he seemed strangely normal, no longer looming like the menacing gatekeeper I remembered. He was barking orders to some men swapping out the horses on a chariot and took no notice of me. I turned to go into the inn with increasing disquiet—maybe Liam really was dead.

Then I saw him, partly hidden by a wall near the entrance to the yard. He stepped forward and held out his hand.

"There you are," I said, suddenly shy. This, even though I'd spent the whole carriage ride—at least when not thinking about his likely murder at the hands of Jencks—imagining with pornographic precision all the things we could do together now that we no longer had to fear our servants. He looked down at me, with no words but a face full of feeling. His hand felt cold and strong wrapped around mine as we went inside.

CAST OUT OF JANE'S ORBIT AND NO LONGER PLAYING OUR PARTS, WE did not know at first how to be toward each other. In the private parlor where we ate a vile shepherd's pie washed down with musty claret, we kept raising and dropping conversational topics. My late-night visit from Jane and her gift of the manuscript. The unnerving scene when Liam had fired Jencks.

"He had such a face on him when I told him his services were no longer wanted. But what did he expect? He'd behaved terribly, yet I paid him off through Lady Day. He was luckier than he deserved."

"What kind of face?"

"Like an angry man disappointed in love and life." Liam's own face lit up with a sudden smile. "I began to think you were right, and he had a crush on me."

"I told you."

"So, the bloodletting. What do you think she has?" Liam asked after a pause.

"There's no way of telling, without lab tests. It was just a hunch. Not very scientific." I had a cold sensation as I thought of just how unscientific it was. Desperate was more like it. Had I lost my mind?

"But what?"

"Bloodletting can hardly make things worse at this point. Unless she gets tetanus from a dirty sharp." Which she easily could; I tried not to think about that.

"But what do you think she has?"

"There's a condition called hemochromatosis when people absorb too much iron from food. It builds up, especially in the liver, and causes problems. She told me a long time ago that she had stopped menstruating last year. That's when it often starts to present in women, when they are no longer getting rid of excess iron once a month. But it was only recently that this idea hit me." I took another sip of my claret and made a face. "Can I tell you the truth? If your only tool is a hammer, everything looks like a nail. I wanted it to be hemochromatosis, because it's one thing you can treat here with some effectiveness."

"Not because you think it actually is?"

"It could be. I'm not saying it's not."

Liam leaned his forehead on his palm, resting his elbow on the table. "And if it is?"

"Bled regularly, she'll improve."

"You mean she'll live longer? Longer than July 1817?"

"Maybe."

Liam looked serious all at once.

"We've already messed with the probability field," I went on. "So I thought, well?"

"Have you not seen any newspapers, the last few days?"

"No, did Napoleon escape again?" I was joking, but Liam's expression chilled me. "What?"

"Wilberforce died on Tuesday."

"What!" William Wilberforce, the renowned parliamentarian and opponent of the slave trade, had accomplished most of his important work by 1816, but he died an old man, in 1833. "That's impossible."

"There are newspapers downstairs if you care to look."

"I believe it if you say so. Only . . ."

"Yeah."

We sat in silence contemplating this. Premature death of a significant historical figure was a macroevent; there could no longer be doubt that we had disrupted the probability field. And I realized, despite what I'd just said, despite what I'd done to possibly prolong Jane's life, that I had not believed it until now.

"Sometimes I think we shouldn't go back at all," Liam said at last, his voice so low I could hardly hear him. "Because, who knows what we may find there?"

This was a crazy idea; every rational impulse in me rebelled. All I said was "What would we do here?"

"What if we went to Canada? No one would know us as brother and sister there. We could start over with new names. We could marry." He paused. "We still have some money. I wrote to some of our London bankers. I don't think Edward did anything there."

"We don't belong in this world," I said slowly. A picture rose in my mind of my neat apartment, its white kitchen and view down Vanderbilt Avenue to Grand Army Plaza. My life there seemed like a dream: a futuristic, sanitary dream where I had running water and electricity, a responsible job and my real name. I imagined my mother, painting in her attic, wondering if I was all right.

"We may find we don't belong there either." I could feel his eyes on me, but I could not look up. Perhaps I was afraid to; if I did, he would talk me into this, using his occult powers of acting and persuasion. "We've kicked off the traces. We've done exactly what we weren't supposed to do, altering history."

"*I* have, you mean. I'm the one who saved Tom; you told me it was a bad idea."

"Oh, Rachel dear, we don't know what it was. It might have been anything, or all of it together. Are you going to beat yourself up forever over one small kind act?"

I finally looked up. He was leaning across the table, long chin propped on one fist, and his gaze was everything I'd feared: ardent, full of longing, and deadly earnest. It's hard to resist an expression like that, even on the face of a skilled actor. I let myself consider that maybe he was not seeking to deceive either me or himself. And what then? What was my responsibility in such a case? I stood up, my heart pounding; with terror, I think.

"Can I have a hug?" I said, and we started to laugh. "Can we maybe talk about this later? Is it bedtime yet?"

"It could be." His arms were around me, my nose in his neckcloth, and I took in the smell of him: like coal smoke and bay leaf soap and something else I could not give a name to. "How I've missed you."

IT WAS LIKE I'D PICTURED IT, AS IF I'D IMAGINED THE SCENE INTO being: the rumpled sheets of our bed in the raking light of a single candle, the vast darkness outside, the sounds of horses below in the yard. Lying naked and talking freely. Until then, we'd seen each other only in bits and pieces and had been ourselves only furtively; this was almost too much, like an overly rich dessert. We made love, talked, grew silent, fell asleep, then woke up and restarted the cycle, until the dim light of morning appeared at the windows and Liam said, "We should take the manuscript and go to Box Hill and read it there."

BOX HILL IS THE SITE OF THE INFAMOUS PICNIC IN *EMMA*: UNLIKE Highbury, a real place, and not far from Leatherhead. In the shadow of the landaulet, sitting on a blanket we'd borrowed from our room, we read the whole thing aloud, taking turns as our voices gave out, though Liam did more because my untrained voice quit faster. When we were done, the day was almost over. I lay back on my elbows and surveyed the tidy green landscape sloping below us: hedgerow and river and road, the long shadows and golden late-day light. The horses stirred and munched grass; the wind sighed in the trees and the birds replied. All the world seemed alive in a shimmering net. I will never forget this moment, I thought, not if I live to be a hundred.

"Well," I said.

"Yeah."

It was Jane Austen, masterfully plotted and psychologically acute, but transformed: her satire turned savage, her fierce intelligence trained on life's injustices, in particular those facing women. In a fit of sisterly malice, Penelope scuttles Emma's engagement with Mr. Howard by persuading him that Tom Musgrave has had her first. Emma is forced to find work as a governess, but Penelope's fate is worse: she ends up a kept woman, first step on her slide to ruin.

"You start to understand why she didn't want to publish it," said Liam, who was sitting with his arms wrapped around his knees, looking dazed.

"It will be huge. It will transform how people think about her."

He gave me a considering look and scratched his back. "Assuming they ever see it."

"It'll be the making of you, remember?"

He leaned over to look down at me. "I don't want to be made. Can I state that more plainly? I would much rather stay here with you. If you would." He flopped down on his back, putting his hands behind his head and looking up at the sky. "A big if, I know." He rolled onto his side to face me. "Just think about it. We still have a few weeks. Don't say anything now."

I looked at the sky, at the clouds gathering in the west as if to send the sun off in style. My wish to believe in him, to say yes, surprised me and scared me into silence. Because, what would that mean? Never to see my own world again, my friends, my mother. To permanently be a second-class citizen as a woman, and to die of something ridiculous, like childbirth; the hormonal injection lasted only about as long as the mission. So why was I even tempted?

"It's cold in Canada," he went on. "You don't like to be cold. I was thinking, what about Italy?"

I pictured hills to the horizon with lines of cypresses marching up and down them. Venice, before it was lost beneath the sea, was said to have been impossibly beautiful. We could live simply, a garden and a little house. With prudence, our money could last; life was cheaper there. I could learn Italian, work as a midwife. We could grow tomatoes.

I said, "They have a big malaria problem."

Liam reminded me we'd been vaccinated against that, along with everything else anyone could think of.

"We don't know how much protection we actually have; the strains might be different."

"If you were so afraid of infectious disease, you would never have come to 1815."

He had me there.

"I don't know," I said, surprising myself again. "How do people know?"

"They never do, Rachel dear. They take a leap."

"Like you did, when you got engaged?" I could not help asking. Stealing someone's fiancé seemed, at the very least, bad luck, a violation of female solidarity. As an image of Sabina, tall and blond and exquisite, rose before me, it struck me that there also was the mystery of how one person could imagine himself in love with two such different women.

He was silent for a long time. "It seemed a sign that I had arrived. The making of me." Another pause. "I think she suspected."

"Suspected what?"

"Sabina's very intuitive."

"What did she suspect?"

"I'd proposed, years before, when I'd just sold my Brummell book. It seemed like I was finally someone that could dare to ask—but she didn't say yes or no. She said, let's wait. I was handy to have around, you see. And then, just before we left, so suddenly for her to suggest—She sensed, I think, what first I hardly did myself. And it displeased her."

"If you don't stop being mysterious, I will kill you with my bare hands. Sensed what?"

"About you. How I felt."

"We were strangers. What could you feel?"

He looked at me. "You seemed especially American: obtuse and overconfident. You talked a lot, and had a weird laugh."

"That's fair," I said, stung. "You're not the first to—"

"When you dislike someone, and yet you're attracted, your mind does strange things. Every good feature becomes another strike against them."

"So I had some good features?"

"That dry way you looked at the rest of us, like you didn't give a damn what the Old British thought. I loved that. So small, so forceful, with a kind of generous outrage. And then, your mad hair, your epic shape. Your nose." He reached over and touched the tip of my nose. "I was besotted; you never noticed? That's good. It would have scared you."

"I don't scare easily."

"We're all afraid of something."

I fell silent, looking at the sky. "So you were taken with an idea of me."

"That day you bought Tom—that was when I knew my idea of you was right."

I turned on my side to look at him. "You were so angry with me that day—" I began, and paused, staring at his arm. He'd taken his coat off, and there was an ominously familiar brown bug crawling down his white sleeve, one I knew too well from Mongolia. "That looks like . . . Is it possible you got lice at the Swan?"

"Anything's possible," he said, strangely calm, as we looked down at the blanket we were lying on and leaped up from it at the same moment, brushing off our clothes, as if that would help.

AFTER WE LEFT THE SWAN, FINDING SPARE BUT CLEAN-LOOKING rooms to let by the week above a milliner's shop in the middle of Leatherhead, it would be fair to say we became obsessed with hygiene. We sent every piece of clothing and linen out to a laundress except those on us, which we burned when the others came back. We took baths daily in a tiny copper tub placed close to the hearth, drawing a screen around to fight drafts and heating water in a kettle on the fire. Hauling water from the pump in the courtyard was a full-body workout for whoever wasn't bathing, since we'd let the servants go. Liam shaved his head—excessive, since he'd not gotten head lice, yet understandable.

Despite all this, disaster struck.

About a week and a half after Box Hill, Liam complained of a headache and refused to eat. Our usual activities at that time consisted of sex, conversation, meals in our favorite public house, walks around Leatherhead, taking baths, and rereading "The Watsons"; on the following day he had energy for none of them and was ferociously thirsty. Lying with my head on his chest, I felt him radiating heat like a furnace.

Five days after the onset of fever, he was presenting with the characteristic rash, the flushed skin, the bleary eyes. I'd been to an apothecary by then and gotten some willow, the raw ingredient of aspirin; and Peruvian bark, the raw ingredient of quinine. Both reduce fever, though they didn't seem to help, or maybe he would have been worse without them.

The course of typhus is a few weeks, followed by a slow and wearisome convalescence. Nothing was unusual, except having no drugs to address the actual ailment, and the complicated mix of feelings I had for the patient.

Depression, lethargy, and weakness are also normal, as I

knew from my experiences in Mongolia. I'd never seen quite so theatrical a presentation, though. Depression is usually boring, a reduction of feeling. Unless you're Liam.

"I'm shit," he muttered between sips of Peruvian bark tea, hand shaking so much I had to help hold the cup. "Shit on two legs. Henry Austen looked at me and knew that I wasn't a gentleman."

"He challenged you! Only gentlemen duel. So that was like the seal of gentlemanly approval, right? Wasn't that why you wanted to stay and fight him?"

His breath came fast and shallow. "Can I have some more— Thanks. So thirsty."

"Don't gulp it, you'll throw up again. Take your time. We've got nothing but time."

"I should never have—I should never—"

"Should never have what?" I wiped the sweat from his forehead and tried to look on the bright side: only one of us had typhus, and it wasn't the medical professional.

"Should never have, any of it. Shitting higher than my arse. I will pay. They told me I would."

"It's not your fault you got sick. It happens."

"Body lice! It's disgusting. *I'm* disgusting. I stink. Of cabbage. You know that's what they told me, my hallmates, at Crofton? I thought they were just being cruel, but when I went home for the Christmas break, I walked into my house and, oh my god—"

"It smelled like cabbage?"

"It stank! And so do I."

"Can I tell you? I love the smell of your skin, the smell of your sweat. First I thought it was your soap I liked, but then I decided it was you."

"The kind of stink that comes from inside, you can't get rid of with washing," he intoned. "The stink of poverty and doom. I'm disgusting. I disgust myself."

"Will you stop already?" I rose from my chair next to the bed and lay down beside him with a sudden wish to cry. "Move over a little." I hid my face in his neck. "I need to smell you." But his smell had changed; it was of rank fever sweat and Peruvian bark.

"You'll get what I have," he protested; his unshaven chin rasped my forehead.

I put my arms around him. "Don't worry. I love you so much. I don't know why, but I do." I felt a weight lift from me as I realized this was true. How had I failed to see it?

"You can't possibly."

"Oh, but I do. So deal with it." He was silent. "Somehow we have to figure out how to make this work," I added, more to myself than to him.

How, though? I tried to envision us together in our own time, introducing him to my mother. Would I move to England for him? Maybe, though my imagination faltered at the details. I tried to picture him in my apartment in Brooklyn, in my neat white bed, and failed. But maybe the problem wasn't Liam: that world had grown so dim I could hardly remember it. Was I getting sick too? I closed my eyes, and saw Box Hill; the long afternoon shadows, the peace and the slowness. Maybe we shouldn't go back; maybe this only works here, I thought, and fell into sleep like falling off a cliff.

CHAPTER 20

SEPTEMBER 5, 1816

Leatherhead, Surrey

W E STOOD IN THE MUDDY FIELD WHERE THE HACKNEY DRIVER had left us, in a steady cold rain, my arm aching from holding the umbrella high enough to shield Liam's head as well as my own. Though this was the field where we'd landed, my spectronanometer was silent. I squeezed it harder, then tried Liam's. Nothing.

I put my non-umbrella-holding arm back around Liam, whose eyes were closed, teeth chattering despite the blanket he was wrapped in. Typhus lasts two to three weeks in an uncomplicated case. But by the end of August, he'd been as febrile as ever, newly delirious, and presenting with symptoms of pneumonia. Discussions about staying in 1816 were over: the problem would be getting him to the portal site.

It rained the whole week before the Opportunity of Return, as well as the day of; the roads were a sea of mud. My worries about the carriage getting stuck had made it hard to decide when to set out. We needed to be on time but not early, otherwise we'd just be shivering there, waiting. But we couldn't be late: the Opportunity of Return, which began at 5:43 P.M., lasted twenty minutes.

The driver had been suspicious; I couldn't blame him. Liam was flushed and blotchy, shivering in his blanket like a ship-wreck victim plucked from the sea, leaning on me as we wobbled down the stairs. A journey with someone so ill was hard to explain, especially one ending in an empty, wet field. I gave the driver a ridiculously large tip and instructions to return in an hour. By then, I hoped, we'd be gone.

Or, if the portal failed, we'd need a ride back. But if we spent an hour out in this, Liam's pneumonia might kill him.

I looked around the field, squinting against the rain, cursing myself for having spent weeks in Leatherhead without coming out here earlier to look for the marker and test the spectronanometers. And why not? Just because I'd sort of wanted to stay in 1816, and had not thought past that? Later, when Liam got sick, I'd been busy, but still. It seemed, in a blaze of painful self-knowledge, that this was how I'd lived always: sleepwalking, unprepared, thinking only of myself.

There'd been a clump of birch trees, and there they were. But where had we been in relation to them? I tried each spectronanometer again, again without result. The sight of the gibbet—today empty—put me on more solid ground; I remembered where I'd been standing when I first noticed it. I'd been so appalled I'd gotten dry heaves, and Liam had tried to comfort me, but something stopped him. He'd been afraid to touch me! The memory made me smile, and I turned to look at him, just as he folded and fell, landing knees first, then hands, then face.

"Hey," I said, sinking to the ground and shaking him. "Don't give up. We're nearly there. I think I know where the portal is now. Come on."

When he lifted his head off the ground, one side of his face was covered in mud. "Just leave me here," he muttered. "Can't."

"Can you crawl? You can do that, right? One hand, one knee, one hand, one knee . . ."

He made it a few feet, blanket unwinding behind him, and sank down. It struck me I should make sure I was urging him in the right direction, so I struggled to my feet, unbalanced by the weight of my newly wet skirt as well as by the oilcloth-wrapped bundle I had in a bag over one shoulder, and squelched off, letting my umbrella fall away. I sank to my knees and waved my hands frantically an inch above the wet ground where I thought the marker should be, encountered nothing, crawled a few feet to the left, and tried again. Useless.

Then my hand hit metal and closed around it. I felt a galvanic shock and heard a vibration as shrill as a bat squeak, followed by a beep from the spectronanometer. I leaped up with a yelp and turned back to Liam—was he in range? But the portal marker grew louder, more insistent, unbearable. I put my hands over my ears, and everything went black.

WHEN I OPENED MY EYES, I WAS IN A BED, IN A ROOM I'D NEVER seen, white and windowless, lit by electricity's cold glow. Hearing a robotic beeping and a faint, relentless hum, I blinked and tried to focus. The air was antiseptic-smelling; an IV in my arm delivered clear fluid from a nearby bag hooked to a metal pole. I was alone. But my mother should be here, I thought; why isn't she? I closed my eyes again.

"Congratulations, Dr. Katzman," Dr. Ping said, dry yet kind. They'd taken the IV out—it had been a precautionary re-hydration, I appeared to be in excellent condition, I was told—and given me a fluffy hooded garment to wear over my hospital gown; I was confined to the infirmary until all the medical results came back. "It's clear the mission was a brilliant success. The Project Team can't wait to hear your account of it all tomor-row. We start at nine, in the big conference room." He paused and added: "Eva Farmer will be there! She wants to have lunch with you."

It took me a moment to remember who Eva Farmer was. "What time is it?" The lack of natural light was disorienting. How did people manage; how did they know when to sleep?

"About four P.M."

"How long have we been back?" I hesitated over the pronoun. But if Liam had been out of range, and I'd come back alone, Dr. Ping's words or manner surely would have told me that.

"The Return finalized at ten-forty-eight this morning."

"And Liam is okay?" I held my breath.

There was a pause before he said: "Professor Finucane is stable. I'm told recovery will take some time."

"He has pneumonia?" He nodded. "And typhus, I'm pretty sure—I'd be happy to fill his doctors in, if they want. Can I see him?"

"Certainly, in a few days, once you're cleared to leave the in-stitute."

"He's not here?"

"He needed more care than we could provide." I must have looked alarmed; Dr. Ping went on: "He'll be fine, don't worry." He gave his dry little laugh. "His wife is worried enough for all of us, I should think; I'm told she refuses to leave his bedside. Quite a scene, in the airlock—you were lucky to be unconscious. You know how she is, how controlled—Old British to the core. The scream she let out, when she saw him! It's still ringing in my ears."

Having lost my powers of speech, I gazed at Dr. Ping's face. His eyes were so dark I could not distinguish pupil from iris, which gave him a serene aspect, furthered by his tidy little nose and perfectly level eyebrows. I waited for him to say more about Liam's wife, but he didn't.

"How do you know our mission was a success," I finally asked, "if we haven't told anyone about it yet?"

THIS WAS HOW: ABOUT TWO MONTHS INTO THE YEAR WE'D SPENT away, people had walked into libraries all over the world, or glanced into their e-book collections, surprised and pleased by the abrupt appearance of seventeen new novels by Jane Austen. As Dr. Ping calmly explained this, I stared at him with horror I did not try to hide. I'd known we'd altered the probability field, yet only then did I realize how little I'd thought through how this might work. Seventeen more books by Jane Austen was amazing in one way, terrifying in another.

For what else was different? I had returned to a world I might no longer know, one where I no longer belonged. One where Liam, it appeared, was already married. Or, had he always been married? Had he lied to me? I began to tremble.

It was a while before I could say: "So you mean to say everyone *knew* of this mission? And we were *supposed* to change—we were sent to do that, on purpose?" I wouldn't be in trouble for altering history, then; I supposed that passed for good news, along with the seventeen books.

"Of course." He looked at me; I saw something change in his expression. "You did not know? But perhaps, then, you come from a version that doesn't—Let me see if—" Bringing a wrist up to his face, he spoke into his wearable. "Dr. Hernandez, Dr. Montana, if you could." I had not noticed the device until then; I stared at it with all the fascination Jane would have shown, though a little more comprehension.

DR. HERNANDEZ, I REMEMBERED ONCE HE CAME IN AND GREETED me, was the Project Team member focused on the psychological aspects of time travel; Dr. Montana, I had never seen. They sat on either side of my bed, looking serious.

"Dr. Ping told us you seemed surprised to find your mission had altered history," Dr. Hernandez began gently. He was a small man, perhaps sixty, with a kind, rumpled face. "Is it possible, when you set out, that you were not instructed to do so? That things were different?"

With some time to be alone and to think between the departure of Dr. Ping and the arrival of these two, I'd grown wary. "What do you mean by 'things,' exactly?"

"Well, that's what we need to determine, isn't it?" Dr. Montana asked. Their exaggeratedly gentle manner made me worry that they thought I was insane. "Tell us about the world you came from, Rachel, and we will tell you about the one you are in now.

And then we will know." She glanced at a monitor behind me. "Let me give you something to calm you. Your poor heart is racing. Don't worry. This is a lot to take in at once."

She was about my age, with skin the color of weathered copper and a long, slender neck. Her eyes, large and dark and thoughtful, rested on me as she took my hand and turned it over. Before I could protest she'd fished out a tiny syringe and injected something, bringing a pleasant numbness to my forearm, and soon to the rest of me. I felt my heart rate slow and my thoughts with it; my fear began to feel a long way off, like a thing that belonged to someone else. And we talked, for an hour, maybe; I'd lost all sense of time.

WE'D BEEN SENT TO TRY TO PROLONG JANE AUSTEN'S LIFE. NOT TO get the Cassandra letters; the subject never came up that day. I would later discover that not a single letter of Jane Austen's to Cassandra had survived here, though dozens to Henry had. And my spectronanometer, useless in locating the portal marker, also had failed to capture images of those letters I'd risked so much for. Nor had anyone here known about "The Watsons"; they were surprised to find it in my bag. My diagnosis of hemochromatosis must have been prescient, my recommendation of bloodletting spot-on. Jane Austen had not died in 1817. She lived, I was astounded to learn, until 1863.

There was more, there was much more, but here was the big thing: this world I now found myself in had no hesitations about changing history. That was just how things were: sometimes confusing and wrenching but ultimately worth it. Since the invention of practical time travel—a decade sooner than in my own world—people had prevented or mitigated certain crucial disasters of the twentieth and twenty-first centuries, resulting in a world nicer in many ways than the one I had come from, but I did not yet understand all that either. Having solved major concerns, people could turn to smaller ones: researching the Bronze Age, say, or saving Jane Austen's life.

"The world is constantly changing," Dr. Hernandez summed up, spreading his hands. "That's what it does."

"I see." I didn't, though. This was more mind-boggling than when Norman Ng had first told me about the secret time travel project, years and worlds ago in the yurt in Mongolia.

They explained that every mission held the risk of what had happened to me, as alternate possible versions of past and future rippled through the continuum. Liam and I had left through one wormhole, from one possible version, and returned to another, a world recognizable yet significantly different. The version we'd come from, I learned, was rare in its squeamishness about changing history. How could anyone expect to travel to the past and not change it? This seemed a fair question, considering my experience. No one was rude enough to say it directly, but I sensed I'd come from an inferior version; a naïve world, maybe.

"You might well want to be rectified," Dr. Hernandez concluded. "Just based on what I've heard right now." I must have looked as dismayed as I felt, for he smiled and said even more gently, which I had not thought possible: "It is safe; it changes nothing essential. The memories causing the trouble, only those, are excised, and replaced with better-conforming ones. Of course, it neutralizes all memory of the time travel mission, and everything connected to it: that's the hinge. Some people like that, if their voyage into the past was traumatic; for others, it's a deal-breaker."

I supposed it made sense. If no one saw any problem in altering history—that is, collective memory—why should the individual's memory matter either? "Must I decide at once?"

"In a few days you'll have a proper session with your mnemosynist—" He gestured at Dr. Montana, who said:

"We'll review your biography in detail. Based on the degree of variance, and your particulars, I make a recommendation. The decision is yours, but the process is irreversible, so it's important to make a choice you are comfortable with. Rectification must be done within three months, because there starts to be a small but growing risk of complication."

"Meaning what?"

"Memories of the time travel voyage begin to entrench, the old and the new versions to commingle. Later, rectification can be associated with mental disorder."

A little silence followed this.

"We'll let you rest now," Dr. Montana said. "Unless you have more questions."

"Just one." I hesitated. Did I want to know? I did. "My mother promised to come and meet me at Return. When will I be able to see her?"

They glanced at each other, and their expressions confirmed my fears, even before Dr. Montana leaned forward and began: "Rachel. I am so sorry."

AFTER A YEAR OF PRIVIES AND CHAMBER POTS, THE BATHROOM was amazing: the gleaming white surfaces, a magical toilet that flushed itself and then cleaned my ass with a spray of warm water, firm but gentle. In the shower, there was pressure you could dial up and down, and soaps and shampoos that smelled almost like things found in nature: lavender, mint, rosemary. I stood under the steaming water and sobbed, there by the rivers of Babylon, resting my head against the clean white tiles.

SHORT-TERM AMNESIA IS A POSSIBLE SIDE EFFECT; THOUGH I never experienced it on Arrival, my memories of the first days after Return were sloppy and vague. What I mostly remember of the debriefing in that big, windowless conference room is pressing my hot hands down onto the long table to cool them, fascinated that such a large piece of furniture was made of metal, as I answered question after question while trying not to think too hard. I told them everything, except what had happened between Liam and me. My engagement to Henry made everyone laugh and fall over themselves with questions.

My lunch with Eva Farmer I remember, but as dreams are remembered: vivid yet surreal. It was in a private dining room at the institute, one I'd never known about, with a view into a small garden I hadn't known about either. An assistant sitting with us discreetly filmed our conversation with his wearable for possible use in a film they were making about her life. Eva Farmer, like the other time I'd met her, left the impression of an enormously intelligent person striving to act like a merely intelligent one; I had a sense of power held in reserve. She asked lots of penetrating questions: about Jane Austen and her family, particulars of daily life in 1815. She seemed interested in what working with Liam had been like; I got the sense that he was a bigger deal here than in the world we had come from, and I resolved to look him up when lunch was over. For the moment, I played along.

"There's something I would like to ask you," I finally summoned the courage to say over the empty espresso cups. My glance went involuntarily to the assistant, and Eva Farmer gave him a nod; he rose and left the table.

"Thank you," I said, surprised.

"I owe you *much more* than that." Eva Farmer smiled slightly and looked out at the garden, then back to me expectantly. "So."

"Something about this I don't understand." She waited, her dark eyes inscrutable. "Do people actually remember the different versions?"

"Why would they? When they have always lived one version?"

"But when history changes behind you—"

"They adapt to it."

"But how?" She went on looking at me with the same half smile, a little sad, I thought, but maybe that was just me. "Let's say, you're a Jane Austen scholar. Your entire body of work has focused on the six. Suddenly one day, there are seventeen additional books! By the person you're supposedly a specialist in, and you haven't even read them!" She made no reply. "Or are you telling me that everyone's past also changes? So, in fact, our imaginary scholar *has* read them, in a past that's now different—" I stopped. My head hurt.

"You're thinking about this the wrong way," Eva Farmer said. "The past is a collective fiction like anything else. Like fiat money, for example. It exists because we *agree* it does. It has no objective reality."

"So you never wanted the Cassandra letters? You never wanted 'The Watsons'?"

"Of course I did." Her gaze was cool and level. "But perhaps they were just means to an end. As you were too, I suppose. I'm sorry it turned out this way for you."

This made tears well up in my eyes, which I blinked back. "In my version, we had a conversation before I left," I began. "We were in the sand room; I'd been on horseback. You mentioned a thing I'd said in my application essay, about repairing the world." I stopped. "Even in that version, you wanted me to save her, didn't you? You secretly wanted that all along."

"Yes, of course."

"Even though it was strictly forbidden to change history." She nodded, and I went on, feeling I'd caught her in a lie: "But why am I even asking you this? In the version you live in, you've *always* wanted to, it was *never* forbidden. So my question should make no sense to you." I paused; she looked amused. It was a look Jane had sometimes turned on me. "There's something you're not telling me."

"'Seldom, very seldom, does complete truth belong to any human disclosure,'" she quoted, increasing my sense of Jane Austen déjà vu. "People, in general, do not remember what's changed. They know, yet they don't. It's hard and it's confusing; they don't like it. But I am not *people in general,* as should be obvious. I invented the Prometheus Server. For all practical purposes, I invented time travel. *I* don't have any trouble keeping the various versions in my head."

"So you understand it all?"

"That depends on what you mean by 'it all.'"

"You wanted to extend Jane Austen's life. You thought I

would be the person crazy enough to disregard the mission directives and do it. And you knew this would result in . . . things being different." Three days back, I was still unraveling all the ways things were different, aside from my mother being dead and Liam married. They were numerous.

"*Crazy* is a harsh term, Dr. Katzman. You did what needed to be done. For which I am most grateful."

I was not sure what to say to this. "So was it Tom?" I demanded at last. "The climbing boy? Was that what did it? Because things were already starting to be different, even before I had diagnosed Jane's ailment. There was the choking incident, and Wilberforce—what about Wilberforce? I don't see how it all connects."

"There is a high probability that it was Tom. That this act of yours somehow set other things into motion."

"But how could you know that I would do that? Or that he would happen along?"

"I don't think you understand. We are talking here of probability fields. Nothing is *known*. Nothing is *absolute*. Those are ideas for children; they are fairy tales." She looked at me with what might have been pity. "You will have a hard time here, I see, unless you get rectified. I advise you do it soon, once the debriefing ends."

"But I will forget everything about Jane Austen, in that case." And Liam, I did not add.

"If I had been able to meet her, I wouldn't want to forget that either." She looked out into the garden again. "But then, millions of people live their lives happily, never having met Jane Austen. They enjoy her work; they imagine what she might have been like."

Her implication, I supposed, was that I should content myself with being like those people. "But I can't—" I began, and stopped, not sure what I wanted to say.

"It would be hard, though, to forget what I had done," she continued. "If I were you, *that* would be hardest. The world will never understand or thank you for the sacrifice you've made; you must therefore take pride in it yourself. To willingly give that up—to erase that memory and be as other people—it would take more than an ordinary amount of humility, wouldn't it?"

THE FIRST THING I LEARNED ABOUT LIAM IN THIS WORLD WAS that he went by William. He'd been married to Sabina Markievicz, pharmaceutical heiress and noted art appraiser, for five years; the couple had two fox terriers but no children. He was something of a celebrity scholar: the author of several works of popular history and a stage actor as well. Fascinated, I watched clips of him, articulate and amusing on Sheridan, Brummell, Regency hygiene. I wondered if he'd been playing down his achievements before, but decided that could not be right. If he'd been, as I learned, the son of a technology executive from Manchester, or in a Shakespeare troupe in his twenties, he'd have said so. His biography was different here.

The more I learned, the harder it became to avoid concluding that in this version he had the success I suspected he'd always wanted, however modestly he might have disclaimed his ambition. My inability to imagine him in my neat white bed in Brooklyn had been prophetic, if not for the reasons I'd thought.

I turned away from the wall screen, sat down on my bed, and rested my head in my hands, feeling I'd made a terrible blunder. But where?

MY BIOGRAPHY WAS DIFFERENT TOO, THOUGH NOT AS MUCH AS HIS. In my session with Dr. Montana, I learned about the person she called alt-Rachel, that person sharing my name who'd traveled back in time with the goal of saving Jane Austen's life. She'd never volunteered in Mongolia or Peru or Haiti, or trekked through the Andes, though she had had a string of unhappy relationships with men, and perhaps that is adventure of a sort. She was a physician, but an endocrinologist. How she'd ended up on the Jane Austen Project Team was a mystery to me; it certainly wasn't for any proven audacity, though we did share a love of Jane Austen.

My mother, in my own version, had been a healthy sixty-seven-year-old. Here, she'd died fifteen years earlier, in an influenza pandemic. My father, still a handsome cardiologist, still an opera lover, had still died when I was twenty-eight. I still had no siblings.

"Your variance is high, as we suspected," Dr. Montana said. "Seventy-five percent. I would advise rectification, but the choice is yours." She paused. I sensed she felt sorry for me, but maybe that was just me feeling sorry for me; this variant of myself, in addition to being an orphan, seemed so boring. I tried to have more compassion for alt-Rachel: losing a parent so young had to do something to a person, to their sense of how random disaster stalked the earth and could strike at any time. I thought about how she'd gone bravely off into the past—just as I had—and was now presumably stranded in some alternate probability where she did not belong—just as I was. My ghostly twin, my unlived possible life.

"Can I decide later?" Rectification was the last thing I

wanted, but I was reluctant to express my opinions openly. I was in an alien land, even more than in 1815; that at least I had studied ahead of time.

"Of course, within the three-month window."

"So what determines it? How different a person's life might be, when they come back?" I was thinking of Liam, but could not say his name. The hushed, awed way people spoke about him here had been amusing at first, then disconcerting; as if this William Finucane really were someone different from the Liam I'd known. I was starting to see what Eva Farmer meant about the past being a collective fiction. "Does it mean something, when a person's biography is very different?"

"A question more for Eva Farmer than for me. But there are different theories. Some people are thought to be more . . . malleable, you might say, more fluid. A small change in early-life circumstances could send them in quite a different direction. Whereas others—it's unscientific, to talk about destiny, but it can seem so. Like something meant to be."

IN THE VERSION I HAD COME FROM, TIME TRAVEL WAS ONCE IN A lifetime, too dangerous psychologically to be repeated. Here, I was an employee of the Royal Institute for Special Topics in Physics: I could participate in research, help others train for missions, or try out to go on another one myself. Did I want to stay on? I had no idea.

I had furlough of twelve weeks to recover; I could think ahead no more than that. Amid debriefing, report writing, and turning down requests for media interviews, I prepared to return to New York. Whether for a visit or to remain, I wasn't sure yet, but I already sensed there was nowhere in this world I could call home.

Hanging over me like twin black clouds were my mother's death and my failure to go see Liam. I kept realizing things I had saved up to tell my mother about 1815, conversations I'd had in my mind that I would never have in reality. Waking up, I would forget she was dead, and then be newly orphaned once more.

I'd hesitated to visit Liam in the hospital, in case it was true that Sabina never left his side, but when I learned he was recovering at home, I realized going there would be worse. His wife, his fame—why should either give me pause? Yet they did.

We'd worked closely together for months; we'd been lovers; I'd cared for him during a serious illness. And each day that passed made a visit harder. Though the institute database yielded his contact information and a home address in upscale Maida Vale, all I did was stalk him online, finding the video clips particularly irresistible. Each one I watched took us further apart: increasing my sense of his importance, flattening the three-dimensional man I had known into pixels on a screen, until his five-year marriage to a tall blond heiress seemed more real than what had happened between us in the nineteenth century. It was insanity, I knew, yet I could not seem to act on my knowledge.

If he wants to see me, I told myself, he knows where I am and could send a word to the institute. I'd go see him at once, if he did. But he's famous, he's married, he's recovering. I thought this until I began to believe it, until I managed to be hurt by his silence. He'd promised once to break off his engagement for me, but that had been in a different world. And was I ashamed of my own behavior? A little. Was I still in love with him? That was a question that seemed to belong to another time and another place.

SHORTLY BEFORE MY RETURN TO NEW YORK, NEW VIDEO APPEARED: Liam had been well enough to let a reporter into his house, a first interview since his time travel voyage. As a voice-over summarized the aims of the Jane Austen Project and the prior accomplishments of William Finucane, the camera panned around an expensive room, high-ceilinged and minimally furnished with antiques, French doors with views of a leafy garden, and came to rest on Liam, looking gaunt but calm, drinking from an early-nineteenth-century teacup. Wedgwood. I recognized the pattern; we'd had it in our house on Hill Street.

"So," purred the reporter, so famous that even I had heard of her, "how does it feel to be the person who saved Jane Austen?"

"I am happy and proud to have been part of the project. I can't claim any credit for the medical—It was my colleague, Dr. Katzman, theorizing—"

"But it is true that you created the atmosphere that made saving her possible? That you were able to infiltrate her life, to win her trust?"

"That was part of the mission." He wore a zippered black sweater with a hood; his hair was still short from shaving his head against lice. I bent forward, bumping the screen with my nose, seeking a clue, a sign—what? He seemed just as when I'd first met him: formal, correct, unassailably Old British. Except now he didn't have to pretend.

"That was the essential part!" Sabina, next to him on the

sofa, came into view. She leaned over and touched his cheek, drawling: "William is so modest. It's charming, but a huge problem," and I turned away not to see his reaction, as nausea surged through me and I broke out in a cold sweat. I staggered to my feet and lurched to the bathroom, leaving the interview to play on as I fell to my knees in front of the toilet and threw up breakfast.

BACK IN NEW YORK, I FOUND I NO LONGER LIVED IN MY OLD APART-ment, but in the top level of the house I'd grown up in. After my father died, alt-Rachel had sold the house for a co-op and kept one floor, which I suppose she'd found comforting, though I did not, since everywhere I looked I was reminded of my mother. I took daylong walks, the only things that made it possible to sleep at night. In the Met, I gazed at the Vermeers, grateful to find something unchanged. I went to the opera a lot.

Not that this version lacked consolations. The Die-off had been less drastic; you didn't have to go all the way to the botanic garden to find a tree. I had seventeen new Jane Austen novels, and two that had been revised. *Northanger Abbey* was a smoother mix of social satire and Gothic parody, while *Persuasion*, now titled *The Elliots*, better fleshed out the Mrs. Smith–Mr. Elliot subplot. *Persuasion* was the title for a different novel from the 1820s, the decade that also saw publication of *Annabelle* and *Vevay*. These were inspired by her yearlong trip to the Conti-nent financed by the success of 1819's *Ravenswood Hall*, about a mysterious brother and sister who come to England from the Indies.

I loved how her writing deepened and adapted as Victorian

mores fell like a shadow across England, how her wit resolved into a more sympathetic but still hilarious understanding of the human condition. Something like George Eliot, whom she lived long enough to meet—perhaps to encourage, since the younger novelist started earlier in this version, with time to write three more books after *Daniel Deronda*. Jane Austen thus lived long enough both to read *Middlemarch* and to have an opinion on the Brontës.

It took me a while to grasp the implications of extending her life, how the arrival of seventeen more books altered her place in the canon. There was a moment when they were new, when no one had read them yet, but this change in the probability field rippled out in all directions, as new memories replaced outmoded ones, and inconsistencies knitted themselves together again, just as Eva Farmer had said. Biographies reflecting Austen's life to eighty-seven, instead of forty-one, began to proliferate, until it became hard to find an old one.

Scholars were busy and happy with all the new Austen novels, but in the popular mind, scarcity has value. One effect of this new abundance was to make her a less significant literary figure, in the first rank of the second tier, not unlike Anthony Trollope, whom she was often compared to. Our mission, like Austen herself, was respected, but not breathlessly esteemed. It was all Brontës here: *they* were the nineteenth-century writers everyone obsessed about. In this placid age, their emotionally overheated quality had an exotic appeal that Jane Austen, restrained, ironic, and prolific, did not.

Another reason for the fascination was that the Brontë Projects—they were up to six—sent to help the family, kept meeting disaster, with time travelers returning mentally ill, infected with drug-resistant TB, or not at all, and with no apparent improvement to the Brontës' short, doomed lives. A mystery. Who doesn't love a mystery?

I COULD NOT REGRET SAVING JANE'S LIFE, YET I HAD A SNEAKING admiration for those Brontës; their refusal to be saved spoke to some uneasiness of my own about changing the past. I was likewise of two minds about what to do next, feeling I'd had enough of time travel, yet hesitant to quit the institute. Maybe this gloom, so out of character, would lift, and I would again enjoy the hungry curiosity and lust for adventure that had made me upend my life for Jane Austen. Near the end of my furlough, having resolved to sublet my apartment and return to the institute at least for a while, I left early so as to stop off in London on the way, thinking it would be fascinating to walk around a city I had last seen in 1815.

But it was all sleek skyscrapers and overpriced coffee bars, punctuated by the odd museum that made the contrast between past and present even more painful. I got lost a lot and was unable to find any trace of the nineteenth century that was not under glass. Exasperated after three days, I took the train to Chawton.

Austenworld was less elaborate than it had been in my version, though the Great House still combined research center and bed-and-breakfast, where I'd booked a room, disconcerted to find that they knew who I was. I'd shunned publicity for my part in the Jane Austen Project; 1815 was something I didn't like to talk about. Not because I hadn't been happy there, but because I had.

"An honor to have you," the woman checking me in said. "I hope you can take the Backstairs Tour, and tell us if you think our new kitchen restoration looks accurate."

"I never saw the kitchens here," I said, but she was not listening.

"Can you imagine, William Finucane was here too, just a few days ago! He told us the wallpaper in the second-best drawing room was all wrong."

"Sorry I missed him," I said, relieved at my narrow escape.

But it could not be put off much longer: when I went back to the institute, chances were Liam would be there too. I could only hope he'd have quit, his present life appealing enough to have put him off time travel.

Or maybe he would get rectified; then we'd all be fine.

Or maybe I should.

"What was it like working with him?" the woman was asking.

"Great," I said, exaggerating my American vowels for her. "Just great."

TWO DAYS OF WANDERING AROUND CHAWTON, WHICH WAS PRE-served like a bug in amber, brought a painful gratification similar to picking off a scab or viewing video of Liam. Differently though no less exasperated than I'd been in London, I impulsively decided to go to Leatherhead. But as soon as I got off the train, I was sorry.

The Swan was still in business, the décor more faux-Victorian than faux-Regency. I took a room for the night, hopeful they'd solved their lice problem by now, and set out with the idea of finding the field where the portal site had been. But a parking lot and a highway confused me; halted by a fence that bounded a golf course, I turned back and headed toward town.

Once there, I realized again my mistake. There was nothing for me in Leatherhead, which unlike Chawton was not trading on its heritage, the buildings such a random jumble of eras and styles that I wondered if something terrible had happened here. Had it been damaged in the Blitz? Then I remembered: Now there had been no Blitz, no Hitler. This was just poor urban planning. I'd walked the scruffy length of the main shopping street twice, unable to decide which building had been mine in 1816, if it was even still standing, before I paused at a corner, staring blindly at a menu in the window of a Peruvian-Persian-fusion restaurant, finally struck by the reality I'd been trying to avoid: there was nothing for me anywhere, at least as long as I went on like this.

What was gone was gone. Jane; my mother; my world; the life I'd had in my world; my time with Liam in the nineteenth century; Liam himself. They'd had their day, they were not coming back. My task was to find meaning in a life that did not include them.

I turned and started back toward the Swan, but consoled now by the ugliness of the streetscape, its architectural incoherence a mirror of my own tangled heart. Weren't we all like that, dragging around scraps of the past that didn't fit, incompletely overwritten versions of ourselves, always hopeful that someday we'd figure things out and put them right?

But we never do. And what instead?

I am not religious, yet I felt a calm bigger than myself, a sense of the interconnectedness of everything. It will be all right, I thought; somehow it will. As I walked on, looking at the sun and the trees and the random buildings, the few pedestrians, it was as if a veil of the sacred had settled over the tragic ordinariness of daily life.

I found I was on a street with a church, an old one, nothing special, except by Leatherhead's low aesthetic standards. God is everywhere, I supposed, even for Jewish atheists, so giving way to impulse, I pushed open the heavy wooden door, passed through the silent vestibule and into the stained-glass gloom beyond. I had not been in a church since 1816 and was stunned by its familiar aroma of old wood and mustiness—the smell of Chawton Sundays. It brought everything back, such a train of feelings and images of things and people lost and gone, that tears stung my eyes and I nearly turned and fled. But then I noticed a side door open, a rectangle of green and sunlight. A churchyard seemed better than a street for bursting into tears, so I hurried through the door and out into the air.

Amid weak English sun, an ancient yew tree, old gravestones leaning at odd angles, grass overgrown, I breathed deeper, calm once more. As I began reading names and dates and epitaphs at random, my urge to cry abated. What is gone is gone; our task on earth is to learn how to deal with that. And should I be rectified? Forget Jane, Liam, 1815? For the first time it struck me as a serious possibility, no longer terrifying.

Looking up, I realized I wasn't alone. At the far end, bent over to study some stones that looked older than the rest, stood a man, dark-haired with a rangy build that reminded me of Liam. For weeks, this had been happening to me. There was no reason he should be in New York, but on crowded subway platforms in Manhattan, in dim sum restaurants in Chinatown, at the opera, I would glimpse an evocative forearm, a familiar walk, a flash of blue eyes, and for a mistaken instant I would see him, embodiment of my failure in forgetting, my guilt for not saying goodbye. A Leatherhead churchyard, why not? It made more sense than a sighting at *Rigoletto*.

Then I looked again, and realized, as the man turned and drew nearer, that this actually was Liam, headed along the path toward where I stood. Disaster! I shrank behind the yew, which could not help for long; the churchyard was too small and too empty.

"Hey!" I said, stepping out of the cover of the tree and into his way. "What a surprise! They told me you were in Chawton—and now here?"

Perhaps three feet away, he froze, eyes widening. His astonished expression would have been funny if I'd been in a mood to be amused. Yet even as I was thinking this, it vanished; his features smoothed out into bland agreeableness, the face of someone used to being looked at.

"Rachel," he said, calm and formal, stepping forward for a cautious handshake. "What brings you to Leatherhead?"

But I could not answer, undone by the strength and coolness of his grip, by the fingers that had known every inch of me. I dropped his hand in dismay.

Finally I managed: "Oh, you know, a little sightseeing, before I head to the institute." The physicality of him, after all the video, was so overwhelming that I couldn't stop staring. He was inconspicuously dressed in black, his hair as short as when we'd landed in 1815. His eyes were bluer than I remembered, and sadder. There was a little scar near his left eye I'd always meant to ask the story of and never had; seeing it stabbed me with regret. "What about you?"

Liam, gazing sideways toward the ground, did not answer. "Are you going to stay on there?" I went on after a long moment: "I don't know how committed I am to time travel, but I thought I'd keep my options open." He said nothing, while I fought the urge to move nearer, take his hand again, bury my head in his chest. "What about you? Probably not, right? Your career's really taken off in this version—that's fantastic." His silence was making me fill the void with random chatter. "Aren't you writing a book about your experiences in the past? I got that impression from something I watched you on." Admitting I watched him on things probably wasn't a great idea.

"No."

There was another pause as I admired his breadth of shoulder and the delicate whorls of the ear I could see. I said desperately: "Have you been enjoying the new Jane Austen novels? Quite a surprise, when we got back—seventeen! Crazy, right?"

He was still staring at the ground at our feet. "Oh, indeed."

Another silence fell. This was how it ended, then: not in drama and recrimination, but in awkwardness. I was preparing to say what a pleasant surprise running into him had been, and to flee, when he looked up and met my eyes. "It's like a thought experiment. What would you give up, for seventeen additional novels by Jane Austen? Would you give up your life?"

The hair stood up on the back of my neck. Why did his voice have to be like that, so rough-edged and low, so musical? "Too late to ask. We did."

"We did." His gaze was on me, steady and cool.

"But the life you have now is great, I think." I could speak; his words had broken some spell. "I'm so glad for you. Everything you ever wanted, right?" I was trying hard to be glad.

"Oh, everything."

His tone left me no traction; was he being ironic? "That's terrific."

"Do you think so?" For a moment he seemed to be seriously considering my anodyne remark, then I felt the sting of his sarcasm. "Is that the word you'd use?"

"Well, I don't see what you have to complain about."

"Indeed." He glowered at me, and I realized I'd been speaking as if nothing had changed—but he was famous now, and important. Perhaps I seemed insufficiently awed; maybe I was wasting his valuable time. "I suppose you think I've no right to complain, so."

"I don't see how what *I* think has any bearing—"

"That I ought to be extremely grateful."

I had no answer to this, and he did not wait for one, but went on with unmistakable hostility: "I'm glad we got a chance to say goodbye, at least. I'm going back to the institute, but only to complete my exit interviews. And to be rectified."

I had thought I wanted this; only at that instant did I realize how wrong I had been. "Oh." I put one hand on a gravestone and leaned against it for support. "Oh. I suppose that makes sense." He had folded his arms across his chest and was still looking at me, expression unencouraging."Your variance was high, right?" I made myself ask calmly. I was not going to fall apart. At least, not in front of him.

"The highest they'd seen." He no longer sounded so angry, but bored, as if this were something he was tired of thinking about. Or, maybe sad. I imagined him waking up, as I had, in our present time in a hospital bed and realizing, as I had, that everything was different.

Why hadn't I gone to see him; what had I been thinking?

"I'd have supposed they'd want to do it right away then, not wait."

"Oh, they did."

"But you refused?" He was silent. "So what changed your mind?" I asked, realizing the relief of nothing left to lose. My mother was dead, my world was gone, I'd blown my chances with the one man I'd ever loved and he was about to erase me from memory. What more could possibly go wrong? "What changed your heart, Liam?" I liked the shape of his name in my mouth; I'd missed saying it. It struck me there was no harm in sleeping with him one last time, since he would forget his infidelity and I would never tell. Maybe that would give me the strength I would need to endure the rest of my life without him. My room at the Swan: nice symmetry. I pictured him, next to me and naked, so vividly that my knees buckled and only the gravestone kept me upright.

But the mournful look he turned on me was a strong clue I wouldn't be seeing any action. "Have you not considered it yourself?"

I hesitated. "Can I tell you the truth? I'm pretty sure nothing in my life will ever compare. So why would I want to forget?"

My words hung in the air for a long moment as we stood there. A faint wind stirred the yew tree; I could hear the far-off rasp of a crow.

"I don't know," he said at last, looking sad. "I can only guess."

Why hadn't I visited him in the hospital; what had I been thinking? Could I have come between him and Sabina when our memories of 1816 were still warm—or at least, have tried? But some things you can't travel back and fix.

"I'm sorry," I said. "I'm so sorry." At this, he looked sadder than before, if that was possible. "I should have come to see you. I was—you know, I was—"

"It's understandable," he said in his chilliest tone. "When you realized—"

"Yes," I managed to say. "Exactly."

Another long silence, the wind and the crow. The sense I'd had before—of the secret sacredness that conceals itself in plain view—came back, stronger now, and then I felt a faint jolt of hope. Was it possible, even after everything, that we'd misunderstood each other?

"I mean, naturally I was intimidated. You're famous now, you realize that, right?" He stared at me. "I'm joking! Of course you do. But I was . . ." I paused. This was hard, and he wasn't helping; he was looking at me like I'd gone crazy. ". . . intimidated."

"You of all people should have known it wasn't me," he said, so gently that I was ashamed. "Are you saying the reason you disappeared without a trace, without a word, is because I was *famous*?" A pause. "Have I understood that correctly?"

I hesitated. "Truthfully? It was more because of Sabina."

"*She* told you to stay away? When? How did she find you?"

"No, no—I mean, I thought—" I stopped but made myself go on. "That in this world—" I stopped, closed my eyes, and opened them again; he was still looking baffled. "That in this world, you belonged together. I thought, you'd be happier. I felt, Sabina is so perfect. So blond. So . . . tall." I stopped abruptly, because my breath had caught.

"So tall that you selflessly gave me up? Like for Lent, except forever?" Liam asked, a note of laughter in his voice. I shook my head, still unable to speak. "When you disappeared, I thought it was because you despised me. You'd seen who I really was. What was I to think?"

And I seemed to know all that would follow, as if I was looking down a corridor of hours and days and years leading back to this moment, which would in the end acquire the heft of legend. If we hadn't happened into that churchyard, I'd say—the same day, the very hour—what would have become of us? And Liam would laugh. But we did. You were about to be rectified, I would protest. No, not without trying to talk to you first. Did you think I would give up like that, so easily? It will be a story to tell our grandchildren, we'd say, as people do, yet eventually this would be true, and we'd tell them.

But all that lay ahead; just then, I burst into tears.

"Wait. Do you mean that you—And Sabina. What about Sabina? Wait. Can this actually work? What are we going to do? How are we going to make this work?"

His arms were around me; he was kissing my wet face. "I don't know, Rachel dear. We'll think of something."

DUE

PRINTED IN U.S.A.

ACKNOWLEDGMENTS

The very existence of this book means I owe an enormous debt of gratitude to many people, living and dead. Among them are Patrick O'Brian, Bill Mann, Jane Austen, Sam Stoloff, Terry Karten, Fanny Burney, Carol Schiller, Adelaide Nash, Sandra Adelstein, Michele Herman, Heather Aimee O'Neill, Lew Serviss, Julia Fierro, Ledra Horowitz, Joanna Karwowska, Czesia Mann, Steve Kenny, John Donne, Kathleen Furin, Mary Lannon, Jennifer Mascia, Judy Batalion, Virginia Woolf, Scott Sager, David Santos-Donaldson, Tauno Bilsted, Nicole Fix, Colter Jackson, Karen Barbarossa, Heather Lord, Danica Novgorodoff, Dina Strachan, Valerie Peterson, Hugon Karwowski, Perla Kacman, Charles Knittle, Geoff Marchant, Geoffrey Chaucer, Harry West, Brian Keener, Sally McDaniel, Catherine Panzner, Timea Szell, and, not least, Jarek Karwowski.

© 2016 Bryan Thomas

KATHLEEN A. FLYNN is an editor at the *New York Times*, where she works at "The Upshot." She holds a Bachelor of Arts from Barnard College and a Master of Arts from the University of North Carolina. She has taught English in Hong Kong, washed dishes on Nantucket, and is a life member of the Jane Austen Society of North America. She lives in Brooklyn with her husband and their shy fox terrier, Olive.